Carnosaur
Crimes

Also by the author
Mesozoic Murder

Carnosaur Crimes

Christine Gentry

Poisoned Pen Press

Library of Congress Catalog Card Number: 2004117563

ISBN: 1-59058-150-4   Hard Cover

Poisoned Pen Press
6962 E. First Ave., Ste. 103
Scottsdale, AZ 85251
www.poisonedpenpress.com
info@poisonedpenpress.com

Printed in the United States of America

For my husband, Milo Rodriguez,
who taught me that courage is grace under fire.

Chapter 1

"We will be known forever by the tracks we leave."
Dakota Sioux

Headlights off, the lone driver steered the Ford pickup parallel to the narrow Red Water River, which surged westward in the stormy breeze like a monstrous, undulating snake. Lightning flickered, and a sonic boom thundered across the sky as he drove along the parched Montana grassland. Hunger had driven a horde of small grasshoppers through a coulee as they scoured the land at midnight. They popped like bubble-wrap beneath the truck's dusty radial tires. Finally the driver halted, then waited and watched. He made sure that no one had seen his approach.

For fifteen minutes, he sat in the darkened cab while the sky flared and bellowed. A thousand feet away, a two-story, vinyl-sided building surrounded by eight-foot chain link fencing lay anchored against the elements. Vapor lamps on poles spotlighted the structure. The only real security measure had been a Bureau of Land Management station a mile south. By driving down an old utility access road, he'd avoided notice.

His anger simmered. Dumb peckers, he reflected as he observed the lay of the land from within his insulated space. Those BLM assholes and their butt-kissing goons could go to hell. Nothing but land-grabbers and rustlers. Just thinking about his hate made this job enjoyable.

When the time was right, he left the truck and stepped onto the prairie. For all the bluster, there wasn't any rain. High-based storm lightning and boomers had pummeled the night skies for a week, and still Lacrosse County suffered the worst drought in years. Summer temps over one hundred degrees, along with no rain for six months, had sparked numerous brush fires and dried up watering holes from Oregon to South Dakota. He had his own problems.

Thoughts of the money he'd make from this job hurried him to the flatbed. He pulled down the back panel and reached for his night-vision goggles and a small toolbox. Next he positioned a plywood ramp, jumped up, and guided an industrial concrete saw down the incline. The self-propelled, twenty-horsepower chassis rolled easily on eight-inch rubber wheels.

He slipped the goggles with head straps over his eyes and grabbed the toolbox. Limping slightly with his right foot, he navigated the saw toward the river. Everything appeared in varying shades of green as the goggle lenses filtered polarized light from his surroundings into his eyes so he could see without light and greatly reduce his risk of attracting attention.

Suddenly a hideous, towering form eclipsed his field of vision. He froze, heart racing. A monster with tree-trunk legs, clawed forearms, and huge sickle-shaped teeth stared down at him. He'd been busted by a life-sized model of an ugly, pebbly-skinned dinosaur.

"God dammit," he cursed, feeling foolish.

Two months earlier he'd taken a tour of this property given by a fat, balding man. He'd listened patiently as the prissy guide told tourists about the ancient fossil prints pressed into a tidal mud flat about one hundred and sixty-five million years before he was born. The dinosaur hadn't been here.

Lightning flashed again, and he jumped as a tremendous clap of thunder exploded. Sweat coursed beneath his long-sleeved shirt and down his ribs. He looked at the sky. The heat storm moved directly over him. Static electricity crackled the air, and his short black hair stood on end.

He pushed the saw toward a flat shelf of exposed sandstone which angled down to the river. As he reached the rocky ledge, he could see a row of three-toed dinosaur tracks stamped into stone. He set the toolbox down and decided which of the two-foot-long, concave prints to take. He chuckled. Like shopping for pickled pig's feet at the grocery store.

He stood behind the machine's handlebars and activated the ignition with the push of a button. The engine turned right over, and a low RPM whine from the twenty-inch-diameter cutter filled the air. The diamond blade could dry-cut an eight-inch deep slice through solid rock at speeds up to eighty feet per minute. He carefully lined up the guide roller for the first of four slab cuts. There would be noise but only for a short time. The storm was a blessing.

He worked the control lever, shifting the transmission into a low forward speed as he watched the depth feed indicator. The blade shaft dropped just as he heard an unnatural hissing sound coming from the five-gallon propane tank. He smelled gas. A split-second awareness filled him with dread. A pressure leak. Fumes.

The blade bit rock and sparks flew for only milliseconds, but he couldn't kill the engine fast enough with his fumbling, gloved fingers. Powdered rock spewed from beneath the chassis right before a loud popping sound echoed behind him. A green luminescence brighter than the sun filled his goggles as gas-laden air ignited into flame. A few seconds more and the propane tank combusted toward him like a vapor bomb.

The concussion deafened him in an instant while a wall of sizzling heat enveloped his body. Before his goggles melted, he watched his arms and legs ignite like dry kindling. The stench of burnt meat assailed his nostrils. Then everything went black, and he felt only the stomach-jarring sensation of being lifted and dropped. He never even screamed.

By the time the force of the explosion propelled him upward twenty feet, he was already a human fireball.

Chapter 2

*"Life is not separate from
death. It only looks that way."*
Blackfeet

Ansel Phoenix's gaze focused on a dried-up, half-acre stock pond as she nudged the buckskin gelding forward with her boot heels. Chunky, so named because he nipped skin from people's hides, picked up speed. Suddenly the mournful bawl of an animal in distress carried across the pasture.

"She'll die if we don't get her out." Ansel eyed her father, who was riding a large leopard Appaloosa named Ditto.

Chase stared hard at the fifteen-hundred-pound Angus cow crying like a newborn calf. The pond, which kept a nearby trough topped off via a wind-generated pumping system, had evaporated into a deep quagmire of mud. The small windmill with frozen blades now stood over a bone-dry tub. Raw thirst had lured the heifer into this death hole despite good cow sense.

"That's the two-year-old Seth couldn't find when he moved the dry stock," he said, referring to cattle not giving milk to calves. Brown eyes flashed from beneath his white straw hat. "I'll work her out so you don't have to get near the pond."

A tingle of apprehension coursed up Ansel's spine. His offer to do the chore alone sent a subtle message: *Stay away from the water. I don't want you getting upset.* She'd almost died from drowning as a child and still suffered debilitating anxiety attacks.

She shook her head. "It's just a mud hole, Daddy."

Chase grabbed a stiff coil of rope hanging from the saddle's horn string with gloved hands. "You're sure?"

"Yeah."

The cow strained toward freedom, then dropped. Muck sprayed in all directions. Wide-eyed and near exhaustion, she lay chest-deep, panting hoarsely and spewing garlands of foamy saliva. Ansel knew that time and dehydration would eventually kill her.

"Gonna be like pulling an anchor out of molasses," Chase groused, moving Ditto ahead.

Ansel reined Chunky to the right side of the cow but several safe yards from the mud hole. She was close enough to use her lariat if needed and out of striking range of a panicked animal. All of her concentration was centered on the cow rather than the shimmering potholes of water.

Chase halted Ditto next to the mud line and uncoiled some of the lariat from its looped end. Holding the remaining coils in his left hand, he stretched his right arm away from his body and twirled the loop in a small circle. Feeding more rope through the slipknot, he opened the loop from small to large, shifting the whirling circle onto its side. He tossed the lasso in a graceful arc so quickly that the cow never even blinked when the loop fell over her head.

Chase tugged the slipknot tight around the beast's neck, snubbed the lariat around the saddle pommel for leverage, and pulled Ditto in reverse. The Appaloosa backed up quickly, stopping automatically when the twenty-five feet of rope went stiff with tension. Chase urged Ditto further back with bit and boots. Ditto's eleven hundred pounds pulled step by step, dragging the cow from the sucking mud.

"Hup, Ditto," Chase encouraged over and over.

The cow shook her head viciously and bellowed. Ditto tugged harder, hooves churning up dead grass as he strained flesh and bone to maintain momentum. Another big yank and the Angus slid forward on bent legs.

"She's dragging free," Ansel said.

Pride rose in her chest as she watched her father work his horse as if their minds were one and the same. Dressed in faded Wranglers, fringed leather leggings, long-sleeved blue cotton shirt, scuffed boots, and cowboy hat with a long white ponytail hanging behind, Chase resembled an old buckaroo riding range rather than the wealthy owner of the twenty-seven-thousand-acre Arrowhead Ranch, which produced the best purebred Black Angus breeding stock this side of the Rocky Mountains.

At last Ditto belly-dragged the cow onto solid ground and the heifer struggled to get her weakened legs beneath her. Chase nudged Ditto forward, slackening the lariat. He dismounted and walked carefully toward the cow, coiling the rope in his hands as he went. The heifer watched him but made no more attempts to rise. Ten feet from her, Chase flicked the lasso loop off her head with one fast jerk. He turned away.

The cow swung her legs beneath her body in one fluid motion, dug rear hooves into the grass, and rose, a maneuver that took only seconds. Once on her feet, the hornless female hopped forward, gained stability, and moved toward Chase's back.

"Daddy," Ansel yelled while digging her heels into Chunky's ribs.

Chunky rocketed forward, head stretched low and tail flying. Ansel reined him toward the cow's rear end and her only hope of saving her father from injury or worse. Her body was pressed so close to Chunky's neck that his black mane blew into her eyes and sweaty horse musk filled her nose. Every second was a millennium. Every inch a mile. She knew a way to stop the Angus, but would it work?

Chase turned, Ansel's shrill cry alerting him to danger. His face contorted with surprise, then fear. The Angus loped at him, head low and eyes rolled forward.

Ansel leaned low off the right side of the saddle toward the cow's whipping black tail. Miraculously, she caught the thick rope of muscle and yanked it toward her as hard as she could before releasing it.

The cow lost its balance and came crashing down on its head and shoulders. Legs flying up and over during a tumbling roll, the Angus landed on her back in a dusty cloud of dirt and grass. Chase blinked, then stared down in dismay at the filthy rump which had come to rest only inches from his pointed boot tips.

Ansel reined Chunky to a stop and leaped out of the saddle. She grabbed her father in a bear hug. "Thank God. I thought she had you."

Visibly shaken, Chase stared at her before inhaling deeply. "I'm fine. Who taught you how to bull-tail?"

"Mom told me. She said rodeo hands did that when there's no way to use a rope on a wild bull. It just came to me. I didn't even think it would work."

The cow rolled onto her side and shook her head from side to side as if to clear it. As she recuperated, Chase led Ansel away.

"I guess both of you saved my life today. I shouldn't have turned my back on a bogged cow with hot blood."

Ansel reached for the nickel-sized azurite stone hanging from a leather cord around her neck. The stone was the fossilized remains of a small Cretaceous sea urchin. It meant the world to her. Her mother, Mary Two Spots, had passed this Iniskim, or lucky stone, on to her before she died. It had once belonged to her grandmother, a member of the sacred Blackfeet women's society called the Motokiks. She wondered if her mother was watching them at this very moment.

Chase retied his lariat to the saddle string. "I'll get one of the hands to round up the cow. You must be bushed."

"A little. I'd forgotten how hard it is filling water tanks and driving them out to pasture."

At dawn she'd helped ranch hands move two large flatbed trucks, each carrying a circular two-thousand-gallon, polyethylene tank with an integrated portable trough strapped to it. The vehicles were left in the largest pasture for two days so cattle could drink their fill. Afterward, they would be driven back to the main ranch well, refilled, and carted out again. Every Angus drank twenty-three gallons of water a day when temperatures went above eighty-eight degrees.

"First year I've ever seen the stock ponds dry up," Chase said, wiping sweat from his brow. "Two years of little rain and another dry winter have really messed things up. No rain this month will put the Arrowhead in the red."

"Are things that bad?"

"They're dicey. Forage is bad because the grass is dead. Got all the stock rounded up in one pasture to get uniform grazing on what's left, and I'm supplementing with feed I should save for the winter. I've sold every animal on the spread I can part with quick, but there's a glut of stock for sale. My payback was dismal. Things don't change, I'm going to have to let some hands go." Chase turned and, placed his boot in a stirrup, and hiked himself into the saddle. "No use jawing about it. Mount up, and we'll get out of this heat."

Ansel was too stunned to comment about the ranch's dire financial situation. She walked past the cow, which had gained its footing and hobbled away from them. As she mounted Chunky, she stroked his neck. "Good boy," she cooed, remembering how the sometimes ornery horse had obeyed her so well.

She frowned and adjusted her black Stetson. The crown kept snagging the top of the single long black braid hanging down her perspiring back. Her wristwatch didn't lie. Only eight o'clock in the morning and temperatures in the west pasture had to be in the high eighties.

They trotted through a cattle gate, exiting the pasture. After reaching her father's white double-cab pickup with a horse trailer attached, Chunky was loaded first, then Ditto. As Chase closed and locked the rear doors, the sound of a car churning up gravel along the ranch road drew their notice.

A custom-painted, pink Lincoln Town Car with blinding chrome trim came blazing toward them. There was no mistaking the owner of the vehicle. Everybody in Lacrosse County knew the spirited, eighty-seven-year-old matriarch behind the wheel.

Ansel's eyebrows hitched up. "Wonder what Permelia wants."

Chase removed his hat while his face puckered painfully. "Probably just to vex me to no end."

A slow smile spread across her face. The loquacious Permelia Chance could talk the vinyl off wood, according to her father, and always spoke her mind. As eccentric as she was, local residents held Permelia in high regard. Childless, she had survived the deaths of three husbands, managed a thriving Longhorn ranch, interceded as a philanthropist for many needy children's projects, and acted as the Grand Marshal for the Mission City Maverick Parade every July.

The Town Car jolted to a stop, dirt and heat roiling off its girth in a billow thicker than pig pen litter. Ansel coughed while Chase fanned dust away with his work hat.

The buzzing driver's window rolled down and a stick-thin, wrinkle-faced woman wearing a pink felt cowboy hat and a matching polyester pantsuit gave them a crooked, pink-lipsticked smile. The smoking Tipparillo clenched in her right jaw made a full-scale grin difficult. On the passenger seat, a ferret-like red dachshund sporting a pink, leather fringed vest and a miniature cowboy hat strapped beneath its throat yapped maniacally. Its ears flapped fast enough to gain liftoff any moment.

"Shut up, Belle Starr," Permelia yelled. The dog stopped in mid-yip. "Howdy, Chase. Ansel. Glad I caught y'all out here."

"Good morning, Mrs. Chance," Chase said with customary politeness. Cold air, heavy with the scents of lavender and menthol, blew into his face.

"Hello," Ansel replied.

Permelia shifted her green, hawk-eyed gaze right on her. "There's my girl. You've always had the most beautiful skin. I can see the bronze blush of native blood in you so clearly in the light. My grandparents were Oklahoma Cherokee, you know. How I wish I had more of those earthy tones. I take after my English half. I'm as pasty as Elmer's glue."

"Thank you," she said before glancing at her father for rescue.

Chase jumped in with both spurs. "What can I do for you?"

Permelia pulled the plastic-tipped stub from her lips. "I want to buy some Angus. Thought I'd spike the ranch gene pool with Scottish blood and get some polled blackies. Got bulls for sale?"

"Well, let me think. How many head you need?" he asked with a poker face.

"At least two, and I want randy ones with balls of steel. My cows will kick a pilgrim stud chin-up toward the moon if he's not as testy as my brush-splitters."

"I reckon I could part with a couple bulls if the price is right."

Permelia cast a sideways glance. "You must be doing better than most ranchers around here, Chase, if you don't need to thin the herd. I know Jim Ruley out to Sidney is practically giving his Angus away because of the drought, but I'm hankering to give you my business. You're closer, and you treat your stock like kin." She fixed him with a friendly stare.

Chase swallowed. "I'll give you a fair price, Mrs. Chance. I can show you two sporting bulls right now. We can go up to the corrals and talk business if you like."

"That's more like it. I'll follow you up." Permelia eyeballed Ansel. "And I'm commissioning you to draw a cover for my book. I'm writing a tell-all monograph about the history of my family and the men I've known, called *Montana Chaps*. I've seen your pictures, and they've got punch. Just what I'm looking for in my cover art."

Both flattered and confounded, Ansel said, "Mrs. Chance, I'm a paleoartist. I draw pictures of prehistoric life forms, not portraits or contemporary subjects. I couldn't do your book cover justice, though I appreciate you asking me."

Permelia emitted a throaty laugh. "That's why I want you. My family is no stranger to the field of fossil hunting. Very few people know it, but my grandfather worked with Barnum Brown in the early eighteen-hundreds."

"Your grandfather knew Barnum Brown of the American Museum of Natural History?"

Brown was no less than the man who discovered the first reasonably complete Tyrannosaurus rex skeleton in the Cretaceous fossil beds of Hell Creek and who made the "Tyrant Lizard King" the most popular dinosaur of all time.

"That's the fella, all right. And my third husband, Elam, bought a quarry once. You wouldn't believe the bones, photos, and papers I have at the ranch. It's a big portion of the book. Sure would appreciate you helping me to sort out all that old stuff, too."

"Barnum Brown," Ansel repeated. "I can't believe it."

Permelia gave Ansel a cagey smile, then reached into a jumper pocket and pulled out a pink business card clutched between rosy fingernails. "Give me a call, and we'll talk wampum." She spied Chase. "Let's go. Belle Starr and I aren't getting any younger."

The window buzzed up, and the skinny dachshund resumed barking and leaping across the pink leather seat.

Chase grinned from ear to ear. "Don't feel bad. She ambushed you."

"Me? She had you rolled and hog-tied in under fifteen seconds."

"We both got stuck and didn't feel the needle," Chase agreed with a chuckle. "You coming to the corral?"

"No way. I'm heading home," Ansel replied, thinking of her double-wide trailer outside the town of Big Toe. "I've got drawings to work on. Oh, give Chunky a special treat when you get back. He earned it today." She kissed her father just as Permelia gunned the car's engine, spewing fumes as incentive to hurry.

"All right, Sarcee," he said, using her middle name.

Ansel took off her Stetson and hopped into the cab of her relatively new blue pickup. The windows were open, but the interior was stifling. She placed her hat on the seat and tossed the pink business card on the dash. She *had* been ambushed, but the idea of hearing about Barnum Brown and his expeditions was enticing. She rolled up the windows and turned over the motor, setting the air conditioning on the highest notch.

Her father pulled the truck and trailer out onto the road and moved past Permelia's luxury sedan. In a moment, the vehicles picked up speed and rushed toward the paddocks where the sale stock was bedded down. Permelia's neon card below the windshield caught Ansel's eye again, and she picked it up.

The flowing black script was large and simple—*Permelia Reading Chance. Diamond Tail Ranch. Quality Longhorns.* No address. No phone. What Permelia lacked with an advertising spiel, she more than made up for with her devil's gift for gab, Ansel assessed.

Still those romantic fantasies of stark Badlands bluffs and never-before-seen dinosaur bones filled her head with gossamer visions. Her nostalgic daydreams about Hell Creek evaporated, however, when the cell phone sitting on the center console rang.

"Hello."

"Ansel, where have you been? I've been trying to reach you for over thirty minutes."

"Cam?" she asked, recognizing the whiny voice of Doctor Cameron Bieselmore.

"Come to the museum."

"What?"

"Come-to-the-museum," he repeated in a stilted tone as if giving orders to an ADD patient.

"No," she bristled. "I'm at the ranch. I've just watered four hundred cows and dragged another out of the mud. You're the museum director. It's your problem, whatever it is."

She fully expected Bieselmore to continue arguing. Nothing. Dead air.

"Cam, are you still there?"

Bieselmore's frantic voice burst through the receiver and nearly blew out her eardrum. "I've called the police. Your Allosaurus killed somebody."

Chapter 3

*"When you have a talent of any kind,
use it, take care of it, guard it."*
Sauk

Ansel slowed the truck along Barnum Brown Road. It seemed prophetic that she was making her mad dash to what might be a crime scene on a street named in honor of the same fossil hunter that Permelia had mentioned only an hour before.

During the drive, she tried to make sense of what Bieselmore had said before hanging up. How could her Allosaurus kill someone?

She supposed the life-sized model could topple and crush a person, but the dinosaur had been securely anchored into the ground with tornado-resistant steel cables and concrete plugs. The mooring method had complied with all construction codes required by the Big Toe Building and Planning Department and had passed muster with the town council.

Ansel gunned through the chain link entranceway to find the tiny museum parking lot brimming over with patrol cars and a fire truck, plus other assorted vans and vehicles involved with the messy business of death. She parallel parked against the fencing, grabbed her keys and Stetson, and jumped out. No one was in sight, but Bieselmore's black Explorer was next to a twenty-one-foot fiberglass replica of a rare Torosaurus dinosaur. Maybe she could find him.

The museum, which was a remodeled two-story farmhouse, also looked deserted. She passed a large wooden sign posted on the grass and went up the steps. A tug on the white steel door revealed that the museum was locked. Undaunted, Ansel proceeded down the sidewalk toward the left corner of the building.

The rear gate was open, and she saw a phalanx of people about three hundred feet away. They stood on the parched grassland next to a twisted curve of the Red Water River where a series of meandering fossil tracks had been imprinted on sandstone by several different dinosaur species. She could also see the upright Allosaurus model, and relief washed over her.

Ansel hurried through the gate and down a long board walkway ending near the slow-moving waters of the tributary. Once she stepped off the planking, she went carefully. Her boots made loud crunching sounds on the dead grass, and inch-long, migratory grasshoppers scuttled from her path. It was too damn hot to fly.

No one paid attention as she joined the group gathered a good ways behind her Allosaurus. Ansel located Bieselmore right away. He stood beside two burly Big Toe policemen and wore his usual black pants and shirt ensemble. His hairless, baby-pink head sweated liquid BBs beneath blistering rays of sunshine.

Ansel took in the county forensics team wearing white smocks or black I.D. tee-shirts. One tech clicked off a volley of 35mm camera shots. Another videotaped the area from every angle. Her gaze raked the ground. Where was the body? All she saw were harried people and two cops arguing in loud voices. Luckily, she knew both men personally.

"First, I want this area roped off. No one goes near the dinosaur, the truck, or the saw until I say so," said Chief Flynn.

"You can lay the tape, Cullen, but this is Bureau of Land Management land," Lieutenant Reid Dorbandt replied, facing the wiry, red-haired officer. "Neither one of us has jurisdiction."

Ansel stared at Dorbandt. He was wearing his usual nappy investigative attire: dark gray suit, pale gray shirt, gray-striped tie, shiny black half boots. A sixteen-year veteran of the Lacrosse

County Sheriff's homicide division, he was very trim and physically fit for a man in his early thirties.

"Oh, that's just what we need," Flynn said beneath the shade of his ten-gallon hat. "Government paper-pushers underfoot. We tell them about this too soon, and we'll be off the case by noon. This property is within city limits, and the Big Toe town council leases this land. That makes this fossil-stealing business my business."

Dorbandt's neatly parted short brown hair framed a tanned, cowboy-rugged face with a square chin and long jawline. He appeared calm and stoic, but Ansel saw how his lean, tense body language radiated a cop's distinctive brand of impatience as he tried to deal courteously with Flynn.

"The crime scene is deteriorating by the minute, and we can't touch it until the BLM says so. You're the responding officer. You should make the call. I've got to call Bucky and let him know about this, too," Dorbandt insisted.

Flynn shook his head and shuffled his feet. Bucky Combs was the elected sheriff and the coroner. Ultimately he would decide the cause of this unattended death after he completed the autopsy. Combs would be another potent ingredient added to this nightmare bureaucratic mix.

"Play your cards right," Dorbandt continued, "and the BLM might not revoke the council's lease. Feds don't like sloppy security procedures, especially when their national treasures are threatened," he said, sweeping his hand toward the river.

Ansel looked there, too, but saw only the hulking span of the dinosaur's rear end. She had constructed the entire beast with cast rubber skin pieces placed over a heavy, fiberglass-frame body, then carefully airbrushed it with acrylic paints to resemble brown, tan, and black skin pigments. Where was the body? She moved sideways several yards, facing the sculpture from another angle.

Something large and black hung from the Allosaurus' three-foot-long, gaping mouth. It looked like a huge chunk of wrinkled, black wadding or burnt wood. For a moment, the surreal tableau disconcerted her. It was if time had reversed, and she was standing in the late Jurassic era observing a giant reptile as it carried a piece of carrion foraged from the riverbed. The truth was more horrible.

Bile rose in Ansel's throat. An incinerated corpse. The cadaver rested sideways across the reptile's burned pink tongue and had no recognizable human features. There was a head-like lump at one end, dangling charred arms and legs, and a rigoristic spine arched in limp defeat. A few tattered strips of scorched clothing flapped like banners marking a holocaust.

How in God's name had it gotten up there?

Flynn's snort of frustration dragged Ansel's attention away. He erased a line of sweat from his sunburnt forehead with a nail-bitten hand. Everything about Flynn, his straight-as-a-plumb-line backbone, squared shoulders, and straddling, two-footed stance relayed his bulldog intention to stand his ground about pursuing the case no matter what the protocols.

Elected as chief for three two-year terms in a row, he was a stubborn Irishman who could trace his ancestors back to Derrylea, but who always presented himself as a level-headed and reliable policeman. Cullen Flynn was also one of her father's best fishing buddies when it came to catching paddlefish out of the Fort Peck Reservoir.

Flynn gestured toward a patrolman. "Dobie, radio Alma at the office and tell her to notify the BLM station about the body. Don't say anything about the fossils. And get Doc Tweedy. The Feds are still going to need the medical examiner."

Dobie, a young man of ample stature shrink-wrapped in a blue and white uniform, nodded. "On it," he answered. The paraphernalia on his Sam Browne belt jangled like alarm bells.

Flynn shot a glance at the fire chief. "Frank, you better stay. We need a ladder for the body."

When she could bear to look no more at the corpse, Ansel scrutinized the rest of the scene. A mass of burnt and twisted metal rested on the ledge in front of the Allosaurus. Smaller charred debris peppered the rocky ground. An orange toolbox sat abandoned on the outcropping, too.

Farther into the grass, a badly rusted 4X4 Ranger faced the river. The tailgate was open, and a wooden ramp was propped against the ground. Even beneath the patina of range dust that covered it, Ansel could see it lacked a license tag.

Ansel moved forward and sideways a bit and tapped Bieselmore lightly on the shoulder. The director's squinty eyes widened with surprise. She held a finger to her lips and motioned him away from the knot of crime scene personnel.

"I'm glad you're here," Bieselmore whispered. "This is disastrous."

"How did it happen, Cam?"

"I arrived at the museum as usual and walked down to the riverbed to check the fossils before unlocking the museum. I found everything just like this: the truck, the machine, and that man in the dinosaur's mouth. I ran straight to the museum and called you, but you didn't answer so I had to call the police. They just arrived."

"Flynn mentioned fossil theft. Are the footprints all right?"

Bieselmore's paunch jiggled as he shuddered. "Yes. Thank heavens. The vandal tried to cut out a carnosaur track with a concrete saw, but the machine exploded. The blast put him up there. Just desserts I say, but do you realize what this is going to do to the museum's reputation? We'll be known as a killing ground. Tourists will avoid us like the plague. Even if Land Management doesn't pull the plug on this place, we're screwed."

"Ms. Phoenix, what are you doing here?"

Ansel flinched. Dorbandt. They had met fourteen months ago during the homicide investigations of two Pangaea Society members. She and Bieselmore still belonged to the paleontology organization, but at the time she'd been the president elect. Her life had been threatened by a psychotic killer, and Dorbandt had handled the case. Since then, they had maintained a loose, personal friendship which waxed and waned as their busy lives crossed paths.

"Hello, Reid. Haven't seen you for about three months. Never thought we'd be meeting under these circumstances."

"You didn't answer my question."

"I came to get some Pangaea Society files," she lied, though Bieselmore did keep the society records in his museum office.

"Yes, that's right," Bieselmore replied. "We're organizing a state conference and Ansel's volunteered to make the contact calls."

"Uh huh." Dorbandt glared at the director suspiciously, then gently grabbed Ansel's right elbow with his left hand. "Excuse us, Doctor Bieselmore, but stick around. I want to ask you some questions."

Ansel didn't protest Dorbandt's touch as he steered her toward the walkway. Little tingles of pleasure had coursed up her bare arm. Though Dorbandt and she had never crossed the line between friends and more than friends, sometimes the cop just set her hormones slipping loose like a fly on ice. *Stop it. You've got to use this opportunity to pump him for info.*

"Reid, tell me what's going on. Do you know who that dead person is? Was he after anything besides the fossil tracks?"

"No questions," he ordered. "You're leaving."

"I have a right to know. My Allosaurus has a body clamped between its teeth."

"And this is my case."

"Really? Chief Flynn seems to think it's his investigation. Maybe he'll talk to me."

Dorbandt bucked to a stop. "Don't do it," he warned.

"Do what?"

"Get involved." He placed a hand on the small of her back and pushed. "This isn't some footnote on the Big Toe police blotter. This is big league. Don't play sleuth."

"I'm just saying that I need some basic information."

His cool sapphire eyes turned icy. "It's what you don't say that worries me. Can you say Federal Antiquities Act? That's what we're dealing with. The poaching of federally protected fossils. Getting caught on the wrong side of BLM policy is a felony."

Ansel smiled. "I know all about the Federal Antiquities Act. It was established in 1906 and it reserves all rights to objects on land held in trust under the ownership of the United States. It also mandates that these objects be excavated for the benefit of recognized scientific or educational institutions who will retain their permanent preservation in public places. In other words, since a fossil is considered an antiquity, you can't remove any fossils from land owned or controlled by the U.S. without a permit."

"Bingo. And the museum sets on property held in trust by the government."

"I know that, too."

"Then don't mess with the BLM. And don't go on some crusade looking for poachers."

"I don't intend to. I've had quite enough of criminals and death, but I don't want the museum shut down. Big Toe shouldn't suffer because greedy bone thugs are raping the land of its national heritage."

"Save the rallying speeches for your society luncheons, Ansel."

"Why don't you ever take me seriously?"

"Listen, when this case blows open, it's going to be dirty, far-reaching, and stink like hell. Get in your truck. Go home." He braked to a halt again. "Oh, shit."

Ansel looked up. A forensic tech had walked through the gate, but it was a group of people further across the parking lot that caught her eye. Several men and a woman exited a white panel truck and headed toward the walkway. The woman and two men wearing casual clothes followed another man in a gray suit. They toted an assortment of large black cases.

She noticed Dorbandt's grim expression. "What's wrong?"

Dorbandt ignored her and stopped the technician about to pass. "Ken, give me your smock," he demanded.

The blond-haired man stopped in mid-stride. "My smock?"

"Yeah, just let me borrow it for a minute."

Ken shrugged. "Sure. I guess." He took off the large white garment and handed it over.

Dorbandt quickly removed the picture I.D. clipped to a breast pocket and handed it back. "Thanks. I'll explain later." As the tech hurried away, Dorbandt passed the coat to her. "Put it on."

"Why?"

"Be quiet, and just do it."

Exasperated, Ansel sighed and pushed one arm into the gigantic smock. On her small frame, the coat sagged past her knees like a white sack. She looked like a bag lady wearing a size forty coat over dusty clothes smelling of horse lather. Muddy boots and a sweat-stained hat just accented her vagabond appearance.

As the trim-bodied, gray-haired man approached with his mysterious entourage, he pulled a leather wallet from his suit pocket with one hand and removed his shades with the other. Ansel's stare swerved to the men wearing identical blue caps, sunglasses, and black nylon side holsters.

"I'm Special Agent Outerbridge. FBI." He flashed an impressive laminated I.D. and a gold shield. "I work out of the Montana Resident Agency under the supervision of the Salt Lake City Evidence Response Team." His grin revealed pearly white but slightly crooked teeth. Deep facial creases bracketed his mouth. Light gray eyes were soft and nonthreatening, yet he stared at the star-shaped badge clipped to Dorbandt's belt with cold appraisal. "Are you in charge?"

Ansel's eyebrows rose. She stole a glance at Dorbandt, who watched Outerbridge with equal curiosity.

"I'm Lieutenant Dorbandt. Lacrosse County Sheriff's Department. Chief Flynn from the Big Toe Police Department arrived first on the scene. He's down by the river. We just barely notified the BLM. Why are you here?"

It was obvious to Ansel that Outerbridge and Dorbandt were at some unofficial law enforcement crossroads with one another. She didn't understand the rules of engagement, but it looked like a good, old fashioned pissing contest between two alpha male coyotes to her.

Outerbridge delayed his response by casually pushing his I.D. into his pocket and turning a speculative gaze toward her.

Ansel stared back, watching him take in her Amerind features without showing any reaction. She said nothing. Neither did Dorbandt.

"We've been monitoring the police bands for calls like this," Outerbridge finally responded. Then he half-turned. "Let me introduce you to my ERT officers. Agents Walthers and Standback."

The rigid, clean-cut academy clones nodded on cue when named. Walthers' face remained set in stone, rigid and un-smiling. Standback smiled at Ansel from beneath a wavy bang of carefully combed black hair. His skin's ruddy color didn't come from the sun, and his broad cheekbones and narrow nose told her that he was Indian, too. She grinned back.

"And this is Doctor LaPierre. She works for the National Park Service." Outerbridge motioned toward the pretty, full-bodied woman.

LaPierre adjusted the tan straw hat above her black pageboy and moved forward so quickly that large hoop earrings clanked against her rouged cheeks. "Everybody just calls me Dixie. Glad to meet you both."

"What's your specialty, Doctor?" Dorbandt asked.

"Paleontology. I'm acting as a consultant."

Outerbridge edged Dixie smoothly aside and peered carefully at his men. "I want this area secured. Necessary personnel and witnesses only. Go over everything grid by grid. I don't want anything missed." At his command, the team headed for the river.

Dorbandt fixed his crosshairs on Outerbridge. "A paleontologist. Exactly what type of case are you working?"

The agent didn't bat an eye. "I'm not at liberty to say, Detective, but this incident has just become part of a larger federal investigation. The BLM will be assisting and advising, of course, but we're in charge of managing, collecting, and preserving evidence. We appreciate your help so far. I'm sure you've done a good job. It's nothing personal." Outerbridge followed up the canned speech with a beguiling smile, then stepped away.

Ansel's heart sank. She watched the group retreat out of earshot, then yanked off the stifling smock. Her sizzling glare should have seared through Outerbridge's skull, but it didn't. She passed the lab coat to Dorbandt.

"For once Bieselmore is right," Ansel admitted. "We're screwed."

Chapter 4

"Even a small mouse has anger."
Tribe Unknown

Ansel sat at her drawing table and stared at the ink drawing she'd lined so quickly.

Funny—in her mind's eye, she had imagined the scene so clearly. Now she didn't like the black and white, prehistoric picture at all.

The clear skies above the Cretaceous coastal marshland were cloudless and hot. Insects flew from a shagbark forest, and dragonflies buzzed over the sluggish wetland waters. Amphibians jumped over the tops of tangled ferns and toppled rotting tree trunks as a dinosaur herd of thirty-inch-high Gasparinisaura skittered to and fro amid the swampy foliage.

A monstrous bipedal dinosaur crashed through the tree line. The Giganotosaurus opened its mouth and roared, a master predator causing havoc and confusion before selecting his prey. The panicked herbivores scattered as enormous snapping jaws—twice their size—came within striking distance. The chase was on.

The drawing showed the vicious attack from a ground level perspective. The towering Giganotosaurus approached head-on, neck low and reptilian eyes gazing down its massive, bumpy snout. A doomed Gasparinisaurus raced ahead, tail whipping sideways, legs outstretched in mid-leap, spiked front thumb-claws splayed, and beaked head turned to watch the slobbering jaws scant inches away.

It was all wrong. A maw of serrated teeth ringed the Giganotosaurus' tongue and a yawning, black gullet cavity. The portrait background was too shadowy. The foreground lacked detailing strokes. Every line and dot gravitated toward accentuating that cavernous mouth, which eclipsed all other subjects on the page. The overall visual effect was gruesome and frightening.

Ansel threw down her pen. Not exactly what the authors of a new book on momentous Argentine dinosaur discoveries had in mind, she thought. She'd been commissioned to create a large portfolio of realistic dinosaur drawings for a U.S. publisher. The majority of drawings had been completed during the last two months. This was the last picture.

Ansel nervously fingered her Iniskim. Her drawings were usually group studies of interacting species or individual action poses showing the natural, daily behaviors of eating, hunting, or nesting. They resembled photographic scenes—so fine was her stroke and so realistic-looking her ink, watercolor, and air-brushing techniques, which she had perfected through years of experimentation and practice.

Her work was well known in scientific circles because her renderings withstood the scrutiny of degreed academics who valued scientific accuracy based on zoology, botany, and environmental biology over subjective, artistic visualizations. She had learned early that their critical support was essential for establishing her professional reputation.

This portrait of a recently discovered Giganotosaurus, however, had a demonic look. In life, the giant reptile stretched forty-five feet long and weighed up to nine tons, bigger than the largest Tyrannosaurus ever found. More lightly built than its North American cousin, Giganotosaurus had long legs, short arms with three-fingered claws, and a six-foot skull.

Ansel glanced at the towering piles of Giganotosaurus fossil photos, specimen drawings, skeletal measurements, environmental notes, and fossil site impressions the authors from South America had sent her. After studying this scientific data for weeks, her Giganotosaurus sketch resembled a tawdry comic book cover: two dimensional and distorted. Something had skewed her perspective and muddled her purpose.

"The poacher," Ansel said out loud, remembering just how much seeing that burnt corpse hanging from the Allosaurus' mouth had haunted her the past two days. Her revulsion and disbelief had spilled from her subconscious and onto the paper like poison weeping from a wound. Her creative juices were tainted.

Disgusted, she rose from the stool and went over to a half-refrigerator beneath a counter in one corner of the room. She opened the door to find slim pickings. A six-pack of canned Coke. Bottled water. A plundered bag of bite-size Snickers. She pulled a Coke from its neck ring and pawed through the cold plastic pouch for the last two chocolate bars. Nervous energy made her ravenous.

Ansel avoided the drawing board and dropped onto the large pit sofa positioned on the other side of the room partitioned inside the large red airplane hangar. She'd purchased the steel building, along with her double-wide trailer, two years before. The large building contained the workshop where she had sculpted the first life-sized model of the museum's Allosaurus and also stored a personal fossil collection. Munching on the first candy bar, she leaned into the leather cushions and stared up at the twenty-foot-high ceiling joists.

Who had tried to steal the river footprints? What kind of man would risk committing a felony to poach fossils? Did he have a wife? Children? Did anyone miss him and wonder what had happened to him? Ansel tore open the second candy wrapper.

The poacher had known what he wanted and how to get it. Carnosaur bones were the rarest dinosaur remains to be found. Since large reptilian herbivores far outnumbered the carnivores, a complete fossil skeleton of a large predator species was considered the holy grail of vertebrate paleontology.

Although a nicely preserved footprint from a North American species like Tyrannosaurus, Allosaurus, or Albertosaurus was considered only a trace fossil, it would still bring in thousands of dollars on the commercial black market. For the right price, a private collector, fossil dealer, or unscrupulous museum director could purchase one with no questions asked. She had to find out what was happening in the case.

The next edition of the weekly *Big Toe Tracker* wasn't out yet, and though the local TV stations had swarmed around the museum like blowflies on sheep, they knew little or nothing about the vandalism or death. The FBI and the BLM had built a Jericho wall of silence around the crime scene that even the soundbites from a newsie's satellite hook-up couldn't crumble. Dorbandt had disappeared, and Bieselmore hadn't called to gab about what the FBI had done.

Ansel got up and tossed the Coke can and wrappers into a trash bin beside her art table. She'd work on the Giganotosaurus drawing when she felt more objective. Her portfolio deadline was near, but a few hours lost today wouldn't make much difference. Better to distance herself than continue drawing useless pictures that would completely clog up her artistic flow.

She set the security alarm, exited the hangar, and walked along a well-worn path through a field of parched grass that spanned several acres behind her blue and white trailer. Usually this strip of land, which had once been a grass runway for the former owner's Bonanza six-seater, burgeoned in the summer with an assortment of colorful, wild perennials. Scorching western winds and dust had reduced everything into a straw-brown mat. Gone were the rainbow hues of beargrass, Indian paintbrush, Astor, columbine, and Dogtooth violet.

As she walked toward the back porch, Ansel glanced at two Langstroth beehives several hundred feet away. Concern for each colony of fifty thousand bees furrowed her brow. Would there be enough pollen to sustain them through the summer and winter? She made a mental note to get Feltus Pitt, a local beekeeper, over to inspect the hives.

Her thoughts intent on the bees, Ansel almost ran into the couple suddenly appearing on the path. Startled, her hand went to her chest. The last thing she expected was anyone walking behind her forty acres of land unannounced. She'd had a bad experience in the past with people sneaking onto her property to do her harm.

"You scared me," Ansel accused, trying to calm her racing heart.

"Sorry," said a blond-haired woman wearing a hat with a Department of Interior patch on the bill. A gun belt accented her uniform. "We knocked on the trailer door, but nobody answered."

"Ansel Phoenix?" asked the tall, stocky man beside her.

"Yes." Ansel squinted against the sun. He wore no hat to screen a short, well-trimmed moustache and chin beard. His belt holster was bigger, and he carried a clipboard with a gold pen on it. His look was all business. "What can I do for you?"

The man pulled out a gold shield from his breast pocket. "We're from the Bureau of Land Management. This is Ranger Eastover from the Red Water station. I'm Assistant Special Agent-In-Charge Broderick from the state office. I'm investigating the attempted theft of dinosaur prints from the Big Toe Museum. I'd like to ask you some questions."

"All right. Let's go inside."

Ansel led the BLM officers through the cluttered back porch and up some trailer steps. The double-wide was roomy and outfitted with nice furniture in shades of blue and brown. Luckily she'd been spending most of her time inside the hangar, so the living room looked clean and orderly. No bowls of fossils percolating in acid solutions on every flat surface, digging tools on the floor, or journals draped over the chair backs to mark her place.

"Have a seat." She sat in her favorite chair, an antique ladder-back rocker beside the bay window. A quick glance through the glass, and she noticed the white and green BLM patrol pickup with topper and light bar parked on the front drive.

Broderick sat on the blue sofa across from Ansel, his stocky legs barely able to fit behind the glass coffee table. He fussed noisily with his clipboard and pen. Eastover sat beside the SAC officer. It was obvious that she didn't enjoy his proximity despite the smile plastered across her pretty, mid-thirties face.

"I'm surprised you're here. I'm not on the museum staff," Ansel said.

"I'm interviewing a lot of people," Broderick stated. "What's your profession, Miss Phoenix?"

"I'm a paleoartist."

"So you have a working knowledge of fossils, their scientific significance, and monetary values?"

"I'm not an expert, but I know a nice fossil specimen when I see it. What's this about, Agent Broderick?"

"You were at the museum yesterday, weren't you?"

"For a bit."

"And it's your dinosaur sculpture by the river?"

"Parts of it."

Broderick's gaze pinned her. "What do you mean?"

"I didn't build it. The Big Toe town council paid a commercial advertising company to construct the shape to my specifications. I just handcrafted the skin, which was fashioned from latex molds of my original sculpture, assembled the rubber pieces over the frame, and spray-painted the exterior with life-like, acrylic colors and lacquers."

Broderick scribbled long and hard. "How long were you working on museum property?"

"About six weeks on and off."

"During that time, did you ever notice anything strange?"

"Absolutely not."

"Ever see anyone working there or hanging around who looked or acted suspicious?"

"I've never heard or seen anything out of the ordinary when I've visited the park."

"Why were you at the museum yesterday?"

"By accident," she lied. "Dr. Bieselmore and I are members of the Pangaea Society. A paleontology organization. We had some business to discuss." Ansel glanced at the ranger, who sat like a statue, hands folded obediently in her lap.

Broderick flipped through his clipboard papers. "You were involved in a shooting last year that resulted in a fatality, weren't you?"

"How did you find out about that?"

"It's my job, Miss Phoenix. Tell me about it."

"I was being stalked by a killer, and my life was in jeopardy."

"I understand, but wasn't there a fossil artifact involved, too?"

Ansel didn't like that question. He was subtly insinuating that she had something to do with stealing dinosaur tracks. Determined not to show her concern, she rocked slowly in the squeaky walnut chair.

"Partially. There were a lot of factors contributing to last year's murders, all of which were beyond my control. I'd be glad to give you the number for Detective Dorbandt at the Sheriff's Department. He'll tell you everything about the shooting incident you'll need to know."

Broderick noisily snapped his pen beneath the spring-loaded clip. "I've already been there, but there's plenty of follow-up work to do." He gazed at her pointedly.

"So what's going to happen to the museum?" Ansel asked, her obsidian eyes fixed on him in return.

"It's closed."

"For how long?"

"Indefinitely. It's part of a crime scene, and my office has to reevaluate the merits of either allowing the property to remain as a special land-use area open to the public or dedicating it as a fully protected national landmark open only to scientists. It's possible the fossil tracks will be removed from the park and placed in a federal repository for preservation and study."

"What federal repository?"

"Probably the Museum of Paleontology at the University of California."

Ansel's cheeks flared red. "Those fossils belong here in their natural state where they can be studied and enjoyed by Montanans."

Broderick shrugged. "Scholars from all over the world go to UC to study their fossil collections. They're always reevaluated. Fresh discoveries aren't made just in the field."

"You still don't understand, Agent Broderick. Our museum generates a lot of income for the city. You can't take Big Toe's livelihood away."

With a nod he said, "You're right. I can't. However, the state director, under a Secretarial Order, can issue a permit for the removal of vertebrate fossils to qualified paleontologists under certain terms and conditions."

"I don't think it's going to come to that," interjected Ranger Eastover out of the blue. She gave Ansel a commiserating look.

"We'll get a fossil specialist out here and see," Broderick pronounced.

When Eastover said nothing further, Ansel asked, "Doesn't the FBI already have a paleontology consultant with them?"

Broderick shook his head. "The BLM uses real field experts, not desk jockeys like LaPierre." He suddenly rose to his feet. "I have everything I need for the moment. If I have more questions, I'll be back."

Ranger Eastover was obviously piqued. Her lips stretched into a grimace that obliterated the deep dimples on her cheeks. She flicked a strand of shoulder-length hair away from her face and jumped up.

Ansel got up, too. "Who was the thief?"

"We don't know," Eastover spoke up, "but he might be part of a poaching ring. Two other places were hit yesterday besides the museum. A fossil supply store in Sidney and a college exhibit in Glendive."

Broderick had just opened the trailer door and he wheeled around. "That's restricted information, Eastover," his voice boomed. "Do that again, and I'll personally see to it that you're no longer employed with the government. Let's go."

Eastover simply turned and met Ansel's eyes for several long seconds. Pulling a white business card from a pocket beneath her brass name tag, she slipped it to Ansel without comment.

Ansel breathed a sigh of relief as the trailer door closed behind Eastover. The whole experience had been nerve-wracking but worth it. She knew exactly what the BLM was up to. Close the museum and remove the fossil footprints? Not if she had anything to do with it.

Time to make some phone calls. The first to Reid Dorbandt.

Chapter 5

"White men have too many chiefs."
Nez Percé

Dorbandt shifted his body and prayed the chair in front of Sheriff Bucky Combs' desk wouldn't squeal like a wounded animal and draw undue attention. He'd been sitting for twenty minutes. To pass the time, he'd listened as Combs groused on the phone to every FBI and BLM law officer that he could lasso with a phone line. Right now Combs was on an ass-rending tear with BLM Incident Commander Bob Carson.

"I know the museum property is on BLM land," Combs yelled, "but you have no authority to close public access thoroughfares. My deputies should have road-blocked Barnum Brown Road. Instead some Utah FBI geek with gun-toting goons waltzed in giving orders which you obeyed."

There was a moment of blessed silence as Combs listened, large right hand clenched on the receiver as if he'd bludgeon something given half the chance. His silver hair, buzzed to old Navy regulations, glittered beneath fluorescent tubes with a failing ballast. As Combs ground his lower jaw, the cleft in his chin did a horizontal dance. A knock at the door saved Dorbandt from zoning out completely as he watched the indentation's hypnotic rhythm.

Combs beckoned Chief Flynn inside. "Sure, both of us should have been notified that the FBI was here. The fact remains that

I keep the peace and I knew nothing about this from you. I'm supposed to be protecting citizens from criminal offenders, not federal hotshots. Any matter involving Lacrosse thoroughfares or municipal properties had better involve my office, Bob."

Combs hung up without further ceremony. "Damn, I'm sick of these federal clusterfucks. Bad enough I stroke the BLM and the USFS all the time, now the Effin-Bee-Eye is in my face telling me what I can and can't investigate."

Flynn, looking nappy in his starched blue uniform, took the seat next to Dorbandt. His hair blazed orange under the jaundiced light tubes. "Morning, Sheriff. Lieutenant. I guess if I'm here, you've decided to do something about it."

Combs shook his head. "No. *We're* going to do something about it."

Dorbandt straightened. He hadn't appreciated being dismissed like an errand boy by Agent Outerbridge. "What did you have in mind?"

"We need to pool our resources. The feds are freezing us out, but I'm going to light a brand fire under them," Combs declared, throwing his stocky bulk against his chair seat.

"I'm in," Flynn said.

Dorbandt nodded. "I'm with you, Sheriff. I just don't know how far the detective division can go. Outerbridge took the forensics evidence and robbery hardware. Even the truck. That makes us blind in one eye from the start."

"We've still got something they don't." Combs picked up a folder. "The perp."

"Howdun's autopsy report?" Dorbandt asked.

The sheriff nodded. "The DB was an Indian male in his early twenties. Height about six feet, one inch. Weight around one hundred sixty pounds. Looks like a faulty gas valve on the propane tank exploded." He opened the file and pulled out four full-color eight-by-tens.

Dorbandt's eyes widened. An Indian. He wondered how Ansel would take the news. "How do you know that?"

"Howdun pulled a handwheel valve out of the vic's stomach. That's the only reason we have it. It's not stamped with the letters OPD. That tells us that the tank wasn't fitted with an Overfill Protection Device. A spark must have ignited leaking gas, and the resulting flame wicked backward to blow the cannister wide open."

"The saw might be a pre-2002 model," Flynn said. "That's when National Fuel Gas Safety Code legislation was passed that said all propane tanks up to forty pounds have to have an OPD device or they can't be refilled."

Combs passed the glossies of the contorted, burnt corpse lying on the autopsy table to Flynn. "Maybe. Or it was a new saw with a cheap replacement tank of earlier vintage. Hell, could be just an old saw with an old tank that wasn't refilled by a certified propane distributor that knew about the laws. Add the fact that the saw was carried in a flatbed during record high temperatures, and you've already got a super-heated, incinerary gas bomb."

Flynn shuffled quickly through the grisly pictures, shook his head with revulsion, and passed them to Dorbandt. "Damn. What a way to go."

Combs nodded. "I won't argue that. He had third degree burns over eighty percent of his body. Burned off his clothes. Even melted his rubber boot soles and night vision goggles. His lungs were congested and showed focal hemorrhage due to the inhalation of hot gas so he was alive until the explosion wedged him into the dinosaur's mouth. A big tooth punched right though his heart. He died from cardiac arrest due to heart trauma and hemorrhaging."

Dorbandt looked up from the photos. "So, technically speaking, the lizard killed him."

"Yeah, I guess you could say the dino did it."

Flynn asked, "What are the chances of getting an ID?"

"Good. We've known his physical characteristics, and we've got skin, blood, teeth, and bone marrow to work with for the dental, blood grouping, and DNA comparisons. I'll push it through computers, but it takes time. We need a facial ID. Without one, we

can't get his picture into circulation so somebody steps forward
to identify him."

Dorbandt concurred. The stiff, inhuman form had only a
charred, skeletal mask, its shrunken, lidless eyes lacking recognizable color. The hair was gone. Dorbandt handed the photos back
to Combs as Flynn asked, "What about personal effects?"

Combs swiped a bear paw hand across his brow. "Nothing
left. Maybe the feds got clues from the truck. I did find some
interesting information in the x-rays, though."

The sheriff pulled out another sheet. "He had a T10-T11
spinal cord injury, multiple rib fractures, a tension pneumo-
thorax, and was missing his spleen. He also had a claw-foot or
curled toes because of a Lisfranc fracture of the right foot. The
bone injuries looked like they'd healed on their own. The surgical
incision was several years old. Our perp was relatively young,
but he'd sure taken a pummeling."

"Think he was beaten?" Dorbandt asked.

"No. His injuries are common to somebody who's been thrown
from horses or bulls several times. Maybe a rodeo rider or a horse
trainer. The spinal injury and the ruptured spleen probably happened when he fell off an animal. The ribs and chest problems
could come from falling against a bucking animal or striking
body parts while on the way to the ground. A Lisfranc fracture
involves the dislocation of the tarsometatarsal joint in the middle
of the foot. It happens when there's a high-energy blow to a boot
or a twisting fall where the foot gets trapped in the stirrup and a
person is hung-up during a fall. Maybe even dragged."

Dorbandt's stomach turned. He'd once seen a fourteen-year-
old boy without protective gear illegally riding a bull at a rodeo
event. The kid struck his head against the bull's head with such
force that he suffered a traumatic brain injury, a spinal fracture,
and multiple nasal fractures, and remained unconscious for sixteen days. He was transferred to an acute care facility. He'd last
heard that the boy remained in a persistent vegetative state. So
far, protective gear designed for bull or bronco riding hadn't been
recommended or even developed by rodeo organizations.

Dorbandt jumped in. "You want me to check the local rodeos and ranches to see if the perp worked nearby, right?"

"Sorry. I think Flynn should do it. He's more familiar with the Big Toe locals."

"I'll get right on it," the chief said.

Combs looked at Dorbandt. "I have another assignment from the Coroner's Office for you. Since I am the Chief Coroner, the feds can't bitch about interference with their case." He showed Dorbandt a block-toothed mouth full of white enamel. "I want you to visit a forensic anthropologist associated with the University of Technology who does facial reconstructions."

Flynn shot Dorbandt a sympathetic look. "Oh, oh. Guess you drew the short straw, Detective."

Dorbandt stared at Flynn, then turned toward Combs. "What's going on?"

"You're transporting the perp's head to Billings," the sheriff said.

A range of emotions surged through Dorbandt's body. Disbelief. Disgust. Resistance. Surrender. "Can we do that legally? Just lop off the head and cart it around?"

"If it will ease your mind, the head fell off during the autopsy," Combs clarified. "And, yes, the medical examiner has total control over what means are used to identify a victim and the cause of death. Doc Tweedy prepared the papers authorizing delivery of the head to the facial recontructionist an hour ago. I'm not signing the death certificate until I'm sure it was an accident."

"I agree," added Flynn. "You saw the cutter, Lieutenant. Those self-propelled concrete machines retail around three to five grand. The night vision goggles run up to fifteen hundred dollars. I doubt he was alone in this get-rich-scheme to rip off tracks."

"Exactly," Combs agreed. "I've heard some whispers that the FBI sniffed around Lacrosse because they're chasing a Montana fossil theft ring. I've got feelers out through our office and the state police to see if it's true. Drop the head off, talk to this expert, and see what she can tell you She'll need time to examine the skull and work up a profile, but something's better than nothing right now."

"When do I leave?"

"Tomorrow morning. The itinerary will be on your desk late this afternoon. I'll talk to Captain McKenzie. You'll report your findings to me. I want a low profile, gentlemen."

Flynn got up. "I'll do my best, but I've got five Big Toe town councilmen nipping at my heels. I'll bear down if it comes to it, FBI or not." He looked at Dorbandt. "Have a good trip." In a second, the Irishman was out the door.

"Can I have a copy of the autopsy report?" Dorbandt asked.

"Take this." Combs passed it over.

Dorbandt flipped quickly through the brief provisional report. One specific paragraph caught his eye. It listed the perp's stomach contents, and his pulse quickened. A clue to the Indian's activities during the last few hours of his life had just leaped out at him. The trilling of his cell phone broke his concentration.

"Go ahead and get that if you don't have any other questions."

"Nothing right now, sir." Dorbandt rose, file in one hand, while pulling the phone from inside his jacket pocket with the other. He moved quickly through the office door and into the hubbub of a harried, central administrative area. "Lieutenant Dorbandt."

"Reid. It's Ansel. Can you talk?"

He made sure his voice didn't betray his surprise. "For a minute. What is it?"

"It's about the museum investigation."

"According to the FBI, I'm officially off the case. I told you to stay out of it."

"I'm involved whether you like it or not. This morning two BLM officers talked to me."

"Only because you brought attention to yourself by deliberately being at a crime scene, Ansel. You knew better. I warned you that you'd be messing with a federal posse."

"You sound like my father. I didn't call for a lecture. I need your help."

Dorbandt sighed. "All right. What did the cops say?"

"So you're interested. If you want to know, you've got to meet me. How about lunch?"

Despite his irritation, Dorbandt's curiosity was piqued—an Achilles heel that Ansel had speared with a woman warrior's eye for blood. Since June the year before, they'd talked occasionally. Nothing but friendly chatter. The last few months had been hectic in homicide, and she'd been busy doing book drawings. Maybe he could get some bonus legwork done on this case before leaving for Billings.

"How about dinner instead?"

"Where?"

"Humpy's Grill in Swoln. I'll give you directions. Be there by eight."

"Swoln? It's on the other side of the county."

"Yeah, but I've got a craving for a buffalo tongue sandwich," Dorbandt replied, slapping the autopsy file against his thigh.

Chapter 6

"Life is both giving and receiving."
Mohawk

Lacrosse County covered approximately seventeen hundred square miles with a total population of three thousand. That boiled down to one-point-eight people for every square mile, Ansel considered as she drove into Swoln, a rooster tail of gumbo dust arching behind the truck's exhaust. Of the three towns—Mission City, Big Toe, and Swoln—why did Dorbandt have to pick this godforsaken place to have dinner?

Swoln, inhabited by about two hundred people, was an isolated livestock range for sheep. The town's name referred to an historical incident. In 1905 the first commercial flock, brought in and accidentally placed in a pasture with clover, ate so much of the tasty plant that every sheep developed a severe case of bloat. Digestive gases expanded their stomachs like balloons, and they all fell over on their sides, feet uphill.

The entire town spent a night rolling hundreds of distressed, glassy-eyed sheep over so their feet faced downhill and they could stand by themselves, or in cutting a single hole in the beasts' rumens so the gases were artificially expelled. Luckily only a few sheep expired, and the associated town appellation of "Swollen" gracefully morphed into Swoln over time.

Ansel followed Dorbandt's scanty directions and cruised down Main Street. If she'd blinked, she'd have missed the whole downtown area. The only sign of civilization in the dark, rolling landscape was a row of dimly lighted two-story brick buildings on one side and a row of contemporary glass-front buildings on the other. The clay monstrosities looked like original town structures—a municipal building, bank, and feed store. As for the other canopied storefronts, Ansel figured that contemporary around here meant the 1950s.

Humpy's Grill wasn't hard to find. Every decrepit truck in town was hunkered in front of it. Only Dorbandt's unmarked white sedan spoiled the pickup conga line. A huge, blue neon sign over the soaped-over store windows flickered the restaurant's name and the profile of a buffalo.

Lovely, Ansel reflected, parking next to the cop car. She fussed with her form-fitting scoop-necked T-shirt and fringed, brown suede vest before grabbing her purse. Out of the cab, she quickly placed her left palm on the sedan hood as she passed it. Aside from residual heat from a broiling hot day, the engine was relatively cool. Reid had arrived quite some time before her.

She moved toward the entrance, hoping that her casual, sexy look would hold Dorbandt's attention long enough to disarm his usually guarded interaction with her. It had worked before. A crude cardboard sign taped to the door read, "If you don't pay, don't bother to runs. *My* bullet is faster than *your* buns."

Ansel sighed and entered. The cloying smells of horseradish, smoke, and dish-washing soap hit her nose as the door slowly closed behind her. She'd expected every dirty, grizzled sheepherder's head to turn and leer at the sight of a Native American woman entering their lair, but it didn't happen.

Everybody was too busy eating. The tiny room was jam-packed with tables full of clean-shaven cowboys and rosy-cheeked women. The men wore dressy western shirts, boot-cut denims, and polished boots. The ladies wore brightly colored gingham and calico dresses with puffed sleeves. An open mesquite grill crackled and smoked along the rear wall.

Dorbandt, also wearing jeans and a long-sleeved shirt, raised an arm. He was nursing a beer. She took the empty seat where a frosty mug also awaited her. "Hi, Reid. Who's the crowd?"

"The Glory Stompers. Square dancing team from the Revelation Baptist Church. I ordered you an ale."

"Thanks," Ansel said, sipping the Moose Drool brew. She settled in and surveyed the ultra-rustic decor—U.S. license plates or horse blankets nailed to the cheap brown paneling as well as peeling red vinyl floor squares and varnished, raw pine-board tables and chairs. "Nice ambiance."

Dorbandt shrugged. "You don't come for the fencing. You come for the grass. The food is great." He passed her a laminated paper with print on both sides. "I recommend the buffalo chili with a side of corn meal dumplings."

"And what are you having?"

He smiled. "A buffalo tongue sandwich, of course. That's why I'm here."

Ansel set down the menu. "That's all? How did you ever find this place?"

"A lot of smokies eat here. So how have you been, Ansel?"

Well aware that he'd side-stepped her innuendo of duplici she replied, "Never a dull moment. One more drawing an done with the Argentine book. Then all I have to wor are eight other pictures for a couple of magazine artic ing a lecture and slide show for a Pangaea Society October, and designing my murals for the new

"That's the science place being built at E

"Right. The Preston Opel Paleohistory tion is in the final stages. It's taken over completed by Christmas if the weath need rain badly. All the ranchers a the Arrowhead is barely operati my father. I've never seen hi

Dorbandt's eyebrows k I can do?"

"Nope. I can't even help. It's in Mother Nature's hands. That brings us to you. How have you been?"

"Great. Busy, like you."

"Still jogging five miles a day?"

"Weather and job permitting," Dorbandt said. "I'd go stir crazy otherwise. It's how I decompress."

Ansel surveyed his trim, athletic form. Everything about Dorbandt was built for stamina and speed, like a high-strung riata mustang. What a waste of manpower, she mused. In the last year, she'd learned that he'd never been married and didn't have a current girlfriend. She really liked him despite his cop attitude and couldn't deny her sexual attraction to him on certain occasions. The problem was Dorbandt's tunnel vision. His intellectual focus upon his job and bringing in the bad guys made him continually suspicious and aloof.

Just like, me, Ansel considered, reflecting on her half Indian ⁖⁓ an Anglo society. No wonder we both attract and ⁓⁓ time. No matter. They were friends,

muu and waist apron approached ⁓rbandt got his sandwich and 'li but passed on the dump⁓r. No ice.

⁓el said, "Are you sure a local In⁓ FBI was ⁓t these BLM guys." ⁓an was an Assistant ⁓om the state office. ⁓ed Water station ⁓ith Broderick." ⁓ut the gears in ⁓at seems like ⁓tened. The ⁓even if the

"Well, Broderick treated me like a criminal. He questioned my work on the Allosaurus model and if I'd ever seen anybody suspicious at the museum. Then he brought up the shooting last year. He was concerned about my involvement with the Pangaea Society murders. I told him to talk to you if he had any problems."

"Good."

"There's something else, Reid. Ranger Eastover slipped up and told me that the attempted fossil theft was one of three that went down Friday night as part of a poaching ring."

Dorbandt's eyes grew larger. "That's interesting. Sheriff Combs is trying to verify if other counties were working on similar cases. Did Eastover say where the crimes occurred?"

"No." In a split second, she decided not to tell him about the fossil thefts in Glendive or Sidney. Those were her leads.

"Well, in the meantime, don't worry about Broderick. He's shooting blanks."

Ansel shook her head. "You don't understand. Broderick told me he's bringing in a fossil expert to evaluate the dinosaur tracks. It's possible the BLM will close the museum and dig them up. They could be sent to another institution for research and preservation. If he manages that, Big Toe will lose its most profitable public attraction. That would be disastrous for the town coffers and the museum."

"I smell a rescue campaign in the works," Dorbandt muttered, looking exasperated.

"You don't live in Big Toe," Ansel replied, coal-black eyes flashing sparks. "I knew Chester Dover, and he'd spin in his grave if he knew the BLM had used his lapsed land lease payments to finagle the ranch away from his relatives after his death. Now they're stealing his dinosaur tracks. The Bureau is no better than the man who tried to rip off those footprints with a concrete saw. At least he wouldn't have tortured people for months while he stole them. Don't you dare tell me not to get involved."

The conversation ended abruptly as the waitress appeared bearing a large oval plate filled by a foot-long loaf of rye bread split and splayed on the platter. The middle of one slice had been scooped out and filled to bursting with smoked, ground buffalo meat mixed with fried onions and black olive slices. The other half was covered with Romaine lettuce slathered with mustard.

Ansel's bowl of buffalo chili with red kidney beans, diced tomatoes, and chopped onions looked puny by comparison. The speedy waitress also set down Dorbandt's second beer and her water, asked if they needed anything else, then left.

They occupied the tense silence by pulling silverware from their rolled up paper napkins and preparing their food. Dorbandt salted his meat, reassembled the sandwich, and cut the one-pound fare into two pieces. Ansel stirred her chili and blew on it as if it was of prime importance just so she wouldn't have to speak first. Her temper had to cool along with the meal.

The gaiety of the Baptists worked as a defusing element while Dorbandt took a big bite of his sandwich, chewed, and swallowed. For several more seconds he fidgeted like he had a burr under his pants, exhaled, and then said, "Sorry I made that crack about a campaign. I know you're passionate about the museum. I just worry about your safety."

Ansel looked up. His blue eyes gazed softly at her. He really meant it, but it didn't stop her from using his moment of vulnerability to her advantage. "I know that, and it means a lot to me. I promise I won't do anything stupid. Can't you at least tell me who the poacher was?"

"Hokay. No name yet, but he was a young Indian in his twenties. He was also pretty battered on the inside. Had a right claw-foot from a past stirrup injury and some other physical injuries that might be related to a rodeo or bronc-busting career."

Ansel swallowed the spicy chili burning her tongue and stared at him. One of The People had ended up in her sculpture's mouth. Somehow, though it was irrational, she felt responsible. She also felt slightly ill despite the delicious food.

"Do you know his tribal affiliation?"

"No. The Feebees grabbed every clue at the crime scene. We don't have much to work with. The coroner's office has the body, but you saw how burnt that was. Can't even do the usual facial ID or fingerprint search."

"So everyone's supposed to sit around and wait for Outer-bridge or Broderick to toss out tidbits of information," Ansel groused, stirring her food with wild strokes.

"Officially, Lacrosse cops are off the investigation, but there are still things we can do."

"What?"

"Dorbandt smiled apologetically. "I'm not at liberty to say, but if you need to reach me, call my cell phone. I won't be in the office tomorrow or the day after."

"Unofficially, you're up to something, aren't you?"

"No. I'm just an errand boy."

They chatted on other subjects for another ten minutes until Dorbandt finished half his sandwich. Then he looked up, found the waitress, and caught her eye. She bustled over, and he asked, "Could you wrap this? I'd like it to go. And bring the bill, please." The woman nodded and picked up his platter.

"You're leaving?"

"Got an early morning tomorrow. Take your time. This is my treat."

Ansel sighed. Dorbandt had decided their chat was over. Plus he could avoid probing questions. Now she didn't feel so bad about not telling him details about the other fossil thefts. He was holding back, and it was fair play that she do the same. As usual, he didn't trust her to keep quiet about their discussion. Would they never erode this layer of mistrust between them?

She picked at her chili while Dorbandt waited for his doggy bag. The Revelation Stompers noisily exited the restaurant en masse, leaving the room strangely silent. After getting his foil-wrapped grub, Dorbandt placed a twenty on the table and stood.

"Stay out of trouble, Ansel. Your father will peg my hide if something happens to you."

Annoyed at his proprietary tone, she said with false sweet-ness, "Have a safe trip, Reid. I'll expect to hear all about it when you return."

"Uh huh," he mumbled in a noncommital tone. "Adios."

The front entrance closed behind the detective, and Ansel finished her ale but not the chili. She wondered why Dorbandt had really come to Swoln for dinner. He'd only eaten half the buffalo sandwich he'd professed such a hunger for on the phone.

When the waitress walked over to take the bill receipt and money, Ansel smiled and asked, "Excuse me, but could you tell me how long the man eating with me was at the table before I sat down?"

The woman's pale face crinkled in thought as she picked up the tab and Dorbandt's crisp Hamilton. "Sure. Came in about an hour before, Sweety. Spent a lot of time jawing with Humpy. Twern't easy for me with the place hopping full of Holy Rollers, either. I had to fuss about the orders not coming up fast enough."

"Humpy?"

"The owner." She motioned toward the grill, cackling a laugh. "Humpy Duval. Can't miss him. Long beard and a bump on his back."

Ansel looked toward the sizzling, ember-spewing pit. Humpy, sporting a waist-long black beard and standing behind roaring, log-stoked flames, chopped raw buffalo steaks into narrow strips, then dipped them into fry batter. For the first time, she noticed the large tent of shirt fabric pushing up between his shoulder blades. Humpy had an abnormally curved spine caused by Kyphosis.

"Do you know what he talked to Humpy about?"

"Asked about some Indian who ate here last Friday night. Talked to me, too. I waited on the fella."

"An Indian? What did he look like? What was his name?"

Forehead scrunching up again, the waitress stared thoughtfully at the water-stained roof squares and drawled a barrage of words. "No name. Young, quiet, and polite. Short black hair. Thin face. Cowboy duds. Ate a buffalo sandwich and left with a limp. Paid in cash. That's all I know. Gotta git to cleaning tables. Come again." She hustled away.

Irritation coursed through Ansel's veins like electric heat. So Reid knew the poacher had eaten at the restaurant the same night he'd gone to steal the fossil tracks. Somehow he'd tracked the man's activities to Humpy's and hadn't shared that information. She didn't like being skunked. Reid wanted to catch more criminals associated with the poacher while she wanted to save the museum grounds from government real estate barons like Broderick. They both had their reasons for learning the poacher's identity.

Ansel left the restaurant a few minutes later. She was unlocking the truck when the dim vapor light on the storefront behind her winked out, and a shadow fell across the driver's door. Someone had moved soundlessly up beside her. Startled, she whirled to her left side, door key poised between her knuckles to be used as an eye-jabbing weapon if necessary.

A man stood next to her, his body haloed by backlighting. He wore a black tee-shirt and jeans. For a split second as her eyes took in the short-cropped black hair and thin Amerind face, Ansel thought the dead poacher had been magically resurrected. A visceral fear engulfed her. This was impossible.

"Relax, Miss Phoenix. I'm Agent Standback. FBI," said the apparition's calm, tenor voice as he brought out a badge from his rear hip pocket.

Ansel sagged against the truck. "What the hell are you doing here?" she cursed, adrenalin anger replacing her fear.

Standback's sienna eyes gleamed in the moonlight. "Escorting you to Agent Outerbridge."

Chapter 7

"Only two relationships are possible—
to be a friend or to be an enemy."
Cree

Never in her wildest dreams could Ansel have expected to find herself where she was at the moment, strapped in a seat and staring past her feet out the tinted windshield bubble of a shiny black Eurocopter 120B as it lifted off.

The noise was deafening. Turbines fired, the rotor drummed, and three humongous blades scythed through the hot evening air. Everything vibrated. The flight deck and the aft cabin containing three passenger seats. The tail. The nose. The updraft produced by the thirty-seven-foot-long helicopter sent jet fuel fumes and grit swirling like airborne banshees.

Ansel's hands gripped the arm rests as the skids abruptly left the ground, toes first. Then the aircraft's nose lowered slightly and began its forward motion via a boost of added engine power. As the craft made a straight-angled climb, the concrete landing pad beneath her grew smaller with amazing speed, and her stomach flip-flopped. In less than a minute they were going seventy miles an hour.

She wished that Reid hadn't talked her into eating a chili dinner. What would he think about this? Ansel wondered as the small agricultural airfield used by crop-dusting planes became nothing but a postage stamp square dotted with pinpricks of light. It was too late now. All Reid cared about was her being a "good girl" while he was away. Fat chance.

As instructed, she'd followed Standback's black Bronco in her truck and parked near the airstrip outside of Swoln. He'd told her nothing except that they would fly a short distance to meet Agent Outerbridge. Since then, Standback had been deliberately evasive with her questions, busying himself with pre-flight inspections, the engine warmup, and then pre-takeoff checklists.

"How are you doing?" he suddenly asked, seated to her right.

Ansel forced herself to look away from the pitch black void beneath her. His head was covered by a helmet with a radio headset and a microphone boom, as was hers. One of his hands operated the cyclic stick between his legs while the other manipulated a collective lever between their seats. His feet also controlled two rudder pedals. Digital screens, knobs, buttons, and engine gauges filled the cockpit. Multicolored control panel lights illuminated Standback's face with an otherworldly neon glow just as surreal as this whole adventure.

"I'm all right as long as we don't fly over water." Her voice sounded muffled through her earphones.

"We'll be over solid terrain all the way," he assured.

"At least the ride is smoother."

"Above a hundred feet, this baby is pretty quiet compared to other copters," Standback said with pride. "The aft New Generation Fenestron tail rotor really reduces noise print in forward flight. As we level off above the clouds and hit one hundred forty miles per hour cruising speed, you're going to get a great view of the full moon and the stars. Where we're going, there won't be any more lights."

"I know we're headed northwest, but where exactly are we going, Agent Standback? I have a right to know. It's not like I can change my mind, open the door, and leave."

A smile cracked his deadpan expression. "True. Grab that map in the waterproof pouch from your door pocket. Then hit that little switch on your microphone. It's a reading light."

Ansel pulled a 12x12 inch map bag from the elastic-topped receptacle on her right. Rather than the typical air chart, the bag contained a folded USGS map. She clicked the mike switch and a flashlight-like red glow encompassed her chest and lap.

When she opened the geological survey map, she was surprised to see a close-up segment of a familiar Montana Badlands area about twenty-six miles north of Jordon. The yellow-green area marked with a "K" delineated the position and areas of contact in the Hell Creek rock formation, a Cretaceous age geological strata which had always been commercially searched by those in search of ore, minerals, and fossils.

"We're going to the Hell Creek State Park?"

"Close to it. Ever been to the area?"

"Not by air. I've driven through it and once I took a pack trip forty miles west through the Devil's Creek Recreation area. It's beautiful, but dodgy to navigate even in good weather. Why does Outerbridge want to meet there?"

"I'll let him explain," he said, clamming up.

Ansel's heart raced with excitement. She studied the bumps and dips on the map for quite a while. There was no doubt that she was going to the same Hell Creek Formation where Barnum Brown had unearthed his two Cretaceous-era T-rex skeletons.

The Hell Creek Formation was a desiccated, dun-colored range of hilly terrain peppered with gumbo buttes and sharp, drop-away canyons eroded by the Missouri River. It was fringed with ponderosa pines leading down to the shores of Fort Peck Lake. During her pack horse vacation, she'd seen elk, deer, eagles, foxes, and coyotes. Waterfowl even inhabited the lakeside regions.

When Ansel put the map away and looked up, her breath hitched in her chest. The forward view out the Plexiglas nose was magnificent. The helicopter had climbed to one thousand feet, just below the clouds which spread over her in wispy, cotton-batting patches. Overhead a gigantic, radiant orange moon, pockmarked with blue-gray mountains and craters, spilled pastel light into an infinity of night. Stars flickered like silver glitter thrown across black velvet.

Ten minutes later, the aircraft's nose angled downward. When the helicopter descended into the wind, everything below was pitch black. Standback was right. There were no city electrical power grids or road lights. Even the moon looked dimmer, slightly shrouded by gray clouds skimming past them.

Ansel's fingers dug into the armrests as her nervousness returned. "We're already there?"

Standback turned his head and smiled again. He was quite attractive, Ansel thought not for the first time. He had narrow lips and straight white teeth. Dimples pierced his cheeks, adding long creases that reached down to the ends of each jaw. His almond-shaped eyes were topped by thick black eyebrows. A five-o'clock shadow of chin and moustache stubble darkened his light brown complexion even more.

"As the crow flies, our ETA was about thirty-five minutes."

She glanced at his hands. He wore no jewelry except a ring on his wedding finger, but it didn't look like a marriage band. It was black and stoneless, resembling something like a plastic kid's ring pulled from a novelty bubble gum machine. Standback probably wasn't engaged or married.

The helicopter's pitch changed as they made a continuous drop toward the ground. Eventually they leveled off. Even with the moonlight, Ansel was unable to define any landmarks. Only the flashing movement of the tallest rock formations five hundred feet below were visible as the ground rushed past the undercarriage. The fine details of spiring pinnacles, fallen boulders, and hidden cutbacks were impossible to see. Her anxiety heightened several more notches. Flying didn't bother her, but they could run head-on into a precipice and never see it coming until it was too late.

"How easy is it to land in the dark like this?" she asked, peering into the darkness.

"Don't worry. We've got a state-of-the-art GPS/navcom unit tied to a TCAM system, which is great for street or low altitude patrols and warns of nearby aircraft. There's also a radar altimeter transponder. I'm going to turn on the Night Sun, too. It's a searchlight that will guide us down so we don't hit rock."

Standback carefully watched the control panel, monitoring RPMs, turbines, rotors, altitude, and airspeed. The ground reached up for them as they continued to descend, then the aircraft evened out again at one hundred feet. He reached for an independent control box with toggles and flicked a switch. Thirty million candlepower of light sliced through the darkness in a blinding flash as the fifty-pound spotlight mounted on the helicopter's belly flared.

Ansel blinked against the sudden daylight glare illuminating the rocky, boulder-strewn hills and barren brush-laden ground, then bouncing back into her eyes from gray-banded shales, mudstones, and siltstones.

He glanced at her. "We're going to come down alongside a hill. The terrain is flat, open, and easy to maneuver so we shouldn't have any unexpected surprises."

"What kind of surprises?"

"The criminal type. Since the spotlight makes us visible for miles, everyone knows we're cops. That makes us sitting ducks for anybody out here with a gripe against law enforcement."

"People would shoot at us? If you'd told me we were coming here and this was going to be dangerous, I'd have brought my Colt pistol."

Standback cocked his head curiously but said nothing. Ansel enjoyed the moment. Obviously he hadn't expected that answer from a female civilian. And she meant what she'd said. She had quite an experienced working knowledge of firearms. More than she liked.

They passed alongside a small bluff, and the searchlight beam zigzagged across the banded strata of a cliff wall riddled with deep fissures caused by winter runoff and occasional thunderstorm washouts. Next the searchlight flickered so quickly over a group of vehicles parked beside the hill that Ansel almost missed them completely. There were lights down there, too.

Ansel pushed her face against the passenger window. "I see people."

"ERT members," Standback responded.

Soon after, he expertly maneuvered the helicopter into a tight turn by pivoting the entire fuselage beneath the spinning rotor and beginning a fast, steep-angled rush toward the ground and into the wind. Ansel cringed, believing they would crash at sixty miles per hour, but Standback bled off the airspeed and slowed the craft into a perfect ten-foot hover before quickly setting the skids gently down on a level grade of shaley ground.

"Wait until I cut the power before getting out, Miss Phoenix."

Ansel nodded. "Can I take off this helmet? It's driving me crazy."

Standback laughed and began shutting down the mechanical beast, spotlight included. "Sure. Hope you enjoyed the ride because we've got a return trip." His eyes met hers, relaying more than just a gentlemanly attention to her presence. He was actually flirting with her.

"I'm looking forward to it, Agent Standback."

Ansel unstrapped the helmet and pulled it off. It was a relief to get all that electronic paraphernalia out of her face and to hear normally. She also released her seat harness. The rotor blades slowly stalled their gyroscopic spin above her head. All vibration ceased, and lights winked off over the control panel. She gathered her purse and sat quietly until Standback nodded for her get out.

As the door opened, the smell of jet fuel and vegetation assailed her nose. A man quickly appeared beside her in the camp's dim lighting. Agent Outerbridge. She hardly recognized him in casual civilian clothes—high, rubber-soled hiking boots, blue jeans, and a long-sleeved blue cotton shirt covered by a dark bulletproof vest. The butt of a large gun in a white holster Velcroed to the right side of his vest shone in the lantern light.

"Good evening, Miss Phoenix," he said, showing his slightly uneven teeth along with a welcoming, creased-face smile. "Glad you could make it." He politely offered his hand to help her down from the seat and over the skid.

Ansel grabbed his palm and jumped down. "Agent Outerbridge," she acknowledged, stepping carefully over the rocky ground in her expensive calfskin half boots. She was not properly dressed for hiking the Badlands at night, but the fresh smell of sagebrush, wheatgrass, and ponderosa pine was like the perfume of a long-lost friend to her. She hadn't been in the field—the true harsh and dangerous environs of Montana—in a long time.

The agent silently led her away from the copter, leaving Standback behind. He stopped by a folding table supporting maps and a lantern. Agent Walthers, wearing identical casual apparel with vest, nodded a greeting, then returned to studying a topographic contour map. Dr. LaPierre stood beside an SUV, sipping from a Styrofoam cup and giving her a quick wave. She, too, wore sensible, cool clothing, overlaid by neoprene and steel body armor.

None of them were taking any chances out here, Ansel realized, feeling suddenly contrite over her glib remark to Standback about packing a handgun. She squelched her shame and concentrated on Outerbridge.

"The first thing I want to know is how you found out who I am," Ansel demanded.

Showing no surprise, Outerbridge said, "Fair enough. BLM Special-Agent-In-Charge Kevin Broderick mentioned your name."

Ansel's eyes widened. "Of course. And I suppose he told you all about me. Let me set the record straight, Agent Outerbridge. I had nothing to do with what happened at the museum."

"I believe you, even if you were trying to pass yourself off as a county lab tech at a crime scene. That's considered falsifying your identity to federal officers, by the way."

"I was leaving. Detective Dorbandt gave me that smock. Ask him why he did it."

Outerbridge shrugged. "It's not that important. I've checked you out. Graduate of the University of Montana with dual degrees in geology and fine arts. Valedictorian of your graduation class. President of the Paleontology Club. Now a nationally recognized paleoartist and past president of the esteemed Pangaea Society. Even the driving force behind the formation and probably the operation of the future Preston Opel Paleohistory Center. Very commendable."

Ansel crossed her arms, nicely accentuating the upper body curves. "Funny how you're leaving out the part about last summer. Broderick seemed to think that my past experience with a murderer was a national incident."

Walthers looked up, casting a concerned look at Outerbridge, who simply said, "I've reviewed the jacket on that case and have my own opinion. I consider your presence at the museum rather fortuitous, Miss Phoenix."

Relieved but dubious, Ansel brushed back her hair. "Really?"

"Yes. I have something to show you. Then I have a proposal, if you're willing to hear it."

"Why in the world would the FBI have a proposal for me?"

Outerbridge grinned like a Hell Creek fox. "Because you're Indian."

Chapter 8

"The good looking boy may be just good in the face."
Apache

Chief Cullen Flynn parked his vehicle on the weed-infested driveway in front of a dilapidated house, shut off the headlights, and cut the engine. The cool air rushing from the vents died with it. The only sound inside the green Range Rover was that of the engine block ticking off a temperature drop second by second. God, I don't want to do this, he thought. But he had to.

It was his job to follow every possible lead in the museum investigation. So far, none of his inquiries had panned out. Coming here was a long shot. So far-fetched that he hadn't even told anyone at the station.

He peered through the grimy windshield, hands dangling over the top of the steering wheel, keys still in the ignition. Nothing had changed in the last three months. A full moon illuminated the house, and the place was still a dump. No doubt about it.

One exposed ceiling bulb cast a feeble light over the rectangular porch with four spindly, leaning pillars that had cinder blocks pushed against their bases. Windows not covered with plywood held no screens, just open casements with a tic-tac-toe alignment of cracked panes. Dirty sheets, pinned inside as curtains, lay motionless in the sweltering heat. Big Sky weathering had made a seborrheic dander of the cheap, white latex paint. The front door, stained an incongruous kelly green, gaped open.

Nobody came out to greet him, even though a primer-splotched green El Camino was parked beside the squad car. Hell, he knew who was inside, all right. Snubbing a law officer was part of the game in this repeating scenario, carefully choreographed for maximum effect and aggravation. And it worked on him every time.

"Damn pain in the ass," Flynn sputtered as the door creaked open, and he stepped into an ankle-deep patch of dandelions. Nothing else could survive the drought.

He slammed the door, adjusted his ten-gallon hat, and walked toward the wood-rotted porch. Blue flies buzzed around the brown bottles strewn across the veranda planking, the yeasty smell of fermenting beer holding the promise of an easy feast. A large rat skittered under a porch corner as he approached, and Flynn popped the safety strap on his holster. All he needed was to get bitten by vermin while trying to corner a pest of another kind.

"Cyrus, you in there?" he called, climbing two warped steps. "It's Chief Flynn. I'm coming inside."

There was no answer so Flynn stepped onto the porch and continued with purpose toward the door. Beyond the opening, everything was dark. No lights. No sound. He slowed and edged against the doorjamb, trying not to make the floorboards squeak. The acrid smell of piss and marijuana wafted from within. No real surprise, but he wished he hadn't smelled it.

Flynn moved through the doorway, middle-aged eyes adjusting to the darkness oh-so-slowly. The tiny space serving as a living room held little furniture. He saw a sofa and the man sleeping on it first. Then the end table and recliner. A small portable TV on a shelving unit made from eight-by-twelves laid between more cinder blocks stacked up on ends. The rest of the room was a disaster of dirty clothes, fast food containers, and faded boxes that had never been unpacked since being carted in the summer before.

He took the opportunity to walk quickly around the house while the man slept. From the open doorways, his eyes scanned for a pot stash or other drug paraphernalia within the filthy kitchen, both bedrooms, and the minuscule bathroom with unflushed toilet. He didn't see anything illegal in plain sight. No weapons either. He passed the basement door as he headed for the living room, considered going down, but decided he didn't want to turn his back on Cyrus too long.

In front of the couch, he said, "Wake up."

When there was no response, Flynn walked over to a scarred oak end table and turned on a pole lamp with a stained, yellow shade. Ochre light washed away little of the room's sloth and despair. The man, wearing only blue jeans, rolled over onto his side, swatted at the long coppery hair falling into his face, then slid back into a deep sleep.

Flynn roused him with a stiff push to the left shoulder. "Get up. We've got to talk."

Cyrus' torso bolted up from the frayed black cushions, blue eyes wide but disoriented. "What the fuck," he yelled as his dilated pupils finally settled on Flynn's annoyed face. He began coughing in hoarse spasms, then stopped. Gooseflesh covered his arms. "What are you doing here, man?"

Flynn surveyed Cyrus' lineless face. Normally a looker, according to the ladies, tonight his skin was pasty beneath a surprisingly well-trimmed reddish moustache and beard. Dark smudges underscored his lower lashes.

"You don't look good, Cyrus. You've lost weight. I saw the booze and I can smell the pot. What else are you jacked up on? Amphetamines? I thought you were clean since Riverton."

Cyrus' gaze solidified into a piercing green stare. "I'm clean enough. I've just been sick. Got the flu or something. The pot helps me sleep. Besides it's all gone."

Flynn didn't bother arguing. He walked over to the recliner, body tense and ready to spring into action. Cyrus could get feisty without warning. "You're violating your parole."

Cyrus snorted. "Things that slow in that cowpunch Mecca of yours that you're checking up on me for the DOC?"

"Don't get smart, laddie."

Wisely dropping his challenging gaze, Cyrus reached toward a crumpled pack of cigarettes on the junk-cluttered table. Besides the trash, an assortment of over-the-counter cough medicines and lozenges peeked out.

"Sorry about the pot and the beer. I promise it won't happen again. So what can I do for you, *Chief* Flynn?"

"I'm looking for information. Have you ever seen or heard about a young Indian with a claw foot who might have worked around the rodeos or somewhere else busting horses or bulls?"

Flynn watched with a mixture of irritation and awe as Cyrus adroitly delayed his response by using a disposable lighter to stoke his smoke. Every turn of the head, hand gesture, and body twist was smooth and slow despite his condition. Cyrus always used his good looks and animal charisma as a lethal weapon. Just as a glossy sidewinder's undulating crawl is malevolent yet mesmerizing, the man knew how to work every muscle so you did absolutely nothing as he made a slick, inevitable approach into your strike zone.

As a cop, Flynn had always been intrigued by the spiritual concepts of good and evil in human beings, as if he could figure it out given enough time and study. He'd known Cyrus since he was a toothless, undernourished baby, and over thirty years of staring and cogitating on the remorseless soul locked inside that pearly, unblemished skin still had him mystified. Mostly because Cyrus had gone bad as an eight-year-old child. What he did know was that, whether through genetic fluke or psychological disease, the man was morally and socially defective and well beyond saving.

Cyrus completed his ritual. "An Indian? No way. I don't pal around with tee pee trash."

Flynn cringed and his thoughts wandered, as they often did around Cyrus, toward Ansel Phoenix. Dark and light. That's what they both represented to him: the in-your-face, physical reality of the differences between what could be either Heaven or Hell on Earth.

"Maybe somebody you know knows him. I want you to ask around."

Cyrus brushed hair away and sneered. "I'm not a snitch."

"This is important. You're going to do it, and then I'll permanently forget about your little indiscretion with the marijuana and the booze."

"You are all lathered up. What's this Indian done?"

"He tried to rip off some fossil tracks at the Big Toe museum. Got himself blown to bits with faulty equipment and burned beyond recognition. It's been on the news and in the paper."

Cyrus' eyes sparked with interest. "Like I said, I've been sick. And when I haven't been laid on my back, I've been working the night shift at that crappy job at the meat packing plant."

Flynn exhaled. They'd had this discussion before. With his brains and looks, Cyrus could have made something of himself. Maybe gotten a degree in agriscience or even a doctorate in veterinary medicine. He'd always had a penchant for tending to animals. Instead he'd led a life filled chapter and verse with petty crimes of assault and battery, misdemeanor drug trafficking, car theft, and B & Es. So far, he'd only ended up in minimum security prisons or places like the Wyoming Honor Farm in Riverton. He'd been lucky.

"Stop scratching an old itch. It's part of the parole package. If you'd kept your sticky paws clean, you wouldn't be where you are today."

Cyrus puffed his cigarette and considered Flynn's words. "And why exactly am I supposed to know the right people? I'm not an Injun."

"Don't play dumb. At Riverton you trained mustangs in the wild horse adoption program sponsored by the BLM for eighteen months as part of your rehabilitation. You know a lot of jailbirds who might know this Indian. I need a lead and I want to notify his family. Every man deserves a decent burial, even a thief."

"You must think he's an ex-con. Why?"

"Don't ask questions. You just pounce on this. Get me some results."

"I might be able to pull in some favors," Cyrus said, sniffing and wiping a hand under his runny nose. "I've got to make some long distance calls, though. You going to pay for them?"

"I think the police department can foot the bill, but stick to business. No bullshit sessions with your old cell mates on my dime. Work with me, Cyrus, and you'll be doing a good thing for once in your miserable life."

Smoke funneled out of Cyrus' nostrils. "I'll get back to you."

"No. I'll get back to you. Don't disappoint me." He pulled some cash from his uniform pocket. "And go see a doctor."

"Sure," Cyrus said, grinding the butt in an ash-filled jar lid and grabbing the money. Then he flopped back onto the cushions, stretched out, and turned his back on Flynn. "I gotta rest. I'm working tonight."

Flynn gave one last lingering look at Cyrus and pivoted toward the door. He paced by a waist-high stack of teetering cardboard boxes when moonlight glinted off metal. He glanced down and saw a key ring probably tossed on the top carton when Cyrus had stumbled into the house drunk or stoned.

The braided horsehair dangle contained several keys and a miniature bottle cap opener. It rested on a pair of black leather Flex gloves and a matching balaclava. What was Cyrus doing with a total-protection night gear hood? Nothing legal, that was for sure. Stupid leaving such things by the front entrance, but Cyrus hadn't expected him.

Flynn moved slow and easy onto the porch, then went down the steps. As he neared the Camino's pickup end, he took a quick glance behind him. Cyrus was nowhere to be seen. Flynn perused the flatbed and saw scattered tools—ten-pound sledgehammer, a shovel, pry bar, an assortment of cold chisels.

Something special caught his eye and he reached in. Bright moonlight illuminated the dark rock nestled inside his palm. He could make out a three-inch-long pitted surface with one broad end and the other tapering into an arching point.

Flynn sensed someone behind him. Too late. The comforting weight of the gun against his hip disappeared as it was yanked from his holster. He spun around, remembering with self-anger that he'd unclipped the safety strap when he'd seen the rat. Cyrus stood a few feet away with the police issue .357

pistol in his left hand and a double-gauge shotgun pointed at him with the other.

"Damn, Cyrus. Have you lost your mind?" Flynn asked as calmly as he could though his heart was pitching against his rib cage.

Cyrus watched him with unblinking eyes as hard and cold as yellow-green stones. Snake eyes. A moonbeam haloed his red locks as he gave Flynn an angelic smile. He pulled the shotgun trigger without saying a word.

An explosion of sound expanded to fill the world as Flynn knew it, then punched through his chest like a Jack mule's kick. Cordite and the odor of burning meat filled his nostrils. Still his body remained standing, which surprised him immensely considering the large, ragged-edge hole in his torso. He knew he was full of buckshot, but where was the pain? Flynn wondered as he stood rooted like a statue, only one step in any direction from death's door.

Flynn opened his mouth but no words came out. With lungs too damaged to push air past his vocal cords, his pleas for help retreated inward as he silently prayed a Catholic psalm.

God, by Your Name save me, and by Your might defend my cause...for haughty men have risen up against me and fierce men seek my life.

When Flynn heard the small fossil in his hand drop, he fully understood his predicament. Technically speaking, he was already dead. His stubborn Irish brain just wouldn't admit it.

Cyrus stared as gravity finally pulled Flynn's moribund weight to the ground. He hit the dirt like a sack of potatoes, sending juices, dust, and dirt flying. His police hat flew off, rolled on its brim, and fell over with a crown-wobbling spin near the driver's door of his Jeep.

The last thing Flynn saw before he fell into a dark abyss was Cyrus lowering the hot-barreled shotgun to his side and shivering violently against a nonexistent cold.

The last thing he thought about was Ansel Phoenix.

Chapter 9

*"Take only what you need and
leave the land as you found it."*
Arapaho

Ansel carefully placed one boot and then the other upon the crumbly, pebble-strewn incline as she followed the jean-clad rump of Doctor Dixie LaPierre up the east face of the bluff. Behind her walked the stern-faced Agent Walthers, an un-smiling bear of a man in his late forties whose towering stature overshadowed her every move. Outerbridge, a quartz halogen lamp in hand, walked point and led them single-file up the fifteen-degree switchback trail. Standback remained in camp as guard, armed with radio, handgun, and night-scope rifle.

What had started as a winding foot trail through an outwash fan near the bottom quickly turned into a wide, machine-rutted roadway. They now followed a bulldozed ledge made by shearing off bluff walls and pushing debris off the edges. Where the bulldozer bucket had cut into the cliff, colored bands of rock strata were revealed like a baker's slice through a birthday cake. Using a loaned battery-powered lantern light, Ansel noted the white sandstone layers and brown mudstone stripes, actually paleosoil, with her geologist's eye.

She also recognized the single darkest band of the famous K-T clay layer located halfway between the others. This was the Cretaceous-Tertiary boundary deposit comprised of clay and iridium, which some experts asserted had come from an impacting meteorite ten kilometers across colliding with Earth. It was possible that when the large-impact crater vaporized sea water and horizontally ejected dust and grit, a devastating environmental change had occurred that led to the extinction of dinosaurs.

Raking her flashlight beam over the intersecting slopes of sediment bands discarded from ancient rivers and streams covering most of Cretaceous Montana, Ansel could tell which way the water had traveled when the grains of sand and mud were deposited. Water had washed left on a bottom sandstone band, then back to the right on a middle mudstone ribbon, changing direction yet again to flow left on the topmost sandstone layer.

It was obvious that Outerbridge was taking her to a fossil dig. She should have been excited, but other factors distracted her. She'd taken off her expensive suede vest and replaced it with the man-sized, steel-plated body armor that Outerbridge had insisted she wear, and it chafed her breasts through the thin fabric of her low-cut top.

Protective apparel for a woman would have taken this into consideration, she thought with irritation. Given the heat, the heavy bulletproof clothing, and the workout her calves and thighs were getting, Ansel also promised herself to try exercising more.

Walthers moved up behind her. "You going to make it?"

This close, she could smell the spicy aroma of his sport cologne. "I'm fine. How much further to the mystery spot I was dragged up here to see?"

"Around this curve."

Dixie LaPierre peered over her shoulder. "Great view from up here."

Ansel glanced at her. It was the first time Dixie had really talked, though she'd given her a quick smile and "Hello" before they started the climb thirty feet below.

Before she could respond, silent heat lightning flashed, and Ansel looked over the trail edge into the flat prairie expanse beneath them. A hot breeze, tainted with the scent of sagebrush, scrub, and wild grasses, blew into her face. The bluff was one of many that rose above the earth's dirty skin like a cauliflower wart made of white, micaceous sandstone. The gravid moon spilled beams across the ground in milky splotches, illuminating a pitted crossbed of calcareous, cement-like sandstone pillars resembling sharp stalagmites or giant toadstool caps.

Above the trail a ponderosa copse clung precariously to the highest elevations, and stars glimmered in an inky sky-pool. Miles away a coyote howled a moon-song across the Badlands. As beautiful as it was, a fall from this height into the maw of boulders and pillars could kill her.

Silence prevailed until they reached a flat shelf on the eastern face of the precipice. The bulldozer had gouged deep into the bluff's underbelly, pushing flora, soil, and rock away from an excavated fossil site. Once hidden beneath tons of sixty-five-million-year-old mud and sand, an exposed bed of gigantic dinosaur bones lay across the ground. Ansel looked upon an excavation site ringed by rechargeable, lantern-style halogens.

"Jesus," she exclaimed, shocked and disbelieving. This was no carefully tended scientific site preserving matrix, fossils, and ecological microsites. This was a grave-looting frenzy.

"Nice work, huh?" said Outerbridge, hands on his hips. "Poachers on a mission, Miss Phoenix. This used to be the near complete skeleton of an adult female T-rex that the University of Montana had excavated for two years. Everything was carefully removed from the ground, catalogued, and jacketed in plaster this spring. Then it was recovered with dirt so it could be removed next spring. Unfortunately, poachers got to it first."

Ansel stepped through a litter of busted plaster jackets spewing huge broken, brown-grey bones of all sizes and descriptions. The containers resembled monstrous hatched eggs. Fossil ribs once as tall as she were now reduced to fractured, oblong chunks. There were smashed vertebrae the size of footballs everywhere. Crushed arm bones and leg bones. Pelvic bones pulverized into dust. Everything ruined by a succession of treaded backhoe ruts and tractor treads as the plunderers hauled choice pieces away for sale at a humongous profit.

"I don't see the skull," Ansel said.

"That's the only thing they wanted," Outerbridge replied with disgust.

Temporarily speechless, Ansel turned around and bent down to pick up a smaller bone. A toe bone. It was heavy and cool to the touch. Somehow it had escaped damage, though it might have been originally preserved with an intact foot or an entire leg. There was no way to tell. The creature it belonged to had used it to run down prey, dig a nest, or to fight for its life against other dinosaurs. It was an irreplaceable treasure that had survived millennia by pure happenstance of weather conditions, geologic forces, and natural erosion.

Acid anger churned in Ansel's stomach. She'd read about such destructive pilfering, but never seen it. This was a most grievous sacrilege of the ancient dead. Obscene and soulless.

She gently set the bone down and noticed an odd circular piece of foil about the size of an eraser head in the dust. It had a flat, green square of material attached directly in its center. It looked familiar to her, but she couldn't place its meaning or purpose with her jumbled mind. Instinctively, she did know that it might be important. Realizing that everyone was quiet and waiting for her response, she palmed the foil tab in her left hand, stood, and turned around.

She looked at Outerbridge. "Why didn't they take the skull and leave the rest?"

"Honey," Dixie said softly, "besides being thieving amateurs armed with shovels, sledgehammers, and crowbars, they're making a point: Don't mess with us. We don't care about anything or anybody when it comes to getting what we want."

Ansel glanced at the newer discarded boxes of plaster and rope which also littered the ground. "Why did they need new packing materials if the skull was already jacketed?"

"Because they placed new plaster over the old jacket," Dixie explained. "The university marked every case with invisible paint that fluoresces under black light. Same with the bones inside. Helps identify them if they turn up in the wrong place. By covering the original jacket with new plaster, the poachers can transport the skull without it being traced. After the jacket arrives someplace safe, they'll open it up, remove the skull, and scrub the paint off so they can sell it."

"So the poachers knew that the university marked the jackets and bones," Ansel considered. "Is that a standard practice these days?"

Outerbridge swatted a mosquito and moved closer. "No, it's not. Which means these people either had access to inside information or they're savvy enough to check for marked goods. All that most legitimate universities or museums ever hope for is to get their bones back. They don't bother to chase down the thieves and prosecute."

"That's no wonder," Ansel said. "The chances of catching poachers is remote, and the idea of criminal prosecution is a joke. The Archeological Resources Protection Act never included fossils, and the 1906 Antiquities Act is completely inadequate for protecting fossils because they don't fit the vague definition of an 'antiquity' under the law."

"You know your history," Outerbridge conceded, "and I agree. Federal legislation has failed miserably at stiffening penalties for fossil heists on public lands, but that's because commercial fossil dealers and certain academic researchers have vehemently opposed more restrictions for fossil excavations."

Ansel scowled. "What do you expect when the government started issuing permits only to fossil hunters doing paleontological research? Legitimate commercial dealers and other amateurs doing fossil preservation and sales to reputable institutions and collectors see this as greedy, academic snobbery. They're being cast in the role of criminals when the real thieves are bastards like those who destroyed this site."

"That's why I'm here," Outerbridge countered. "To catch these bastards."

Ansel wasn't buying it. "So let's say you do catch them. Even I know that if a poaching case gets as far as a misdemeanor indictment, it won't stand up in court under the Antiquities Act. And if thieves are ever convicted, they'll get nothing but a modest fine or minimal prison time."

Outerbridge sighed and stared thoughtfully into the night beyond the bluff. When he turned around, his face looked older, his gaze penetrating, but weary.

"The federal government owns six hundred and twenty-two million acres of public land held and protected in trust to every person in the United States, Miss Phoenix. We can't allow this wholesale looting. Restricting the removal of any fossil from public land through permits is the only stop-gap federal law enforcement has got, and it's all I've got to work with while I do my job. The only other thing I can fall back on is making arrests backed up with solid judicial evidence of illegal fossil poaching and sales. And I need your help."

"Because I'm Indian? You told me you'd explain that comment. I'm still waiting."

"I'm conducting a sting operation, and I need somebody with your experience and ethnic background to do some front surveillance work."

Ansel was floored. She couldn't breath as her thoughts whirled. She had to finish the last Argentine book drawing, which would take another week, at least. Besides, this was dangerous work. She wasn't qualified. What would Dorbandt say? Her family? This was preposterous. She couldn't possibly do it. She wouldn't.

She sucked in a lung full of bone dry, hot desert air and swallowed. "No way. I'm not a token Indian for your war games against crime, Agent Outerbridge."

Outerbridge said nothing, but Dixie walked over. "Ansel, this is no game. Forget all the rhetoric, politics, and bureaucratic bullshit Outerbridge is selling. Do you know what this poaching scum calls historic fossil sites? Bone Orchards. Like they can come in and pick them off the ground by the bushel, haul them away in pickup trucks, and sell them on the black market by the pound. And that's almost what they do unless somebody stops them somehow, some way."

Dixie looked down at the carnage, crossed her arms, and shook her head. "When all the fossils are gone, they're gone. We can't make any more. We need your help for a couple days."

The silence was deafening, even in the middle of the Badlands where night birds called, predators howled, and insects sang. Outerbridge watched her closely. Walthers scratched his jaw and tried to look half as looming as he was. Dixie stared at her pitifully with large brown eyes.

Ansel felt like a heel. She could at least listen to an explanation of what they wanted of her. They seemed sincere, and they appeared quite united in their desire to right a grievous wrong. In principle, she agreed with them one hundred percent.

"All right. I'll listen to what you have in mind, but I'm not promising anything. Got it?"

"Understood," Outerbridge said. "I'll contact you again soon. We'll go over the operation contingencies then. Right now, let's get you home." He walked away. Walthers followed. Ansel remained a moment longer, inspecting the disarticulated and ruined bones a last time. The foil tab inside her balled fist felt like fire. If she got caught taking it, there'd be hell to pay.

Dixie pulled up beside her. "Relax," she coached, a red-slashed smile showing perfect, to-die-for teeth. "You know the best part of this operation?"

Ansel shook her head.

"Honey, you get to work with Agent Standback, and he's got the cutest tush in this pack of hair-trigger belly-gunners."

Chapter 10

"It is not good for anyone to be alone."
Cheyenne

Dorbandt prayed that the Indian's head hadn't defrosted. He gazed at the heavily sealed, medium-size, liner-board box covered with biohazard stickers on the passenger seat. Five early morning hours of speeding from Mission City to Billings with the Freon pumping hadn't guaranteed the appropriate transport conditions.

The sedan was griddle-hot on the outside, temperatures hitting a record one hundred one degrees, and the interior wasn't much cooler. He hoped the five kilograms of dry ice surrounding the leak-proof polystyrene box inside this one were holding up—he was sweating like a steam pipe beneath his dress shirt.

"This can't be right," Dorbandt spat, scrabbling for the manila envelope containing the official papers needed to comply with a chain-of-custody report. He peered at Bucky Combs' cover scrawl. Yes, this was the street.

Billings was his home town. He'd been born and raised here. Once a frontier cattle town with five mountain ranges visible from its northern borders, it was now an urban sprawl of one hundred thousand people. He knew the area like the veins on his hand, and this wasn't anywhere near Montana State University College of Technology. This was a suburban area growing a bumper crop of five-acre ranchettes cooking in a dust-bowl dip carved out of the landscape.

Dorbandt turned left, past a horse-shaped mailbox bearing the name BIRCH. That fit. He was supposed to hand over the head to a Doctor Birch. The sedan cruised down a long, dusty drive toward a split-level wood house with Shaker shingles and a garage.

He parked beside a blue Chevy Lumina van. When he got out, a wall of heat hit him, but he staunchly grabbed his jacket and put it on. He retrieved the paraphernalia from the front seat and went to the door. A cathedral chime rang as he straightened his suit and continued the process of sweltering two notches closer toward unconsciousness.

The door opened in a flash. After his cop's gaze raked over a pretty lady with short, platinum-blond hair, Dorbandt did a double-take. His heart lurched into his throat. He couldn't believe his eyes. The long auburn locks he'd once known were gone, but she looked just like… No. Surely he was mistaken.

The woman stared back, blue eyes shocked with surprise before her face transformed into delight. "Reid? God, I can't believe it. It is you."

"Hi, Chloe," Dorbandt said like a tongue-tied teenager.

Chloe didn't stand on decorum. She moved through the door, wrapped her arms around his waist, and gave him a quick hug. Dorbandt nervously balanced the evidence box and thick envelope at the same time. He also enjoyed the tingling that the feel and scent of her produced.

Sixteen years later, and he still remembered Chloe's velvet touch and gardenia bath oil smell. A pang of deep-seeded regret jabbed him. It seemed only yesterday that she'd hugged him and told him without rancor that their relationship was over. At the time, he'd agreed with her.

Chloe drew away. "You look wonderful," she replied as she appraised every lean and well-toned bit.

"Thanks. You, too. I've brought you a head," he replied, then wanted to kick himself. "I mean, I'm supposed to deliver this to Dr. Birch. Is he here?"

Chloe laughed. "That's me. When we dated, I was using my stepfather's surname of Masterson. After my mother divorced him, I went back to her maiden name. I guess we've got a lot of catching up to do, Reid. It's been a long time. Follow me to the studio, and we'll talk."

He went eagerly. They crossed the parched front lawn to the detached garage, and Chloe motioned him through a heavy steel side door. "Make yourself comfortable."

Between the rush of air conditioning and Chloe's unexpected presence, Dorbandt was feeling better about this trip. He'd anticipated a hasty and dreary delivery job without any perks, not even time to visit close friends or relatives in the city. Instead he'd stumbled into a bonanza of opportunities to reconnect with a woman he'd almost married years before.

He watched with appreciation Chloe's long legs stride beneath her ankle-length corduroy skirt as they entered the single-room workshop. Chloe was tall and slender, what his mother had once described as willowy when he'd brought her home to meet his parents. He'd always liked that—dating a woman as tall as himself, plus athletic.

"Let me put this someplace cool," Chloe said, pointing at the box in his hands.

"Good idea. Here's the paperwork you requested: crime scene report with photos and drawings, clothing inventory—what there was of them—the postmortem photos, and the autopsy results. We weren't on the case very long before the FBI took over so the forensics are nil."

"That's what Sheriff Combs told me." She took the box with the folder into her smooth, long-fingered hands. "If I work fast, maybe I can give you a face to go with the remains."

Chloe headed toward a large refrigerator next to a stainless steel gas oven, a short countertop, and a row of overhead cabinets—a functional mini-kitchen not meant for preparing foodstuffs but rather human body parts. There was even a long block table with stacks of old newspapers, surgical instruments, rubber gloves, and large plastic bags.

Dorbandt looked away and took in the rest of the workshop, which smelled heavily of artist's paints, cleaning solvents, rubber, and clay. Several small tables with stools before them filled the room, each with a single wooden block with a vertical dowel upon which a human head was attached. All were in varying states of completion.

Some busts had human skulls stuck with protruding rubber pins. Others were covered with pins and clay, half-completed faces, and craniums where the heads looked caught in the process of generating their skins and features all over again. Still more heads, fully completed, dotted the room on wall shelving, larger tables, and the floor. The studio reminded him of Ansel's hangar where she created her dinosaur drawings or other paleosculptures. But there were differences.

Ansel kept a neat and orderly workshop. Here everything was randomly dispersed. Surfaces were stippled with the rainbow hues of dripped paint or dust from colored clays and cluttered with duplicate sculpting tools strewn next to busts in progress. Unframed sketches of dead human faces of all genders, ages, and races were hastily tacked to the walls, while Ansel preferred to keep stacks of preliminary sketches under tight control and her artistic milestones lovingly framed and displayed.

The women definitely had different personalities, Dorbandt assessed. Though both were artistic and surrounded themselves with the bones of the dead—animal and human—he had to admit that Chloe's chosen profession was more disquieting. A hundred human eyes stared back at him, giving him the uncomfortable feeling of being watched from every angle in an abattoir of the dead. He wondered what Ansel would think about Chloe.

As he surreptitiously searched the room for personal mementos or pictures that might reveal if Chloe was married or had children, she said, "Your sheriff told me that the body was badly burned. A gas explosion, right?"

Dorbandt didn't see anything telling. "Yes. A propane tank from an industrial concrete saw. Probably accidental. The perp was poaching dinosaur tracks from a riverbed on BLM land."

"Sounds like a real bad character," Chloe said as she sat down on a metal stool, crossing her long legs at the ankles. "Have a seat."

"Thanks." He sat across from her, his back toward a table bearing the gracile, recreated bust of a black child. He noticed Chloe had no wedding band. "When did you get into all this?"

"I prefer to think that it got into me," she corrected with a dazzling smile. "I suppose this is quite a shock for you. When we broke up, I was just a lowly dispatcher for the local sheriff's department, and you were a trooper climbing the tin-plate ladder. Sheriff Combs told me he was sending a homicide detective, but I had no idea who it was."

"You ducked the question. What happened to get you into facial reconstructions?"

"Oh, I decided that being just an observer of the criminal action wasn't my calling. After you left, I quit the department and got a Ph.D. in physical anthropology at MSU Missoula. Next came enough forensic experience to get me certified by the American Board of Forensic Anthropology. Afterward I went to the Scottsdale Artists' School and got certified in forensic reconstruction. I worked in Arizona for quite a while but ended up in Billings a year ago as an associate professor with the College of Technology."

Dorbandt stared into her deep blue eyes. "Sounds *very* impressive to me, Chloe."

She shrugged. "It's worked out all right. I teach some 3D computer imaging classes, get access to their facial reproduction and photo superimposition software, do research, and run my studio business helping police, coroners, and pathologists identify faceless people."

"You're a miracle worker. It takes a focused intuition and lots of fortitude to make the conscious determinations used to recreate a human personality from nothing but cold bone. I'd never have the patience for it. Sitting for hours on a stool would kill me. I'm a mover."

"I remember," she replied fondly, "but the real miracle is that I do what I love and manage to make enough money to survive financially. This is strictly a labor of love, Reid. There's always some lost human soul calling out to be recognized and named. Their numbers seem endless, and I often feel I'm not working fast enough. Sometimes I have to be careful not to go plum crazy thinking about it. Now what about you? How do you like Mission City?"

"I love it. It's a small town with big ideals. Of course, I like coming home once in a while so I can brush the cow patties off my boots and tromp around the Rimrock Mall, eat Greek food at the Athenian, or listen to live jazz at the Golden Pheasant. I haven't gone native yet."

"Any family?"

Dorbandt hesitated, though he was glad she'd broached the subject first. She seemed curious in an anxious sort of way. He took that for a good sign. "No. Not yet."

"Still haven't settled down, huh? I've been married and divorced. No kids."

"Sorry to hear that."

Chloe sighed. "Well, my career didn't help. I've been obsessed about it. I was juggling a lot of things, and Cody got lost in the shuffle. How long are you staying in Billings and where?"

"I'm bunking at the Motel 6 until the day after tomorrow. That should give us time to discuss the case in detail. How are you doing the reconstruction?"

"Since this is a rush job, I'm going to do a completely computer-generated photo rather than the usual clay bust. Clay requires at least ten to fourteen days of very concentrated work, and is more labor intensive than digital work. Besides studying the skull characteristics, placing the twenty-one skin markers, and filling in with clay, I've got to make a mold of the completed head with synthetic rubber reinforced with fiberglass plaster, sand it, paint it, and retouch the bust. Your supervisor wants a quicker turnaround."

"How long will the computer work take?"

"About a week. I've got classes to teach in between. When the photo is finished, it'll give you the fastest shot at getting the face recognized from police fliers, newspapers, and TV spots."

"Got time to go to dinner tonight?" Dorbandt grinned. "Sort of a reunion celebration to the forces of serendipity."

Chloe cocked her head in consideration. "I'd love to, but I've got to macerate another skull before I start your reconstruction. That means first removing the skin and muscles with dissecting tools, scraping away tissue, separating the jaw and removing the teeth, boiling everything in separate pots with a bleach solution, and then carefully simmering the pieces again in water for up to eight hours."

Dorbandt looked at his watch. "How about a really late meal?"

"Well, the trick is making sure I don't boil and cool things too much, especially the teeth, or they'll crack. And if I don't get the tissues, grease, and odor out of the bone, leftover bleach can degrade the bone surfaces even after drying. Any unremoved grease will smell, seep through the bone, and attract dust and grime. I can't risk careless processing which would damage the bone and obscure or remove morphological traits. Worse, I could create 'pseudotrauma' that could be mistaken for real perimortem trauma."

"Is that a yes or a no?"

"Yes. I guess we can do a late supper. I have to eat sometime."

"Great." His cell phone rang. "Hold that thought, Chloe." He grabbed it from inside his suit pocket. "Lieutenant Dorbandt."

"Reid, it's Odie," boomed the deep voice of fellow detective Oden Fiskar. "McKenzie told me to call. Get back here pronto. All hell has broke lose."

Dorbandt looked at Chloe, his excitement over having dinner at a five-star Billings restaurant, and maybe something else, with a charming ex-girlfriend dashed to smithereens. "What's happened?"

"Chief Flynn has disappeared."

"What do you mean?"

"He's gone. Dropped off the edge of the earth. Flynn was last seen leaving the police station at seven last night. He never got home. The city cops have been trying to locate him since ten last night when his wife called them. Now the search has spilled over to us. Sheriff Combs thinks it may be related to the poaching case."

"Hokay," Dorbandt replied. "I'm heading back." He replaced the phone.

"Trouble?"

Dorbandt nodded. "Always in this business. Listen, I've got to leave. I'm sorry about tonight." His eyes locked onto hers. He felt terribly cheated by fate.

Chloe smiled. "I'll accept a rain check. Don't worry about it, Reid."

"Give me your phone number, and I'll call you."

She pulled a business card off a table and passed it to him. Then she bent forward and pecked him lightly on the right cheek. "I'll be waiting. Drive safely."

Dorbandt hurried from the studio and slammed into the summer heat, but this time he was floating on hot air.

Chapter 11

"All who have died are equal."
Comanche

The phone next to Ansel's bed woke her from peaceful slumber with brutal efficiency. She jerked upright like a marionette, eyes wide, heart pounding, and brain disoriented. Jesus, what was happening? Eight rings. Why didn't her answering machine kick in? Nine rings. Ten.

Groaning, she rolled toward the night stand, flailed her right arm, and snatched the device. "Hello," she said, projecting the angry tone she intended.

"Ansel, this is Permelia Chance. Sounds like your belly cinch is too tight. You all right?"

Damn. She'd forgotten her promise to call Permelia. Ansel rubbed a hand over her face, then pushed back strands of tangled hair. The digital clock-radio blinked an erroneous twelve o'clock. There must have been a power outage. Everyone was maxing out their air conditioning, and Montana Power and Light was hard-pressed to match supply with demand.

"Sorry, Mrs. Chance. I'm under the weather. I was going to call. What time is it?"

"Only eight o'clock. I'm impatient but at my age the glass is three-quarters empty."

Gaining her bearings, Ansel knew she needed more sleep, and she ached all over. "No problem. We should meet, talk about your book cover art."

"How about today? Starr and I are free all afternoon."

Ansel mentally reviewed her schedule for the next few days. There was only one good time to make the drive to Permelia's ranch. "I'm booked this afternoon. Tomorrow morning?"

"Sure. Come over about ten o'clock. You know your way?"

"Yes. See you then, Mrs. Chance."

Permelia said farewell through Starr's yapping echo. Ansel clicked off and speed-dialed the ranch. Every day at the Arrowhead began at four a.m. She listened as Pearl's affable, taped voice requested her to leave a message. Her stepmother of fifteen years was a no-nonsense, liberated woman who could draw straws of semen from high-strung Angus bulls for artificial insemination one minute, then turn around and speak in a guileless, ladylike voice that sounded as if butter wouldn't melt in her mouth.

"Pearl, it's Ansel. Ask Daddy to give me the name of a good attorney who handles land trust cases. Leave a message if I'm not here. Hope everything's all right. Love you both. Bye."

Ansel pushed back the covers, her leg muscles protesting with bolts of fiery pain and reminding her of her night in the Badlands. Agent Outerbridge had revealed nothing more about his mysterious sting operation, and she'd made a helicopter trip back to Swoln with Standback.

Agent Standback, she thought with a smile while rounding up khaki pants, a beaded shirt, and a basket-stamped belt from closet and drawers. The FBI pilot was an enigma.

Standback had stuck to his routine of polite dialogue peppered with provocative glances. It was obvious he liked her, but he'd never asked her anything personal. He'd promised to see her again, which was a given if Outerbidge was returning with a pep talk. Otherwise, she didn't even know Standback's first name. Nor had he given her any clues to his Indian heritage.

That's what stumped her. Indians usually conversed first about their family ancestry—what tribe they were from and their clan affiliations. It was important to know one's relationship to clan strangers who could be tied to you by extended lineages as intricate as the strands of a spider's web. She didn't deal with such tribal customs daily, but was surprised that Standback hadn't acknowledged they were Amerindian kinsmen in an Anglo-dominated world.

Ansel put on her makeup and grabbed a bowl of cereal and a cup of instant coffee. As she ate, she pulled the neatly manufactured foil tab from her purse and studied it. Curious. The quarter-inch foil circle with the smaller green square on the shiny side taunted her as it lay in her hand. If the FBI team had searched the area, how had they missed it? Maybe being under the toe bone had obscured it, or maybe somebody had left it behind after the land was combed for forensic clues.

Pushing the tab back into a plastic photo wallet sheet and replacing the billfold in her purse, Ansel planned her day. She'd lined up a full schedule of chores, not the least was continuing to work on the Giganatosaurus drawing. First, she had some investigating to do.

Within the next twenty minutes, she'd grabbed some things and primed the trailer security system. She was shocked by the broiling heat outside. Dust billows generated by northeasterly prairie winds and the crispy, straw-matted wasteland of what had once been a verdant spring-green landscape engulfed her. Even the ponderosa at the end of her drive were turning sienna under the broiling sun. An end to the drought didn't look anywhere in sight.

Things didn't get better as she drove toward the Big Toe Natural History Museum. Pastures withered, watering holes steamed away, and dirt-powdered stock animals cast skeletal shadows across a dying earth. Ansel had never seen a drought this bad, so fierce and unrelenting.

When she reached Barnum Brown Road, she drove slowly, keeping an eye out for cops of any variety. She wasn't sure how the FBI, county police, or BLM officers had beefed up security. The front gate was chained and padlocked. A large, yellow NO

TRESPASSING sign had been wired to the chain link. The parking lot was empty. No sign of Bieselmore either, who'd get the bum's rush as curator if the BLM decided to close the place.

There was a dirt service road to her right bordered on both sides by a fence line of thick chains strung between wide posts. The side road entrance was also blocked by a timber drop gate securely padlocked at one end. Ansel didn't care about the museum compound. She was interested in the riverbed.

Ansel switched gears and reversed the truck down Barnum Brown Road until the chain barrier ceased. Then she gunned the four-wheel-drive vehicle around an end-post and made a diagonal grassland crossing to intersect with the service road.

She was officially trespassing on BLM land, but if she was quick and unobtrusive, she could get in and out without being spotted. She wanted two things: a closer look at the ground surrounding the fossil tracks and to scrutinize the damage done to her Allosaurus sculpture.

The gravel drive stopped on the west side of the compound, but Ansel continued off road onto the grass. No one could see her from the parking lot. This was what she wanted, as had the poacher. She carefully negotiated the truck between the riverbed and the dinosaur sculpture and parked. Her destination was the rocky incline where the fossil tracks had nearly been pilfered.

Most of the grasshoppers were gone. Some starved and listless insects remained amid the occasional dead husks of their brethren. Birds, small mammals, and reptiles must have finished off the majority, Ansel guessed. Nourishment was at a premium right now.

The Red Water River was as sluggish as the crawling pests. Low-level waters barely rippled as they moved southwest past the rocky riverbed to feed a fan of streams and creek evaporating as fast as they were filled. The thought that death was everywhere saddened her.

The FBI had done an efficient job of scouring the crime scene area. Except for the trampled and tire-furrowed dirt, the grassland looked deceptively void of all signs of criminal mayhem.

Nothing remained of the exploded saw debris or combusted human remains.

Ansel walked onto the sandstone ledge with eyes scanning the Cretaceous bedrock. The footprints were from an undetermined carnosaur species, but it made them no less valuable in terms of rarity and geohistorical value.

She stood looking down at the charred ground surrounding the single despoiled dinosaur track and frowned. A deep, slicing gouge ran along one side of it. The diamond blade hadn't cracked the matrix supporting the footprint, but the foot-long cut would have to be filled and patched in order to prevent irreversible destruction from edgewater erosion and weathering. Already sand, grit, and pebbles were lodging into the crevice.

A quick scan of the rest of the ledge revealed a hodgepodge of scraps, dings, and pits caused by exploding saw debris. A particularly odd-looking groove caught her attention, and she bent to examine it. The narrow, two-inch-long groove had left a white scar along the brown sandstone as tiny silicon crystals had been sheared off at high speed. More shrapnel, she decided.

Moments later she was in front of the Allosaurus' pimpled stomach skin, staring up at its jaws. Burnt and peeling rubber latex streamers hung down from the snout and looked like strips of decaying flesh. Major repairs there, Ansel thought. And the mouth cavity and teeth were completely blackened by soot damage.

Ansel winced, not envying the firemen who pulled the corpse from those resinous, three-inch-long serrated teeth. How long and hard would any of the law enforcement agencies search to identify a faceless Indian thief who bungled a robbery attempt and got himself killed in the process? Certainly their prime motivation would be to try to outsmart one another for jurisdictional vanities and glory rather than to gain closure for the man's family and friends.

As she shifted position to view the dinosaur in profile, Ansel saw a flash of brilliance out of the corner of her eye. Glancing up again, she saw nothing. Then, there—sunlight glinting off silver near the beast's lower chest. She located the source of the sunlit sparkle eleven feet above her, within a badly charred section of rubber skin just beneath the clawed forearms. There was no way she could reach it.

The crunch of footsteps on parched grass behind her was unmistakable. Her urge to bolt didn't lessen when she saw BLM agent Broderick coming toward her. He carried his clipboard, too.

"Miss Phoenix." His mouth presented a wide smirk. "Why am I not surprised to see you?"

His vehicle was nowhere in sight. Ansel decided that he must have parked in front of the museum and walked down to ambush her. She smiled gaily even as her shaking hands hung limply at her sides. "Good morning, Agent Broderick."

"You're trespassing. Do you have a problem understanding this is a crime scene?"

"No. I'm sorry. It won't happen again. I thought only the museum was off limits. I'll be glad to leave." She took a quick step around him.

Broderick moved sideways to block her. "Not so fast. What are you doing out here?"

"I was looking at the sculpture. Assessing the damage. I'll be repairing it when the museum reopens. I need to order materials before then."

"If it opens, you mean."

Ansel's eyes narrowed. "I guess I'm just an optimist at heart."

Broderick raised his clipboard and took the pen from beneath its clasp. "What a coincidence. Me, too. I'm hoping you've learned your lesson. That's why I'm not taking you into custody, just issuing you a citation."

"You're giving me a ticket?"

"Uh huh." He scribbled across the pad.

"For what?"

"For crossing through the brush with an off-highway vehicle to get past a clearly marked and closed Land Management access road. You'll have to go the same way out of here. Off-highway vehicles such as yours can only be operated in BLM areas designated for OHV use. Unauthorized OHV use leads to serious environmental degradation, Miss Phoenix."

"All right. I could see you giving me a warning, but a ticket seems excessive."

"You are contributing to the destruction of a prehistoric site. As a paleoartist, you should know that by enforcing the proper recreational laws, permits, and citations, the BLM is safeguarding public lands for future generations." He grinned and passed the completed form to her. "Please sign at the bottom."

Ansel carefully took the board with pen in her right hand. The fine was for one hundred dollars. Silently fuming but anxious to depart, she had no choice. Her signature was an illegible scrawl.

Broderick took the board and tore off the top copy. "The payment instructions are on the reverse. Mail it on time. The BLM appreciates your cooperation."

"Of course," Ansel replied, taking the citation. "Are we through, Agent Broderick? It's stifling out here."

"Almost. I see that you've been making close friends with the FBI."

Ansel tensed further. His relaxed, sarcastic demeanor had changed for the worse. His gaze was razor-sharp, and his fist holding the clipboard at his side was turning white with squeezing pressure. He was angry.

"What do you mean?"

"Midnight jaunts in helicopters. That's what I'm talking about. Where did you go with Outerbridge's lackey?"

"How do you know about that?"

"Answer me. Where did you go?"

"Ask Outerbridge."

This time Ansel took several quick steps before the agent reacted to stop her. She got past him, but he was fast, too. Broderick backpedaled and thrust his face up to hers again, effectively sending her backward in mid-stride. He was smart,

Ansel assessed—wasn't going to touch her and leave marks or risk an assault charge.

"I will ask Outerbridge, Miss Phoenix, but you can be certain that I'm going to know every move you make with the FBI. Count on it. This is BLM territory. Nobody's shoveling the ground out from under us. Not the sheriff's department, the FBI, or you."

"Either arrest me for trespassing or get out of my way."

"And if I don't?"

"If you don't, when I get out of jail I'm going to every newspaper, TV station, and radio show I can and talk about how you bully Native American women BLM-style. That should do wonders to screw up any relations the BLM has going with tribal authorities from Big Toe to Butte."

Broderick's face went ashen, then he simply moved away from her, eyes glaring. Ansel rushed past him. Only near her truck did she dare to look over her shoulder. The mercurial agent stood in the broiling sun like a statue watching her. She jumped into the cab. Seconds later, she drove past Broderick, never glancing into the rearview mirror. The drive down the access road and through the grassland brush to Barnum Brown Road was done in another minute. She noticed the BLM truck parked by the museum gate as she sped away.

Finally she calmed down and focused on her next mission—visiting Glendive and Sidney, where the other fossils had been stolen.

Chapter 12

"No answer is also an answer."
Hopi

Ansel opened the door leading into the Glendive Community College Library and almost got trampled by a noisy herd of students exiting en masse, their backpacks full of notebooks and their arms burdened with textbooks. It was the first week of fall term and lunch hour to boot.

It hadn't been difficult to locate the school where Ranger Eastover had informed her that fossils were nabbed. The small Dawson County institution, which offered limited curricula for obtaining bachelor degrees, was the only campus in Glendive that was displaying them.

The intellectual and physical excitement generated throughout the campus was palpable in the air around Ansel. Slumbering memories of the rigors of academia life rose like a leviathan in her chest and feelings of nostalgia overwhelmed her. How hopeful these young scholars were, so sure of their dreams and their places in the world. Like salmon swimming upstream, she thought, watching their purposeful swerves and dashes.

All of their energies were devoted to chasing a chosen goal, an undefined destiny waiting always just out of reach but forever within sight. Many would fail to ford the rough waters ahead. Others would simply grow weary of the competitive, driving tempo and choose to quit. And those who made it to the end-run waters would probably find the reward less satisfying than all the racing to get there had been. Was it worth it? Ansel had no answer to that question even for herself.

She certainly loved what she was doing as an artist, but any career could become nothing but a breeding ground for stale successes which turned into carefully constructed death traps for the soul. Twelve years after graduating with dual degrees, had she really gotten what she needed out of life?

She'd been one of those blessed students, surviving the trials of university life and even surpassing her career goals in the real world, but she was still unhappy and unfulfilled on other emotional levels. She had her family, but no children. She had money and possessions, but she shared them with no one. Fame certainly didn't fill her home with happy voices. Fortune didn't warm her bed at night.

Ansel quelled her maudlin thoughts and allowed the cool, calm atmosphere of the brick and glass library to envelop her. She crossed a veldt of green carpeting toward the main checkout desk and skirted the usual gaggle of study desks, carrels, computer stations, periodical stands, and towering rows of bookshelves. A gorgeous panorama of the Yellowstone River Valley complete with grassland expanses and a river view was visible through large arching windows along the northeast wall of the room.

The front counter was empty except for an elderly gray-haired lady wearing an Assistant Librarian name tag. She looked up expectantly. "Hello. How may I help you?"

"Hello. My name is Ansel Phoenix. A woman from the administrative office sent me over here. I'd like to speak with Director Bogart, please."

The librarian's eyes widened. "Not Ansel Phoenix the dinosaur artist?"

"Why yes, I am. Don't tell me somebody from administration called you."

"Heavens, no," she replied with a light chuckle. "I recognize your name. We've got one of your prints up on the wall." She pointed a knobby index finger behind Ansel's shoulder.

Ansel glanced around. A large, signed limited edition print of an adult Albertosaurus tenderly nuzzling a clutch of eggs was situated over a potted plant. She'd painted the original oil and canvas artwork for display in a Butte gallery, where it quickly sold to a well-known Montana celebrity and avid dinosaur fan.

Soon after, an art publishing house had contacted her about producing the painting as a limited edition print of five hundred. She'd always had a soft spot for that particular artistic creation. There was something almost mystical about the vision of such a fearsome meat-eater tending so lovingly to her unborn young that always tugged at her heartstrings.

"What a nice surprise," Ansel said.

"It's a wonderful picture. You wouldn't believe how many students enjoy it. There was a red-haired young man here the other night who stared at it for quite a while. He seemed positively entranced."

She faced the librarian again, thinking that if the man had been an Indian with a limp, she'd really have something concrete to work with. "The truth is, dinosaurs are what I want to speak with your director about."

"Really? Goodness. Unfortunately she's gone for the afternoon. Maybe I can help you."

"I wanted to ask her about the T-rex foot bones that were on display. I just found out at the office that they were stolen last week, which is unfortunate. I'd planned to do some sketches of them today. Research for a drawing I'm doing. You wouldn't believe how much preliminary sketching goes into these paintings."

The librarian's face turned dark. "Yup, they stole the foot right out of this big case we had over by the front door, all right. Don't know how they carted it away so fast. Everyone's upset about it. Mrs. Bogart will be very disappointed that she missed you, Ms. Phoenix. And missed the opportunity to have you working here in our library. Listen, you know, Dean Knowles is here. Back in audiovisual. He could tell you all about it."

Pleased at her continued luck, Ansel said, "I'd like that very much. I won't be long."

"Oh, he loves to talk. I'll get him."

The woman left the counter and hurried into another room behind an alcove. She soon returned with a short, frizzy-haired man wearing brown pants and yellow shirt with a horseshoe bolo.

"Ms. Phoenix, this is Dean Knowles," the assistant said.

Ansel held out a hand. "Nice to meet you, Dean Knowles. Hope I didn't disturb you."

Knowles smiled effusively, his pudgy face a green-eyed vision of delight. He grabbed her palm and pumped it several times. "It's my pleasure, Ms. Phoenix. Absolutely. Elke tells me that you want to know what happened here last week. Very bad news. Terrible. The college is going to suffer the repercussions from this for some time. The foot wasn't ours. It was on loan for display purposes from the Makoshika State Park. Worth about five thousand dollars."

"Well, I don't mean to pry, but I'm horrified that something like this has happened to you. A similar incident occurred in my town of Big Toe. Somebody tried to steal fossil dinosaur tracks from a museum the same night. Fortunately, they didn't succeed."

"Yes, I read about that in the papers. What a coincidence. Amazing. Small world. The police here believe that the two events are related, you know."

"Do the police know how many people were involved in your theft?"

"More than one. They cut the alarm system, battered down a rear security door to the library, sledge-hammered the Plexiglas case apart, and grabbed the foot. Nothing subtle about them."

"I'm not being critical, but didn't security guards see or hear anything?"

"We're a small campus, just fifteen hundred students even on a very busy day. In the middle of the night, we're locked down with minimal security resources," Knowles admitted. "It was Friday night. Most of our trouble on campus, if it happens, comes from the dormitory. By the time the guards realized the library had been breached, the robbers were long gone, unlike your situation. The poacher at the museum was killed, right?"

Nodding, Ansel cast a glance at Elke, who still stood by them listening avidly. She needed to get the dean alone so she could talk more frankly to him. "Yes. Accidentally. Could we sit down, Dean Knowles?"

Knowles blinked, then clucked his tongue. "Absolutely. How thoughtless of me. I'm still reeling from all this. Let's go to a table, shall we? Elke, I won't hold you up. I know you've got a thousand things to do."

"Not right this minute," Elke said, grinning at Ansel.

"We'll be fine. You run along," Knowles insisted gently to the woman as he turned Ansel toward a long wooden table with four empty chairs.

"Thanks for your help," Ansel said to the kindly librarian.

"You need anything else, Ms. Phoenix, don't you hesitate to ask me," Elke responded anxiously. "I love your work."

Knowles pulled out a chair for Ansel, and when she was comfortably seated, he yanked out another, sat down in it, and crossed his legs as if settling in for a while. "As I was saying, there's no telling where these thieves came from. They can find you if they want to. I have a friend who stumbled upon some nice smaller dinosaur fossils on his own property, and a month later his house was broken into and they were stolen. The police think that his own excitement over the fossils did him in. He discussed the find with people he knew and word of mouth got around until somebody decided they wanted them. Whoever it was used his license plate number and hacked into DMV records to get his home address. You've got to be very careful these days when you go someplace with fossils or go looking for them."

"I had no idea things were that bad."

Knowles nodded. "Well, at least your museum footprints are safe. I doubt we'll ever retrieve the T-rex foot. It will probably end up on the international, multi-million-dollar black market and sold to some Japanese businessman in Tokyo. With buyers like that, it's no surprise that museums and exhibitions, even a tiny one like ours, are fair game for smugglers."

Ansel looked at her artwork. Nothing was sacred. She'd heard once that fossil eggs were a hot commodity. Each egg in her drawing symbolized up to fifteen hundred dollars in the real world of illegal fossil trading. Entire nests were pandered to foreign buyers. Years ago she'd read that a Los Angeles undercover operation had grabbed an illegal shipment of one hundred Chinese dinosaur eggs and nests worth four hundred thousand dollars, exactly the kind of wholesale destruction that Outerbridge was asking her to help eliminate.

"And then, there was that other fossil theft incident in Sidney, just north of us," Knowles added.

The Sidney theft was exactly what she wanted to know more about. She feigned ignorance. "Another robbery? Do you know where it happened?"

The dean grimaced. "I certainly do. A fossil store called Earthly Pleasures. It's run by Hillard Yancy."

"You aren't fond of him, I gather."

With a shrug, Knowles replied, "I'm not fond of his business practices. It's nothing personal. Calls himself a private commercial dealer. I've only dealt with Yancy through college affairs. He's approached us several times. I hear he's solicited every campus in the state, trying to sell his fossils as educational tools."

"How does he contact you?"

"He sends me catalog lists. Anything from dinosaur dung in bulk at a dollar per pound up to a Triceratops skull for sixty thousand. If I don't respond, which I never do, he gives me a personal follow-up call."

"Is he a certified dealer?"

"Yes. He's got all the proper credentials. He's even a member of the AAPS. That doesn't make him a saint."

Ansel knew that the American Association of Paleontology Suppliers had a code of ethics which stated that its members would strive to place specimens of unique scientific interest into responsible hands for study, research, and preservation, but their policy wasn't purely altruistic.

A lot of dealer-excavated fossils from private lands were fragments which had no scientific value for institutions, museums, and repositories and were sold to customers who wanted "something beautiful" and which they could relate to. Many AAPS members firmly believed that fossils weren't rare at all and that commercial sales by dealers ultimately reduced bone prices by finding more fossils than academics could ever hope to excavate.

"Do you suspect Yancy's involved with any illegal fossil hunting activities?"

"I couldn't say one way or the other, but he's an original Jurassic Shark in my mind. He hunts down fossils, gobbles them up, and digests the cash to get fatter and fatter. All the while he claims he's saving fossils before the forces of nature or poachers destroy them."

"Did you tell the police this?"

"Absolutely, but they didn't think Yancy would be involved in robbing the campus library and burglarizing himself at the same time. According to them, his supply store got ripped off for a lot more fossils than the foot bones taken from this college."

Knowles grunted. "Serves Yancy right though. Even if he is on the up and up, he's doing a lot of damage to the academic and scientific community he professes to serve. He may be properly excavating a fossil, but I bet he's not doing the research and paperwork that should go along with it. A lot of contextual knowledge about bone locations and the biology around them is being lost, and it's irreplaceable. Education isn't displaying fossil curiosities on a wall to be ogled, Ms. Phoenix. It's collecting scientific data and disseminating it to the public. Maybe the theft will put him out of business for good."

Ansel took all this in with a grain of salt. It was the same old story she'd heard before from academics in the Pangaea Society. Commercial dealers are bad. Scientists are good. Dean Knowles was a nice man, but he was a typical soapbox advocate for stricter fossil regulations. Things weren't always so black and white.

She felt sure that when she talked to Hillard Yancy, he'd be a rabid advocate for government deregulation of fossil excavation laws. The dealer probably believed that he was exerting his god-given right as a businessman to search for bones on private lands where he had owner permission, contractual or otherwise, to excavate and sell his inventory for profit. The problem was that neither side of the sell/not-sell coin bought positive results when it came to stopping illegal poaching on public or state lands.

"Thank you, Dean Knowles. You've been very kind," Ansel said, rising.

"Don't mention it. You're going to visit Yancy?"

"Of course. You've raised my curiosity, and shopping for fossils is my passion."

"Just don't be fooled by what you see," Knowles replied with a wise smile. "I may be a college dean, but I'm also an old cowboy at heart. If there's one thing I know, it's when to pull on my galoshes while mucking through a barn. Wear your boots, Ms. Phoenix. Absolutely."

Chapter 13

"A good man does not take what belongs to someone else."
Pueblo

On her way out of town, Ansel passed road signs pointing south toward the eight-thousand-acre Makoshika State Park, where the stolen foot bones had been excavated. She wished she could stop. Makoshika's water-eroded terrain had exposed the Hell Creek Formation and a rich record of fossil life, including Triceratops and Tyrannosaurus.

Two years ago Pangaea members had hiked the Cap Rock Nature Trail, which dropped one hundred sixty feet along the canyon walls. They had spent the day viewing a short natural bridge, pedestal rocks, a gumbo sinkhole, and the fossil beds. The group had also enjoyed the many wildlife areas that contained a notable summer population of Badlands turkey vultures.

Ansel veered northeast along State Road 16 toward Sidney. To her right, the scenic white waters of the Lower Yellowstone River paralleled her journey. Once in town, she made a quick stop at the Eagle Café to get Chinese take-out and directions. Half an hour later she arrived.

The outside of Earthly Pleasures suited a small up-scale antiquities business rather than a fossil warehouse. The two-story building had a decorative column portico, white stucco walls, and huge picture windows. Through the spotless glass frontage, Ansel saw dinosaur skulls and bones sitting on custom, laminated stands. Also visible were numerous sets of brass and glass display shelving units showcasing a variety of tastefully arranged smaller fossils.

An old-fashioned brass bell tinkled. The spacious interior was mostly oak wood: flooring, wall shelves, and storage cabinetry. All were situated to call direct attention to the ancient, museum-quality artifacts for sale around her. The store was empty except for a man standing beside a long glass counter twenty feet away.

"Good day. Welcome to Earthly Pleasures. I'm Hillard Yancy," he said in a soft, squeaky voice before stepping toward her, hand extended.

Despite Dean Knowles' opinion, the middle-aged Yancy looked more like a trustworthy insurance salesman than a fossil broker with shady connections to the black market. He was short and stocky, his short brown curls springing in a ringlet across his head. A set of thick glasses perched on a flat nose. She shook his immensely strong and very calloused hand. All that digging, she surmised.

"Hello. I'm Ansel Phoenix. Phoenix Studios," she added, passing him a business card.

Yancy released her hand and took the card. He glanced at it quickly. "The paleoartist? Well, this is a pleasure. Glad to meet you, Miss Phoenix. Your work is quite extraordinary. Have you come to sell me some of your paintings? I could use a couple in the shop."

"You're very kind, Mr. Yancy, but I've come for more altruistic reasons."

"Well, I can't help but notice that very unusual pendant you're wearing. That five-fold radial symmetry on top tells me it's a sea urchin. Looks like *Rhycholampus gouldii* if my memory serves me right."

Ansel touched the Iniskim. "That's right."

"And that marvelous blue color," Yancy said, cocking his head sideways to stare at the echinoid fossil. "Is that copper-based chrondorite?"

"No. You're close. Azurite."

"Ah, of course. Goes to show I'm strictly a bone man. You might be interested in my custom jewelry. They're made by local artisans." He swept his arm toward another nearby counter. The shelves contained beautiful gold, silver, and copper necklaces and bracelets with a variety of polished fossil pendants and dangles.

Ansel saw mostly the ancient waterborne invertebrates such as trilobites, blastoids, crinoids, ammonites, cephalopods, starfish, mollusks, and snails. However, the display included some interesting oddities, like strands of carved amber beads, fossil coral, and mammoth tusk. Fossil bone and insect inclusions rounded off the assortment of glittering accessories quite nicely.

"They're beautiful," Ansel said, eyeing a hadrosaur bone ring.

"Thank you. Is there anything in particular you'd like to see, Miss Phoenix?"

"I'm just looking."

"Then you should take one of these," he said, reaching onto the counter and taking a thick glossy pamphlet. "This is my sale catalog. Let me know if anything interests you."

"All right. I also came to talk to you, Mr. Yancy."

"What about?"

"Your business. I'm the former president of the Pangaea Society. Have you heard of it?"

A wariness flitted across his jovial features. He smiled thinly and crossed his arms. "Yes."

"Well, I understand that your shop was robbed last week. There was a similar attempt to steal fossil dinosaur tracks from a museum in Big Toe the same night. Fortunately, it failed."

"I heard about it and the robbery in Glendive. What's this got to do with me?"

"Two things. I'd like these poachers caught and punished, just like you. Second, I'd like to save the fossil tracks that the robber didn't get from our museum property. The museum is on leased BLM land. It's being threatened with closure because of this incident, and the footprints may be removed to another institution. My town can't afford to loose the Bureau contract that allows the museum to operate as a public attraction, and the society is greatly concerned about this new development. Generally, we support the preservation of Montana fossil sites in their natural state, not hauling them off to distant federal archives."

"I agree with you so far, but I don't see how I can help."

"I need some information about what was stolen from you and what you know about any illegal poaching going on around here. Perhaps through word of mouth or your field experiences."

"What makes you think I'd know anything about the black market?"

Ansel was surprised at the hostile edge in his voice. "I'm not casting any aspersions, Mr. Yancy. Your line of work is far different from the scholarly members I usually work with. You have a different perspective on things, and I'd like to hear it."

"Then pardon me for being blunt, Miss Phoenix, but I'm the last person your scientific society would invite to join because I'm strictly a commercial dealer. In their minds, I'm probably considered a thief despite the fact that I carefully excavate fossils from private land with owner permission. I have detailed documentation for every piece I take—who was involved, where it came from, and who I sold it to. I don't know a damned thing about the black market, except that I've been victimized by it."

"I'm not representing the society. I'm trying to get leads on the poacher who vandalized the museum so I can give that information to my local sheriff's department."

Yancy rubbed his chin. "Then I'll tell you what I told the Sidney cops. Start with the Internet if you want to tap into the black market. You can get any fossil you want online through fossil chat rooms or auctions. They don't have any verifiable pedigree, but rabid collectors don't care. Or you can go highbrow and buy your fossils directly from Christie's of London, Butterfields, or Bonhams at Knightsbridge. Get a complete fossil turtle for nineteen thousand or even a whole Allosaurus dinosaur for a seven-hundred-thousand-dollar bid. Who knows for sure if it's legally excavated or the provenance is real."

Yancy's eyes flashed hot. "Those are the real big-money crimes, and you don't see the feds or scientists hassling these people, do you? Yet I'm often accused of using legal loopholes to steal fossils. It's crap, and I'm really tired of it."

"I didn't mean to upset you," Ansel consoled. "I'm trying to enlist your help."

Yancy's tight, angry face slackened. "I've already been through this with the FBI, the police, and the insurance company. They ran me through a grinder."

"Could you at least tell me what was stolen?"

Yancy sighed, then nodded. "All right. Come back here, and I'll show you."

He moved away and Ansel followed as he went to the rear of the store and through an oak door. The storefront was deceiving. Once beyond the grandly decorated showroom that customers saw, the building dimensions went straight back for another hundred feet. She took in everything she could as quickly as possible. Yancy wasn't going to put up with her snooping for long.

The room had a concrete floor and unpainted drywall panels. Large, heavy wood tables crisscrossed the area, all of them covered with fossils in varying stages of cleaning, preparation, and mold casting. Assorted crates and boxes were crammed everywhere. The place smelled of plaster, dirt, and solvents. Yancy stopped next to a table holding some huge fossil vertebrae.

"This is my workshop. Some of these pieces I excavated myself and hauled back here to clean. Others I order piecemeal or wholesale uncleaned, finish preparing, and sell through mail order. If I don't move the fossils via that business, they go into the showroom. Usually things don't last long out there."

"What did the robbers take?"

"Nothing from out front. From back here they stole some unprepared artifacts easy for a couple people to carry out. I lost a complete, eighteen-inch-long Albertosaurus foot, a fifty-one-inch-long T-rex humerus and a thirty-eight-inch T-rex footprint. Other items they broke and left behind for spite. It makes me sick just thinking about it."

Ansel looked around. The only entrance into the room besides the showroom was a large steel garage door and a staircase on the right. "How did they get in?"

"I live upstairs. I wasn't home last Friday night. They broke in through a second-floor window after cutting the alarm wires. Once they got down into the workshop through those stairs, they opened the rear garage doors and loaded what they wanted."

She moved around the room, weaving between the work tables before stopping by a bench holding a complete dinosaur arm and plenty of cleaning tools, glue bottles, and non-abrasive solvents. A piece of paper on the table identified the piece as a Maiasaura limb being prepared for Montana State University. The dinosaur once called "duckbill" was a vegetarian that nested in huge nurseries which were first made famous in Montana by Jack Horner of the Museum of the Rockies.

"You do nice work, Mr. Yancy. Do you do a lot of fossil cleaning for outside facilities?"

Yancy shrugged. "It seems that way sometimes. It's a nice income when the shop sales are slow. Helps to pay the bills."

"Before the break-in, did you see anyone suspicious?"

"The police asked the same question. Didn't see anybody or anything suspicious and, believe me, I watch for such things."

"Did you ever notice a young Indian man with a limp in your store before the robbery?"

"No. Why do you ask?"

"He's the man who died while trying to steal the museum tracks. He was badly burned when his concrete saw exploded. Unfortunately, the Lacrosse authorities can't identify him."

His snort was derisive. "The local police are no match for poachers, Miss Phoenix. They're high-tech now. Helicopters, ATVs, night vision goggles, surveillance cameras, electronic bugs, computers, and Uzis. Fossils are the new stolen art of the twenty-first century. It takes a SWAT team to take them out."

A vision of Outerbridge and his agents wearing body armor and toting their heavy-duty law enforcement gear through the Badlands jumped into Ansel's head. An eye for an eye.

"You make them sound invincible," she replied. "I don't believe that."

"Not invincible. Industrious," Yancy corrected. "They never give up. They'll watch your dig sites, your shop, your home, and you. They'll find out your vulnerabilities and capitalize on them. The average fossil hunter, dealer, or curator can't fight back, and personal confrontations with these thugs turn deadly."

"You're right, Mr. Yancy. Fossil collecting is a very dangerous business these days. So why are you in it?"

"I guess I just like to play in the dirt," he replied, smiling for the first time in a while.

The loud tinkle of the shop bell interrupted Ansel's next question. Yancy looked toward the open showroom door. "I've got to get that." He disappeared, leaving Ansel alone.

She busied herself for about a minute, scouting the rolltop desk near the door and looking at the paperwork visible across the tiny wooden top. There was nothing interesting. Invoices. Computer printouts. Sales lists. Topographical maps of northern Montana.

"Don't touch anything."

Panic gripped Ansel as the voice resonated beside her. In an instant, her stomach withered into a tiny ball. Reid Dorbandt, an Earthly Pleasures catalog clutched in one hand and his wallet with gold badge gleaming in the other, radiated his aura of all-powerful jurisprudence directly toward her.

And he looked absolutely, positively pissed.

Chapter 14

"One 'Take this' is better than two 'I gives.'"
Unknown Southwest Tribe

"Tell me everything you've done," Reid demanded. "No lies, no half-truths."

Ansel swallowed the lump in her throat. She sat in his passenger seat looking through the front windshield at a Sidney convenience store, where a field littered with bottles and trash, an overflowing Dumpster, and scavenging grackles provided the view. That was better than a side window shot of the cedar-shingled Quik-Pik studded with neon beer signs and loitering Indians who crossed the North Dakota line ten miles away looking for work or booze.

Ansel fingered her Iniskim and watched an Indian man in holey jeans and shirt gulp down a beer and stagger toward the Dumpster. She winced inside. She'd had her own minor battles with liquor. Booze had always clouded her judgment where men were concerned and sent her into a downward spiral of self-pity.

After cornering her inside Earthly Pleasures, Reid had ordered her to wait in her truck until he finished questioning Yancy. Then he'd stomped to her driver's window and gruffly commanded her to follow him. He'd picked this wretched, depressing place to scold her.

Ansel tried to focus on the bright side. Reid was angry but going to listen to what she had to say for a change, and he smelled good, a bittersweet combination of musky cologne and male sweat. It was also kind of cozy being together, even if the police radio crackled out garbled code alerts while tepid air conditioning blasted their faces like a desert zephyr.

"Of course," she said, fixing him with a serious stare. "I thought you were gone."

"Hokay. Lie number one. Not a good start," Reid huffed. "Three strikes, you're out."

"Not everything's my fault."

Reid's eyes went squinty. "Lie number two."

Ansel flopped against the seat. "All right. It's a long story. First there was Agent Outerbridge," she began, then explained in detail about being flown into the Badlands and shown the destroyed fossil T-rex. Except for grinding his teeth like an ornery stallion, Reid was quiet until she told him Outerbridge wanted her to join his sting operation.

"What?"

"I haven't agreed to anything. Outerbridge will contact me again and give his sales pitch."

"When?"

"I have no idea. He needs me because I look Indian and know dinosaurs."

"He's got LaPierre for chasing down fossils," Reid said thoughtfully. "Why the tribal link?"

"Dixie mentioned that I'd be working with Agent Standback, and he's Indian, too."

"So was our poacher. I'll get back to the subject of Outerbridge. What's the next adventure you had after the FBI meeting?"

"I had a run-in with Agent Broderick this morning."

"Go on."

Ansel relayed how she'd gone to the museum to look at the riverbed and her Allosaurus model. Reid stared and let her ramble. Probably thought she'd spill more info that way than by interrogating her, Ansel decided.

"When I was looking at the Allosaurus, Broderick showed up. He was pretty nasty, Reid. He threatened to arrest me but issued me a citation for driving off-road on BLM land instead."

"You were lucky he didn't lock you up and toss the key."

"Thanks a lot. Broderick will do that if he catches me again, but what he really wanted to do was question me. He also became a physical threat."

Reid's face finally registered another emotion besides calm disgust. Concern knitted his brow. "In what way?"

"Muscled his smirking mug right into my face, that's what. Said he knew that I'd been talking to Outerbridge and demanded to know what was going on. When I refused to tell him, he almost lost it. He's crazy because he thinks the sheriff's department and the FBI are trying to steal the thunder from his big poaching case. He said he'd be watching me."

Ansel peered into his eyes. "It was pretty hairy for a few moments. I told him to get out of my way or I'd raise hell about it to everyone who would listen. He backed down, and I got out of there fast."

Reid was looking into her eyes as well. His face softened dramatically before he placed his hand on hers, which rested on her lap. "I'll take care of Broderick," he said in his authoritative detective voice. "He won't be bothering you anymore."

Reid's hand was very warm, and an electric heat surged up Ansel's arm. This was the first time that Reid had ever touched her in a truly personal way. Sure, he herded her around by the elbow or shoulder all the time while getting her out of his hair, but this was different. More friend and protector than dutiful cop. His voice may have been all business, but his expression and his body language said something else. And she didn't mind at all.

When she smiled at him, Reid drew his hand away and straightened up in the driver's seat, suddenly realizing that he'd been leaning toward her in a very unprofessional way. He swiped a hand through his brown, slightly spiky hair.

"So, how did you end up at Earthly Pleasures, Ansel?"

"I found out where the other fossil robberies occurred."

"And how did you do that?"

"Ranger Eastover told me."

He glared at her. "And when were you going to tell me?"

"When you told me that you knew the Indian poacher had eaten at Humpy's before trying to steal the tracks," she countered. "All that crap about wanting a buffalo tongue sandwich was a lie, so don't give me a speech about honesty and sharing information for mutual benefit."

Ansel glared back at him and was pleased to see him squirm in his seat. He cocked his head sideways and cleared his throat. "You've made your point, but that wasn't a definite lead. That was a hunch I still haven't verified through the lab. So you went where with Eastover's information and did what exactly?"

"I went to the Glendive Community College and spoke with Dean Knowles first. He told me about the theft of a T-rex foot on display in the library, but didn't see any Indians hanging around before or after. He also told me about Hillard Yancy's break-in at the Sidney shop. That's why I went there."

"And what did Yancy tell you?" he prodded.

"He denied selling fossils that he couldn't back up with paperwork or knowing anything about a local black market. Still, there's a lot of money tied up in the pomp and glitz of his store. The fossil inventory alone is staggering. I'm wondering where all that financial backing is coming from," Ansel admitted. "Plus Knowles thinks Yancy is nothing but a fossil plunderer chipping down the walls of scientific knowledge because of greed."

"I'll rake through both their backgrounds with a curry comb. You can count on that."

Ansel's gaze gravitated toward the Indians outside. During the last year, she'd been cutting back on her drinking. Alcoholism ran in her mother's family genes like a poison, especially through relatives living on the Blackfeet Reservation in Browning. She loved her heritage, but had to admit that most of her driven behavior came from trying to outrun the inherent social pressures of being a Native American. Still her personal decisions were her own.

Ansel swivelled toward Reid. "Listen, I'm going to hear Outerbridge out on his sting operation, and there's nothing you can do to stop me."

"I don't plan to. I want you to help Outerbridge."

"You're not going to argue?"

"No. I also want you to tell me what the FBI is up to. I expect a full report when you get back from the meeting as well as any other activities you engage in with the Feebees."

Ansel stared a few seconds before responding. "You want me to be a spy?"

Reid shrugged his broad shoulders and grinned. "I'm a realist. Outerbridge has shut my department out. You keep me informed about the sting, and I'll tell you what I learn about the Indian from my out-of-town source. We'll collaborate, and you'll have the added bonus of me watching your back in case you get in too deep."

"Sounds like coercion rather than mutual trust. It stinks."

Reid shook his head. "You just don't give up, do you? What are you always trying to prove with this Miss Independent routine?"

"Nothing. I want to know who that poacher was. The future of the museum depends on a positive resolution from the legal fallout of that attempted robbery. The FBI holds all the cards, and Broderick's an idiot. Your department hasn't identified the thief either. Time is wasting. Don't be mad because I'm willing to follow up any clue, no matter how far-fetched it seems, in order to save the museum."

"When are you going to get it through your head that this is dangerous?" Reid exploded at her. "You want to end up with a Teflon bullet through your chest or captured by a group of international criminals who'd use you up and throw you away like a disposable cup? How about some intelligent and rational thought here? For once, let somebody help you, Ansel. I'll get you the answers you want, and you'll live to do something with them. After what's happened to Chief Flynn, I'd think you would get the message."

That brought her up short. "What did you say?"

His expression was dubious. "Don't tell me Big Toe's master sleuth doesn't know that Flynn has been missing since last night? It's been all over the radio and TV stations."

"No, I didn't. I was on a desert bluff yesterday evening and left Lacrosse County this morning. Broderick didn't say a word to me about it," Ansel fumed. "What's happened?"

"Flynn worked his usual shift on Sunday and left the police station around eight o'clock in the evening. He never got home. Nobody knew about it until Mrs. Flynn called the station looking for him at ten. Flynn's just dropped off the earth. No sign of him or his green SUV. We do know that he spent the day before his disappearance chasing down leads about the poacher. Sheriff Combs is about to call in the state police to help with the search."

"You think he found the poachers and got in trouble?"

"That's what we think. Flynn wouldn't disappear like this. He's an excellent officer. Experienced and reliable."

She couldn't believe it. She'd known Cullen and his family since she was a little girl, when they'd attended many parties at her parents' ranch. Those were the days when her mother had been alive. Cullen had been there the Thanksgiving day she'd almost drowned to death.

In fact, she'd been underwater for forty minutes before the EMTs arrived, then rushed to the hospital where she was miraculously revived. The extremely cold temperatures of the pond water had shocked her body into a hibernation-like coma and ultimately saved her life.

The irony was, she'd almost died from complications; bacteria-laced water caused an infection in her lungs that took weeks to abate. The residual side-effects had been more insidious. Her entire life was spent battling chronic anxiety attacks triggered by the most innocuous sights, sounds, scents, or touch of water.

Just thinking about the incident whirlpooled her memories to the surface. She saw a vision of the large snow-covered stock pond. Her breathing quickened, then her heartbeat. She remembered the feel of frigid wetness squeezing her skin. The slippery, unyielding hardness of ice beneath her tiny hands.

"You're right," she managed to say. "Flynn would never put his family through that." She dug into her purse. "Take this. I found it at the dinosaur dig site. None of the ERT saw me pick it up. Don't know what it is, but it's unusual." She fished out the foil tab from her wallet and passed it to him.

Reid took it in the flat of his palm, careful not to touch the item with his fingers. "Looks like some sort of memory chip."

"No kidding? I didn't think of that. What from? A computer?"

"Can't say. Maybe we can read it. I'll have it analyzed by the lab. You did the smart thing by turning this over to me. Thanks." He took a napkin from the dash and carefully wrapped the tab up, then placed it in a suit pocket.

Reid started the ignition, and the engine turned over. "I've got to get going," he said before flicking on the windshield wipers. He followed the motion by another that automatically sprayed water over the dusty glass. Rivulets snaked down the incline like speeding water bullets. "We'll do things my way. Agreed?"

Ansel shot a wide-eyed glance at Reid. He was totally unaware of the effect the squeaking wipers smearing dirt across the glittering silver bands of fluid would have on her. God, not now, she screamed silently. She had to get out of this claustrophobic space. Now.

Speechless, she turned and clawed for the door handle. She wasn't familiar with this car. She couldn't remember. The white noise on the radio became the low whooshing sound of water filling her ears. A mucky, mud smell wafted up her nose, and a visceral panic spread through every organ and muscle.

"Ansel, what are you doing?" Reid demanded.

She couldn't see his face, didn't want to. She flailed at the door, at the window glass. A thick blackness edged her vision, telescoping inward across her eyes. A flashback. She knew the symptoms so well.

"No, no, no," she whimpered. *Don't let him see me like this.* Tears rained down her cheeks. Suddenly it wasn't glass at all. It was a sheet of ice covered with hoarfrost. She couldn't see through it. Impossible. She knew that, but it didn't squelch her growing hysteria.

"What's wrong?" Reid's voice echoed from far away, receding speedily.

In an instant, she was underwater, her vison filled with murky green fluid swirling with brown algae, dead plants, and decaying matter. Dim light from the ice hole above speared into an infinity of darkness below. No sounds except the splash of liquid and the gurgle of air bubbles coming from her screaming mouth and running like mercury beads along the underside of the ice. And the cold. Bone deep. Mind numbing. Can't breath, Ansel realized, her fists bleeding from striking the ice. Momma. Daddy.

Something clawed at her shoulders. She was being sucked down, down, down. Into the darkness and mud. No use. She couldn't fight anymore. She curled into a fetal position and sank like a stone.

"Ansel, listen to me. Open your eyes. Right now." Something shook her violently. "Listen to me. You're all right. Open your eyes."

Her eyelids fluttered, than popped open. Reid was staring into her face only inches away, his gaze focused despite his grim expression. He'd turned her around in the front seat and was holding her shoulders with both hands. She was back in the car. A wave of hot shame enveloped her. How could she let him see her like this? He'd think she was crazy and would never believe anything she said to him again.

"Calm down," he instructed softly. "It was just a flashback. Everything's all right. I'm sorry. I didn't realize about the wipers."

She fell against him, weeping her heart out with embarrassment, disgust, and anger. It seemed the only thing to do. Her father had explained to him several months before what had happened to her as a child, and he had the good manners not to push her away. In fact, he held her quietly as she sobbed all over his carefully pressed suit and hiccupped against his shiny badge for several minutes.

"I'm taking you home," Reid stated. "I'll drive your truck and leave my car here. A deputy can pick it up."

She pulled away from him, swiping at her puffy, red eyes. She couldn't look him in the eyes. "You must think I'm some helpless female. Well, I'm not."

He peered at her critically. "You, helpless? Never. Just indisposed."

"God dammit. Don't patronize me. I'm fine," she protested, sniffling again uncontrollably.

Reid didn't release his hold on her. "Now you've done it. That's lie number three," he said, not unkindly. "Give me your truck keys."

Chapter 15

"You can't get rich if you look over your relatives properly."
Navajo

"God Almighty, I pray that Cullen's not dead."

Chase Phoenix sipped his scotch and stared blankly across the sarsparilla wood dining table. Pearl cast a worried glance at Ansel, her short gray-blond hair shining beneath the Kokopelli-style swag lamp above them. Ansel lifted her eyebrows, relaying her own feelings of anxiety to her stepmother.

Reid had taken her home. A sheriff's deputy was already there to drive him back to the station, and they parted after she promised to tell him when Outerbridge made contact with her. She'd caught a couple hours of sleep to regroup her emotions before driving to the Arrowhead in time for an evening meal. She was exhausted, but knew that Flynn's disappearance would play havoc with her father's worries.

As things stood now, Chase had barely touched his supper: a quick fare of son-of-a-gun stew made from sweetbreads, vegetables, Mexican beans, and calf meat with sourdough biscuits and salad on the side. Even Pearl's offer of a slice of contest-winning sweet-potato pie for dessert had been rejected. This was a sure sign that, between the drought and his friend's disappearance, he felt his luck was running kind of muddy.

"We're all praying that Cul's all right," Pearl said. "Let's not get spooked. There could be ordinary explanations why he's out of touch."

"Tell that to Katherine," Chase replied, referring to Cullen's wife of twenty-six years. "She must be suffering aplenty. Cul's been gone about twenty-four hours now."

Pearl fixed him with a curious gaze. "I told you I talked to Katherine this afternoon and offered to stop by, remember? She's holding up all right. Shea and Erin are staying with her tonight along with the grandkids."

"I forgot," Chase admitted.

"You're tired. You've been doing chores from dawn until dusk. Counting some sheep tonight will make everything look better in the morning."

"That's right, Daddy. Cullen will turn up," Ansel reassured, though she had her doubts. If they knew what she knew about fossil poachers, they'd be horrified.

"Can't convince me of good news with neither shuteye nor blather," Chase pronounced. "I've got the willies tonight, ladies. And we all know what that means."

"Lordy, here comes that old tale about your mother being a Blue Child," Pearl groused. "You're just a superstitious old cowpoke, Chase." She rose and started clearing dishes.

Ansel said nothing. There was no doubt that her grandmother, Renee Phoenix, had been born with uncanny intuitive gifts. Some family members said she had been a Blue Child, not a baby tangled up in her own umbilical cord as the name suggested, but one with a special connection to unseen forces from the misty beyond. A lot of people had called Renee a psychic. Others had labeled her a specialist in synchronicity, always guessing right with the odds in her favor. Personally, she had no recollection of grandma Renee, who died a year before her mother and father met.

"My mother knew things before they happened," Chase insisted, "and I've got a little of her juice in me, Pearl. I don't get the willies that often but when I do, somebody's going to get hurt. Can't say who or how or when, but it happens every time. Sarcee knows, don't you, darlin'?"

Ansel nodded. "I've seen him get the willies three times. Once before one of our cowhands got drunk and died when he drove off the road straight into a John Deere Harvester sitting in a wheat field. And another time he knew somebody was in trouble before Howdy Adams' wife committed suicide. She threw herself in front of a locomotive on a Great Northern spur line. Daddy also felt the willies when something was wrong with my mother. He was at a stockman's conference in Jordan and left right away. Wasn't until he got to the ranch that he knew for sure what had happened."

Ansel stopped there. A stiff silence invaded the room. Nobody really wanted to go into Mary's sudden and protracted diabetic coma and eventual death. It had devastated her father and changed her life as a little girl forever.

"Let the sheriff's department do their job," Pearl urged Chase. "Don't borrow trouble you'll loan to your stomach. You'll get an ulcer." She hustled toward the kitchen, her hands stacked with plates and serving dishes.

"I know something bad has happened just as sure as I'm sitting here trying to deny it to myself," Chase mumbled.

"I wish you'd foretold that you weren't going to eat a lick of supper," Pearl scolded over her shoulder. "I wouldn't have cooked all this food. It's a good thing Ansel came over."

When she was gone, Chase swallowed down his drink and watched as Ansel stood and collected the remaining odds and ends left on the table.

After several moments of silence, he said, "How are you doing? You look tired."

"I am. Long day."

"Are you still working on that Argentina book?"

Ansel shrugged. "Should be. Seems like everything else keeps getting in the way." She had no intention of telling him about her experiences with the FBI, the BLM, and Dorbandt. His blood pressure would spike for sure. "For example, tomorrow morning I'm going to Permelia's to discuss her book cover."

A slight smile crinkled the corners of Chase's mouth. "Good luck with Starr. That dog makes more noise than a jackass in a tin shed. With all the barking, you'll probably only hear a hundred words for every thousand-count Permelia throws at you. Maybe that's a blessing. She wheedled down my sale price on two stud bulls using tongue oil alone. She's a regular word bandit."

Ansel laughed as she walked to the kitchen. "I have my own selfish reasons for helping her. I want to see her Barnum Brown memorabilia and her dinosaur fossils."

As she set the plates on a tiled island counter inside the spacious kitchen, Pearl peered at her. She stood at the double porcelain sink rinsing dishes beneath the tap. "Ansel, I'm worried about your father," she whispered. "He's not acting like himself."

Pearl's expression was pensive. Deep furrows raked her brow, and her blue eyes were intense with unspoken emotion. She'd stopped in mid-swipe, and water from a soapy plate dribbled down to her elbow. She didn't even notice.

"What do you mean?"

"He's been moping around hardly speaking and he's distracted. I talk but he's not listening. He's also having trouble sleeping. Been using over-the-counter sleeping pills for two weeks now, and they don't help at all. He's bushed, that's true. The ranch work is busting him good, but that's not all it is."

Ansel looked at the open kitchen door and moved closer to Pearl. "He's real worried about the Arrowhead. He told me the ranch is working in the red. That's never happened before."

Pearl turned back to rinsing the soapy dish. "The ranch is a major problem," she agreed. "But there's something else going on."

"What?"

"I don't think he's feeling well." To her right, the dishwasher door beneath the counter was open. She dropped the plate into a rack slot. "It's more than just aches and pains for his age. I catch him wincing like he's in serious discomfort when he thinks I'm not looking."

"Did you ask him about it?"

Pearl nodded. "Several times. He just smiles and makes light of it in his customary way. Says he's fine, and I'm a mama cow trying to give milk to a bull. You know him. His damn pride won't let him complain."

Ansel pursed her lips at this disturbing news, then crossed her arms. "I'll talk to Daddy. Maybe I can pry some information out of him."

"Good. I feel better now. I just had to tell you. The ranch will survive. I can't let something happen to Chase," Pearl confided. "I don't know what I'd do. Somebody's got to talk some sense into him and find out what's wrong."

Footsteps resounded on the oak-slat flooring outside the kitchen and Chase popped through the door, hands ladled into his jean pockets. "Sarcee, I forgot to talk to you about that attorney referral you wanted. Got a minute?"

Just what she wanted. The perfect chance to corral her father and pounce on him about his health. "Sure."

Pearl wiped her hands on a dishtowel and turned around. "Maybe you two will reconsider having some pie afterward," she suggested with a grin. "I'll leave it out just in case."

Ansel and her father walked through an opposite kitchen door and directly into a hallway in the east wing of the four-thousand-square-foot spruce log home. A quick jaunt to the right and they reached a heavy cedar door. Ansel walked first into the study with its floor-to-ceiling bookcases, an antique redwood desk, plenty of cushioned chairs, and a fireplace. Chase gestured her toward another archway on their left, which led into a smaller room containing a luncheon nook and a solid wall of casement windows. A single folder lay on the wooden table.

Ansel took a seat in one of four leather chairs, glad that it was night and she could see no further outside than the white light cast by decorative patio lamps. The wall before her faced the south pasture where horses grazed. The stock pond where she had almost died was out there, too. Today of all days, she certainly didn't need to view it.

Chase sat across from her, back to the windows, and grabbed the file. "You know that the Arrowhead covers fifteen thousand deeded acres, plus another twelve thousand BLM lease parcels that I use for grazing land," he began, opening the folder. "The lawyer I've used to handle my Bureau affairs for the last five years is Noah Zollie. He's in Billings."

She took the sheet of paper he passed to her. It was an advertisement for law services with Zollie's letterhead on top. "I was hoping for someone local."

"He's one of the best in the state. I don't like messing around with fly-by-night lawyers when I'm courting the Bureau of Land Management," Chase explained. "Too many things can go wrong. You going to tell me why you need a land trust attorney?"

"I'm looking for basic information about the way BLM land leases operate on paper."

Chase eyed her carefully. "I can tell you that."

Ansel folded the letter. "There are all sorts of land agreements between private, state, and federal groups. I need a complete overview. It's just research work. I'm not getting personally involved in anything."

Chase closed the folder and leaned back in his chair. "I'm going to guess it has something to do with the Big Toe fossil robbery. Am I right?"

She tried to keep her game face on, a smile plastered across her lower jaw like a stiff rubber mask. Maybe he was a bit psychic. "Lucky guess. Okay, I'm trying find out how to prevent the BLM from revoking the museum land lease and removing the fossil tracks to a federal repository. They've threatened to do that. I'm just fishing. What can that hurt?"

"Nothing," Chase conceded. "To tell the truth, I never liked the way the BLM moved in on Chester's land after he died. His kin never had enough time to arrange for personal loans that would pay off the back revenues he owed under the terms of his Conservation Reserve Program contract with the government. The whole deal stank. I'd like to see things set right."

"I think the Bureau was always more interested in the fossil tracks that flash flood exposed before Chester's death than getting their money back," Ansel declared. "The fact that the town council approached them with the idea of leasing the farmhouse and some of the property to start the museum was just icing on the cake."

"Well, Noah's the man to call if you want to plumb your angles," Chase insisted. He pushed back his chair and slowly stood up, a slight stoop to his stance.

As she rose, Ansel noticed his gritted teeth. "Are you all right, Daddy?"

He smiled, his leathery, tanned face suddenly vibrant. "I'm a little off my feed, but it's nothing a few good bucketfuls of rain won't cure. Things will change for the better. They always do."

When he came around the table, Ansel walked over to him. "Pearl says you're in pain, but won't admit it. I want to know the truth."

The annoyance on Chase's face shadowed his grin in an instant. "I know she means well, but she's fretting over nothing. I'm fine. I wish everyone would leave it be."

Ansel realized she'd get nothing out of him by direct questioning. Making him angry wouldn't help. She stood on her booted tiptoes and kissed him on the cheek. "I'm glad to hear it. There's a beautiful moon out tonight. Do you want to walk me up the hill? I'd like to see momma's grave."

Her mother was buried in a small family cemetery which began in 1878 and contained many Phoenix ancestors, some of whom originally immigrated to America from Germain-en-Laye, France. At the top of a low ridge overlooking the Missouri River was a white marble tomb with a six-foot-tall Indian Angel carved in her mother's likeness on top.

Chase's face relaxed as he chuckled. "You're about as subtle as an Arkansas toothpick," he said, referring to another name for a Bowie knife. "Trying to scare a confession out of me?"

"Not at all. I've got to leave early in the morning. This will be my only chance to go."

"All right, we'll go see Mary. Then we'll make Pearl happy by having some pie."

"I love you, Daddy," Ansel said.

"And I love you, Sarcee."

Chapter 16

"When the wisdom keepers speak, all should listen."
Seneca

Ansel sucked in a warm lungful of the air that rushed through the open driver's window. The sky was cloudless and azure blue, typical for Big Sky country, and she was determined to enjoy the comparably cool, high-seventies temperatures while she could. According to the news, the sun would be a wood-burner by noon.

She peeled the truck along a Diamond Tail dirt road and surveyed Permelia's drought-ravaged grasslands. They looked like the Arrowhead's except they were stippled by red and white Texas Longhorns rather than Black Angus. Permelia operated one of the few Montana ranches that bred the registered heifers, steers, and seedstock bulls.

She knew a little about the breed from her father. They were originally descended from cattle brought to Spain by African Moors, then imported into Mexico and America. Both sexes carried lengthy horns spanning up to eighty-four inches. Ansel watched as older genders trundled across the pastures, looking ready to topple onto the ground from sheer top-heaviness.

She reached the late 1800s vintage farmhouse constructed from ponderosa planking painted bright white and parked by a corral where Permelia stood beside a tall bay horse. Gone were her fancy, neon pink clothes and accessories. She wore denim ranch duds, navy boots, and a floppy blue hat. Despite her years and rail-thin stature, she released the cinch buckle around the horse's belly, slid the heavy western saddle off, then tossed it onto the top rail as easily as a young cowhand.

Ansel dragged her large leather portfolio case out of the truck. Dust swirled with every step she took, while the smell of hay, horse lather, and dung assailed her nostrils. It made her long for the days when she had ridden War Bonnet, a birthday gift from her mother twenty years before, over coulees and through cottonwood stands. That was impossible now. The old paint stallion had laminitis and spent his days paddocked or brushing grass with his tail.

Permelia patted the gelding affectionately and joined her near the porch. "Howdy, Ansel. Glad you could make it. Gonna be another neck-blister today. I hear there's a passel of Canadian forest fires and dust storms up north. Hope Saskatoon dust and smoke doesn't blow our way."

"God forbid," Ansel said, with abhorrence.

Between fires and dust storms, the black blizzards of the Dust Bowl days were most feared by everyone. Lands ravaged by fire renewed themselves. Not so with the dust tsunamis that churned across rangelands with winds up to eighty miles an hour and flattened everything from power poles to sixty-five-foot grain bins. Worst of all, the winds stripped topsoil and rocks from local fields or dumped it in dunes behind windbreaks. The results left only sandy soils behind and removed all the nutrients needed to grow healthy crops.

"You throw a mean saddle, Mrs. Chance."

"Call me Permelia. I've known you since you were in my beginners' riding classes. Only strangers and gentlemen call me by my married name, and I don't trust any of them. Especially the men. You do what I do, Ansel. Always throw your own saddle. Taking responsibility for yourself makes you strong. It's as true with life as it is with riding."

Ansel smiled as she remembered taking a summer's worth of classes from Permelia when she was ten years old. Permelia had instructed girls in the skills of western riding for over thirty years, and she was still teaching them.

"I intend to."

"Good girl." Permelia scanned the heavens. "Curse this heat. L.C. Smith died this morning from it."

"Oh, I'm so sorry," Ansel proclaimed. "That must be a terrible shock. Was he here long?"

"About seventeen years. He went down sudden-like. Saw him yesterday and he was Jim Dandy. Got to be crucible-hot to bring down a Butler bred stud that'll go for days without water and live on weeds, cactus, and brush. Let's wet our whiskers."

Only then did Ansel realize she referred to a deceased Longhorn, not a respected top-hand. Chagrined, she followed across the porch and through a squeaky, wood-scrolled screen door. As soon as they entered, the maniacal yelps of a dog locked inside a room echoed down a hallway.

The noise receded in Ansel's mind as she marveled at the inside, which looked like a sitting room straight out of the early 1900s. Gazing at the well-worn four-piece hardwood parlor suite upholstered in three-tone floral velours with bottom fringes, fancy bindings, and rococo brass gimp ornamentation was like time traveling.

Her eyes also took in the graceful lines of a birch parlor cabinet with ornamental wood shelves, two center bevel-plate mirrors, and narrow legs. In the dining area sat an immensely heavy golden oak table with five-inch hand-turned and fluted legs with matching chairs. A combination sideboard and glass closet was filled by flowered china with gold edging. Ansel was yanked back to the present by Starr's vocables, which had become keening howls.

"Just have to breed them heifers to somebody else," Permelia continued at warp speed. "Maybe Six-Shooter or Pistolo. Got my foreman dressing down L.C. Smith right now. We'll have meat aplenty and another hide and set of horns to sell to city folk. Take a seat, Ansel," Permelia directed, tossing her hat on a spring-loaded parlor chair. "Any news about Chief Flynn?"

Ansel sank into the couch that looked as if a thousand rumps had kept it warm for her and adjusted her case so she could paw through it easily. She shook her head. "Nothing much except that the state police are involved now. It looks like foul play."

"Seems like somebody might have ambushed him, all right. I'm praying for him and the family. I remember when you could ride anywhere alone for days in Lacrosse, stop at any ranch along the road day or night, and be guaranteed a friendly welcome whether they knew you or not. Got nothing worse than mean gossip and bad grub. The world's turning sour."

Permelia's hawk-eyes shifted to Ansel. "Guess you know about Rusty Flynn?"

Ansel's head snapped up from her fussing with the portfolio zipper. She hadn't heard that name spoken around her in years. Everyone made a point of not repeating it to her. Rusty Flynn had been eight years old when he pushed her into the pond.

"Rusty? He's in prison."

"Not anymore. He got out a year ago. He's living in Swoln. Used to come by here every once in a while last fall. Sold me braided horsehair key chains he learned to make in the Wyoming hoosegow. I'd buy a few from him and give them out to the sick kids at the hospital. It's uncharitable for me to say it, but Rusty's an oily one. He's always polite and charming, but he's got the 'dare me' eyes of a sand scorpion. I don't trust him and I quit encouraging him to come around. Now I'm wondering if he has anything to do with the Chief gone missing."

Anger flushed through Ansel's veins as she tried to wrap her mind around the fact that Rusty was in Lacrosse. Had been for quite a while, and her father and Pearl hadn't even told her. No wonder her father had the willies if Rusty was hunkering in the background shadows of Cullen's affairs.

Cullen had always kept an eye on his only nephew after his brother Colm died. It was the Irish way to overlook your clan be they sparrow or hawk. As Cullen's friend and confidant, there was no doubt in her mind that her father was informed the minute

Rusty returned. The paternal betrayal of trust bloated her rage. What if she'd accidentally run into Rusty during her travels? "I didn't mean to rile you," Permelia assured. "I thought you knew. Let's forget about it. How about something to drink? What's your pleasure? Coffee, iced tea, soda pop, water?"

"A Coke would be fine, if you have it," Ansel said, feigning joviality.

"I believe I do. I'll be back. Make yourself at home."

Starr quit howling and went into stage three of her disgruntled repertoire. It featured fierce, low-level growls and claws scratching against wood. The howls could have been her own, Ansel thought, stewing over Permelia's news. She ignored the dog and tried to calm herself by observing the mementos around her. The old-fashioned gray wallpaper festooned with old-rose daisies with green foliage supported a passel of framed black and white photos. The pictures showed horses, mules, cattle, and scenic views of mountain ranges and large river bends.

Some other photos of men were set along an ancient side-board table against a wall. Each was distinctive in his own way. One clean-cut young blond man wore a 1940s Marine Corps uniform. Another long-haired, older man wore his best cowboy dress, and a third brown-bearded man wore a nice suit and tie. Permelia's three husbands, Ansel surmised, each as different in face and stature as the other.

Elsewhere Indian pottery lining ceiling shelves around the room added more gay colors to the mish-mash of busy floral fabrics covering the old furniture. A corner shelving unit beside a window was crammed with verdant succulents: aloe, flowering cactus, or hen and chicks.

Everything was neat and orderly, what she'd expect from Permelia, who was well known for her simple and punctilious business practices. The woman was a whiz at investment foresight and market speculation. She had to be or she would never have survived keeping the original Diamond Tail land parcels intact amid the predatory circling of government officials and nature conservancy advocates, who had great disdain for the old ranching traditions like open range grazing and private water rights.

Permelia returned bearing a small wood serving tray with two tall glasses filled with ice and a quart glass pitcher filled with fizzing brown Coke, forks, and two dessert plates, each containing a freshly cut square of home-baked crumb cake. She set it on the white coffee table. "Help yourself. I quieted Starr down. Gave her a dried cow hoof."

Ansel noticed that the house was quiet. Hands shaking from anxiety, she poured Coke into her glass and said, "I brought my portfolio so you could see my artwork styles, which include pen and ink, watercolors, acrylics, oils, and air brushing. I wasn't sure what you had in mind for the medium, composition, or design of your book cover."

Permelia poured herself a drink and grabbed one of the plates. "When it comes to style, I'm not picky about the fixings, just want a full belly. I'm sure you know best about those things, Ansel. What I'm looking for in a cover is something that looks like Montana and will grab your eye like a fish hook when you're passing by it at the store. Let me see what you've got."

"I'm sure we'll find a technique you'll like," Ansel assured. "What I'll do today is concentrate on the underlying picture, not the lettering for title, name, and so on. I'll design that later. Keep in mind that these are mostly dinosaur subjects, but I can do any landscape or animal you're interested in. Portraiture takes me longer because I don't do much work in that area."

Ansel unzipped the case and pulled out drawings she'd done over the years which reflected her different styles. She passed them one by one to Permelia in between sips of her drink and bites of her delicious crumb cake. They ran through twelve pictures very quickly. Permelia was decisive about what types of perspective, shadowing, and detailing she liked. She didn't care for line drawings at all, no matter how detailed the subject. Nor did she like black and white. She wanted full color and tended toward realistic textures and methods rather than abstract or surrealistic techniques.

Knowing this, Ansel pulled out a recent full-color acrylic test drawing of an Argentinosaurus that was rendered on smooth illustration board with dry brushed paints and air-brushed watercolors.

"Now this is what I want," Permelia declared. "This critter looks like you could touch it and feel the bumps. How'd you make it look so real?"

"That's an old painting technique called gouache. The ancient Egyptians, Greeks, and Romans painted with the precursor of modern gouache. This style relies on carefully controlling the painting of colors from dark to light or light over dark. Special paints and colors are used as very thin opaque layers continually placed on top or around each other. I often intermix gouache with watercolors as stains and air-brushing with regular acrylics in my projects that require absolute, photo-like realism."

"Pharaohs and Caesars? You don't say. That settles it. This is the brand of paint I want on *Montana Chaps*."

Ansel grinned and took the illustration board from Permelia's tan, wrinkled hand. "Great," she said, muscling the large, stiff board into her case. "Gouache it is." As she fumbled with the preliminary drawing, the open end of the portfolio dipped off the sofa toward the floor. A whole sheaf of materials piled out, including one pen and ink drawing she didn't know was in there.

The sketch of the Giganatosaurus she'd drawn the morning after the museum robbery flew across the floor directly in front of Permelia. Ansel cringed. Somehow she had unknowingly grabbed it when she filled the case with drawing samples from her workroom. She should have thrown the damn thing away.

"Oh, I like this," Permelia crowed, grabbing the drawing off the rug. "Somebody rang the grub bell. Look at them jaws. Hey, I got an idea. Let's use this for *Montana Chaps* except replace the little lizard with a cowboy on horseback. You know, a wrangler back-trailing from this critter. That cover will get attention, all right."

Ansel's eyes widened. "I thought you wanted a very realistic cover. Perhaps a photo-like drawing of your homestead with longhorns or a collage of images. Maybe even something more symbolic? Maybe the Diamond Tail brand," she offered hopefully.

"You can make this look real," Permelia countered. "You've sure got the talent, gal. And this idea has the grit and gristle I'm looking for, especially with my family being involved with dinosaurs. Kinda draws the bones and broncos together, don't you think?" She leaned back and stared at the painting, her eyes sparkling and a grin stretching her lined face into a younger version of herself. "Can I keep this?"

Just the thought of the drawing circulating the local dump annoyed Ansel, let alone that Permelia wanted to put such a garish creation on a book stand. But what could she do? It was a work for hire. Maybe she'd even get a quirky new following of art fans who would be into Phoenix Studios comic book art. Yeah, fat chance. Could this week get any worse?

"Of course," she said, clenching her teeth and pushing the remainder of her artwork into the portfolio.

"So what will I owe you?"

"I'll do some figuring and send you an estimate within the week. We'll talk again. I can't start the cover art until after I finish a prior book deadline next month. Is that agreeable?"

"Surely is." Permelia rose and put the drawing down tenderly on the dining room table. "Now that we're done talking business, I'll show you that hodgepodge I've got from Barnum Brown's dig that my daddy left me. Bet you're itching to see it."

"I certainly am," Ansel enthused, a bright spot shining on her gloomy day at last.

"Did I tell you that my second husband, Elam Gruell, bought quarry land outside Jordan?"

Ansel nodded. "Yes."

"Well, Elam got the bone bug in 1950 and bought four-hundred acres of range in the Badlands. Said it was part of an ancient creek bed and bursting with potential. Thought he could run it as a sideline besides ranching Herefords. He worked it for a year, then lost interest. After Elam died in a farming accident in 1954, I married Loren Chance, you know.

"Loren decided in 1963 to switch from Herefords to Longhorns, which is what my first husband, Kenny Knox, started the ranch with after World War II," Permelia continued as they walked past the kitchen. "Anyway, in the sixties, Loren found out that the Texas breed was on the brink of extinction with only fifteen hundred left in national parks or zoos. Before the open ranges disappeared, about six hundred thousand were driven to market every year. People talk about the buffalo going extinct, but Longhorns stampeded that dead-end trail first. Loren died from cancer ten years ago, and I've been herding the critters alone."

Ansel barely focused on Permelia's words because the kitchen they passed held her enthralled. She took in the vintage, black iron gas and wood-burning stove, white kitchen cabinetry with old porcelain sinks, and original 1940s Linoleum flooring with amazement. She wondered what the bedrooms and bathrooms looked like.

"Did Elam ever find anything good in the quarry?" she finally asked.

"Oh, he found a lot. Big bones and little. Plenty more left behind, I reckon. Still own that parcel. Don't know why I keep it. Maybe you'd like to putter around on it some day."

"I'd love that, Permelia. Thank you for offering."

"Now what I'm going to show you is the stuff my daddy, John Reading, helped Barnum Brown with from June to July 1908 around Big Dry Creek. That's where Brown found the most complete Tyrannosaurus out of three, plus a lot of other bones. Daddy was in charge of the horses they used to prospect for bones and to haul the wagons carrying out the plastered bones."

They'd walked along a narrow hall with dark gray wallpaper and stopped at a thick, white door. "Here you go," Permelia exclaimed. She grabbed a white porcelain doorknob and pushed the portal open.

Ansel nearly tripped when Starr, wearing a hand-sewn outfit of matching blue denim shorts, vest, and bandanna bolted between her feet. She was barely able to brace herself against the wall with one arm as the ten-pound dachshund keened like a canine wraith, then raced around her legs in toe-scrabbling circles on the tongue-and-groove floorboards.

"Shut up, Belle Starr," Permelia hollered loud enough to split firewood.

Starr quit but began an incredible, two-foot-high rabbit-hop against Ansel's knees. The dachshund's tail wagged like a joy meter and cow hoof drool sprayed her boots.

"You two are sure gonna have fun," Permelia cackled. "Go on in."

Ansel dared a step forward. She suddenly felt like she was entering a temple of doom.

Chapter 17

"There is nothing as eloquent as a rattlesnake's tail."
Navajo

Detective Odie Fiskar shifted his massive, muscular body against the driver's seat, exhaled loudly, and adjusted his bear paw hands on the steering wheel. Reid Dorbandt looked up from his small leather notebook. Odie had been trying to find his saddle seat for the last thirty minutes. Compact sedans weren't designed with giants in mind.

"Almost there," Reid said, staring through the gumbo-dusted windshield at the crispy sheep land surrounding them. "I'll fill you in on Flynn's nephew. His parole officer says he works the midnight to eight shift at Swoln Stockyards. Best to corner him when he's home for shuteye."

"Worth a try, I guess. The jailbird nephew is all we've got," Odie said woefully. "Sheriff Combs will keep busting our chops until we find the Chief."

Reid stared at his notebook again. He was actually thinking of Chloe Birch. He hadn't had a moment to call her since he got back from Billings, and she'd been on his mind a lot. He hoped to go back into town to reclaim the Indian's head and see her again. Out of nowhere, Ansel's scowling face popped into his head like a subconscious chimera.

Yesterday had been a roller coaster of emotions. First he was furious with her, then he was practically making a pass at her.

And last but not least, he'd driven her to tears with his insensitive actions with the windshield wipers. He'd never meant to upset her. What a disaster.

Odie's voice slammed through his wall of confusion. "Hey, you napping on me?"

Reid blinked and blew air out his mouth. "Hokay, here we go. Flynn, Cyrus Kelley, thirty-three, white, male, five foot eleven, one hundred eighty pounds, red hair, green eyes. No warrants. Now, that is," he added. "Possession of drugs, 1984. One year probation. Possession of drugs, 1985. Thirty-six months. Possession of drugs with intent to sell, 1988. Thirty-six months. Criminal mischief, 1991. Thirty-six months. Theft, 1995. Twenty-four months. Burglary, 1997. Thirty-six months. Burglary, 2000. Thirty-six months. Prison release from Wyoming Honor Farm in 2003 with two-year probation."

Odie guffawed, sending a deep boom across the front seat. "He's like a Bosch painting done with fingerpaints. Sounds like a simpleton."

"Bosch. Isn't that a soup?"

"Not borscht. Heironymous Bosch. He was a famous artist who portrayed the evil of man in scary images—demons and half-human animals and machines."

Reid closed his notebook with a snap. "Stop it, Odie. You're the one that scares me when you flex your brain muscles. You've been doing too many *New York Times* crossword puzzles again." He peered through the windshield. Ahead was a disintegrating wood house. "Here it is."

Odie parked the car next to a green El Camino in the dirt drive and killed the engine. Then he reached for the radio mike and called dispatch, notifying them of their arrival. Meanwhile, Reid got out and surveyed the place: an overgrown yard with a gray-white house sporting a badly leaning porch and broken windows.

Reid walked around the sedan and surveyed the area for signs that other vehicles had been there recently. Hard to tell because the long, dead vegetation in the drive was constantly crushed by Flynn's car going in and out. Nothing else looked amiss.

He wandered over to the El Camino in front of the sedan. The doors were locked and the windows up. Nothing on the inside except holey, gray fabric seats and faded blue carpeting on relatively clean floorboards. Unusually fastidious for a con driving a junk heap.

The same wasn't true for the outside. The flatbed was empty but badly dinged and rusting. Reid surveyed the truck body, which was caked high up with gumbo dust and dirt. The wheels' undersides and chassis, however, were gummed over with globs of black mud. That intrigued him. Where in the middle of a drought did you find mud? Against the dark splatters, something pink on the right rear undercarriage caught his eye. He squatted and peered closer. A tiny speck of fluffy material was pinched between the decorative metal molding and the wheel well.

"Find something?" Odie stood behind him.

"Maybe." Reid used his fingernails to pinch the fibers up, then stood.

Odie moved in closer. "Looks like shotgun wadding."

"I'd bet it is."

It wasn't unusual to find such wadding in areas where a shotgun had been fired. He pulled a small glassine envelope stored inside his suit breast pocket for just such treasures, and bagged it. They looked at each other and silently headed across the knee-high weeds to the house.

Once up the rotten porch steps and onto the creaking, warped planking, Odie pounded on the green door with a sledgehammer fist. Reid wandered toward an adjacent window with cracked glass and peered around the dirty sheet doubling as drapes. He could see a small living room containing cheap furniture and unpacked boxes. Odie knocked again.

The front door whipped open and a man with wet, long red hair, beard, and moustache glared at them. He wore blue jeans and a baggy red pullover sweater more suitable for fall temperatures than summer. "Yeah?"

Reid stepped quickly to the door. "Cyrus Flynn?" he asked
as the distinct smells of mildew, rotten fruit, and human waste
wafted past him.

"Yeah."

"I'm Lieutenant Dorbandt. This is Detective Fiskar. We're
from the sheriff's department. We want to ask you some questions about your uncle, Chief Cullen Flynn."

Reid kept smiling and took in Flynn's sallow face, red-rimmed
eyes, and puffy nose. Cyrus looked like he was either strung out
or had one doozy of a cold. He made a mental note to check
Flynn's jacket for a list of drugs the con had used and dealt.

Cyrus casually placed one hand on the door frame, effectively
blocking the entrance. His face morphed into a mask of dire
sadness. "Oh, man. My uncle. I've been worried sick about him.
Have you found him?"

Reid doubted the sentiment but held his friendly expression.
"We're working on it. We need to come in."

"I'm trying to sleep. Just got home from a job about fifteen
minutes ago. Anyway, to be honest, I can't tell you much. I
haven't seen or heard from Uncle Cullen since last April. Given
his line of work, he's not too fond of me."

"To be honest with you Mr. Flynn, because of your record,
we've got to probe a little deeper into what you've been doing
lately," Reid said. "We can do that here and now," he said, looking
pointedly at the door, "or we can do it at the sheriff's office."

"It *would* be more expedient to do it here, Mr. Flynn," Odie
added, towering over the smaller man.

Cyrus coughed, sniffled, and then pulled the door open.
"Sure, okay. Excuse the mess."

Odie went in first, entirely filling the doorway. Reid didn't
really want to enter, but he did. The place was worse on the
inside. It looked like Cyrus had quit housekeeping months ago.
The carpet was full of dirt and the dingy, fading wallpaper swallowed what little light came in through the makeshift curtains.
It was hard to tell whether Cyrus had gotten stalled moving in

or out with all the boxes. There was no air conditioning either. The room was a miasma of stale air.

Flynn immediately sat on a black sofa that looked like he lived in it. Magazines, empty soda cans, non-prescription medicines, and unwashed food dishes spotted the floor around the sofa and the coffee table in front of it. "What can I help you with?" he asked agreeably.

Reid forced himself to take a nasty-looking recliner on the right side of the sofa. Odie remained standing. This was how they operated. He'd ask the questions while his partner slowly circulated the room. Odie would peruse the immediate area within eyesight for anything suspicious or telling, and if Flynn bolted, Odie would nab him in a second.

He pulled out his notebook and a pen from an inside breast pocket. "Exactly when was the last time you talked to Cullen Flynn?"

Cyrus watched him carefully. "The end of April. The thirtieth, I think. Pay day for both of us. Uncle Cullen brought me some extra cash."

"How often does Cullen do that?"

"Not much. Maybe twice a year. Like I said, we aren't close, but he helps me out."

Odie shifted to the left and walked around the sofa. Reid held Flynn's attention. "Do you ever argue with your uncle?"

Cyrus shrugged. "Sure, sometimes. He gets on my case about my past. He's a cop. I'm the black sheep of the family."

Cyrus looked over his shoulder at Odie, who had moved beyond the sofa toward the kitchen. "Hey, I thought you just wanted to ask questions."

Odie turned around and smiled, but kept walking toward the kitchen entrance and a closed door against one wall. "This place sure brings back memories. My grandmother had a house like this. What year was it built?"

"I don't know," Cyrus said, eyeing the detective warily. "I rent. I'd prefer it if you didn't wander too far, okay?"

"You ever have a serious disagreement with Cullen? One that got physical?" Reid said.

Cyrus' head snapped around. "What? No. He yells at me and I yell back. That's it. He was a pain in the ass sometimes, but I've never hurt him."

"Was?" he asked, staring carefully.

"I mean is, of course," Cyrus corrected, rubbing a hand across his face. "I'm tired. It's been a long night, and you're making me nervous."

"You just got off shift from the slaughterhouse, right?"

Cyrus snorted and leaned back against the cushions. "They call it a beef kill, not a slaughterhouse. You know what I do? I'm the shackler. It's the filthiest job in the whole plant, man. Cows come in three at a time, and another guy called the knocker shoots a three-inch-long spike through their heads before they drop down, twitching and kicking, into a pit with me. I wrap a chain around their left rear legs so they get hoisted thirty feet over my head and moved to another guy who cuts them throat to breastbone. Bleeds them out."

Cyrus glanced at Odie, who had returned near the sofa. He heaved his shoulders dramatically and then gazed hard at Reid, "Hell, I stand in that bloody piss and shit hole eight hours a day, and you guys wonder why I can't talk straight?"

Reid had listened with one ear as Cyrus rattled on, and he had perused the room with both eyes. The sympathy ploy was standard fodder for ex-cons. When they weren't jiving, hustling, or lying about one thing, they were wheedling, whining, or wowing you about something else. So far, he'd only seen one item in the house that interested him.

"You're using drugs, aren't you Cyrus?"

"No, dammit. I'm clean."

"You don't look it. What is it, crank? Crack?"

"I've got a cold. You can test me. I'm clean," Cyrus flared.

"How about a gun?" he asked, going straight for Cyrus' jugular. "Got one stashed here?"

Cyrus' face went flat. "No. What are you doing? I haven't done anything wrong."

"You've got a gun-and-ammo magazine on the coffee table," Reid pushed.

"I used to hunt a lot. A man can read about guns, can't he?"

"Ever use a shotgun?" Odie queried.

Cyrus calmly reached for a pack of smokes on the table. "Oh, now you've got me, boys," he retorted, as he pulled a cigarette out and stuck it between his lips. "I confess. I used one plenty before becoming a guest of the states of Montana and Wyoming. Gut shot three deers and a turkey if I recollect right. Is that illegal these days?" He used a lighter to stoke the smoke between a few congestive coughs.

"Lying to a sheriff's detective is," Reid snapped. "If I have to come back again, it will be with a search warrant, a DAF swat team, and an army of sheriff's deputies. Get smart, Cyrus. Is there anything you want to tell us about your uncle's vanishing act before we leave?"

Cyrus glared back, cigarette burning between his pale, trembling fingers. "I don't deserve this. I'm out of jail and off the drugs. Just trying to straighten my life out, man. You should be detecting what really happened to Uncle Cullen, not harassing me."

Reid closed his notebook and stood. "Don't leave Swoln." He headed for the front door at a jaunty pace, Odie's heavy footfalls behind him. Cyrus didn't bother to leave the couch, just sucked on his cigarette with short angry puffs as they opened the door and departed.

Once at the sedan, Odie said, "He's lying."

"Like a cur dog in dirt," Reid agreed as they both slid into the car. "Have you ever been to a slaughterhouse?"

Odie shook his head. "No. Why?"

"Well if you had, you'd know that anyone who works there smells like blood. They can't come home and wash it away. It's in their clothes. It's in the skin. It's in their hairs. Cyrus had taken a shower, but he still didn't smell like blood, feces, or urine.

Either did that house. Makes me wonder what he's really doing at Swoln Stockyards."

"Yeah, I see what you mean. What's next?"

Reid strapped on his seatbelt and grinned. "Today we'll stop in Swoln and ask some questions. See if anybody saw Chief Flynn's Jeep pass through town the day before yesterday. We'll also ask about the Indian with a gimp. I got the lab results back from Butte. My buffalo tongue sandwich matched the poacher's stomach contents. He was at Humpy's all right."

"That was good work, Reid," Odie said reverently.

"If you like that, you're really going to like this. I've got an idea how we might slap a face on the poacher without having to wait for the reconstruction from Billings," he said, thinking as he had been for the last few days about Chloe Birch. Who knew when he'd get back to see her again with the Cullen Flynn dilemma?

Odie started the car and backed down the drive. "How's that?"

"There's a bank across the street from the restaurant with a money machine. It has a closed circuit camera on it. Maybe it catches people going in and out of the restaurant. That means he's on tape."

Odie's large, square teeth gleamed like white Chiclets. "Sweet. And maybe the lab can tell us something about the wadding from the jailbird's car. Somebody shot a gun near it. The only problem is, it doesn't mean it has anything to do with the Chief's vanishing act."

Reid nodded. "True, but I'll bet you a bucket of cluck from the Chicken Barn that this week was payday at the Big Toe police station."

Suddenly a cell phone rang. "That mine or yours?" Odie asked as he sped down the gumbo road.

"Mine." Reid pulled it out of his jacket. "Lieutenant Dorbandt."

"Hi, Reid. It's Chloe."

"Well, hello. This is a surprise." Reid turned his head toward the passenger window.

Chloe giggled. "A pleasant one, I hope."

"Very. How are you progressing on your reconstruction, Dr. Birch?"

"Oh, so formal. You're not alone, I gather."

Reid looked at Odie, who grinned wolfishly at him. "No."

"All right, I get the message. I've been working day and night since you left. Even begged off some of my college classes on other professors who owe me favors. I know how badly your department needs this completed. Besides, it's really for you," she said meaningfully.

Now Odie was grinning at him. "And I appreciate your efforts."

Chloe laughed again. "I've scanned the skull and finished placing the skin depth markers this morning. I'm going to convert those measurements into a computerized program this afternoon."

"Great."

"As I mentioned before, this is a radical approach that sometimes gets negative press as not being as accurate, but I think that's just subjective resistance to change."

"Do whatever you have to. The poaching case may tie in with something else I'm working on. It's imperative that we get some leads. Chloe, this is great news."

"Chloe, huh?" Odie echoed.

Reid shot him a stern look, which partially dissolved when he saw the man's broad, clownish mug. "This couldn't come at a better time," he told Chloe.

"Just trying to help. I'll call when the reconstruction is done."

Her voice sounded anxious and excited about the idea of speaking to him again soon, and Reid smiled. "Thanks, Dr. Birch," he said and clicked off. He glared at Odie. "Don't say a word. Not one, *New York Times* puzzle word."

Chapter 18

"Man's law changes with his understanding of man.
Only the laws of the spirit remain always the same."
Crow

Ansel's phone rang beside the art table and she scooped it up. "Phoenix Studios," she said, critically surveying the new pen and ink sketch of a Giganotosaurus she'd use as a template for the Argentine book drawing. "How may I help you?"

"Tell me what you'd get if you crossed a dinosaur with a herd of cows?"

She stiffened. "Daddy, you told me that joke when I was six years old. You get a dinosaur that isn't hungry anymore."

Chase laughed. "You're no fun, Sarcee."

"Why are you calling?" Her simmering ire about Rusty Flynn was bubbling over.

"Just wanted to say that Noah Zollie will phone you. I talked to him this morning."

Ansel didn't care about Zollie. "I didn't need your help. I'm perfectly capable of running my own affairs. Stop doing things behind my back. I don't like it."

A heavy silence prevailed until Chase said, "I'm missing something. What's wrong?"

"Why didn't you tell me that Rusty was back in Lacrosse?"

Another long beat. "Shoot. I was going to. Who told you?"

"It doesn't matter. What matters is that you *didn't*," Ansel declared. "How could you let me wander around town not knowing he'd been back for a year? A year! What if I'd run into him? What if he did something to me? How would you feel? You and Cullen Flynn. Neither of you bothered to tell me. How could you do this, Daddy?"

Chase sighed his distress. "I can see how much you're hurting, Sarcee. Your flashbacks are still strong, and…"

"Don't throw psychology at me," she screamed. "And don't call me for a while. I've got to forgive you first."

She disconnected, then sat clutching the device in a white-knuckled fist. Tears of anger and frustration pooled in her eyes, and she blinked them back. Cut the waterworks, she thought. It had felt good and she was right. Rusty could be very dangerous. Her father had been patently wrong to keep her in the dark. As she glared down at the drawing, the phone rang again.

Reluctantly, Ansel grabbed it. "Phoenix Studios. May I help you?"

"Is this Miss Ansel Phoenix?"

"Yes."

"Hello, this is Noah Zollie from Land Commerce Partners in Billings. Your father asked me to call you. I gather you need some legal advice."

"Hello, Mr. Zollie. Yes, I have some questions regarding land trusts. Do you have time?"

"I have plenty of time for Chase's daughter. What is it you'd like to know?"

Ansel inhaled and stilled her inner turmoil as she explained to Zollie about Chester Dover's problems with his BLM contract, how the land became trust property, and why the Big Toe city council leased the museum grounds. Then she told him about the attempted fossil theft.

"I need to know how solid the BLM contract is, and if the council would have any legal leverage to keep the museum business and the fossil tracks intact. Is it possible to find out?"

"Sure. I'd see if the land records for the parcel are secure and valid up to the point the BLM repossessed it and placed it in trust. I'd also research the current covenants, conditions, and restrictions in the Big Toe contract that would prevent termination of the lease agreement."

"Could you find out that information right away?"

"Certainly. We're experts on governmental land laws including land transfers, trusts, and exchanges with the Federal Bureau of Land Management, the U.S. Forest Service, public agencies, and private clients. I can do the usual land patent, title, and BLM archival document searches for the property right away. It's all available under the Freedom of Information Act. Then I'll review the data and give you my opinion. How does that sound?"

"Wonderful. How much will this cost?"

"For you, nothing, Miss Phoenix. Chase has paid me well over the years, plus the BLM state office is right here in Billings so all the research can be done very inexpensively."

"Thank you. That's very generous of you, Mr. Zollie. How long will this research take?"

"All I need is the museum address, and we can begin collating the public documents today. I should get back to you within a week."

Ansel felt much better. She gave him the information. "I'll wait to hear from you."

His hearty chuckle warmed the line. "Call me Noah."

"Only if you call me Ansel."

"Agreed. Talk to you very soon, Ansel."

She turned off the phone and focused on her work. The new sketch was better, depicting the Giganotosaurus from a side view. The carnosaur chased a herd of Gaspirinisaura across a watery, coastal marshland. In the sky, a flock of small pterosaurs flapped upward, startled by the life and death drama unfolding below them. The drawing was action-packed: a stalking predator, leaping prey, scattering observers, splashing water, and flying dirt.

Next she would redraw the sketch onto a larger sheet equal in size to that of the final artwork dimensions. Then she could transfer the entire image onto smooth illustration board, which was the best surface for achieving precise detail with a plate-finish that looked like eggshell.

She winced as her thoughts drifted toward the Giganotosaurus cover she was supposed to design for Permelia, but the memorabilia she'd seen from Barnum Brown's 1908 fossil expedition brought a smile to her face. Permelia had a nice collection of bones her father had been allowed to keep from the quarries, mostly Ankylosaurus and Triceratops fragments.

There were also vintage photographs of the roving Montana campsites along Big Dry Creek that showed the plow, scraper, and dynamite work required to wrest huge fossils from the sandstone bluffs during the early nineteen-hundreds.

Most interesting to her were the photos of the skull, jaws, and pelvis of an otherwise limbless Tyrannosaurus rex being removed with primitive tree trunk braces and rope winches, then hauled away by continuous trips on a six-horse-team wagon. Barnum had originally discovered this specimen in 1906 and covered it until he could return and excavate much later.

She also viewed old pictures of Barnum wearing a snappy hat and a full-length fur coat, which he was known to wear to quarries on occasion, plus other members of the digging crew, such as Peter Kaisen and C.H. Lambert. All in all, Ansel decided, even spending a few hours with Belle Starr had been well worth the aggravation. It had given her great insight into Permelia's family history and would definitely flavor her creative inspiration for the better.

Still, dark thoughts about Rusty Flynn intruded again. Ansel shook her head. First an emotional breakdown in front of Dorbandt and then yelling at her father. The urge to grab a few beers to erode away the rough emotional edges occurred to her. *Don't go down that road. You have work to do.*

A loud and low thrumming noise coming from outside the hangar drew her attention. There were no windows. She looked up and listened. The sound grew exponentially. It was a mechanical whine resonating with deep cyclic bursts of power.

Ansel rose and headed quickly out of the art room, through the front sculpture room, and opened the personnel door. The noise was deafening, and gusts of sweltering air and dust blew past the open doorway. One step outside and she could see the sleek black helicopter landing on the grass several hundred feet from the east side of the hangar. The FBI chopper.

Her heart beat faster. Not because of Outerbridge's unexpected visit, but because Standback would be piloting. She was dressed in her painting clothes, an old tee-shirt beneath paint-stained jean coveralls. She wore no makeup, and her hair was hastily braided with Indian-style pigtails down to her waist. She looked like an overgrown child from a Rocky Mountain bootlegger's camp who'd been interrupted painting the outhouse.

That didn't stop her from walking toward the copter through a wall of swirling dirt as the chopper made a smooth touchdown and the rotor blades and turbines decelerated. The aft cabin opened first, and Agent Outerbridge, carrying a large steel briefcase, stepped down. Dr. LaPierre followed, carrying a duffel bag. Ansel saw Standback's helmeted head and sunglass-shrouded face through the front windscreen as he continued his post-flight operations. Walthers was missing.

Outerbridge wore his suit again. Dixie had dressed in casual jeans, short-sleeved shirt and black pumps. Outerbridge turned and spoke to Dixie, but Ansel couldn't hear what he said. Then he turned with that fox grin on his face. "Miss Phoenix."

Dixie gave a little wave. "Hi, Ansel."

Ansel crossed her arms. "This is a surprise."

Outerbridge nodded. "It's time for that talk I promised you."

"Quite an entrance. Doesn't the FBI have cell phones? I might not have been home."

"We knew you were here." He raised his briefcase. "Is there somewhere we can talk?"

Ansel glanced at Standback, who exited the flight deck and rounded the helicopter nose. His tall, slender form looked good in stone-washed jeans, navy blue tee, and boots. "Hello," he said as sunlight bounced off his pilot sunglasses.

"Hello, Agent Standback." She gazed at Outerbridge. "Sure. Follow me."

It was a solemn procession. Ansel led them to the rear trailer porch, contemplating that she'd had no time to notify Dorbandt that a meeting with the FBI was pending. A neat tactical maneuver by Outerbridge, she considered. It made her invulnerable to negative outside influence while she considered whether to help them. Or maybe it was pure loose-lips paranoia on his behalf, making sure that few people knew what he was up to.

"Take a seat anywhere," she directed as they entered the living room.

Outerbridge sat in the recliner beside the sofa and laid his briefcase on the coffee table. Dixie grunted as she fell into the sofa, settling into the cushions as if for a long stay. Standback whipped off his glasses, winked at her as he passed, and took a seat on the sofa beside Dixie. Ansel couldn't help grinning back before sitting in the rocker opposite them all.

"So tell me what this is all about, Agent Outerbridge."

Outerbridge leaned over and popped the chromed briefcase latches. "This is about Operation Dragon, Miss Phoenix." He pulled out a manila folder. "Basically my team has been set up as a paleo-task force designed to go undercover and apprehend the people involved in a major fossil poaching ring operating on public lands throughout Montana and Utah. The group we're after is specializing in the rare meat-eating dinosaurs which are in greatest demand by collectors or dealers, sell the fastest, and always go for top dollar. For example, we suspect that this gang recently sold a complete Tyrannosaurus skeleton for five million dollars to a private corporation. Along with other multi-agency operatives, we're infiltrating this network of marketeers, filming or recording their illegal transactions, and collating other evidence that can be used in court. We're going to close them down."

He pulled out some glossies and handed them to her. "This is where the poaching ring started three years ago. Those are the larger complete or partial fossil remain sites which have already been plundered. The most recent is the Hell Creek site you saw the other night."

Ansel looked at the eight graphic photos in her hands one by one. Like the ravaged Tyrannosaurus skeleton she'd viewed, what remained of these excavations was little more than bone kindling, savagely destroyed for sheer pleasure after prime portions had been carted off by bulldozer, loader, and truck.

She noted the legends typed beneath each: *Albertosaurus, Allosaurus, Ceratosaurus,* and *Tyrannosaurus.* The sites included prestigious U.S. properties like Charles M. Russell National Wildlife Refuge, Dinosaur National Park, Badlands National Park, Fossil Butte National Monument, and public lands adjacent to them.

She felt sick to her stomach and handed the photos back. "These are all geographically isolated areas with large, naturally occurring bone beds. What makes you think your poaching group was involved with the Big Toe, Glendive, and Sidney incidents?"

"They aren't above quick smash and grabs," Dixie piped up. "If he showed you reports on all the places they've hit in the field and out, and what they've taken, you'd need all night to read them. Right now the methods used in the Glendive and Sidney robberies are consistent with our poachers."

"But not the museum?" Ansel pressed.

"No," Outerbridge confessed, "but we haven't discounted it."

"So what *do* you know about the museum heist?" Ansel peered hard at the agent.

Outerbridge refiled the photos. "Not much," he confessed. "We've traced the concrete saw via its vendor registration number to a rental store in Billings. They were robbed a week ago, and the only thing missing was the cutter. We traced the truck VIN to a man in Billings, too. Same story. The pickup was stolen from a fenced construction site the night before the museum incident. We lifted prints from both the saw and the truck, but got no results on national or international I.D. systems. Still don't know where the goggles came from. That's it."

Ansel sighed. "And you have absolutely no idea who the Indian man was?"

Standback shook his head. "His limited personal effects didn't tell us anything, and without a facial ID, it's a wash right now."

She eyed Standback carefully. He looked as disgusted as she felt. Out of everyone in the room, she was prone to believe him. "All right, you're on the trail of this poaching gang. What do you need me for?"

Outerbridge took over again. "We've been monitoring Internet fossil groups out of Montana and Utah for months. That includes email posting boards, chat rooms, and online fossil sales of all types. A computer operative using a false identity has made friends with a person connected to a black market dealer who belongs to our poaching ring. It's taken six months of building mutual trust and buying several small illegal fossil items from this person through the mail, but it's paid off. Our operative has put in a request for something bigger to buy. An Allosaurus skull of specific size and characteristics. One that we know was stolen along with other skeletons in Utah a month ago."

He sat back in the recliner. "This agent has received instructions to go to a specific shop located in Billings and meet with somebody who will continue negotiations. Probably a poacher-dealer who assesses the situation before sending someone directly to the seller with the skull. Normally, I'd have Dr. LaPierre go in with our contact agent, but I can't this time. The front man expects to meet an Indian man. We've deliberately set it up this way so the buyer seems as unlikely to be helping the police as possible. Standback is going in as the buyer, and you're his wife."

Ansel nodded. It made sense, but it was scary work. "What am I supposed to do?"

"I'll do all the business talking," Standback said. "You mostly look and listen. You're the fluff to make it look legit and to make sure that what this guy tells me is true. You've got the working knowledge of fossils. We'll be shown photos and documentation for the skull. You've got to clue me before we leave that we're going to get the stolen Utah skull we want along with bogus paperwork. It's evidence that they're selling black-market merchandise."

"Once we crack the first link in the chain, we can follow where it leads," Outerbridge interjected. "Right up to the major players organizing this poaching ring and raking in the money. This is the first step, and with us, the IRS, Customs, and the National Park Service cooperating, these thugs will go down hard for theft, fraud, customs violations, and a host of other crimes."

"That's it? I go in one time, look pretty, and cross-reference what I know about the Utah skull's morphology with the info we're given?"

Outerbridge smiled. "That's it. A couple hours of work."

"Aren't you forgetting something? Like how you're going to record what happens while Agent Standback and I are in there?"

Outerbridge leaned forward, his eyes bright. "Agent Walthers has already checked out the shop by going undercover as your average rockhound. Turns out the building's got surveillance cameras inside and out just to watch who comes and goes. We're going to use their own video system to record everything they do with us, and they won't even know about it. Kinda like letting them hang themselves."

"How is that possible?"

Outerbridge pulled a square white plastic device from his case and passed it to Ansel. "That's an X10 nanny cam. It's a mini-wireless surveillance camera that you can buy for under one hundred bucks. They're popular for watching babysitters, property, and anything else you want to keep an eye on. We set up close to the shop and use a hand-held directional antenna connected to a laptop with a video card and intercept the shop's wireless video signals. Then we watch and record to DVD on our laptops the same thing the shop nanny cams are sending to the their TV security monitors. We already know where their shop cameras are. Inside the shop, both of you will be well within a one-hundred-foot radius of their cameras in any direction. That's all we need."

Ansel was totally intrigued. "Isn't highjacking the signal illegal?"

Standback smiled. "The act of wiretapping sound recordings on tape without permission is a federal crime. Not so with the interception of wireless video signals, as long as it's lawful. We're trying to prevent a crime, so the video images are even admissible as evidence."

"So are you in or out at this point?" Outerbridge asked, taking the nanny cam gently from her.

Ansel could tell that he'd said all he would about Operation Dragon. Now it was time for her to ante up. Well, Dorbandt wanted her to go through with it, didn't he? And she didn't see anything wrong with giving the FBI several brief hours of her time. This could be very interesting.

"I'm in," she said firmly. She looked at Standback for an instant, and he gave her a heart-stopping, supportive smile. Dixie, too, grinned from ear.

"Welcome to our team, Miss Phoenix," Outerbridge exclaimed as he snapped his briefcase shut like a happy man who'd completed a job well done. "We'll go in tomorrow. Dr. LaPierre will be staying with you tonight and briefing you about the Utah skull, the shop layout, and the undercover scenario," he commanded before standing.

Ansel's mouth dropped open, her idea of working on the book drawing all night blown to smithereens. "Is that necessary? Couldn't we do it now?"

Outerbridge fixed her with a firm stare. "No. I want you well acquainted with FBI procedures. This isn't a game. I need a flawless negotiating session with these people. No mistakes. If they smell a rat, they'll disappear into the woodwork and six months of undercover work will go down the tubes."

Standback got up. "See you soon, Ansel."

"This will be great, honey," Dixie added, remaining on the couch. "It'll be just us girls tonight. I'm really looking forward to it."

Before Ansel had assimilated that Standback had called her by her first name, he and Outerbridge had exited the trailer with quiet expediency. She turned and looked at Dixie's pretty face, feeling outfoxed yet again.

Somehow she'd have to notify Dorbandt where she was going before she got spirited away to Billings.

Chapter 19

"Those who lie down with dogs get up with fleas."
Blackfoot

Ansel noticed the odd-looking ring on Dixie's left hand right after the agents left. Its dark gray tones stood out against the paleness of LaPierre's skin, and it was the only finger jewelry the paleontologist wore. A thick, non-metallic band with a flat round top. No stone, just that clear, circular plastic cover piece with pinwheel-like cutouts. It was exactly the same as Standback's, which she'd seen the night he piloted her to the bluff. She'd forgotten to look and see if he'd been wearing it today.

Dixie sat across the dining room table from her, explaining the sting operation. Two folders were open on the tabletop, pulled earlier from her duffel bag. All Ansel could think about was that ring, and she glanced inconspicuously at it whenever she could. Why would two people on Outerbridge's team be wearing those?

Dixie looked straight at her. "Basically you and Parker will be going in as an Indian couple that just won three million in the Powerball lottery."

Ansel's attention diverted from the ring. So Parker was Standback's first name. Now she could finally associate some personal information with the agent's face. She focused totally on what Dixie was saying as the woman pulled out a baggie with plastic cards inside.

"The FBI's got everything set up with the lottery commission for verifying your names as winners should anyone check out your story. You've also got fake IDs and histories in place which include social security numbers, licenses, license plates, multiple bank accounts, and plenty of high balance credit cards. Dump your own stuff and carry these. These guys may check you out by trying to trip you up with questions so memorize your new data, as well as this prepared sheet with both your biographies."

She slid the baggie and typed papers across the table. Ansel picked them up. According to her license, which sported a picture of her head taken right off her commercial Phoenix Studio website, her name was Angela Georges and she lived in Billings.

"What if they decide to go to my fake home at 5498 Midland Road or to phone there?"

"Not a problem. That's an FBI safe house. A female agent dressed as a maid will answer in either case and tell them you and your husband aren't home."

Ansel smiled. "That's pretty slick."

"The idea is that you're upper-income, Native American professionals and your newfound wealth has made you spend-crazy. You've decided to build a new house and you want to decorate it with all sorts of expensive art and sculptures." Dixie grimaced. "You know the type, Yuppies who think fossils make fashionable conversation pieces during cocktail parties."

"Sure," Ansel agreed. "I went once to the home of a private collector who had a complete pterosaur skeleton set in a limestone slab on the wall of his home office instead of a painting. He claimed that the ninety-one-thousand-dollar price was a bargain compared to a traditional objet d'art of the same quality. It was an investment for him, along with thousand-dollar apiece mudstone dragonfly fossils cut into accent tiles for his bathroom and a twenty-one-thousand-dollar, phallic-looking mammoth tusk over his bed."

Dixie shook her head. Long, silver dangle earrings whipped back and forth. "It just makes my blood boil. It's the pretentious jerks with that mindset who make poaching profitable. If they're not buying fossil trophies from any source they can, they're taking fossil souvenirs right off the ground from the national parks. I see it all the time."

"What park do you work in?"

"I work at Dinosaur National Monument. Been there five years."

"That's in Utah. Did this Vernal skull we're buying come from near you?"

Something dark flickered across Dixie's shining face. "Fossils are stolen from all over Utah. As far as my park is concerned, a lot of park visitors just don't know any better, think taking a tiny piece of bone or rock won't hurt anything. The problem is, thousands of people come there every month. What if they all took something? Others are just plain greedy. They're private collectors who know what they're doing and don't care. On top of that, we're always battling to protect the fossils from poachers. It's a never-ending cycle."

Ansel wasn't fooled by Dixie's attempt to steer the conversation away from the precise origins of the Allosaurus skull. She made a mental note to do some research on Dinosaur National Monument and Vernal, Utah.

"Sure sounds like a wonderful job," she said, shifting gears.

Dixie looked up again and smiled. "Yeah, I love it, despite the problems with keeping it safe from thieves, vandals, and tourists."

Dixie blinked and got back on track. "Anyway, Ansel, you'll need to dress the part of a rich, frivolous wife: high-end, casual clothing and accessories, jewelry and makeup. Parker will carry the conversation. You stick near him and look over any potential sale materials. Like Outerbridge said, make sure we're getting the Allosaurus skull from the Vernal heist and let Parker know you're satisfied with the deal. Simple."

"Not a problem. What type of pathologies am I looking for on the skull?"

Dixie picked up another folder with quick, thick fingers. The gray ring caught Ansel's eye again. God, the mystery of the bauble was going to drive her nuts all night long. She really wanted a closer look. She could ask LaPierre about it, but her instincts told her not to. The rings served some important purpose to the team if both an FBI agent and a NPS employee wore them. They weren't telling her something.

"Here's some glossies of the skull shot by park personnel before it was stolen from its dig site. They show the lateral side which was facing up out of the ground. Looks like a male." She slid the color photos across the table.

"The skull is thirty-six inches long, very high, and laterally compressed," Dixie continued. "There are the usual brow horns behind the eyes, plus the snout ridges. The teeth are almost fully intact, normally laterally compressed, and recurved. Two posterior teeth on the lower lateral mandible are missing. Visible pathologies seen upon initial excavation included two scar marks across the cheek and a half-inch-diameter hole in the brain case, directly behind the ear hole."

Ansel looked at the jumble of bones partially imbedded in fine sandstone as represented by the first photo. The large, brown-gold skull was nestled inside its own pelvis and surrounded by a cross-hatch of huge rib bones. This was its natural skeletal disposition. Geological drift over many centuries had moved the Allosaurus skull completely away from its original death position at the top of the neck. Now that skull was gone. Stolen by crooks and being sold on the black market to her tomorrow afternoon.

She looked at the next picture. It was a close-up lateral view of the entire skull with its huge eye socket and long jaw rows of upper and lower teeth. The bone scarring behind and to the side of the triangular orbital opening was easily visible as deeply gouged grooves. The very noticeable puncture behind and toward the top of the ear hole was also apparent.

Ansel gazed at Dixie. "Looks like this guy was in a fight. Tooth puncture in the rear and smaller teeth marks along the face." She gave Dixie the photos. "Wonder if this is what killed him."

"Could be. Infection or brain damage might have made him unable to function even if he survived the initial attack. Anyway, thanks to those wounds and the missing teeth, you should be able to verify the skull as the one we want." She gathered up the folders and then rubbed her shoulders. "I'm starved. Should we order out tonight? I'll foot the bill."

Ansel looked at her watch. It was late. Nearly seven o'clock. "I'm sorry. I should have offered you something. We can either order out or I can throw something together. Whatever you'd like. And I need to show you your bedroom."

"I don't want to put you to any trouble, honey. Let's get take-out. What are our choices?"

"Well, there's either pizza from Ancient Pasta in Big Toe or hamburgers and sandwiches from the Maverick Corral in Mission City. The Maverick food takes a while to get."

"Pizza it is then," Dixie replied. "Got any wine to go with it?"

"Sure. Red and white." Just what she needed, Ansel thought, to be holed up with a social drinker the night before the onset of Operation Dragon. She didn't need the temptation to imbibe when she was really under stress.

"Red's fine. Let's order and break out the bottle. I need to cut loose. Been with those straight-laced government boys for almost two weeks." Dixie got up and left the table. From her duffel bag sitting on the floor, she pulled out a pack of cigarettes. "Mind if I smoke?"

Ansel kept her mouth shut and blinked away the first thing that wanted to come from her mouth. She'd never smoked and didn't care for the habit anywhere in her personal space. The seconds dragged by as Dixie waited.

Keep her happy and off guard, Ansel reasoned. As soon as the woman turned her back and gave her a chance, she was going to check out that duffel bag. And that ring if she could.

She flashed a magnanimous grin. "Make yourself at home."

Ansel rolled over in bed and looked at the blood-red numbers on the digital clock radio. One in the morning. Her long wait was over. Time to move. She threw back the covers and rose, treading barefoot across the bedroom carpet to the closed door. Then she grabbed a small penlight she'd left on the bureau before going to bed. The catch opened without a sound as she turned the knob and stepped into the hall.

Her master bedroom was on the west side of the double-wide and at the end of a hall coming from the living room. Two more bedrooms and a full bath were on her left. Dixie was sleeping in the guest bedroom next to hers. The hallway looked clear. Dixie's door was closed. The bathroom door next to that was open.

According to Ansel's calculations, Dixie should be fast asleep by now. The paleontologist had consumed liberal portions of wine during their pizza meal and later banter in front of the TV. She'd kept refilling Dixie's drinking glass while merely sipping her own throughout the evening. Finally Dixie had wobbled down the hall to take a shower, then retired.

Ansel closed her door and went to the bathroom. As she suspected, Dixie had left her traveling paraphernalia there. Moonlight spearing through the small frosted window revealed a bundle of stripped clothing and shoes on the floor. The open duffel bag was perched precariously on the countertop beside the sink. A hodgepodge of beauty aids and dental hygiene products lay strewn across any other available counter space. Dixie's earrings, a gold necklace, and the grey ring caught her gaze. She'd been hoping that Dixie had removed the jewelry before stepping into the shower.

She closed the bathroom door and picked up the ring. Using the penlight, she examined it more closely. The clear plastic pinwheel capped off a hollow interior and looked as if it could be easily popped out of its recess. A flash of silver in the hollow depths caught Ansel's eye, and she worked the tiny light beam back and forth through the lattice design. In the bottom there was a square green chip stuck to a circular foil backing, just like the one she'd found on the bluff.

She set the ring on the counter and mulled over this revelation. She'd have to check and see if the ERT wore these rings the next time she saw them. The most she could hope for was that Reid got back to her soon with some info about his foil tab. What were these things? Even as she asked the question, a nagging suspicion tickled her psyche. It was connected to college and her classes on geology, but the final connection between its design and purpose still eluded her.

Frustrated, she went for the duffel bag, probing with her right hand deep inside for unusual items. She found some folders and yanked them out. Two header tabs were labeled *Biography* and *Allosaurus*. Dixie had used these to explain the sting operation and the skull pathologies. She flipped through them and found nothing new. The third file read *Medicine Line*.

Ansel recognized the name and it completely surprised her. The Medicine Line was the American Indian name given to the 49th Parallel, or simply the United States-Canadian border above Montana. Montana was fortunate enough to share more than five hundred and forty-five miles of adjoining land touching British Columbia, Alberta, and Saskatchewan.

The Medicine Line cut through rivers, glacial mountains, thick timber, and endless fields of wheat, marked by nothing but an imaginary line or short white pillars stating that the spot was an international boundary. The U.S. Border Patrol was responsible for law enforcement on the stateside and the RCMP monitored the Canadian side. Elk and moose wandered unchecked from one country to the next, so crossing back and forth illegally could be easily accomplished in these remote areas. The Border Patrol was constantly monitoring for such activities.

As she reached to flip open the cover, she heard and felt the trailer's tremble from heavy footsteps coming down the hall. Her head snapped up. Dixie. Adrenalin shot through her body in a single burst of primal panic. She jammed the files into the duffel bag and threw clothes over them just as the footsteps stopped outside the bathroom door. The doorknob grated loudly as it was twisted, and Ansel's fear-laden paralysis evaporated. She had to hide, as impossible as that seemed inside the tiny bathroom.

Ansel bolted toward the tub with shower curtain, bare feet soundlessly stepping onto cold porcelain as she smoothly tugged the opaque, blue plastic curtain with yellow rubber duckies on it closed. She crouched near the water faucet, knees to nose so that her standing form wouldn't be back lighted by the ochre light coming in through the window. The door creaked open.

The sound of Dixie's heavy breathing and quick, cumbersome steps reverberated through the bathroom. Ansel held her breath, praying nothing caused the woman to open the curtain. The noise of clothing being slid away, loud yawns, and sniffles was soon followed by the physical weight of a human body settling upon the toilet. Ansel placed her hands over her mouth in an effort to contain her dismay and total discomfort with this turn of events. Only a couple of feet and a thin polyvinyl sheet separated her from viewing Dixie's ablutions in all their glory.

The rushing sounds of liquid hitting porcelain thundered in Ansel's ears, and it seemed to take an eternity before Dixie emptied her bladder. The acrid odor of urine just added to the overall torturous effect, along with the cramping in her legs from sustaining such an awkward position. Finally Dixie gave the toilet paper roll a spin. The toilet suddenly whooshed and Ansel used the resulting cacophony of noise to shift her feet forward a bit to sit on her rump. Icy cold but better.

Dixie coughed and muttered lowly to herself, messed with things on the countertop for a few moments, then opened the bathroom door and exited. Ansel didn't move an inch. And she didn't intend to until she was sure that Dixie wasn't coming back. She sat there for a long time. Eventually, she rose stiffly from the tub and dared to peek around the shower curtain. The bathroom door was open again and the duffel bag was gone.

Ansel crept to the door and listened. No sounds. Once she stuck her head into the hall, she could see that Dixie's bedroom door was closed. The coast was clear. She sprinted down the hall, opened her bedroom door, and slipped inside. Her back pressed against the door, she closed her eyes and exhaled her relief. Shit, that was close. Too close. Still, if the duffel had been there, she would have risked taking another look at that file.

Dorbandt. She had to call him and tell him about the sting operation in Billings. Dixie had watched her like a hawk all evening, and she couldn't risk using the bedroom phone until she was sure Dixie was asleep. It was late, but she could leave a message.

Ansel went to the night stand and picked up the phone. She turned it on and auto-dialed Reid's number. Dead air. She pulled the phone away and looked at it. Turned it off. And on again. And off. And on. There was no dial tone. She slammed the phone. Her cell phone was in the truck. Of course, there was no guarantee it hadn't been disabled as well by Agent Outerbridge. Only he could have orchestrated this coup to neutralize her ability of communicating with anyone while LaPierre babysat her.

Ansel steamed quietly and flopped down on the bed. Outerbridge and his damn FBI gophers. They were probably staked out in a car somewhere zapping her phone lines with a remote antenna at this very moment: slurping coffee, eating doughnuts, and laughing at her. Then she thought about Standback. Well, maybe he wasn't laughing, she considered. A tiny smile creased her face. Parker Standback. No, he was definitely not laughing. Tomorrow she'd get to be with him.

Before she knew it, she fell asleep sideways across the bed.

Chapter 20

*"Good and evil cannot dwell together in the same
heart, so a good man ought not go into evil company."*
Delaware

Ansel's pulse quickened as Parker maneuvered the black Lexus on
loan from the Billings FBI carpool, into the parking lot of Accent
on Antiquities. Nearby, Outerbridge, Walthers, and La Pierre were
copying the shop's closed-circuit video system signals on a laptop.

"Are you okay, Ansel?"

She looked toward Standback. He assumed her silence was a
sign of anxiety. Far from it. She was mulling over the events of
the night before and this morning. Her check of the ERT members' hands had confirmed that everyone was wearing a gray ring
except Standback. Reasonable since he was going undercover.
His left hand was adorned with a gold wedding band just like
hers. Dixie was also in her thoughts. The paleontologist, thank
God, didn't seem to have a clue about the rifling of her folders
or their up close and personal bathroom encounter.

"I'm fine."

She fussed with four concho buttons on her black moleskin
skirt. Its split front nicely displayed her knee-high, black calf-
leather boots. She'd hot-curled her hair before the helicopter
flight to the Billings airport, and wavy tresses fell beneath her
black gambler hat with concho hatband, contrasting nicely with
the short-sleeve, white turtleneck blouse accenting her curves.

She'd worn her best jewelry: a silver and gold three-horse cuff bracelet, diamond rope-knot earrings, and a thick collar necklace with matching three-horse silhouette cut-outs. Gone was her mother's Iniskim, which she wished she could wear. However, after piling on makeup and appraising herself in the mirror before leaving, she realized that she really looked the part of a spoiled Yuppie with frivolous but expensive home decorating tastes.

Parker eyed her as he drove into a parking spot beside a silver BMW. He wore a brown shirt, black slacks, black boots, and a gaudy Texas Star belt.

"If you've got any questions, ask them now," he said.

Ansel smiled and fingered the oversized wedding ring on her finger. "No. Let's do it."

He chuckled and turned off the engine. "Yes, ma'am."

Parker exited the Lexus, walked to the passenger side, and opened the door. The sudden no-nonsense look on his face was daunting. The game was afoot. Ansel grabbed her small, black saddle purse and clasped his outstretched palm. The sun was scorching bright as she shoved on her Ray-Bans with the other hand.

Accent on Antiquities was very plain. Just another store in a run-down strip mall with concrete block and tempered glass architecture. A misaligned row of pot-bellied clay planters filled with ferns dotted the concrete walkway beneath an overhang, and the broken Spanish roof tiles looked completely out of place. This was a far cry from Hillard Yancy's gallery, and two very noticeable nanny cams on each corner of the store watched as Parker opened the dirty, swinging glass door for her.

The inside was cool, well lit, and rather small. It also smelled of new carpeting and a strong, fruity deodorizer. An eclectic assortment of antiquities such as pre-Columbian ceramic pots, South American sculptures, African carvings, woven Indian rugs and wall hangings, and Indonesian wooden masks was packed everywhere, along with pockets of various fossil flora and fauna curiosities. Everything Ansel saw looked to be of top quality, but of moderate price. Nothing extremely rare or outrageously expensive was in sight.

Only two-thirds of the store was filled with merchandise. Near the back, a long, wall-to-wall tile and wood counter separated the room. A brown-skinned man wearing a plaid shirt stood behind the counter laden down by thick three-ring catalog binders, collectible books, a computer station, electronic register, and lots of accumulated junk. He looked Indian. Two more nanny cams spied on them from rear corners of the room.

"Can I help you?" asked the large man with steely brown eyes and a noticeable gap between his two front teeth. He didn't budge, and he didn't look particularly friendly.

Parker gave a cool glance in return. "I'm Peter Georges. I'm supposed to meet William De Shequette and discuss buying an Allosaurus head."

The Indian's gaze raked from left to right over both of them, especially Ansel. Then, without a word, he quickly clomped through a pass-through gate and ignored them totally as he walked to the front door. With a single twist of a deadbolt, he locked the front entrance and turned over a CLOSED sign.

As he paced toward them, Parker spoke, his voice imperious. "What are you doing?"

"Just being smart," the Indian said gruffly as he walked behind the counter. "Billy's in the office." He stared at Ansel. "Put your purse on the counter, Mrs. Georges."

"What?" Ansel sputtered, making an obvious move to clutch her shoulder strap closer. "I will not. This is outrageous."

"We aren't exactly selling goose eggs here. You both know what you're asking to purchase isn't a usual piece of merchandise." He lifted his eyebrows. "You don't have anything to hide, do you? Just put the purse on the counter so I can check it out or you might as well leave." His square head swivelled toward Parker, eyes like black shotgun pellets. "You, too, *kola*," he said, using the Sioux word for friend. "Empty your pockets."

"Let's just get it over with, Angela," Parker ordered.

Ansel huffed indignantly and dropped the black handbag on the counter. "Be my guest."

The Indian unceremoniously dumped the contents onto the countertop and took several moments examining them. First, he carefully checked out her wallet with all her ID, then slowly surveyed everything: inside makeup containers, a pen, hair clip, small bottle of perfume, and even an open packet of tissues. He did the same with Parker's keys, wallet, and penknife. Probably searching for electronic bugs, Ansel assumed as she watched, and she'd have to Lysol the whole lot when she got home.

Eventually he pushed the mound of items toward them. "Okay. Wait here."

He turned around and went to a closed door behind the counter, knocked three times, and waited. A lock turned, and the man disappeared. Ansel and Parker were left alone to gather up their possessions.

Knowing they were being monitored, Ansel made a show of angrily picking up her belongings and throwing them into her purse. "I hope this skull is worth all this trouble," she groused, giving Parker a soul-spearing look.

Parker stuffed the wallet into a pants pocket. "Believe me, it will be. Stop complaining. He's right. A complete Allosaurus skull just doesn't fall from the sky." He imprinted an eager, excited expression across his handsome features. "This is going to be great."

A few minutes later, the Indian appeared. "Come on back. Billy's ready for you."

They entered a small office outfitted with a nice gray and black executive desk, workstation, and credenza. Two black fabric chairs with curved tube bases and armrests sat before the desk. The closed armoire-style TV center drew Ansel's gaze. She'd bet that the TV monitor and VCR recording equipment for the nanny cams was stashed there. The walls were basic white and filled with auction posters of beautiful antiques and cultural antiquities sold at Christie's or Lloyd's of London. Another nanny cam eyed everything from behind the desk.

"Howdy, folks," said the friendly, gray-haired man standing just inside the door. He grabbed Parker's hand and shook it. "I'm Billy De Shequette. Nice to meet you, Mr. Georges."

Parker grinned. "Hello, Mr. De Shequette. Wasn't sure if we were going to see you. The guy out front wasn't very hospitable."

Billy's smile became wolfishly inviting. "Oh, don't pay Claude any mind. Just a security precaution. We've got a lot of valuable antiquities out front. Can't be too careful." He turned toward Ansel. "And you must be Mrs. Georges." He held out his hand expectantly.

Ansel pulled off her sunglasses and took his large-knuckled hand in hers. Billy looked sixtyish, tall, thin, and well-tanned. Unlike the thug out front, he was quite average in appearance. His Montana duds made him appear down-home trustworthy. She looked straight into his gray eyes beneath bushy silver eyebrows, wondering all the while what possessed such a wholesome, grandfatherly-looking man to become a slime ball.

She quickly shook his hand, then disengaged herself. "Hello, Mr. De Shequette."

That maneuver completed, Billy lost all interest in her, homing in on Parker. "And congratulations to both of you for your recent good fortune. I can't imagine what I'd do if I won the state lottery. How much was it?"

"Three million," Parker said. "Sure surprised the hell out of us, too."

"That's wonderful. Please, sit down." Billy gently coaxed the agent toward the desk with a feather light touch on the shoulder. "You're really going to love the Allosaurus head we discussed by email. Your timing was perfect. It's a wonderful fossil specimen from Utah that just came on the market through a rancher whose land it was excavated from at his own expense." The lie rolled across his tongue like clover honey.

Parker sat in the left chair and Ansel took the right. Billy hustled around his desk and sat in his executive chair before beaming his Cheshire grin again as he pulled open a lower lefthand drawer and removed a manila envelope. "I think we covered the general details about the skull, so I'll show you all the legal documentation."

"We discussed everything but the price," Parker interjected. "What do you want for it?"

Billy chuckled. "Well, I'd prefer you look at the papers before we discuss the bottom line. It gives you a better appreciation about what you're getting for your money, Mr. Georges. After all, it's not the cost, it's the pride of owning an irreplaceable piece of antediluvial history, isn't it? Something to savor every time you look at it and to cherish for a lifetime. It's also going to become a considerable financial asset over the passing years, so what you're paying today will be only interest on the capital of tomorrow."

Ansel wanted to gag. "Where is it? Are we going to see it?"

Billy opened the envelope and pulled out the materials. "It's much too large and fragile to retain in the store, but it's being housed nearby. I have some pictures here so you can see its condition as you'll receive it. If you're interested in purchasing it, I'll make arrangements for you to view it. It's been professionally excavated and prepared by people who are experts in this field. The rock surfaces have been carefully cleaned, strengthened with glues, and shellacked with top-quality materials and products. All of this requires a lot of time, patience, and skill. These factors must be figured into the price." He passed four large color photos to Parker.

He grabbed them and flipped through them quickly. "This is the real deal, right? I don't want a fake or a replica. I'm looking for an old dinosaur head for my new house," Parker demanded. "I want those jerk-off managers in my office to piss in their pants the next time they come to my house for a corporate bash."

Billy laughed. "Actually, this skull is one hundred sixty million years old. And it's damn real. All one hundred fifty pounds of it."

"It looks good to me." Parker passed the photos to Ansel. "What do you think, Angela?"

The color pictures Ansel surveyed showed the excavated skull from four views: both side shots and a top and bottom shot. They were taken in a very dark space with a bright flash. However, the skull appeared to be adequately cleaned and prepped. The two last teeth in the lower lateral jaw were missing, and there was a hole behind the ear hole, along with two teeth gouges on the cheek.

Amazingly, there was no other damage she could attribute to rough handling while being ripped from the ground by poachers, cleaned by amateurs, or hauled around the country for illegal sale. The only characteristic that bothered her was the startling bright yellow color of the skull. The fossil had been a more normal looking golden-brown in Dixie's Vernal dig site photos.

Fossils reflected the colors of the minerals and sediments that had replaced the original bone with new materials during the slow and delicate process of fossilization. Jurassic Morrison Formation fossil deposits were usually brown or gray with intermixtures of black, red, blue, gold, and sometimes peach colors. The yellow tint wasn't a lighting defect or the result of using improper solvents during cleaning. It looked like a geological anomaly, almost as if organic phosphates deposited by ground waters had moved through the rock beds where the Allosaurus remains had been fossilized.

Ansel scowled. "It's broken, Peter. There's a hole on top, marks on the side, and missing teeth."

Billy swivelled his head toward her. "There are no perfect fossils, but these flaws are all indications of its authenticity. This once living creature was brought down in its prime by fierce competition from other predators. You not only have a validation of that fact, you also have an amazing story to go with the skull." He looked at Parker. "Your work associates will marvel at it, Mr. Georges."

"I don't care," Ansel quipped. "It's too big. And that color. Yellow doesn't even go with the powder blue decor of the living room." She grimaced as Parker's sloe eyes widened.

Billy jumped in like a pig in mud. "Well, I don't know about you, Mr. Georges, but I'd change the room colors rather than let this wonderful specimen slip through my fingers. Fossils are precious objects of joy, transcending time and space. No offense, of course, Mrs. Georges, but the Jurassic era didn't come on a color swatch. Actually that delightful buttery hue is somewhat of a geological rarity." His smile was wide enough to gobble up Montana.

"He's right. Who cares?" Parker retorted. "Is that your only objection?" His double meaning was obvious. He wanted a definite sign that he should proceed with the buy.

Ansel sighed and tossed the photos on the desk. "Yes. Get it. Forget I said anything."

Parker leaned forward. "Let me see the rest of your papers."

Ansel kept quiet, just watching the show. The rest of the convincing-the-mark stage was done solely for Peter Georges' benefit and went very quickly. Billy produced a wealth of paperwork verifying the skull as having come from a ranch in Bonanza, Utah. There were legal papers of sale and transfer of ownership between a rancher named Henry Davis and William De Shequette of Accent on Antiquities.

The provenance of the Allosaurus skull was impeccable on the surface. There were permits and licenses. Contracts and sale receipts. Parker's false grin got wider and wider, while Billy's back-hinged, serpentine jawbone reached exponential proportions. Then he got to the discussion of price.

"And you're going to get this beauty for just a hundred fifty thousand. Now that's a deal, considering a whole Allosaurus skeleton can go for as high as two million. So are you sold yet?"

Ansel sensed she should get to work again. She glared at Billy. "A thousand dollars per pound? That's too much."

The toothsome orifice on Billy's face shrank. "On the surface, I suppose it looks that way. However, as I mentioned before, Henry Davis paid to have the skull excavated out-of-pocket. Between the costs for equipment, travel fees, shipment, and paid labor, Mr. Davis has had an overhead of forty thousand dollars. He needs to turn a profit, and I need to make a commission. I assure you that the sale price is fair market value under the circumstances."

Ansel looked at Parker. "Honestly Peter, we could get an original 1900s vintage Remington bronze for that price." Parker shot her a fierce glance. "I don't want a sculpture. I want a dinosaur." His tone was that of a petulant little boy who wasn't going to get the department store toy he wanted. She shook her head. "It's still ridiculous." Parker ignored her and faced Billy. "I want it. What's the next step?"

Billy De Shequette didn't miss a beat. "I'll need a small deposit today. Say twenty-five thousand. It guarantees we'll hold the skull until you see it and make your final decision. Standard practice in the antiquities market. It's refundable. Will you pay by cash, check, or charge?"

"Check." Parker pulled his checkbook out and signed on the spot.

Ansel hunkered in her chair and pretended to sulk while the men concluded their deal. Inside she breathed a sigh of relief. She'd done her part. Now she could fly home and draw.

Billy gave Parker a receipt for the deposit and explained how he'd contact them within the next few days about setting up a meeting for viewing the fossil skull. It was all quite cloak and dagger: a special phone call to their home with specific instructions on how to identify themselves as the buyers to the mysterious rancher, Henry Davis. At least, she wouldn't be there. Finally Parker stood up, clasp envelope in hand, and shook Billy's palm. Ansel rose and stiffly nodded her farewell.

Billy opened the door for them. "Don't you worry about a thing. I'll call as soon as I speak to Mr. Davis. Here's my personal card for both of you should you need to contact me. Have a great day, folks."

Claude led them to the front door, flipped the CLOSED sign over, and stepped aside as they left. They were both firmly ensconced inside the baking Lexus before either of them spoke.

"I'm glad that's over," Ansel said.

Parker started the car, turned on the air, and shifted the vehicle into reverse. "You did great. You really got me with that bit about the yellow head not matching the paint scheme."

"Thank you. I was impressed with your tantrum. 'I want a dinosaur.' That was classic."

"Well, I'm glad I'm not married to you. Angela Georges would drive me to violence."

Ansel pulled off her wedding band and dropped it into a cup holder on the dash. "In that case, I'm divorcing you here and now."

Parker grinned. "I guess marriage ain't what it used to be."

Ansel took a chance. "Nope. So are you?"

"Am I what?"

"Married."

"No. The Bureau keeps me busy. I'm not in one place very long."

"Where's your home town?" She was on a roll.

Parker's smile evaporated. "Don't have a home town. Just the Crow Agency. I'm from the rez. You're half Blackfoot, right?"

Ansel could see that the reservation was a touchy subject, and she wondered why. "Yeah. I suppose Outerbridge discussed my file in detail with everyone. Nice."

Suddenly the two-way portable radio stashed on the floor beneath Parker's seat crackled to life. "Unit One to Unit Two. Over."

Parker listened, then said, "Speak of the devil." He pulled out the black Motorola VHF radio and pressed the call button with one hand as he drove. "Unit One. 10-24. Over."

Outerbridge's voice filled the car. "What's your 10-20? Over."

Parker turned a corner and peered at the street signs. "10-8. Corner of South Twenty-fourth Street and King. Over."

"Unit One, 10-25. Zero, zero, Midland. Over."

Parker glanced at Ansel. "Unit One. 10-4."

She noticed his odd expression and watched as he placed the radio on the console between them. "What was that all about?"

"We're going to meet him at the Rimrock Motel on Midland."

"Why? I thought we'd head back to the airport."

Parker avoided her gaze. "I guess not."

Ansel smelled a rat. A big, fat, half-decomposed one. "Listen, I want to know what's going on. I signed on for a couple hours, remember? I fulfilled my part of the bargain."

"Hey, we'll both have to see what the boss says. Besides, would being with me a little longer be such a bad thing?"

He turned and flashed her a beatific smile full of secret meaning, and his eyes were absolutely sparkling with mischievous intent. Ansel waded into those sexy, glistening brown pools with her bikini on. God, he looked knee-weakening adorable. When guilty thoughts about Dorbandt splashed cold water in her face, she simply dove away from them.

She was attracted to Reid, but he was hopeless. Chasing him would be an emotionally exhausting and unappreciated endeavor akin to stalking a person trying to dodge your every move. Life was too short. She wasn't a spring calf anymore.

Her expression softened. "No, I guess I could live with that."

"Good," Parker replied, staring ahead at the road. "Oh, give me Billy's card."

Damn, she'd hoped he would forget it. "Card?"

"Nice try. His business card. In your purse. Hand it over."

She opened the handbag, fished around inside, and pulled it out. She'd never even had a chance to memorize it. Parker snapped it from her hand before she could get a glance.

"Thanks, Ansel." He quickly shoved it into a shirt pocket.

"That wasn't very sporting, Agent Standback."

"Please, call me Parker. We've already been married and divorced. Just doing my job."

Where had she heard that before? She settled back in her seat and speculated over what new tortures would spring from the hands of Agent Outerbridge.

Chapter 21

"Not westward,
but eastward seek the coming of the light."
Dakota

Reid slammed down his desk phone. "Damn it, Ansel. Where are you?"

Both Odie and another detective stared. Then Odie displayed an amused grin. He was still needling him about Chloe in his own companionable way. Danny Landstrom was another story.

"Female troubles, Reid?" the younger, blond-haired Landstrom jibed before nickering like a wheezing horse.

A tendril of acid curled up Reid's throat. Everybody in the department was aware of his ill-advised friendship with Ansel Phoenix, the woman whom his immediate supervisor, Captain Ed McKenzie, hated with a passion. McKenzie was a racist and always bad-mouthed the whole Phoenix clan because of the Indian associations. Not to mention that Chase Phoenix had butted heads with McKenzie years before over a murder investigation. Chase had almost gotten McKenzie, then a rookie cop, thrown off the police force. Landstrom was McKenzie's toady.

"Shut up, Danno," Reid snapped. "Women aren't your strong suit. The only thing you've ever kissed is McKenzie's ass."

"Ahhh, good one," Odie guffawed, swiveling his massive, buzzed skull to stare at Landstrom with anticipation.

Landstrom's face turned bright pink. "Bite me, Dorbandt. You're lucky the Captain's gone." He turned away and pretended to be immersed in writing a case deposition report.

Odie shook his head. "A disappointing retort from Landstrom. Zero points for originality and only one point for contextual impression. Reid, I salute you. You are still the Royal Rejoinder."

A tiny smile edged across Reid's face even as he perused his monumental stacks of paperwork. A hundred loose veins on several current cases needed to be tied off before they bled out, and he didn't have the time to do it. The Cullen Flynn case had taken precedence, and nobody had the tools to cauterize that spurting artery. How could you fix what you couldn't find?

There was no sign of Cullen or his vehicle. The sheriff's department, the Highway Patrol, and the Big Toe police department had turned up zip, zilch, nada respectively. Odie and he had questioned everybody they could rustle up in Swoln, asking if they saw a green Jeep go through town. Nothing. It was as if Cullen had driven into the sunset and evaporated like Clint Eastwood in *High Plains Drifter*. Was Cullen dead? His heart said no way. His head said yes.

Reid shifted paper mounds across his desk and picked up Cyrus Flynn's jacket. Flipping through it over and over hadn't led to any investigative inspirations. Cyrus' illegal substance abuse had included marijuana and methamphetamine. His drug sales had been loosely tied to a larger drug operation out of Billings which had possibly been protected by an even bigger Helena influence. Nothing was ever proven one way or the other.

Cyrus was a small-time junkie-dealer who couldn't ply his trade without getting caught. When he bombed at that, he sustained his existence by stealing private property and selling it on the sly. The slaughterhouse job was a career boondoggle for Cyrus. It was the first legitimate employment he'd ever held and he'd managed to keep it for almost a year.

Still something stank, and it wasn't just the packing house, Reid considered. Cyrus had a gun and he knew it. He'd checked federal gun registrations and nothing came back under his name, but cons had their own set of procurement rules. The shotgun wadding had gone to the state crime lab in Missoula. He expected it might not tell him much.

Odie interrupted his thoughts, appearing in front of his desk like an up-thrust mountain range, folder in hand. "Reid, I got the info you wanted on Swoln Stockyards."

Reid closed Cyrus' file. "Tell me what you've got."

"The stockyards are owned by a corporation called Allied Beef Exchange out of Helena. The packing house used to be privately owned, but sold out in 1987 because beef consumption in the U.S. dropped fourteen percent, and they were going bankrupt."

Helena. A red flag slid up a synaptic pole in his brain. "Hokay, go on."

"Cows going in as USDA choice sell for seven hundred a head, about sixty-one cents a pound. The place processes up to seventeen hundred cows a day with ninety-two employees working one of two eight-hour shifts. The current operations director is Frank Carigliano. I spoke with him directly. He confirmed that Flynn works there as the shackler Mondays through Fridays on the eleven-to-eight a.m. shift. Said Flynn was doing great. Never late for the job. Gets along well with everyone." Odie passed him the file. "Flynn must work in a bubble suit because he's the cleanest shackler in the history of the beef industry."

Reid grabbed the faxed papers. There was a completed application for employment, DOC prison release authorization, parolee employment agreement, and an employee performance review signed by a Swoln Stockyards foreman named Jessup Frost. They were all in order. It didn't mean anything.

"Carigliano's covering for Flynn. The question is why? Run a computer check on him, Frost, and Allied Beef Exchange through NDIC and Interpol. See if there's any drug connection."

"Drugs? Where'd that come from?"

"Flynn's file. He dealt with pot and meth, and there was mention of some heavy hitters supporting a drug channel out of Helena that went through Billings, where he got his street supply. Maybe he's found the perfect niche for himself. Like old times. He uses and cruises in a circle of fellow junkies that are part of a bigger picture."

Odie's face was grim. "You think Chief Flynn stumbled into that?"

Reid ran his hand across his face. The prickly stubble of five-o'clock shadow surprised him. Another day had flown by, and he didn't feel like he'd accomplished anything. Cullen had been missing for four days. His trail was stone cold. Maybe this was the break they'd been waiting for, but a black hole formed in the pit of his empty stomach. He liked Cullen. Though he didn't socialize with the man, he'd worked with him on various cases during the last few years. Straight board-feet law officers like Chief Flynn were hard to find.

"I don't know, but he sure is git-gone. That's SOP with drug cartels that need to eliminate a problem." He passed the file back. "Eventually we've got to visit Carigliano, but I don't want to tip him off that we're spotting the plant operations as well as Cyrus."

"Got it, Reid." Odie paced away.

Reid grabbed up the report on Hillard Yancy. No criminal record, court appearances, or bad press. Yancy was from a rich family in New York, so the question of his funding for the shop was a no-brainer. Despite the gold apron strings, Yancy had gone to college at Utah State for a degree in geology, then worked as a paleogeologist for Wonsits Valley Oil and Gas. He'd retired after twenty years and was now the proprietor of Earthly Pleasures.

He'd even looked at Yancy's glossy sales pamphlet, which contained color fossil photos, long lists of indecipherable Latin names, and sequential catalog numbers. Before he could exhale his frustration, a shapely, uniformed file clerk dropped another sheaf of papers on his desk.

Dorbandt threw up his hands. "No more, Jasmine, please."

The harried, auburn-haired woman barely gave him a glance. "And the beat goes on," she sang in a Cher-like voice. "La-dee-da-dee-dee. La-dee-da-dee-da." She sped out the division doorway. So much for fraternal bonding.

Reid dropped Yancy's file and picked up the six-page lab report. He was surprised to see that it was the brief analysis from Trace Evidence concerning the foil tab Ansel had given him. That was fast, which meant that the object had been easily identified by one of the Missoula techies. He skipped the parts regarding the material evidence designation number, background recovery information, and the item's physical description.

Findings

The evidence from the crime scene (Case 04-08-29-H-0011) in Big Toe, Montana, is consistent with TLD chip (thermaluminescent dosimetry) badges, bracelets, and rings used to measure exposure to radiation due to x-ray, beta, and gamma rays.

The radiation passes through a thin layer of aluminum oxide and different filters. A circular TLD chip mounted on Kapton foil is further attached to a small aluminum disc containing a miniature, circular bar code with a six-digit number which is personalized for identification of each person. The TLD chip assembly is inserted into a disposable, plastic finger ring and protected by a clear Teflon cover plate. This design is convenient to wear, comes in small, medium, and large finger sizes, and can be cold sterilized for multiple use in surgery.

For readout, the ring is opened by a semi-automated device and up to four bar-code discs can be inserted into a modified standard TLD card for automatic processing by Harshaw readers model 6600 or 8800. The reader contains a video bar code identification system based on a miniaturized CCD camera and image processing by special PC software. The circular bar codes are mathematically linearized and decoded directly from the enhanced grey scale picture obtained with optimized illumination by power LEDs.

> Rings are usually issued on a 3-month, calendar-quarter basis and serve to distinguish between different types and levels of radiation exposure. They are worn at all times when exposure from ionizing radiations are likely and exposure to the extremities is a possibility Typically, these are issued to persons working with significant amounts of P-32 or other hard beta-gamma emitters.
>
> TLD detecting elements are reusable and expensive. They are not waterproof and must be protected by plastic or latex gloves if immersed. Personal dosimeters are issued for use by the named person they are intended for. They are not to be used by any other person. If damaged, they must be returned for replacement. If lost, the person they belong to is usually charged for replacement costs.

"Wow." Reid sat back in his chair. He had to think. If this TLD chip had belonged to one of the FBI agents as Ansel suspected, it meant that the feds weren't just chasing fossil poachers but something radioactive as well. And if the device hadn't belonged to the Feebees, who did it belong to? He wondered if there was a way to read the bar coded chip and find the person the dosimeter had been issued to. But did it matter where the original ring came from?

For all he knew, the chip could have come from some x-ray technician who visited the museum to take a gander at the dinosaur tracks. Just because Ansel said the agents were proficient at forensic recovery didn't mean squat. The wind was thorough, too. Given the heat boomers and dust blows going on the last week, a prairie gust could have blown that foil tab in from the next county.

"Ansel, where are you?" he whispered. He needed her. He'd left her phone messages all morning and afternoon. She'd better not have done something stupid like traipsing off with Outerbridge and not telling him about it.

Reid slipped the TLD report into the Indian poacher's file. Just looking at that gave him another harsh reality check. That case wasn't exactly being cross-whipped either.

Odie and he had gone to the bank and checked out his money machine theory. Yeah, the machine had a camera, and it did eyeball the door to Humpy's Grill across the street if the traffic was sparse, but the video was broken. Had been for a month. No one had bothered to have it repaired. The idea of too much government control was anathema to people in the heartlands, and one less Big Brother camera watching people's private financial transactions and conversations was not a priority at the Swoln Credit Union. God bless America.

Reid looked toward the exit door and wondered if he could escape just as Jasmine had. Then he saw Agent Adam Broderick pass by the opening. He'd never met the man, but he'd made sure to pull up everything he could about the guy. He'd been waiting for this moment since Ansel told him about her unpleasant encounter. He'd also pulled up Broderick's license photo from DMV records, and there was no mistaking that distinctive mug or taupe BLM uniform. Reid leaped from his chair in an instant and jetted past Odie's desk into the hallway.

Broderick had stopped to use the water fountain and was bending over in a most vulnerable position as Reid reached him. The urge to kick the agent's permanent-pressed butt was a powerful temptation. Instead he crossed his arms and waited until Broderick turned around.

The agent rose and started visibly upon seeing Reid face to face. "Sorry. Didn't know you were there." He shifted his weight and moved around Reid. When Reid moved directly in front of him, Broderick stopped. His face tightened. Reid held his ground and smiled. They were pretty evenly matched in terms of height, but Broderick outweighed him by about thirty government pounds.

"Is there a problem," Broderick said.

"I have a message for you."

Broderick eyed Reid's I.D. card clipped to a shirt pocket. "Do I know you?"

"Leave Ansel Phoenix alone." His stare bored into Broderick's widening eyes.

The hall was fairly busy with other cops, clerks, civilians, and office personnel. A few stopped in mid-stride to view this unexpected entertainment. Surprise wiped the smug expression off the agent's face, but he knew he was being watched, and snorted through his nose.

"I don't know who you are or what you're talking about. Who's your supervisor?"

Reid pointed a finger scant inches from Broderick's pointy nose. "Leave her alone." He turned and walked through the growing knot of onlookers and back into his department. Broderick could have followed but didn't. He didn't care. Nobody was going to steamroll Ansel as long as he was around.

Odie, oblivious to the confrontation outside, sat at his desk nodding into a phone receiver. When he spied Reid, he motioned wildly. Reid stepped toward him, still feeling his blood pounding like a hammer against his left temple.

"He's just walked in, sir. I'll put him on the phone." Odie covered the earpiece and mouthpiece with one Herculean hand. "Bucky."

There was no way Broderick could have gotten to Sheriff Combs this fast. Reid took the device. "Lieutenant Dorbandt."

"Lieutenant. Dr. Birch called. The reconstruction is done. She's faxing me head photos as we speak. Go to Billings and gather up her final report, our papers, and the skull. I just got an official request sent to the coroner's office from the state FBI in Glasgow. I have to transport the remains there immediately. I need that head to go with the body even if it is cleaned to the bone. Those bastards can't grouse if the deed is already done."

Reid looked at his watch. Five-thirty. He could be in Billings by ten if he hustled. He could see Chloe. "Will I spend the night?"

"I don't see why not. Get back here by five tomorrow. Clock your travel time and don't worry about completing a request for expenditures. Just get receipts. You've been putting in a lot of overtime, and I promise you'll get some time off when these pressing cases are closed."

"I'm leaving now. Thank you, sir."

Sheriff Combs hung up and Reid handed the phone to Odie, who'd been listening to every word. "The reconstruction is done. I'm leaving for Billings to get everything. Be back late tomorrow. Find out all you can about the slaughterhouse."

"The info will be on your desk," Odie assured him, grinning.

"What the hell are you smiling at?"

"Nothing."

"I know what you're thinking."

Odie beamed. "I know what you're thinking, too. Have a good trip, Reid."

"Oh, I will." Reid grabbed the essentials he'd need to make the drive: shoulder belt holster, cell phone, beeper, and suit jacket. He already had a pre-packed bag in his car trunk for traveling emergencies. In seconds he was ready to depart, energized by his excitement about seeing Chloe. The evening promised to be very special.

First he had to get out of the station before Agent Broderick got to Sheriff Combs.

Chapter 22

"Our first teacher is our own heart."
Cheyenne

Ansel sat beside Parker on one of the double beds Room 110 of the Rimrock Motel, swinging a crossed leg back and forth like a metronome. Outerbridge had just informed her and the ERT members, minus Agent Walthers, that they were not leaving Billings for another eighteen hours. The small consolation that her split skirt showed a tantalizing amount of leg between boot top and thigh, which Parker seemed to be enjoying, was Ansel's single high point in this entire Machiavellian drama.

Outerbridge, wearing thin, silver-framed reading glasses, sat at the tiny round table just inside the door. The sale papers from the clasp envelope were splayed across it. Dixie sat across from him, puffing on a cigarette with carefree abandon. Smoke rose to the ceiling of the pocket-sized, industrial-grade room like steam. She seemed oblivious to the fact that this was a non-smoking room.

"There's been a lot of activity since you two left the store," Outerbridge intoned. "Plenty of people coming and going. We're getting some solid information about co-conspirators in this group. Walthers is taping everything. I don't want to pull up stakes until we've gleaned every piece of evidence we can. Then agents from the local office will continue monitoring things. Sorry for the inconvenience, Ansel. We'll get you home soon."

He sipped from a Coke can and continued. "Walthers is on surveillance through tomorrow morning. After that, we're flying out of here. We won't be back until De Shequette sets up the skull viewing appointment. Parker, you'll be the only person going in on that. Questions?"

Ansel waved her hand. "I have to make some phone calls tonight. There will be people worrying about me if I don't make contact. No one knows I left Big Toe."

"That's usually not possible in cases like this, but I'll compromise. I can let you contact one person. Decide who needs to know your whereabouts the most."

Ansel didn't like it. She'd never reach Dorbandt at this rate. "I'd like to call my parents."

"Fine. After we finish this meeting, you can do that." His quick brown eyes surveyed the rest of the group. "Anything else?"

"What's next after we leave here?" Parker said.

"I'm not sure. We'll have to wait and see how long before the suspects set up the skull sale and how it goes down. Then we'll have plenty of new information to process. There is, however, a chance we'll go back to Utah right after the Vernal buy."

Ansel wasn't sure she understood Outerbridge correctly. "That's after you bust De Shequette and his gang, right?"

"Not exactly."

Ansel looked around the room. Nobody seemed to be as confused as she was or acted the least bit annoyed. "You will prosecute them, correct?"

Outerbridge nodded. "Eventually, yes. We'll take possession of the skull in any case. We'll pay for it, and De Shequette can deliver it to Parker a.k.a. Peter Georges. It's essential evidence for conviction, so we must regain possession of the Allosaurus skull at all costs. It's also important that we follow the poaching links to the top of the food chain. That's the only way we'll break it."

Ansel checked her anger. "Are you saying that you have no immediate interest in prosecuting bottom feeders like Billy and Claude?"

Outerbridge pulled off his glasses. His expression was bland. "Prosecuting a bottom feeder takes just as much effort as prosecuting a shark, Ansel. The same amount of time, money, and back-breaking footwork with the same lack of evidence, resources, and judicial or legislative support. I'd much rather filet a twenty-foot Great White than a three-foot channel cat. It's a matter of profit per pound."

Ansel sat there stunned. She hadn't offered to help so creeps like Billy and Claude could plea-bargain their way out of trouble by offering to rat out their higher associates in crime, but what could she do? It was the legal system, not Outerbridge, who set the conviction bar so high.

Outerbridge took advantage of her silence. He pulled out three room keys from his suit pocket and tossed one to each of them. "We'll stay here for the night. I'm in this room. I've got phone calls to make the rest of this evening and I don't want to keep anybody up. The rest of you are upstairs. Dixie, you and Ansel will bunk together again. Parker, you have Walthers' room to yourself. He won't need it tonight. The three of you have the evening off. Enjoy it. Just stay on your toes and keep a low profile. We'll regroup at eight tomorrow in my room. That's all."

Dixie got up quickly and headed for the door. Obviously she wanted first dibs on the dubious amenities the Rimrock could provide. Ansel felt too tired to move that fast.

"How about some dinner?"

Ansel looked up. Parker's smile was as inviting as his offer. "All right. I have to use the phone first."

"I'll wait outside." He gave her the second wink in two days and hurried out the doorway into the first-floor hallway.

Outerbridge got up and closed the door behind Parker before turning to look at her. His accompanying sigh was long and audible. "You think I'm a real sell-out, don't you?"

"No. I think I made a mistake coming here."

He chuckled and his face crinkled at the corners of his eyes, nose, and mouth. "Me, too." He walked toward a small black suitcase sitting on a collapsible stand, unzipped it, and pulled out a pint of Jack Daniels. "I'm off duty. Want any?"

"No, thanks. I'm going to make that call." She reached for the phone positioned on a night stand between the two beds.

"Not that one. Use my cell." He pulled the blood-red device from his suit pocket and walked over to pass it to her. "Keep it to a couple of minutes."

As she dialed, Ansel watched Outerbridge remove the shrink-wrap from a plastic cup on the bureau, pour Coke from the can into it, then add two fingers of booze. She only had seconds to think about what she was going to say to Pearl or her father, but her worries were fruitless. The answering machine kicked in. Outerbridge sat down in the chair again. When the machine began recording, she left a brief message explaining how she'd left Big Toe the night before to do some research for one of her drawings and would be back by the next afternoon.

Outerbridge reviewed the dinosaur papers again, but Ansel knew it was a ruse. He was listening to her every word. She hung up, feeling frustrated by her lack of control over the situation but glad that her parents wouldn't worry.

She stood and approached the table. "Thanks."

He set down his drink and accepted the phone with a brief, sad smile. "You did a terrific job today. It does count. No matter what you think."

Ansel didn't agree and might never. He was rigid, opinionated, and fiercely loyal to a bureaucratic system that couldn't support the weight of its own dogma, a federal cop through and through. To most Montanans she knew, Outerbridge was a trickster, bamboozler, and destroyer of the American Dream and everything westerners held dear.

Well, he'd loaned an Indian woman he hardly knew his private property without a second thought, and she figured that's all she needed to know about the Special Agent Outerbridge inside that government suit. She had to respect him for that.

Ansel gave him a brief, heartfelt smile. "Goodnight, Agent Outerbridge. See you in the morning."

◇◇◇

Parker was waiting as he promised, leaning against the hotel wall outside the door, legs and arms crossed. "We'll have to order in, but I know some really good take-out places here." He gazed into her eyes. "Your place or mine?"

Ansel grinned. "Hmm. Let's see. I'm sharing a room with Dixie, and you've got one all to yourself. Which should it be?"

"May I make a suggestion?"

"Certainly."

Parker pointed a finger due east. "That way. I'll lead."

And he did. They walked down the hall to a foyer where an elevator took them up to the second floor. They said very little on the way up, mostly because Ansel was too nervous to make even idle conversation. They exited and Parker stopped at Room 215 to unlock the door, where he motioned inward.

"Welcome to Chez Parker."

Ansel stepped inside. The room was a clone of Outerbridge's, right down to the laminated fiberboard table. Parker came up behind her, slid past her, and flicked on the orange, ginger-base lamp on the night stand between the beds. It was much cooler in this room. Goosebumps hitched up along her arms. Then he closed the door.

She wasn't sure if it was the temperature drop or her sense of arousal that gave her the shivers. She knew what this could lead to. How far did she want to go with this man? She knew nothing about him, except that he was Crow, an FBI pilot, good looking, and intelligent. And she'd been celibate for over a year. The last man she'd slept with had been murdered.

Parker returned to her side. "You're cold." He ran his hands briskly over her bare arms, then moved away. "I'll boost the temperature."

Ansel felt as if his warm hands had been coated with fire during that brief moment of touching. She swallowed back a gasp of sheer pleasure and stood almost paralyzed as he fiddled with the thermostat controls beneath a metal flap on the central unit beneath the picture window. Was he going to try to kiss her or not? she wondered as he dragged the flowered curtain closed along the rod and then came toward her. She didn't move. She couldn't even speak.

"I've wanted to do this for a while," Parker said, his voice husky.

He leaned toward her and kissed her. Just like that. Smooth and easy. No pressure. No abrupt motions of indecision or hesitation. His lips were soft and feather light on hers, and she responded instinctually by kissing him back more powerfully—an open invitation to continue in any way he saw fit.

Still, Parker never used his hands to caress her or his arms to envelope her. Only his lips. Ansel restrained herself, too. No other limbs. No other body parts touching. Only their lips joined as one in a long, soft, sensuous expression of mutual exploration. Suddenly Parker drew away. Disappointed beyond reason, Ansel opened her eyes and peered at him questioningly.

He smiled impishly. "First, we eat and talk. Japanese, Chinese, or Greek?"

Relieved that he had rejected her only for gentlemanly reasons, she replied haughtily, "Steak. The Black Angus restaurant down the road is great. My father raises those, you know."

"No, I didn't. *That*," Parker said facetiously, "wasn't in your file. How did the Bureau ever miss it? Steak it is. I'll call and order a couple of thick, carbohydrate and cholesterol-filled beef slabs for both of us." He headed for the phone. "I'm ravenous."

Ansel walked forward slowly and exhaled. "Parker?"

"Yeah."

"What about the others?" She stood by the bed nearest him.

"Others?" The phone receiver was in his hand.

"The crew. You know." She shifted her eyes to the left meaningfully.

"Oh. You mean…"

"Yeah. Should we be doing this? I don't want Outerbridge to freak out."

Parker shrugged. "I'm off duty, Ansel. I have a life. Pathetic though it is, I am allowed to have one. Don't worry." He patted the bed. "Relax."

And she did. Parker made the call and placed the order while she pulled off her knee boots and turned on the TV to find a news station. She wanted to see if there had been any information about Chief Flynn, but the fifteen-second sound byte she saw about the investigation revealed only that there was no news. She could see what was happening as plain as day. Flynn was no longer a big story. Without sufficient gore spin, Cullen's fifteen minutes of notoriety were winding to a close.

When Parker left for a bucket of ice and some sodas from a vending machine, Ansel toyed with the idea of using the phone to leave Reid a message, but it would be long distance and appear on Outerbridge's hotel tab. Not possible. Besides, Parker could appear momentarily. A flash of irrational guilt scorched through her. No matter how attracted she felt toward Parker, Reid's face seemed to superimpose itself over the pilot's when she least expected it.

Dammit. I don't owe Reid anything. *Except your life*, a tiny voice tittered in her ear. So? I'm indebted to him for my mortal life, not my love life. *Splitting hairs, aren't we?* He doesn't like me enough to even kiss me. *Maybe you should have kissed him.*

Further self-recriminations were impossible when Parker returned. "You look like somebody kicked your dog," he said, staring at her oddly. "Everything all right?"

"It's been a long day. I'll be better after I eat."

"Why don't you take a shower. I'll watch TV and wait for the chow." He went to a pouch on the floor and pulled out a black tee-shirt. "This ought to cover the most critical spots." He tossed it to her, his expression totally serious.

The thought of a long, hot shower almost made Ansel purr with delight. She grabbed the shirt off the end of the bed and looked at it. How would Outerbridge feel about her strutting around half-naked in this? *Oh, the hell with him, too.*

"Maybe I will get cleaned up. Thanks."

Once in the bathroom, an oversized closet-space with a wall counter, toilet, and combination tub and glass shower stall, Ansel flicked the light switch and closed the door. Her reflection in the wall-spanning mirror under the harsh white lights was not a flattering one. She ignored it and stripped off her clothes, pantyhose, and jewelry.

She had no energy for a tub bath, and a twist of a single knob to the right setting sent a splatter of deliciously warm water cascading out of the shower head. A pre-pack of herbal shampoo provided by the hotel would have to do for her hair.

Ansel stepped into the tub, slid a frosted door across the upper portion of the stall, and simply stood in the wash of hot, cleansing liquid. She'd just turned to wet her hair when the bathroom door opened. She stopped abruptly and tried to stare through the steamy tempered glass.

Instinctively, she knew it was Parker even before his shadowy outline filled her vision. When his left hand reached out and slowly slid the glass partition away, she merely stared. He wore nothing, and steam curled around his brown physique as misty caresses. She positively couldn't take her eyes off of him. He was beautiful. Every inch of him.

His own masculine gaze was filled with heat. "Mind if I join you?"

She wanted to say something witty, calm, and collected as he stood there feasting his eyes on her wet, naked form, but her brain wasn't connected to her body anymore and her knees felt like rubber. This was crazy. Insane. But the thought of tomorrow didn't exist for her. The ache inside her lonely heart and the throb in her groin taunted her mercilessly. She needed him more than anything else in the world right now.

"Parker," she whispered.

He stepped into the hot spray of water in one sinewy motion, arms encircling her with raw maleness as the fullness of his form pressed against her. She was engulfed in a wash of pure carnality as Parker kissed her again, this time with such passion and hunger that she was pushed against the back wall of the shower.

She responded to his touch, taste, and smell in kind with a blatant urgency unknown to her in many months. Parker's strong, powerful hands roved across her body and she surrendered, melting sensually into him with every part of her: skin, muscle, and vein. Warm, gushing rivulets blessed their union and drowned out their cries.

And, God help her, she wished he was Reid.

Chapter 23

*"The eyes of men speak words
the tongue cannot pronounce."*
Crow

She had to get out of here.

Ansel rolled on her right side and stared at Parker. He was lying on his back, the wrinkled white hotel sheet covering his body from the waist down. His eyes were closed, his breathing soft and even. After their love making in the shower, the Black Angus take-out had arrived. They'd gorged themselves on Delmonico steaks, baked potatoes, corn on the cob, and spinach salad. Then they'd made love again in this very bed, more slowly and more intimately.

Both satisfied, they'd talked for a while but piloting the early morning chopper flight to Billings and the undercover work at the store had taken their toll on Parker. He'd apologized for his flagging attention span. He needed sleep and so did she, but she hadn't been able to rest. Suddenly Parker's dark eyes opened and darted in her direction.

"I didn't mean to wake you. Go back to sleep," she whispered.

"I got a couple hours of rest. I feel better. Why aren't you sleeping?"

Ansel shrugged. "Too much to think about."

Parker smiled. "Me, I hope."

She languidly stroked his hairless chest. "Yes, but not what you think."

"I'm disappointed." He turned on his side and took her chin in his right hand. "What's bothering you?"

"I think I'm out of my league with an FBI pilot. I don't even know you."

"You want to know about me? I'll tell you." He sat up and swung his legs out of bed before Ansel knew what was happening.

"Wait, where are you going, Parker?"

"I want to show you something."

The room was dark with the heavy curtains pulled across the window, but Ansel could still see his naked form as he traversed the room to a bureau set against an opposite wall. He grabbed something and came back, sliding in beside her under the sheet, then turning on the lamp next to him. The glare stunned Ansel's eyes.

"Ouch. Do we have to do this now?" She sat up in bed, pulling the sheet over her breasts.

Parker's face was tense and determined. "It's the perfect time. I don't know how much we'll be able to speak with each other tomorrow."

"You mean today, don't you?" He'd brought over a brown leather trifold wallet, not the fake one he'd used at Accent on Antiquities.

"Yeah, today." He opened it and flipped to some plastic photo sleeves. Pointing to a picture, he passed the billfold to her. "I was seventeen years old and an only child living on the reservation with my grandmother who raised me. My parents died when I was twelve."

Ansel looked at the picture and hardly recognized the thin, angular-faced teen as Parker Standback. His thick, ebony hair fell below his shoulders and across a faded jean jacket with a dirty red tee beneath it. His boy-man face was sullen and unsmiling under long, black eyebrows. He looked angry and suspicious with clenched jaws and a sideways stare, like the weight of the world had been dropped squarely on his shoulders. Most disturbing were Parker's large, brown eyes. They were dilated and flat. Dead eyes providing a window into a conscienceless spirit, like those frightening mug shots she'd seen of hardened felons filled with anger and hatred.

"I can't believe it's you."

Parker stared at his photo. "I was getting into trouble. Lots of it. I skipped school. I drank. I fought. For a while after this picture was taken, I was even huffing paint. Anything to either vent or escape my problems."

"What problems?"

"Reservation life. You name it, I hated it. I felt like a trapped animal caught inside my own skin. Being Indian disgusted me," he admitted quietly. "I was trying to claw my way out of the poverty and despair any way I could." He looked at her. "Probably sounds corny to you, huh?"

Ansel brushed his cheek with her fingers. "No. I just don't know what to say. I didn't live on the reservation. I can't even pretend to know what it was like. You probably think I'm a spoiled little Indian girl who's had everything nice handed to her all her life. And you'd be right. My mother's people are still on the rez in Browning. I don't even know them that well. My mother left the reservation physically but kept it near her soul. She instilled in me the power to be proud of who I was and where I came from no matter how despairing the reality."

Parker smiled. "I think you're blessed. I would have given anything to be you."

"So what happened? How did you end up becoming a chopper pilot?"

"I almost got sent to reform school after I threw rocks through the windows at the Tribal Council building, but an Indian coach at the local high school stepped in and said if I could throw rocks hard enough to crack glass, I could surely throw baseball pitches. In order to skip reform school, I accepted his offer to attend the school and play for the team. Thought I'd slum for a season, then run away. Damn, if I didn't like the game and was good at it. I stayed in school and graduated by the skin of my teeth—not because I was a bad student, but because I'd done a kamikaze job on my GPA up until high school."

"Then what?"

"I went to junior college and got a degree in criminal justice. Straight from there, I went back to the rez. I was a tribal policemen for four years. I liked the work but not the environment. That made me very ambitious. The next step seemed to be trying to get in with any sheriff's department that would take me. I was accepted as a Big Horn County deputy and took flying lessons on my own time. Eventually, I got my private and commercial pilot licenses."

Ansel smiled with him. "Next step the federal government, right?"

"You bet. And here I am. The point I'm making is that this guy," he said, tapping his teen photo, "has nothing to do with this guy." He flipped the sleeves and showed her his driver's license. "Except that neither of us is going back to the reservation. I'm out and I'm staying out."

She regarded Parker carefully. The pronouncement made her very sad. She was proud of her heritage. She couldn't imagine disavowing hundreds of generations of ancestors because you were born into a bad situation.

"You can't change who you are, Parker. You've risen above your negative experiences and you have a lot to be proud about, but being Indian isn't the problem. It's being treated like you're less than human by people who aren't Indian. You sound ashamed of your people."

He closed the wallet and set it on the night stand. "Ansel, I'm not ashamed of them. I'm realistic. It's an Anglo world, and I want to advance in it. That's all." He leaned over and nuzzled her on the neck, signaling that the conversation was closed. "You taste very good."

Ansel wasn't satisfied with his answer, but decided to change the subject. "What happens now? You'll take me back to Big Toe tonight, right?"

"Uh huh," he said between kisses along her shoulder.

"And will we see each other again?"

"You can count on it. This isn't just a one-night stand. I don't operate that way." His eyes peered deep into hers with desire and truth. "I'm normally stationed in Hardin. When things settle down with Operation Dragon, I'll be back. I mean that."

Ansel believed he believed it, but Parker had been the first to admit that he was always on the move with the FBI. What kind of relationship could they have? "If you're being totally honest right now, I'd like another truthful answer from you."

"What answer?"

"Tell me why everyone in the task force is wearing a gray plastic ring." He didn't bat an eye, but Ansel could see the meditative wheels turning behind them.

"I'm not wearing a gray ring."

"You were. I saw it the night you flew me to the bluff. Don't play head games with me, Parker. If there's one thing you should know, it's that I make my livelihood from observing small details and placing them on canvas. Somebody on the ERT lost or damaged their ring because I found the foil tab with a chip on it from inside one at the T-rex dig two nights ago."

Parker blew air through his lips. "You should be a cop, but you're not, Ansel. This detail is FBI business."

"Am I just FBI business?"

"Of course not. I just told you how I feel about you."

"Then please tell me about the rings."

He snorted through his nose and shook his head disparagingly "You shouldn't put me in this position. I can't talk about it."

"Oh, but you can put me in the position of being flat on my back in your bed," Ansel countered. "Very nice, Parker."

He reached out to her. "That's not the way it is."

Ansel jerked away from his attempt to touch her arm. "Liar."

"All right." Exasperated, Parker threw his hands up in the air. "They're dosimeters."

It all made sense to her in an instant. She leaned against the headboard, amazed that she'd forgotten all about her college training in radioactive geologies until this moment, but the multiple gray rings and the odd yellow color of the Vernal skull they tried to buy told her the true story. Occasionally, Morrison Formation fossils hosted for radioactive mineralization because bones in particular stayed in the ground for long periods of time and had a tendency to bind with mobile, radioactive elements distributed by ground waters.

She stared at Parker. "The Allosaurus skull is loaded with uranium, isn't it?"

"Yeah. Or, as the gamma spectrometric analysis says, a load of one hundred fifty million-year-old parent uranium and radioactive decayed daughter nuclides containing bismuth, lead, and radium 226."

"How many rem per minute?"

"About eighty."

Ansel was horrified. Radiation caused atoms to lose electrons, and when that happened in the human body, the ions damaged cells. That damage could come from either a low radiation dose over a long period of time or a high dose in a short period of time. If the cell damage was low level, the human body could repair itself. If it was too much, radiation sickness was the ultimate result. At eighty rem, you should definitely wash your hands after handling the stuff.

"Anything over one hundred rem per minute is a time bomb dosage waiting to explode into a death sentence, depending on how long you were exposed to it," Ansel said. "That skull could be deadly."

Parker sighed. "The Vernal skull isn't the real problem. A whole load of radioactive bones were stolen from the Vernal area, not just specialty pieces like skulls, claws, and feet. A couple of complete skeletons came up missing. If everything is being stored in the same place, they're pumping out radiation hot enough to cook anyone who gets near them. That's why we're wearing the rings."

Ansel had listened and watched his body language very carefully. He was calm and direct, looking into her face, showing no indication he was overly nervous or lying. She believed him.

"Shouldn't the FBI make a public plea requesting the return of the fossils because they're a health hazard?"

"Why? These people are criminal scum. Anybody dealing with stolen radioactive merchandise deserves to be microwaved from the waist up as far as I'm concerned."

Ansel squinted at him. "Even criminal scum have children. What if they're storing the fossils somewhere near their kids or somebody else's?"

Parker placed his hand on her arm and she didn't pull away. "You can't save somebody who doesn't want to be saved, Ansel. Crime is a volunteer profession. When people cross the legal line, they know it. Don't waste your sympathy on them. They'd kill you and your children just as soon as look at you."

She didn't agree, but at least he'd been honest about the rings. It was too late to argue. She folded herself against him. He smelled like the hotel shampoo. "Turn out the light. We've got to get some sleep."

Parker tilted his head and kissed her, tongue probing in such a way that sent shivers down her spine, while his arm reached out and fumbled with the lamp switch. In seconds a cocoon of darkness enveloped them, and Parker slid down with her into the sheets. He wrapped his protective arms around her.

"I'm going to miss you while I'm away, Ansel. "

She ran her fingers through his hair. "Don't worry. You can't get rid of me that easily."

Parker laughed. "That's a given." In a few minutes, he was sound asleep.

Ansel hated clock watching, but that's what she did for the second night in a row. She could see the digital clock provided by the hotel on the night stand quite clearly if she lifted her head a bit and got her line of sight just over Parker's rising and falling chest. When the clock said one-fifteen, she began her slow disengagement from Parker's outflung arm over her waist with snail-like patience. No way was she getting caught in the room by Agent Outerbridge in the morning.

Ansel slowly slid away from Parker, and his hand fell with a low thud to the mattress. She froze, watching to see if he jolted awake. He didn't, and she continued to move sideways away from him and toward the far side of the bed. Then came the lower body swing to get her legs off the edge. A quick feet-on-the-floor push-up and she was standing. Parker still hadn't budged. In seconds she had grabbed her boots, cowboy hat, and saddle purse from near the bed and hurried into the bathroom. Closing the door left her in total darkness.

When she flicked the overhead light switch, every cell in her eyeball screamed bloody murder to her optic nerves. The tiny bathroom looked positively ugly, sterile, and washed out by yellow light. Peeling off Parker's tee, she groped for her clothes folded on the toilet tank.

Five minutes of fumbling and stumbling with her clothes, especially buttoning the split-front skirt, were finally rewarded with victory. She used her brush to tame her wild, frizzy hair, applied some powder, blush, and lipstick. Next she put on her jewelry and twisted her hair up into a top knot before donning her hat. At last she was presentable for entrance into Dixie's domain.

Ansel turned off the light and opened the heavy door as quietly as possible. Parker was snoring. A good sign. The front door opened with a low, nasty mechanical squeak. Damn. She halted in mid-movement, hand gripping the knob and praying for mercy. A wait of another minute gave her courage to try again. This time she swung the door open very quickly, went through the opening, and closed it behind her with a loud click of the electronic lock.

The hall was well lighted and completely empty. A flowery red and gold carpet stretched past an infinity of identical yellow doors. No roving FBI agents in sight. A fresh bed and some real shut-eye awaited her in Room 216 across the hall. Hopefully Dixie would be zonked out and never know she'd come in. Ansel turned on her heels and dug into her purse for the room card. Bliss was only a card swipe away.

As she scooted past Outerbridge's room, the elevator ahead of her chimed its arrival. Two cowboys, laughing loudly, clomped into the hall. Ansel looked up at them as they spoke to each other in the small confines of the hall foyer.

"Shit, this is the wrong floor," said the smaller, blond-haired man wearing a white Specialist hat.

"Man, we've got to get back before daybreak," whined the second man. "I don't have time for this crap."

She couldn't take her gaze off the taller guy wearing faded jeans and a powder blue, long-sleeved ranch shirt. The pale white face framed by bright red hair, thin moustache, and beard was impossible to miss as it turned to stare directly at her.

Ansel froze in place, feet bolted to the floor halfway to the safety of her room and eyes riveted to the malevolent green-eyed gaze of Rusty Flynn.

Chapter 24

*"The dead add their strength
and counsel to the living."*
Hopi

Reid stood in Chloe's studio carefully studying the full-color computer-generated image of the Indian poacher. It was eerie having a mortal face to go with his implanted memory of the inhuman, immolated corpse he'd seen at the morgue.

The bust of a dark-skinned young man with a thatch of short black hair parted along the right side, broad forehead, narrow jaw, and square chin filled out the face, but it was the personal features that held Reid captive. The Indian's dark oval eyes closely set beneath thick black eyebrows and above a broad nose and thin lips gazed back at him challengingly. *So now you see me. Give me back my name.*

"Explain how you did this, Chloe. It's amazing."

It was almost one-thirty in the morning. Chloe sat next to him on a stool positioned in front of a long table where the paperwork he'd take back to Mission City was neatly stacked. The skull was resealed in the packing box as well. She'd waited for his late arrival. He couldn't believe how pretty Chloe looked during the middle of the night in jeans and peasant shirt that clung low over bare shoulders. Her smile was radiant.

"Basically, a Cyberware color laser scanner captured the 3D images of the cleaned skull as it sat on a platform linked to a computer. While the platform rotated, a digital wireframe matrix was generated which simulated the dimensional contours of the skull. It's really simple computer tomography scanning, and it permits me to make more accurate measurements of potential tissue depths. I can virtually reconstruct a face from separately scanned skull pieces if I have to."

"Like a CT scan the hospitals use."

"Exactly. The only facial features I can't get from scanning skull contours are the nose, eyes, mouth, skin texture and color, so I add them with another program. That software is based on known tissue depth measurements collected on standardized charts associated with past cadaver facial studies compiled by age, sex, build, and ethnic group."

She shook her head. "Still, because I'm unable to digitize some of the personal features directly from the skull bones, it makes the most fundamental features a person possesses nothing but subjective guesswork on my behalf. That's where my artistic training kicks in the most."

"You've done a damn good job."

Chloe stared at the photo. "The digital 3D reconstruction technique has its faults, but it's repeatable and fast, unlike my traditional clay reconstructions. Hopefully, if I'm off on the character details, the drawing will still stimulate a recognition response in somebody who knows this man." She peered at Reid. "You're bushed. I have a spare bedroom. You could stay here tonight."

Reid saw that her expression, though warm and inviting, held no promise that sleeping over entailed anything more than just a good night's rest. And that was all right. He wasn't plunging into anything. He'd just reconnected with Chloe under the most bizarre of circumstances and was drawn to her by old memories. Chloe had changed and so had he. He had to get to know the woman again and redefine their relationship past, present, or future.

He placed the photo on the other papers, then picked them up along with the box. "I appreciate the offer, but I checked into a hotel before coming here. I owe you a meal, remember? If it can't be dinner, how about breakfast?"

"I'm teaching a class at the university tomorrow, but breakfast is doable. When are you going back to Mission City?"

"Not until noon."

"All right. Let's do it." Reid smiled. "I'll pick you up. What time?"

"How about seven-thirty?"

"Perfect. I guess I'd better go."

"Sure."

Reid went to the door and Chloe followed. Once there, he gazed back at her. "Get some sleep yourself. We have a lot of talking to do."

Chloe smiled back. "I know."

He stepped through the doorway, which was the last thing he really wanted to do. Their time together had been all too brief. "Goodnight, Chloe."

"See you in a few hours, Reid."

This time he didn't get a kiss on the cheek before Chloe shut the studio door. He wasn't sure how to interpret that. Was Chloe secretly mad because he didn't stay? Was she playing coy? Was *he* reading something into nothing?

Irritated, he swiped a hand through his hair. He'd never been good at the dating games women played with a prospective suitor. His timing was always off. When women wanted action, he hesitated. When they wanted personal space, he blundered in and dominated. Subtle clues flummoxed him every time. He was a guy used to spotting the straightforward lies, deceptions, and inconsistencies of his fellow man, not to perceiving the tangled ambiguities and abstruseness of his fellow woman.

That's why he always screwed up with Ansel, he reflected as he slid into the sedan and dropped the papers and box on the passenger seat. She was a bright, rough-edged lady with so many raw emotions and hang-ups, and so much stubborn willpower that she usually turned him off completely.

Yet there was something about Ansel that abraded away his irritation like the scrape of fine sandpaper against skin. You never bled, but the itch to take notice as she worked her way into your system was always there. A grim smile erupted. Indian hoodoo. And where the hell was she?

He pulled the cell out of his coat pocket and punched her home phone number as he backed down the driveway. The phone rang, then her answering machine droned in his ear. Disgusted, he turned off the device. He wasn't leaving another message, and it was too late to call the Arrowhead and chase her down through her parents.

He had a bad feeling in the pit of his stomach. Ansel must have bailed on her deal to keep in touch with him about Outerbridge. Maybe she was angry over the wiper incident. Why did she do this to him? He should be enjoying his time with Chloe, not stewing over Ms. Anselette Phoenix. *Stay focused.*

Reid glanced at the poacher's picture setting on the seat. Why did you go after fossil tracks at the museum alone, without your gang buddies? You were well prepared. No amateur chisels, picks or pry bars for you. Just a top of the line concrete saw and expensive night vision goggles. Clean, quiet, and efficient. You weren't a user either. No drugs or alcohol in your system.

Most important, you didn't pick the remotest place to strike, or slink around in the dark avoiding the police. You were braver than that. You went right past the BLM field station with your old truck that could never outrun anyone. You were daring them to catch you, weren't you? Like the old days when Indians counted coup against their enemies by passing up the opportunity to kill and simply tapping their foe's body with a coup stick instead. This act demeaned your opponents and gave you power over them.

Enemy. The word bounced inside Reid's head like a ping-pong ball. Having an enemy was a personal thing, and he knew he'd just figured out the real motivation behind the Indian's plans. It wasn't about poaching fossils for financial profit. It was all about getting even, stealing something that meant a lot to somebody else.

Reid was almost at the Rimrock Motel, but he stared hard at the digital man. Speak to me. Who was your enemy? The

BLM in general or somebody at the station? And he had another thought. Chester Dover. The fossils were found on his land. His land? Maybe not.

He knew nothing about the history of Dover's cattle ranch. He'd check out all angles, from property history to possible relationships between Dover and field station employees, or any other BLM agency. Plus local tribes. Maybe the calm waters of the Red Water River ran deeper than anybody imagined. If the Indian wasn't connected to the fossil poaching ring, it was one less puzzle piece for him to fit into a larger picture.

He pulled into the motel parking lot so deep in thought that he inadvertently drove around the back side of the building. Stupid, he realized an instant later. He should have parked out front near his room. That was when he noticed the green Jeep parked beside the Dumpster near the employee entrance to the kitchen.

"Son of a bitch."

He slammed on the brakes, tires squealing as the unmarked car bucked to a halt and completely blocked the Jeep's reverse exit from against a wall parking slot. Reid turned off the engine, pocketed the key, and considered his options. He was out of his legal jurisdiction and it was the middle of the morning. Better to check this out quietly before rousting local cops for backup.

He wasn't wearing his holster and he grabbed it from under the front seat. It took a minute to adjust it over his right shoulder. Then he pulled his jacket from the back seat and slipped into it. A moment later, he was in the parking lot looking at the Jeep while one eye watched the building in case somebody came out and noticed him.

The entire rear of the vehicle was encrusted with black mud. The Montana license plate was practically unreadable, but it was not from Lacrosse. It was local. Switching plates was common with stolen vehicles, but the mud intrigued him. It was the same type that Cyrus Flynn had all over his El Camino.

He quickly inspected the Jeep back to front. There was nothing that indicated the vehicle had belonged to Cullen Flynn.

Any decals, bumper stickers, or personal items belonging to a police chief were gone, or he had the wrong Jeep. The front seat was a mess of garbage, including empty beer cans, overflowing ashtrays, and fast food trash. The back seat had old newspapers and two beat-up fabric suitcases on it. Reid squinted at the headlines through the rear passenger window. A *Sky Sentinel* newspaper from Mission City was visible beneath a *Billings Gazette,* and he felt an adrenalin rush.

He left his sedan where it was and headed for the rear lobby entrance. Time to talk to the night clerk and find out what room the Jeep's driver was occupying.

Chapter 25

"What is past and cannot be prevented
should not be grieved for."
Pawnee

Rusty Flynn took a slow, staggering step toward Ansel. "What are you looking at?"

She blinked, comprehending that after dreading this moment for so long it would come down to a freak crossing of two lives in the most unlikely of places and under the most preposterous circumstances. There was a dark, cold humor in all this, as cold and dark as the murky depths of the ice pond into which he'd thrown her as a helpless child. Well, she wasn't helpless anymore.

Flynn was only a few feet away, staring at her with a smug sneer of curiosity and amusement. "Maybe you want some satisfaction," he suggested, his gaze raking over her outfit from top to bottom. "That why you're hanging out in the hall? You a hooker?"

A spark of anger flared inside Ansel, fanned by the outrageous ramblings of a nasty little boy wearing a man's skin. A bully, even now, but less powerful and intimidating. Her dangling hands knotted into fists as a seething hot anger raced through her veins.

He was either drunk or stoned, and his adult face, which might be handsome under better conditions, was drawn and pale, sickly. He was pathetic, really. Nothing but a swaggering brawler with a monkey on his back. Ansel took a step toward him, staring him down with two and a half decades of hate. She waited with anticipation, second by excruciating second, for him to acknowledge who she was and what he'd done to her.

She didn't expect an apology. Oh, no, never. All she wanted was his full, undivided attention so she could prove to him that she'd survived his almost fatal cruelty and not had her spirit crushed by his ignorant bigotry. She had been wounded, yes, but battles weren't fought without scars. Judging from his appearance, the ultimate war victory was definitely hers.

"Cyrus, leave her alone. We've got to check out." The blond man behind Cyrus jabbed several times at the elevator button in frustration, trying to get the door to reopen.

Something in her face must have scared Rusty. He halted in mid-step, emerald eyes squinting with the effort of focusing more clearly on her. He finally pointed a slender, shaking finger at her. "Shit, I don't know who you are, bitch, but you stay away from me. I don't like your looks." Rusty turned and stumbled away.

Ansel stared at his retreating back in total shock. He didn't even recognize her. How was that possible? She relived the day he had almost killed her with every other thought, tear, and breath.

What sort of soulless monster was he? Any other thoughts she had were truncated when the elevator chime pinged, and the stainless steel doors opened.

Reid stepped into the hall. First he looked at the blond man, then his gaze speared through Cyrus Flynn. Next his stare flickered over Ansel, and his blue eyes widened into quarters. Ansel held his gaze for a second, and it smarted down to her soul as he relayed his disturbing inner message to her: disbelief, distrust, suspicion.

Flynn simply bolted toward Ansel, grabbing her by the arm so fast with his right hand that she didn't even see it coming. Sheer revulsion made her yank away from him, but he propelled his body behind her, threw his left arm around the front of her throat, and locked her into a vise-like choke-hold with his forearm.

Reid's eyes turned steely black. "Let her go, Flynn."

The blond man acted, too. He backpedaled from Reid, reached down to his right ankle, tore at his jean cuff, and pulled at a small gun hidden beneath its folds. Reid went for his own gun and managed to grab the weapon out of the holster. He aimed it at the blond man's chest just as a small caliber pistol was leveled back at his own head.

The blond man smiled. "Mexican standoff, buddy," he warned Reid.

Reid held his fully extended arm as steady as an iron bar. His calm, cool expression broke into a small grin. "Not really. Give it up. I've got you surrounded."

The man cocked his head sideways and sneered. "Hey, Cyrus. Who is this asshole?"

"A cop from Mission City," Cyrus called back. "Put the gun down, Dorbandt, or I'll snap her neck."

Ansel halted her struggles as she watched this dire turn of events. Cyrus was pressed tightly against her back, and his foul breath reeked of beer and vomit. She wanted to claw his eyes out, but this wasn't the time. She'd endure anything to keep Reid safe. They pressed up against the door to her room, and she prayed that Dixie wouldn't sleep through all the noise. Or maybe somebody would call hotel security.

"I told you not to leave Swoln, Cyrus. After I shoot your friend, I'm going to shoot you."

Cyrus yanked his arm tighter, and Ansel choked as her windpipe closed. "You'll have to get the bullet past her first. Put the fucking gun down." He started shuffling slowly down the hall, dragging Ansel with him. "Kill him," he ordered his accomplice, "and let's get out of here."

Cyrus' buddy obliged and cocked the trigger. Suddenly from around a far T-turn in the hall, Parker leaped out, feet straddled, his automatic supported in both hands, and fired. A loud blast reverberated a second after a bullet slammed into the blond man. His hoarse yelp faltered even as he hit the floor with a thump. The bullet had struck his shoulder.

Reid was dumbfounded, but safe. That was all Ansel needed to see. She instantly went rigid in Rusty's dragging grip and stomped on his right toes with the nice square heel of her boot and one hundred and twenty pounds of grinding torque power.

Rusty screamed and released her with surprising speed, then abandoned any efforts to subdue her further. Without a word, he half-bolted and half-limped down the short hall toward an exit stairway while she steadied herself against the wall and rubbed her sore neck.

Parker rushed past Reid and the fallen man, gun in hand, and toward Ansel. He quickly looked her over and placed a comforting hand on her shoulder. "Are you all right?"

Ansel looked into his inquiring eyes. "Yes, I'm fine."

Reid took this in with a critical stare, then focused on Cyrus, who was getting away. "Shit," he exclaimed before picking up the blond man's tiny pistol and pocketing it. "Keep an eye on him," he yelled as he bolted first past Parker and then a myriad of sleepy people who were opening their doors and sticking their heads out.

"I've got to go," Parker told Ansel. "Call an ambulance and then Outerbridge."

She nodded as he disappeared down the hall. Her room door opened, and Dixie wandered out wearing a satiny black pajama outfit, eyes half-shut and hair askew. She looked to the right, eyes going wide at the sight of the older blond-haired man prone on the floor. "What's happened?"

"He tried to shoot Detective Dorbandt. He and Parker went after another man. Get an ambulance," Ansel repeated as she walked slowly toward the man bleeding onto the carpet. "And Outerbridge."

Dixie didn't move. "Dorbandt shot him?"

"No, Parker did. Hurry up, Dixie."

"OK. I'm right on it." She hurried into the bedroom.

Ansel bent down beside the man. He wasn't bleeding too badly, and his breathing was slow and even. It looked like a flesh wound more than anything else, but the man had been under the influence of either alcohol or drugs and being shot had totally zonked him out. That was good news. He needed to live so Reid could question him. Maybe he knew where Cullen Flynn was.

"Jesus, what's happened?" asked a skinny old man wearing boxer shorts and a white undershirt.

"This is a crime scene. Please stand back. Help is coming. The FBI are here."

The man scooted back about five feet. "No kidding?"

"What's your name?"

"Jerry Atwater."

"Listen, Mr. Atwater. I'm going to get a blanket so he doesn't go into shock. Can you keep people away from this end of the hall?"

"Sure." He swivelled his head toward the growing crowd of onlookers and peered over the top of his glasses. "Back off. The cops are coming." He looked at her and grinned. "That okay?"

Ansel stood up. "Great."

She went straight into her room so fast that Dixie, who was sitting on the far bed with her back to the entrance, didn't even know she was there. Dixie was on the phone and Ansel couldn't help but hear her.

"Get up here, John. Parker just shot Jessie Frost." Dixie waited a moment, then said, "I'll keep her busy."

After Dixie hung up, Ansel made no effort to hide her presence as she whipped down the coverlet on her unused bed to reach the blanket beneath. Dixie twisted quickly around. "Shoot, you nearly made me pee my pants, honey."

Ansel clutched the fuzzy green blanket to her chest and glared at the woman. She was in no mood for games. "Who the hell is Jessie Frost?" When Dixie simply stared back, speechless, she said, "Go ahead, Dixie. Tell me what I should have known from the beginning."

The paleontologist bit her lip and continued to look as guilty as sin, but said nothing.

"Fine. I'll find out all your dirty little FBI secrets anyway." Ansel walked toward the door, then half-turned. "Oh, and don't you ever call me 'Honey' again."

Chapter 26

"Never go to sleep when your meat is on fire."
Pueblo

Reid shot through the second-floor exit door and started down the stairs toward the lobby. He'd bounded down half a flight before realizing that the pounding footsteps he heard were actually above him. Dammit. What kind of moron ran away from cops by going upstairs?

Just as he started back up, Standback bulleted through the door onto the second-floor landing, gave Reid a sour glance, then bounded ahead of him up the stairway toward Cyrus' fleeing form. Reid cursed and took the steps two at a time, reclaiming lost ground.

The sound of an opening third-floor doorway echoed through the stairwell. Flynn had gone back into the hotel. On instinct, Reid shot back through the second-floor entrance and down the hall. He planned for Standback to tail Flynn while he cut the jailbird off at the opposite end.

Reid sprinted past knots of hotel hawkers and the man still lying on the floor. An old-timer wearing boxer shorts yelled at him as he jumped over the unconscious cowboy, sprinted down the east hallway, and slammed through the door into the stairwell. He was up the steps and through the third-floor entrance in moments. This hallway was blissfully quiet, and he sped down it, seeing no sign of Flynn or Standback. Suddenly Standback veered around a corner of the elevator foyer. Standback saw Reid and looked doubly exasperated.

"Where have you been? He's on the elevator." He darted past Reid toward the stairwell.

Reid shot into step behind him. "I'll handle this. He's my suspect."

"Who says?" The agent hit the door hard and headed pell-mell down the stairs.

"I'm working the Chief Flynn case. This is his nephew."

Reid matched Standback's speed, and they flew down the stairs side by side. Parker held the inside railing and a distinct advantage around the turns. They made the stairwell turn just beneath the second-floor landing.

"It belongs to the FBI now."

"In your dreams, Standback."

"Just stay out of my way, Dorbandt."

Reid grinned. He knew something that was going to work to his advantage. Once they hit the ground floor, Standback raced toward the stairwell door, bee-lining for the lobby elevators.

Reid hesitated a few seconds, allowing the agent to take the lead. That's what he wanted. As Standback tore into a hallway leading to the front desk, he stopped, turned around, and went out the first-floor street exit. From there he coursed past the front of the hotel and around a corner into the darker reaches of the rear parking lot.

The foul smell of rotting fish wafted into his face from the overfilled Dumpster next to the kitchen entrance as he raced over the asphalt, his eyes scouring the area for signs of danger. He saw his sedan and the Jeep, but there was no sign of anybody, especially Cyrus. Reid slowed to a walk and pulled his gun out. Maybe the guy was faster than they thought and had already gotten into the Jeep. Once inside, Cyrus could pull a weapon from anywhere.

The sound of an ambulance siren out front wailed over the hotel roof line. Reid shook his head. The place would be a zoo in a few moments, plenty of opportunity for Cyrus to melt into the confusion and slip through a two-man search team. Where was Outerbridge?

Reid walked carefully up to his car, using the vehicle as a shield between him and the Jeep, with his gun ready. As he moved closer and could see inside the Jeep, he realized that nothing looked amiss. Everything was closed and locked. Nobody inside or under the vehicle. It looked like Cyrus hadn't headed this way.

The thought that Standback might have collared the con in the lobby made him hitch up his mouth in disgust. Worse yet, what if that little weasel had eluded them? Cyrus knew what had happened to Cullen Flynn. He had his uncle's Jeep. Reid knew that he should have muscled Cyrus at the house when he had his chance. Leaned on him until he popped.

Soft footsteps coming across the asphalt jarred Reid into action. He crouched beside the Jeep's passenger door and pressed himself against it with his pistol gripped in both hands, cocked and ready. The footsteps moved around the hood of his sedan and down the length of the Jeep's driver side opposite him.

Reid licked his lips, every fiber of his body listening and evaluating the movement of shoe leather on gritty asphalt only eight feet away. When he felt that the moment was right, he leaped up, located his target, and pointed the gun across the roof.

"Hold it right there or I'll shoot."

Standback, brown face criss-crossed with dread, stood across from him, his own gun raised uselessly in mid-air. When he recognized Reid, his lips puckered with disdain.

"Bang, you're dead," Reid said, enjoying the moment.

"Very funny." Standback re-holstered his gun in a left shoulder strap. "You'd be dead if I didn't shoot the other guy first. We're even." He glanced at the inside of the Jeep. "Chief Flynn's missing car. When did you find it?"

Reid pushed his gun into his holster and walked to his sedan. "Thirty minutes ago. It was right under your nose. Looks like I've been one step ahead of you."

"Did you happen to see the perp while you were cavorting around the parking lot?"

"Not a red hair. You?"

Standback stood beside him. "Nothing. He's gone."

"How could you lose him in an elevator?"

"He stopped it mid-floor. By the time I got back to the second floor, he'd taken the elevator up to the third. When I got up there, he was a ghost. I even checked the roof. I came out here hoping to lock onto him again. Where the hell were you?"

"Right here waiting for Cyrus Flynn to show up, of course. Outerbridge is going to pitch a shoe over this."

"Sheriff Combs isn't exactly going to give you a commendation."

Reid smirked. "Oh, I don't know. I found the Jeep. Once my department examines its contents, we may have a lot to go on. Too bad for you."

"Mind telling me what you're doing at this hotel in the first place?"

"Just came to Billings to get a photo of the museum poacher's face. I don't suppose your team has identified him yet, right?"

Standback got serious. "To tell you the truth, he hasn't been a high priority."

"I guess that's a no," Reid said. "Well, you'll find out all about it anytime now. I brought the skull here to be digitally reconstructed a few days ago. The facial photo has already hit the police networks, especially the reservation computer banks. We should get this little loose end tied up for you Feebees in no time."

"You know, all this macho, competitive repartee is getting old, Dorbandt. You have a personal problem with me?"

"Wrong question, Standback." Reid crossed his arms.

"What's the right question?"

"Is Ansel Phoenix going to have a problem with you?"

Standback shifted his feet and cocked his head sideways. "What's Ansel to you?"

Reid scratched his temple, looked at the ground, then glared back. "I'm a friend. Just want to know what she's been doing here with you."

"She's working with our task force. Since you've blundered into our operation, I'm sure Outerbridge will tie up that loose end for your sheriff's department." He walked away.

Reid didn't move. "I'm not done."

"Well, friend, I think you are."

Reid didn't like what he was feeling because he wasn't sure what it was. Envy? Jealousy? It didn't make any sense. Where was he going with this? Ansel was an adult. She had her own life. And he had the promise of Chloe coming into his. He was way out of line and he knew it, but the words just tumbled from his mouth before he could stop them.

"Don't hurt her or you'll answer to me," he called across the parking lot as Standback went to the lobby entrance.

The Indian didn't respond until he had one hand on the glass door. Then he turned slowly. "You're a good detective, Dorbandt, but a lousy realist. Ansel couldn't be any safer with anyone but me unless she was with you, which she's obviously not." He was gone in seconds.

Reid spun around and punched his fist against the door of his car, wishing it was Standback's face, then grimaced in pain. He spent the next minute shaking his hand and flexing his aching fingers. He felt like a fool.

All right, if Ansel had been with Standback, there was nothing he could do about it. He told her to come on Outerbridge's mission. He'd also told her to keep in touch, which she hadn't. Deliberate evasion or not, she'd apparently been attracted to Standback during their time together. Maybe because he was Indian, and that was something he could never change in himself.

Two tan-uniformed men came around the hotel corner and spotted him. They approached him cautiously, hands on their belt holsters. "Excuse me, sir," said the young, fresh-faced one. "What are you doing back here?"

"I'm Detective Dorbandt, Lacrosse County Sheriff's Department. I'm going to reach for my badge." He pulled his wallet from his inside jacket and flashed his shield. "I need you guys to stay here and guard the Jeep. It's a stolen vehicle and evidence in my case. A perp associated with the shooting inside may try to get to it. Keep an eye out. I'll be back in a bit. I'm going to leave my car here, too." He replaced the wallet and pulled out his cell phone.

The cops nodded, radioed their position via shoulder radios, and took positions around the Jeep as he walked toward the lobby entrance. He hastily dialed the main number at the Lacrosse station and talked to the desk sergeant, catching him up with what had happened in Billings. Primarily, he was going to work with the local sheriff's department to seize and impound Chief Flynn's car, since it was no longer occupied by a suspect and had been left in a public place.

From there, the news that Cullen's Jeep had been found and that Cyrus Flynn and another man, as yet unidentified, were possibly involved in the Chief's disappearance would filter up and down the chain of command. Soon a felony warrant for running from an officer would be issued for Cyrus Flynn.

Reid also received information back. There was only one pressing message. Odie had done his homework on Carigliano and Allied Beef. The sergeant delivered a summarized version of the important info, and Reid listened with total concentration. The news was quite illuminating, and he licked his lips in anticipation. Agent Outerbridge and he needed to talk.

His last instructions to the sergeant were to have Odie start the ball rolling on an affidavit for a search warrant on Cyrus' house and car, and to contact him as soon as he came on duty in a few hours. Reid closed the conversation by promising to be back in Mission City as soon as possible. He wanted to be back in Lacrosse for the house bust. Silently, he cursed.

There was no way he could make that seven-thirty breakfast with Chloe.

Chapter 27

"Listening to a liar is like drinking warm water."
Tribe Unknown

Ansel watched from her room as the paramedics lifted the cowboy onto a stretcher and strapped him in. The hall was littered with medical equipment, and excited people swarmed the area: EMTs, police, sheriff deputies, hotel security and staff, and curious onlookers.

Outerbridge had arrived a few minutes after Dixie's phone call. He conferred with her briefly, then hustled over to stand guard beside Jessie Frost while Walthers, who'd apparently been called away from surveillance, kept the crowd away. Dixie had avoided Ansel at all costs, slinking toward the far corner of the hallway behind Outerbridge.

Ansel rubbed her arms and leaned wearily against the doorway to her room. Her eyes felt like sandpaper, and her tight clothes chafed at her skin. She needed sleep, even if it had to be in the same room with Dixie. The only thing that kept her standing was hoping Reid would return. They had to talk, and she didn't care what Outerbridge thought.

Ansel saw Parker first. He appeared from the west end of the hall, nodded briefly in her direction, then went straight for Outerbridge, who was talking to a police sergeant. Her heart sank. By the scowl on his face, it looked like he hadn't apprehended Cyrus. At least he was safe. When Outerbridge saw Parker, he pulled him aside and began an animated conversation that didn't look pleasant.

Ten minutes later, Reid pushed through the crowd. At least he was uninjured, too. He'd almost been shot right before her eyes. By the time he reached her through the throng, his expression was stony. No matter his frame of mind, she had to tell him what she'd found out about Operation Dragon. It might help locate Chief Flynn.

Without thinking, Ansel stepped forward and hugged him. "Thank God, you're all right. I thought that thug was going to shoot you. Did Cyrus escape?"

Reid stiffened in her embrace and pulled away. "You know Cyrus Flynn?"

"Of course. He's Cullen's nephew. He pushed me into the pond when I was five."

Reid shook his head. "Wow, I had no idea."

"There's no reason you should. I never told you. You didn't catch him?"

"I will."

"Reid, what are you doing here in the first place?" Ansel demanded.

He looked around the hall. "We need privacy. This way." Abruptly, he steered her through the open bedroom door.

He didn't answer her question, but she suspected what was coming. "Listen, I would have called you, but…"

"I don't care about that."

"What's wrong?"

Reid released her forearm and shut the door. The hubbub from the hallway became a dull drone. "I want you out of this fiasco right now. I'll tell Outerbridge you're leaving. You'll ride back to Lacrosse with me."

Ansel wasn't surprised, considering what had happened, but did she want to leave Parker so soon?

"Reid, I think I should see this through. I can learn more information about what's going on. I don't expect you to stay."

His face darkened. "It's too dangerous. Things are going down that you're not aware of."

"I wouldn't doubt that, but I've already found out some of Outerbridge's little secrets."

"Such as?"

"The microchip. It came from inside one of the gray rings all the ERT are wearing. They're actually dosimeters used to measure high-level radiation."

"I already know that. The chip analysis came back last night."

"But I know why they're wearing them. They're worried about high radium counts. Some of the fossils stolen from Utah sites are dangerously contaminated with uranium deposits. Exposure to a cache of these bones for more than one minute can kill people, Reid, and they're not even concerned about anything but themselves. The important thing is, if Chief Flynn was taken by poachers, he could be exposed and suffer from radiation poisoning."

Reid shook his head. "I think Chief Flynn may have bigger problems than radiation sickness or poachers, Ansel."

"What are you talking about?"

A heavy knock sounded at the door, and both of them gazed at the barrier suspiciously. Reid finally reached out and opened it. Agent Outerbridge stared at them ominously. "Am I interrupting something?"

Reid frowned. "As a matter of fact, you are."

"Tough." He walked into the room. "Close the door, Detective. Time for a little chat."

Reid looked at Ansel. "You'd better wait outside."

Ansel crossed her arms. "No, thank you. I have a few things to discuss myself."

"Since you two obviously know each other, I think you should stay," Outerbridge agreed. "Especially since both of you have compromised my sting operation and put my task force in jeopardy."

Ansel didn't like the way Outerbridge stared at her in particular. She knew why he was singling her out, and her cheeks flared

red. Parker. God, if Outerbridge mentioned that she'd spent part of the night with the pilot, Reid would blow a gasket. She didn't dare leave without being able to defend herself.

Reid's grin was flat. "Which operation? The fossil smuggling ruse you've pandered to Ansel or the real one?"

Outerbridge's head snapped toward him. "The only FBI mission I'm in charge of is called Operation Dragon. My task force is working under the direction of the Department of Justice, and we're investigating a fossil poaching ring operating throughout Montana and Utah. That's it, period."

"Bullshit," Reid insisted.

Outerbridge pursed his lips. "Anything else you've heard is wrong, Lieutenant Dorbandt. You've just exposed an FBI presence in this area with your Lone Ranger act out in the hallway. Thanks to you, I'll be lucky if I can complete the illegal fossil buy I've worked hard to accomplish for months. I'll be discussing that with Sheriff Combs and the State Attorney."

The threat flew over Reid's head. "I'll loan you the quarters, Outerbridge. I have every right to pursue suspects who have stolen a Lacrosse County police chief's vehicle, pulled a weapon on a sheriff's officer, committed an aggravated assault on a civilian, and run from law enforcement during an arrest. Quit blowing smoke up my ass."

Ansel had listened to all the posturing she could take. "Wait a minute. What other FBI operation are you talking about, Reid?"

The stare Reid flashed at Outerbridge was hotter than a branding iron. "The one probably cooked up by the U.S. Attorney in Washington. Tell us about Frank Carigliano."

Outerbridge didn't twitch a muscle, but Ansel could see the cogs turning. She knew that anything coming out of his mouth would be a lie.

"You're way off base. I don't know him," he said.

Ansel focused on Reid. "Who is he?"

"Carigliano is the operations director of Swoln Stockyards, where Cyrus Flynn works. I just found out from Montana

Department of Criminal Investigation files that in 1999 Carigliano was suspected of calling the shots for the beating-murder of
a deputy county attorney from Sidney whose body was dumped
across the North Dakota line. Nothing was ever proved, but five
witnesses fingered him, two of them drug dealers."

Outerbridge simply shrugged. "That has nothing to do with
Operation Dragon."

"I'm not done. The murdered attorney, Lewis Lovell, was
involved with a local banker in a money-laundering scheme.
Sicilian mafia drug monies were siphoned into the bank and
processed out to purchase stolen objects of art, antiquities, and
fossils. Converting illegal cash assets into legitimized collectibles
with a history and verifiable pedigree was a good business until
Lovell wanted out and threatened to expose the whole scam."
He stared at the agent. "The illegal fossil dealing is right up your
avenue."

Outerbridge snorted. "So what?"

"Swoln Stockyards is owned by a dummy corp called Allied
Beef Exchange. Tracing the real owners is like unraveling a bird's
nest, but the corporate trail goes out of the country through
Helena, then into Canada. From Vancouver, British Columbia it
heads toward South America, probably to a mafia cartel operating in Belize. Mafia drugs like cocaine, heroin, and marijuana
coming into this country take the reverse route and land in Chi-
nook, Montana, for distribution throughout the U.S., Mexico,
and Latin America."

"Still has nothing to do with my task force," Outerbridge
insisted.

The startling wealth of information Ansel had heard caused
her head to spin, but certain facts stuck in her brain like colored
tacks. She pinned Outerbridge with her own stare. "So who's
Jessie Frost?"

Reid's head twisted toward Ansel. "You know Jessup Frost?"

Ansel watched the FBI man before speaking. He was nervous, unconsciously rubbing his right thumb across his index
finger. "No. I overheard Dixie telling Outerbridge that Parker

shot Jessie Frost. Obviously the FBI knows who he is. Let me guess. He's a poacher digging up bones for eventual sale to the mafia, isn't he?"

Outerbridge swallowed. "I'm not allowed to answer that. It's restricted information." He turned and headed for the door.

"I went to Dawson County College, where the T-rex foot was stolen," Ansel continued. "A librarian told me that a man with red hair and a beard had been there a few days before the robbery. I didn't think anything about it until now. It was Cyrus Flynn. He was casing the place. Both of them obviously work together since they're at this hotel. Probably came to Billings because of our Allosaurus sale through Accent on Antiquities."

The agent ignored her, but Reid's smile was broad as he watched Outerbridge try to make an escape. He had the agent by the scruff of the neck. "I'll tell you who Frost is, Ansel. He's a foreman at Swoln Stockyards and an ex-con heavy into meth-amphetamine, like Cyrus. You think the feds didn't know that? Or about Carigliano and Allied Beef? This is all about drugs. We've been suckered."

Ansel was furious. She'd opted to help the FBI because she believed she was saving plundered fossils, not to be used for some backdoor poaching bust when the real agenda was to trap drug runners through a lesser felony charge. Like convict-ing Capone on IRS tax evasion crimes rather than for being a multi-murderer.

As Outerbridge reached for the doorknob, Ansel stepped up behind him. "I want the truth. Is this operation nothing but a Department of Justice ploy to go after a drug cartel?"

The agent spun around. His face was bright red, and he fixed her with a glare. "All right, Miss Phoenix. I'm not ashamed of doing my job any way I can. Operation Dragon is a double-edged sword. We're after a fossil poaching ring that sells its stolen goods to a drug cartel and gives them a way to hide their illegal cash assets. With luck, we'll bring down a two-headed monster: a fossil smuggling ring and a drug pipeline. As far as

I'm concerned, a felony is a felony. I don't care how I get one as long as it sticks."

"You should have been honest," Ansel parried.

"If you're squeamish about details, then you were just giving me lip service when you spouted your indignation over black market bone smuggling. Either you want to stop the destruction of fossil artifacts or you don't. Fortunately, equivocation about the methodology isn't an option in my line of work."

The rebuke shocked Ansel, but it didn't negate her outrage over the deception. "I get it. That Great White you told me you wanted to filet is a big drug player. That's why fossil dealers like Billy De Shequette at Accent on Antiquities will skate past felony charges if they rat out the mafia drones buying bones from them for the money laundering scam."

Reid jumped in. "Exactly. Want to tell us who the big fish is you're after?" When Outerbridge failed to answer, he said, "I'll guess. It's the high ranking state official in Helena that Attorney Lewis Lovell threatened to expose before he was set up to die by Carigliano."

A light went on in Ansel's head. She gazed at the agent who stood stonily by the door. "When you gave me your pitch about the operation, you told me that the fossil poachers sold a T-rex skeleton for four million dollars to somebody. Who was that?"

Outerbridge shrugged. "A Dutch businessman."

Ansel sighed. "Was the skeleton radioactive?"

A tic jumped on Outerbridge's left cheek. "We believe so. You don't expect a cartel to care about what happens to people, do you? It's all about money with this scum."

"Hokay, somebody was the go-between for an international black-market sale of that magnitude. Who brokered the deal stateside?" Reid demanded.

"I don't know."

Reid moved up to Outerbridge's face. "You might as well tell me. Sheriff Combs can phone the U.S. Attorney of Montana, too. Right now you're withholding information that could lead to the identification of felons who may have Chief Cullen Flynn as a hostage. Your actions are obstructing justice and interfering with a major county investigation. Play ball with me, Outerbridge."

Outerbridge held his features rigid for several long moments, then his line-etched face relaxed. "I'll tell you on one condition. Information goes both ways. I understand you have Chief Flynn's missing Jeep under sheriff's guard down in the parking lot. I could confiscate it because it's part of my investigation, but I don't need the hassle. I want copies of all the Lacrosse county forensics and vehicle contents reports on the Jeep sent to me electronically. I also saw the digital reconstruction photo of the museum poacher's face, but don't know who he is or how he fits into all this, so I want to know immediately what you get back from your tips and sources."

Ansel's mouth dropped open. "You have his picture?" she asked Reid.

"That's why I'm in Billings. It's been in circulation for several hours now." He glanced at the agent. "It's a deal. Now who is the prime target from Helena you're going to bring down?"

Outerbridge smirked. "Lewis and Clark County Attorney Cody Masterson. I understand that you know his ex-wife quite well, Lieutenant."

Chapter 28

"Thoughts are like arrows: once released,
they strike their mark.
Guard them well or one day you
may be your own victim."
Navajo

A loud knocking reverberated through the hotel door. Ansel rolled over, staring blearily in that general direction as she tried to orient herself. After Reid and she had cornered Outerbridge, she'd collapsed in bed to grab a few hours of sleep before he would drive her back to Big Toe. She looked toward Dixie's bed. The covers were twisted but empty. She had yet to see or hear from the woman. The raps resumed.

She wiped the fuzziness from her eyes and slowly trundled to the door in her wrinkled dress clothes. "Who is it?" No sense taking chances with Cyrus on the loose.

"Parker."

She was too tired and cranky to be excited about his presence. "What is it?"

"I need to talk to you. I haven't got much time."

Ansel looked at her wristwatch. It was almost nine. Parker must have finished the group huddle with Outerbridge scheduled the night before. She was no longer in the FBI loop. Reid had told her he had an appointment to catch before they left town, and he wouldn't be back until after eleven. She wished they'd already departed so she could avoid seeing Parker at all.

"Ansel, open up."

Despite her better judgment, she unbolted the door. When she opened it wide, Parker stood eyeing her warily. He was wearing a fresh outfit of jeans, black tee, and boots. He looked tired, too. "Can I come in?"

"Sure." She retreated into the room. "I'll be back in a moment."

Parker stepped in and closed the door while Ansel headed for the bathroom. Once inside, she locked the door. He wasn't going to slip inside again so easily. She used the toilet first and then brushed the foul taste in her mouth away with some of Dixie's toothpaste and her index finger. Leaving home without the minimal toiletries was a major inconvenience. A review of herself in the mirror revealed a nightmare vision of an Indian wraith with spiky hair, smeared makeup, and two matching pouches of dark FBI baggage under her eyes. Parker certainly wouldn't be pawing her clothes off in passion, she mused.

He knocked on the bathroom door. "Come on, Ansel. You can't hide in there."

Ansel opened the door. "Are you sure you want to talk? You won't like what I say."

Parker reached out to touch her. She expertly dodged his hand and slid past him. He turned and watched as she walked stiffly into the center of the room. "Why are you mad at me?"

She faced him, raising her eyebrows and crossing her arms. "Cyrus Flynn. Jessie Frost. Frank Carigliano. Allied Beef Exchange. Sicilian Mafia. County Attorney Cody Masterson. Should I go on?"

Parker sighed. "You're blowing this out of perspective. My job is to fly a chopper. I don't contribute to the game plan."

"But you knew the game plan, Parker. I didn't. It's bad enough that I was tricked into this operation with all those honorable platitudes about bone orchards and the noble fight against wanton destruction of fossil artifacts, but you really played me for all I was worth."

"That's not true. It may seem that way, but it's not." He came toward her again, a pained expression drooping his usually stoic face.

Ansel backstepped. "Don't touch me. You all shared the scoop on me in one of your neatly labeled federal files. You had to know about my childhood accident and who was involved. When were you going to tell me that Cyrus Flynn was tied into this mess? Did you ever think of my feelings about finding out or seeing that sicko bastard after what he did to me?"

Parker halted, dismayed by the venom in her voice. "You're right. I should have told you even if it compromised the op. I was wrong and I apologize. How can I make it up to you?" His eyes were beseeching.

Ansel trembled with rage and rubbed her arms briskly to calm herself. He was trying to appease her, but it wasn't enough. A cold, slithering snake of reason lay coiled in the back of her mind that she couldn't chase away, and it hissed to her that Reid Dorbandt would never have done this to her. Not even if they'd just met and jumped into an intimate relationship. Reid would have told her about Cyrus. Warned her.

Unlike Parker, it would have come down to a matter of honor with Reid, not servitude to a higher force. Parker had decided long ago that currying himself to Anglo men in power advanced his rank in the pecking order. To keep Outerbridge's secret about the drug cartel connection, Parker hadn't dared to mention Cyrus to her.

"Get out, Parker."

"You don't mean that." He rushed forward and grabbed her shoulders before she could avoid it. "You're tired and upset. I've got to leave in half an hour. The task force is flying back to Glasgow. I'm not going with this hanging between us."

Ansel didn't pull away this time, but she didn't dare look at him. One glance would start melting her resolve. Already his hands were like red heat on her body. She focused on the floor.

"I mean it. I don't want to talk about this anymore."

"Then we won't. I'll call you like we planned."

Tears started at the corner of her eyes. She squeezed them shut. She refused to let him see her cry. "Just go," she ordered.

Ansel sensed his body shift forward as he placed a tender kiss upon her lips. She stood unyielding, determined to be stone against his fiery liquid sexuality. Her lack of response discouraged him, and Parker pulled away.

"Be safe, Ansel."

She listened as his footsteps treaded across the carpet and the door opened. The soft click of its closing was like a smooth stiletto piercing her chest, and it angered her that was so. "You, too," she whispered.

And then the floodgates within her eyes opened.

"You're awfully quiet." Chloe sipped her espresso and fixed Reid with a curious stare. "Tired?"

Reid sat at the black marble table across from her feeling physically ill. There was nothing wrong with the small restaurant situated near the College of Technology. The tiny bistro was crowded but clean and cheerful. The gray slate walls guarded by an army of potted plants supported huge single-pane windows overlooking the rolling, landscaped campus. The breakfast food and drink was excellent, served with glazed stoneware dishes and mugs.

Still Reid could barely force himself to talk or eat. A few hours before, when Odie called as requested, he'd ordered the detective to do a complete background check on Cody Masterson and Chloe Masterson Birch. He wanted to know what ties, if any, Chloe had maintained with her ex-husband. The thought that she might be involved in fossil poaching or drugs had driven him to this point. It was a cop's mentality and, though he berated himself for it, it was as much of who he was as the normal social pleasantries he now forced himself to do.

Reid sighed. "It was a long night. I'm not looking forward to the drive back either, but that's the demands of the job. Speaking of which, you did a great job on that reconstruction."

"You keep saying that. I'm just a messenger. My work will only be a success if somebody uses the information to come forward and identify the man."

Reid nodded and picked at his scrambled eggs. "The photo was distributed electronically early this morning, especially to the tribal police agencies. We'll get a strike soon."

Chloe's hair shone like spun platinum beneath the sunlight coming in through the window as she reached across the table and placed her left palm over his hand resting along the table edge. "I hope you get bonus points with Sheriff Combs," she said with a wink. "That would make my long hours of slaving over a hot computer worthwhile."

Reid felt worse. She was making all the right overtures about still caring for him, and he was about to manipulate her trust for selfish reasons. "Must have been tough for you."

Her brows crinkled together. "What?"

"Finally finding something you love to do and that you're really good at, but it has this humongous down side—it negatively affects your life, even your marriage."

Chloe removed her hand and gestured off-handedly. "Oh, that…Well, like I said, Cody wasn't entirely to blame. We were both career-driven fiends. Not that he didn't have his faults. He had a lot of mood swings and bouts with depression. I didn't have the time to coddle him, and he found other ways to pull himself together without me." She looked at him, her face pensive. "I know what you're thinking. Other women. No, he never cheated on me. I know that for a fact."

Reid sensed an underlying current of evasion about Cody's faults. He'd have to probe deeper. "How did you meet him?"

"I met him at MSU in Missoula. He was getting a law degree. He wanted to be an attorney. We clicked right away when we found out that we were both interested in the criminal field. After dating until he graduated, we decided to get married. Soon after we lived apart on and off because he got an attorney job in Havre for a small law firm while I continued my schooling, graduated with an archeology degree, and then decided to go into forensic reconstruction. After that, things fell apart."

"What's he doing now?"

"Cody's the county attorney in Helena. He prosecutes big-time criminals."

Or protects them from prosecution, Dorbandt thought. Masterson had a lot of power, like the ability to dismiss cases he deemed lost causes. How many mafia stooges, poaching accomplices, or personal criminal buddies had he let loose by failing to allow cases to move forward into a Lewis and Clark county courtroom?

"He sounds very ambitious," Reid replied, barely containing his consternation. How could Chloe have gotten involved with this man?

She inhaled deeply. "Definitely. You know, it seemed like the more Cody succeeded from small-time attorney to deputy county attorney, and then to county prosecutor, the more our marriage disintegrated."

"He moved up quickly, then?"

Chloe nodded. "Almost like opportunities fell into his lap. And he's still hungry for more. His ultimate goal is to get the U.S. Attorney position for Montana."

Reid took a sip of coffee as he considered Chloe's words. Corrupt local and state government employees were the bane of law enforcement when it came to weeding out drug enemies. Masterson had probably made his connections with the mafia in Havre as a fledgling attorney. All kinds of narcotraffic went through that border town straight from the Canadian line. Sometime during a fragile period when a brassy, ambitious attorney's soul could be tarnished black, Masterson was seduced by the prospect of easy money, future career advances, and power. Love of self had replaced his love for Chloe.

"Chloe, did Cody ever use drugs?"

Chloe looked at him sharply, a shadow crossing over her eyes. "Why on earth would you ask me that?"

"You said that Cody had mood swings and bouts with depression. Sounds like a substance abuse issue."

She looked down at her near empty plate once filled with puffy slices of French toast slathered with hand-harvested maple syrup from Vermont. "Once a cop, always a cop. Sure, Cody had his bout with recreational drugs when he was in college, but that was it. His real problem during the marriage was alcohol. I pushed him into rehab once, and he passed with flying colors. All of this was before we decided to part ways. As far as I know, he's still on the wagon. Why this deep interest in my ex?"

Reid knew that he'd pushed far enough. He grinned. "Guess I'm curious about the competition."

When she gazed at him this time, her expression was mirthful. "There is no competition, Reid. I don't even speak with him anymore. Does that make you feel better?"

"Yeah, it does."

Chloe looked at her watch. "I've got to get going. I have some papers to correct before class." She gathered her purse and briefcase together.

"I wish we had more time."

"Me, too, Reid. When will you come back to Billings?"

Reid swiped a hand across his face. "I don't know. I've got a heavy case load right now, but I'll have some vacation time soon. I could come back and visit my parents and brother. Haven't seen them in quite a while."

Chloe stared into his eyes. "I'd like that. Call me and let me know what you're doing. I'll clear my calendar." Chloe stood and so did he. The bill had already been paid so they left the bistro and forged out into the suffocating heat.

Since they'd met there, he walked her to her van, feeling awkward, sad, and excited at the same time. "Well, here we are," he said as they stood by the Lumina's door.

Chloe leaned close to him and kissed him briefly on the lips. It was not a passionate move, but not just a peck on the cheek either. "I'll miss you, Reid. Come back quickly."

Reid searched her eyes, wondering if she felt as he did that they'd just turned some invisible corner with one another. He placed his hand on her arm and pulled her close again. This time, he kissed her and drew away. Her response had been just as he remembered it to be so long ago as she leaned into him, cool, soft, and smelling of lavender. It was like a time warp, as if fifteen years hadn't passed at all.

"I'll call when I get back to Mission City," he said.

Chloe laughed. "You'd better. I don't want you to disappear on me." She unlocked the van with a remote and slid in, then shut the door, waving quickly as she started the vehicle.

Reid watched, feeling ten feet tall, as she backed out and left the parking lot. It had been a long time since he'd been in a serious relationship with a woman. Work had consumed him. The long hours on the job filled his head and his hours. It was time that he started enjoying life more, he decided as he watched the van turn into a blue dot amid downtown traffic.

Maybe it was time to turn his compass toward home instead of toward infinity. He wasn't getting any younger. He did want a wife and kids. Early thirties and he was sightseeing life on cruise control rather than with his hands guiding the wheel. Maybe Chloe was always the woman he was meant to marry.

His cell phone rang and he scrabbled for it. "Detective Dorbandt."

"Reid? This is Pearl Phoenix."

Though Ansel had pressed him into meals at the ranch a few times and he'd liked her parents very much, they had never called him directly. "This is a surprise. How are you?"

"Not well, I'm afraid. I'm sorry to call your cell phone, but a nice man named Detective Fiskar at the sheriff's department gave me this number when I told him it was an emergency."

"What's wrong?"

"Chase is in the hospital. He's had a heart attack. I need to speak with Ansel, Reid. Do you know where she is? I've called her home phone and the cell all night, but she doesn't answer," she said in a rush of words.

Reid assimilated the bad news and the effect it would have on Ansel in a split second. He was thankful that he would be the one to break the news to her. "It's a long story, but she and I happened to meet here in Billings."

"Billings? Well, can you contact her and tell her to call me?"

"I'll call the hotel where she's staying. Where are you?"

An exhalation of relief echoed through the receiver. "Thank God. I'm at the McCone County Hospital ICU. Tell Ansel to call my cell phone. She knows the number."

"What's Chase's condition?" Reid asked, knowing that ICU was a red flag of danger.

Pearl's voice cracked with emotion as she replied, "Very serious. He's critical."

Chapter 29

"One has to face fear or forever run from it."
Crow

"You still mad at me?" Dixie said through her headset microphone.

The FBI Eurocopter banked to the right, rotor blades drumming like thunder while Ansel's fingernails dug into the rough, navy-blue fabric on the armrests and her seatbelt clip cinched into her abdomen from the sudden shift in centrifugal force. Parker wasn't wasting any time lifting off and speeding his four passengers toward Glasgow with a short side-trip to the McCone hospital heliport beforehand.

"No," Ansel replied, barely able to respond. Her conversation with Pearl on the hotel phone was all she could think about, and her stepmother's words echoed through her head.

"Chase is in ICU, Ansel. They just brought him up from the emergency room. He's unconscious. They want to stabilize him. Dr. Welman say's it's a myocardial infarction. Please, hurry."

Fortunately, she'd received Reid's call relaying the horrible news about her father before the ERT had departed for the Billings airport. She'd rushed to Outerbridge's room and asked to be taken to the hospital by air rather than make the long drive with Reid. The agent was very sympathetic and obliging considering their previous confrontation, but she would have begged on bended knees if she had to. This flight would cut her travel time by more than half.

She sat in an aft passenger seat this time, right behind Parker. He couldn't see her, but she didn't care. Dixie occupied the middle seat to her left. Walthers inhabited the far left seat behind Outerbridge, who rode shotgun with Parker. The quarters were cramp and claustrophobic, their backs pressed up against a vibrating rear wall next to the tail boom, but Ansel's anxiety had more to do with her internal demons rather than a fear of her surroundings.

She was paralyzed by the black dread that her father would die before she saw him. All she could see in her mind's eye was herself yelling at him about not telling her that Rusty was back. Guilt and sheer mortification gutted her insides at the very thought of it. She'd argued with her father before, but never like that. Never with such a cold hate in her heart and such venom in her voice. Had she upset him so much that she'd caused his heart attack?

Without warning, her internal self-control mechanism misfired, and Ansel began to sob openly, hands over her face, head bent, which wasn't easy with the bulky helmet and headset.

Dixie came to her rescue. The paleontologist handed her a wad of tissues taken from her duffel bag beneath a seat and patted her on the back. "Ansel, don't worry," she said, her voice tinny through the earphones they wore to communicate above the thumping din. "We'll get you to your daddy."

Ansel gratefully took the tissues and wiped her puffy eyes and red-splotched face. The interior scene would have been comic under other circumstances. The beefy, self-assured Walthers grimaced nervously as if dealing with a despairing woman was above and beyond the call of duty. Outerbridge feigned total ignorance and stared through the sun-filled windshield where toy-sized ranches and farms filled a tinderbox landscape moving quickly past below.

She could also see every twist and turn of Parker's body as he surreptitiously tried to cast glances toward her over his shoulder. His movements intensified as she cried, and she imagined every twitch had something to do with his frustrated efforts to either see or console her without Outerbridge noticing. Dixie just kept talking.

Ansel ignored all of them, leaned back into her seat, then stared out her window like a zombie. Finally Dixie quit trying to rouse her into good cheer with a few hope-and-faith one-liners about her father's prospective recovery, and the only sound inside the cabin was generated by the engine, rotors, turbines, and wind.

Her fragmented thoughts drifted briefly toward Reid, whom she hadn't seen before leaving Billings. Nor had she seen the photo reconstruction of the Indian poacher's physical identity, something she'd been longing to discover for over a week. Now it didn't seem important.

Time passed with the slowness of a freeze-frame slide show. They'd traveled northeast for about an hour before the flat topography began to break apart by the appearance of large dun-colored humps. Ansel looked at Dixie, who was dozing beside her.

"Is that the Badlands?"

Dixie jerked to attention, peered out the same window, and nodded. "Sure is. Should be right near Hell Creek again. Looks clear out here now, but I hear there's an honest-to-God storm front coming in. We might get some rain."

The unexpected good news nibbled away at the dark abyss filling Ansel's soul. Above the copter, visibility looked unlimited. The sky was azure and relatively devoid of clouds. It didn't look as if there would ever be relief for the drought-ridden terrain.

"When's that supposed to happen?" Ansel asked.

Parker's voice shot through the earphones. "About four o'clock. All that dust in Canada helped a weather system develop some convective storms. Sometimes dust serves as condensation nuclei for water vapors. That's going to make your father happy."

"Parker, have you noticed any bogies following us?" Outerbridge said suddenly.

"Negative. Saw a light plane behind us about five minutes ago. That was it."

"Well, there's a black chopper coming up fast from below. It's headed right at us."

Ansel looked out her window but couldn't see anything.

"I see it," Walthers said from his left end seat as he peered out Outerbridge's side. "No call letters."

"I'm going to take a look," Parker replied. The copter executed a smooth lefthand turn so he could observe the approaching aircraft through the lower front windshield.

Ansel saw it, too. It was slightly larger than the Eurocopter with a similar styled, teardrop-shaped fuselage, glassed-in cockpit, long tail boom, and enclosed tail rotor. The chopper climbed toward them at a forty-five degree angle, its current trajectory placing them on a collision course.

"It's a Gazelle with outriggers," Parker said, his voice tense. Abruptly, he banked the chopper back to their previous heading and increased his flight speed with a burst of power.

Outerbridge stared at Parker. "What's an outrigger?"

"The external stores racks on either side of the fuselage behind the cabin. Could be carrying nothing more than smoke markers and flares. Or it might be hauling 36-mm rockets, TOW missiles, machine guns, or side-mounted miniguns. I don't like it."

"Maybe they're military," Walthers added.

"Uh uh. They're unmarked. The Gazelle is a reconnaissance and attack helicopter mostly used against armored troops. We're out in the middle of nowhere. They shouldn't be here. I'll try the com and see if they respond." He began a calm, purposeful inquiry across the radio airwaves, requesting that the unidentified helicopter on an approach below make contact.

Ansel listened to all this with a sinking feeling in her stomach. If Parker was worried, so was she. They were much closer to the Hell Creek bluffs now. That would be a bad place to encounter trouble. She gazed at Dixie. The paleontologist stared back at her, eyes wide and frightened.

"They're still coming," Walthers volunteered as he watched out his rear window. "I see two people in the cockpit. Can't be more than five hundred feet away now. Looks like they're moving over to come up alongside."

Parker abandoned his mike. "They aren't responding, and I don't want them too close."

Outerbridge nodded. "I agree. Let's get out of here."

Parker increased the collective, and their flight speed jumped yet again. Ansel watched as the other copter appeared below her window and began to drop back appreciably because of the Eurocopter's acceleration. On the ground, the first of the Badlands' bluffs came into view, and she tensed. "Shouldn't we avoid the rocks and stay over level ground?"

"Not necessarily," Parker responded. "If things turn sour, we'll need cover."

She leaned forward. "What do you mean?"

"He means we're a sitting duck out in the open." Outerbridge had swivelled his head around to stare at her. "Somebody's coming after us, Miss Phoenix."

"Who?"

"Take your pick. The mafia. Black market dealers. Local poachers. We've spooked somebody out of the woodwork," he replied angrily. "Just keep your head down and do whatever we tell you. No arguments."

The second copter began to catch up. They were being chased, she realized. Nothing made that fact more real than seeing the black helicopter heading straight for her. She also noticed that Parker had started to decrease their altitude. The eroded Badlands were only a mile ahead, and they made a dashing descent toward them. As they got lower, the other copter moved into a position several hundred feet behind their tail.

"I want everybody to stay calm and don't panic," Parker ordered. "Keep your helmets and restraints on at all times. Make sure loose items are secure. If we have a forced landing, you'll have to assume a crash position. Bend over with your chest on your thighs. Place one arm under your thighs and the other grabbing the seat. Feet braced on the floor and slightly apart. I'll get us down safely no matter what."

He turned to look at the aft seats. "Everybody got that?" Ansel couldn't see his eyes behind the sunglasses, but didn't have to. She could feel his energy directed toward her despite his generalized question. She gave him a brief acknowledging smile and a nod before he looked away. In that fleeting moment, she wished she could have touched him and apologized for what she'd said to him, but now was not the time or place.

Behind her, the sudden noise of gunfire exploded. A whizzing strafe of bullets hailed down on them an instant before the copter lurched abruptly sideways and shot for the ground. Nothing hit the fuselage during the short barrage as Parker managed to adroitly avoid the first volley with lightning-fast reflexes. Below, the first towering ridges and plateaus scythed by at fifty miles an hour. Above, Ansel could plainly see the chasing copter with two occupants inside. She could also see the outriggers and mounted miniguns.

"Shit," Dixie exclaimed. "Get us out the hell out of here, Parker."

"I'm trying." He'd navigated the copter down to two hundred feet and was weaving in and out of ravines, passes, and Badlands rock corridors like a combat pilot.

Another volley of bullets pinged past them, and Ansel saw the flashes and smoke fanning out from the gun mounts with crystal clarity. The black copter was slightly above them and shooting at the tail boom. She couldn't believe this was happening. All she wanted was to get to the hospital and see her father. Another strafe came at them. This time, something hit the copter and there was a explosive concussion that sounded like a firecracker going off inside a tin can.

"Set us down," yelled Outerbridge, "before we fall down."

Parker frantically struggled with the controls. "Don't have a choice now. We can't go up again. The hydraulics were hit. We're losing pressure and tail rotor elevator controls by the second."

Outerbridge scowled. "Find a place to land, dammit."

As they lost altitude and speed very quickly, the stony ground reached up for them. Ansel swallowed back her panic. If the crash didn't kill them, the ten-story-high crags would. She forced herself to peer out her window. Clustered bluff tops ringed by tall ponderosa would be impossible to land on. So would the deep gullies and calcareous bluff bottoms. "There's a box canyon to our right. The middle is flat. Can we reach that?"

Everyone except Parker looked toward her. "Looks about three hundred acres wide. Should work if I can get us there," he yelled back. "I haven't got much directional control in forward."

"Just do it," Walthers shot back from the back seat.

Parker struggled with the sluggish controls, and the copter slowly turned to the right. Behind them the Gazelle closed in. Miniguns fired. High-velocity bullets skimmed past the turning fuselage and struck rock walls, surrounding them with explosive smacks that chipped off stone, felled tree limbs, and raced along the canyon rim in a lethal swath of destruction. In the midst of this, an alarm sounded throughout the cabin, warning of some incipient danger with the copter's functions.

Dixie screamed and covered her ears. Walthers squeezed his eyes closed. Outerbridge clenched his armrests and leaned against the copter's semi-controlled and sharply angled turn. Ansel put her hands over her ears and prayed they survived long enough to attempt a crash landing.

"Crash positions," Parker yelled.

The right turn never stopped as the copter dropped beneath the northwest rim of the box canyon, barely missing a direct hit against the cliff wall. The nose kept spinning right, and the left side of the tail struck rock like a decelerated hammer. Metal dragged across bedrock as a deafening, cacophonous screech.

A thud that felt like God had swatted the copter threw Ansel against the fuselage despite her leg-hugging stance and iron grip on the seat. Screams and hoarse grunts of shock and surprise echoed through the cabin right before the copter nose tilted down, and the craft dropped like a stone.

Then the long, scraping fall to the boulder-strewn canyon floor began in earnest.

Chapter 30

*"Make my enemy brave and strong, so
that if defeated, I will not be ashamed."*
Plains Indian

Something tugged on Ansel's shoulders. Her eyes flickered open, then closed though she was vaguely aware of a loud crackling sound and the smell of smoke. A cough welled in her chest as acrid air invaded her lungs, but a heavy drowsiness kept her from stirring too much. Only a sharp yank near her stomach irritated her enough for her to open her eyes again.

She saw the blurry outline of Parker's smoke-shrouded face hovering above her. He was reaching down, frantically trying to release her seatbelt. Only then did she realize that she was hanging sideways with Dixie and Walthers below her. The copter had come to rest on its left side, and Parker was actually on top of the overturned fuselage trying to get her out through the open right passenger door.

"Hurry up," he ordered. "This bird is smoking. Hold onto my hand, and I'll pull you out." He unclipped her buckle and suddenly Ansel's dangling weight was free.

Her body dropped onto Dixie's unconscious form still strapped in a seat. The smoke inside the cabin became much thicker, funneling up past Ansel and through the overhead door. It smelled of acrid burning plastic and fuel. She glanced down and could barely see Dixie as she struggled to upright herself with feet on her seat's now sideways leg struts and the gray-carpeted cabin floor against her belly. Coughing several times, she grabbed Parker's right hand. He moved further back on the exterior fuselage, struggling for footing, and pulled her through the opening. When she was almost out, long split-front skirt and all, Ansel settled on her rump and swung her legs onto the copter's fiberglass hull.

"Slide down to the ground, then get back near those boulders. The copter might blow. There's a hot power plant with an engine compartment leaking sixty gallons of fuel beside us."

Ansel half-slid and half-jumped the many feet to the ground and her sore back complained. She noticed Parker's red duffel bag thrown on the ground. He must have gathered his belongings before leaving the flight deck and rescuing her. Luckily, she had placed her saddle purse diagonally over her shoulder and chest when she'd buckled into her seat.

"The others?" she called up. "Are they all right?"

Parker prepared to jump directly into the passenger deck this time. His face was grave. "Just Dixie." Without another word, he sat, dangled his legs into the smoking hole, and then disappeared.

Dixie? What about Outerbridge and Walthers on the bottom left side? Ansel wondered. Instead of leaving the copter, she quickly circled it, her boots sinking into the soft dirt churned up by the crash velocity. The copter had sustained a lot of damage, but she couldn't see anything or anybody through the front windshield. It was opaque with roiling gray smoke and partially compacted on the left side from some catastrophic impact too great to withstand.

Everything in front of Outerbridge had buckled inward six feet. Even with the smoke, she could see the huge blood splatters coating the indented, spider-webbed windshield. The gruesome sight confirmed that Special Agent John Outerbridge and Agent Daniel Walthers were dead. The copter's forward ground speed, almost vertical drop, left-sided impact, and the hard-packed terrain had doomed them.

With new horror, she vividly remembered how the left side of the nose-down copter had dragged more than seventy vertical feet down the sandstone canyon wall as the engine accelerated them forward even faster. Then there had been that tremendous tilted crash to the earth when she must have lost consciousness.

As if that wasn't enough, the thirty-foot-long main rotor blades had snapped, either from striking the canyon cliff or by surviving the drop only to have the nosedive against the ground catch the blade tips in mid-spin. The tail boom was missing its rear portion, which had landed several feet away from the main fuselage.

Ansel looked at her watch and rubbed her lower back. Only eleven minutes had passed since the copter hit the canyon wall. Now two people were gone. No matter their treatment of her, neither FBI agent deserved this. Tears stung her eyes, but she didn't have the luxury of losing it out here in the one-hundred-and-three degree heat with two killers probably out to finish off the rest of them.

Suddenly Parker reappeared through the door, coughing and covered with black grit. He'd revived Dixie, whose head popped out. She was sputtering for breath and clawing at the fuselage sides, her duffel bag in tow. Ansel ignored Parker's instructions and hurried to help get Dixie off the copter. The paleontologist had a bruise on her left forehead but looked physically well otherwise. Ansel tried to ignore the bloodstains smearing Dixie's clothes. They had must have come from Walthers.

Parker stared down at the two women. "Get further away. I've got to go back in."

"Parker, no," Ansel said. Toxic black smoke now spilled from beneath the copter and out the passenger door, and the air around the craft felt hotter, fiery.

"I forgot something," he said, distracted. "I'll be right out."

"Let's move back," Dixie agreed. "He knows what he's doing."

Ansel reluctantly left. Dixie and she walked toward the canyon wall some eighty feet away. As soon as Dixie reached the shade, she pulled a cell phone from her duffel and punched in a number. As Ansel watched, amazed at the idea that Dixie thought she could just dial up the equivalent of Triple A to come and pick her up, the paleontologist's face twisted into a grimace and she snapped the cover plate shut. "I tried calling an operator. No signal. Great. No food and no water. I didn't sign up for this."

Next Dixie sank to the ground and leaned her head against a huge boulder providing shade and scrabbled through her bag for matches and a cigarette. She lighted the tip with badly shaking hands, puffed several times, then stared angrily off into the flat brown acreage filled with brown scrub brush and prickly pear enclosed by a solid ring of sienna and cream skyscraper cliffs.

Ansel leaned against another chunk of rock, fanning her face with her hat. "Relax. Even with these temperatures, if we stayed in the shade and moved from dusk until dawn, we could last almost six days without either, but it probably won't come to that. We'll find something to eat, and there's a rain storm on the way."

Parker soon jumped to the ground from the destroyed aircraft and joined them. He was carrying his duffel and Outerbridge's steel briefcase. "We're going to need this," he said, "or everything we did will be meaningless."

The bill of sale for the Allosaurus skull and the store security camera recordings were in the briefcase, Ansel considered with admiration. She'd forgotten all about them. She scanned the canyon. Everything looked normal—lifeless and isolated, but she knew that things weren't always what they seemed in the Badlands.

"Where do you think the other copter went?" she said.

Parker wiped sweat from his black-smudged forehead. "If we're lucky it's gone, but with all that smoke, they can come back and find us anytime they want."

"So can the FBI," Dixie asserted. "And doesn't the copter have a distress beacon?"

"Sure, I manually activated an emergency locator transmitter before we crashed, and it should broadcast a radio distress signal for quite a while. The problem is that the copter's not just smouldering, it's on fire near the engine compartment. It's only a matter of time before it blows. Plus, we're in a box canyon. A CAP plane or any other aircraft would have to be directly over us in order to pick up the distress signal. We can't depend on the ELT."

Ansel nodded. "I've got to get to my father. So which way is out?"

"I've got the survey maps for this area and a GPS unit. We should be able to find the entrance to this box canyon pretty easily. After that we head toward civilization. First, we take stock of what we've got so everyone knows who's in charge of what supplies."

They all sat on the ground and went through both the duffels and her purse, garnering a catalog of items necessary for the trek. All in all they were in pretty good shape except for their food and water situation. Parker had taken an emergency medical kit, safety strobe, flashlight, matches, two inclement weather ponchos, and three guns from the copter—his own, plus Walther's and Outerbridge's. Parker and Dixie chucked most of their clothes and toiletries, replacing valuable duffel space with important papers, maps, two cell phones, and other essentials. Ansel's purse was rifled, too. She removed all her jewelry and tossed it inside after taking everything else out except a tiny bottle of expensive perfume which she couldn't bear to part with, a mirror, and lipstick to keep her lips from chapping.

Parker took the strobe, flashlight, and guns. Dixie took the ponchos and whatever protective clothing remained. Ansel got the medical kit, which fit perfectly inside her purse and merited the thick leather protection. Outerbridge's briefcase was the only tote left intact. By silent, mutual agreement, the case seemed somehow sacred—inviolable until it was given to the proper authorities. Ansel carried that.

Behind them, the helicopter suddenly flared with a sizzling whoosh of flame that engulfed the interior cabin and the men left behind. Tongues of fire shot out of the open doors on the right side, hissing and smoking. The noise sounded like perverse cackling to Ansel as she watched the helicopter become a funeral pyre.

Dixie stared hard at the aircraft while fashioning a makeshift head covering with a large yellow tee-shirt. She stretched the neckline tight across her forehead and tied it behind her head with the short sleeves, then let the rest droop behind her neck and back.

Dixie stared at Parker. "Maybe we should have taken them out of there."

Ansel shook her head. "Couldn't bury them. They'd be eaten by animals."

Parker said nothing but watched the fiery spectacle, his face ashen. Ansel couldn't imagine what he must be feeling. Guilt, anger, horror. He'd known those men better than she, and she imagined that the deep, fraternal bonding between federal agents was something unfathomable and unquantifiable by her standards of experience. When the copter finally exploded, sending a hellish fireball of orange and black smoky flame into the sky along with a rain of small debris and gagging fumes, he turned away.

He occupied the next several minutes consulting a Hell Creek geological survey map and orientating himself with the GPS. "West to east, this flat area is about a half mile long. There's only a deep ravine at the east end that leads out of the canyon."

"That's not too bad," Dixie admitted. "Maybe our cell phones will work outside these bluffs."

Parker sighed. "I wouldn't count on it." He reached into his duffel and pulled out a light blue windbreaker. "Ansel, put this on. I don't want your bare arms getting burned. I'll wear a long-sleeved shirt." He passed her the jacket and stripped off his sooty tee, replacing it with a vibrant red plaid western shirt. Then he carefully strapped on his shoulder holster.

Ansel pulled the windbreaker over her thin white top. "Good idea. Dehydration is going to be our worst problem."

Parker started walking. "There's not much shade anywhere so we'll take the fastest way across and see how it goes. Stick together. If that copter comes back, find some cover or hit the ground. If everything goes all right and we get out of here, we'll concentrate on staying in the shade the rest of the afternoon and building a shelter at dusk."

They began the long walk across the small prairie, one behind the other. Parker led, Ansel followed, and then Dixie, who tended to lag anyway. It was fast going since the land was relatively flat and the normally tall grasses and scrub were reduced to near nothingness. The worst was the prickly pear. They zig-zagged a lot, avoiding these thick succulent patches. The foot-high cactus had long, stiff thorns that cut with a wicked efficiency and could cause infection.

They hadn't walked more than five minutes before the drone of helicopter blades sounded beyond the eastern ridge. Parker's head snapped upward as he scanned the ponderosa-covered eastern bluff they were headed toward. Ansel and Dixie froze in place, listening. The *whomp-whomp* of rotor blades increased with every passing second.

Parker calmly turned and looked at Ansel as he handed her his duffel bag. "Run into the rocks," he commanded. "Now."

Ansel accepted the baggage, but stood her ground even as Dixie bolted past her to start the long run from the center of the prairie toward the nearest plateau on the southern side. "What are you going to do?"

"Decoy them away from you two."

The black helicopter appeared over the bluff top. "Bullshit. I'm not letting you be a target. Come with us."

Parker grabbed her arm and pushed her roughly away. "You've got to protect that briefcase. I'm depending on you. God dammit, get out of here." His face was red with anger as he pulled his gun from his holster and looked up at the copter headed straight for them.

The briefcase in Ansel's hand felt like lead. She didn't want the responsibility of being the caretaker of Outerbridge's covert strategies and dogmas, but she couldn't deny Parker his request. He trusted her implicitly, and she wouldn't let him down. Her face softened. "All right, but make this quick. I've got to get to McCone, and I expect you to take me there."

Ansel turned and ran with every fiber of her being. Her last vision of Parker was that of him standing feet spread and arms locked straight with automatic weapon aimed at the sky.

Overhead the Gazelle swooped toward him, miniguns blazing.

Chapter 31

*"Treachery darkens the chain of friendship,
but truth makes it brighter than ever."*
Conestoga

Safely at the boulders, Ansel slowed and watched the scene unfolding behind her, heart jackhammering against her rib cage. The copter was low, coming at Parker with tremendous speed as a strafe of bullets tore across the ground. Parker fired several rounds at the copter's windshield while dirt, plants, and rocks before him fanned upward in a linear spray.

One bullet hit the Plexiglas and Ansel saw the helmeted pilot jerk abruptly. Suddenly the copter swerved right, and the deadly strike ceased. Parker threw himself to the left, rolled away from the turning aircraft, then jumped to his feet and started running toward her. The copter gained altitude in the turquoise sky and headed north.

Parker reached her out of breath. Ansel dropped his duffel and the briefcase to give him a joyful hug. "That was amazing, but don't you dare do it again."

A lopsided grin encompassed his face. "I think I gave them something to think about."

Dixie appeared from behind a boulder wall. She watched the horizon, her demeanor leery. "You were lucky. They could have made beef jerky out of you. Then what good would you be to us?" She walked stiffly into the prairie.

Parker stared after the paleontologist. "What's eating her?"

"She's not happy to be here. Let's get moving. I've got to reach my father."

Parker checked his ammunition clip and then reloaded. "I'll get you to him. No more heroics. I promise."

They made the rest of the journey across the prairie in record time. When they reached the east rim of the canyon, they were tired and hot. Just that bit of exertion under the broiling sun had taxed them greatly. Parker used the GPS to find the exact location of the exit ravine. They found it just beyond an unusually green and grassy spot with a perfect ring of huge white and brown puffballs. The fungi grew out of a loamy pile of decaying plant matter and fallen limbs that had washed off the cliff above.

Parker cleared the accumulated dead fall and discovered that the exit path was nothing but a narrow, three-foot-wide swatch cut between two towering bluff walls. It served more as a drainage gully for winter run-off than as a pass through. On top of that, the cut-out was riddled with scrub trees, fallen rocks, and small boulders for as far as their eyes could see. Walking through or over the jumble of debris would be a real physical challenge.

"We'll never get through that," Dixie groused upon seeing the dark, tiny, overgrown pass. "Like trying to squeeze through a bottleneck filled with gravel."

Ansel sucked in a breath. "We going to have to. At least it will be out of the sun. I'll lead."

"No, I'll lead," Parker declared. He stepped in front of her. "I have the upper body strength to move things."

Ansel stepped back and searched the ground, looking for anything that could be used as a walking stick. She found a sturdy ponderosa branch which had fallen from a hundred feet above and stripped the smaller, dried limbs from it.

"Use this to poke the area ahead of you. Watch for snakes, bees, wasps, spiders, and scorpions. I fossil hunt in places like this. They're full of critters that can kill you. I'll carry your bag."

Parker took the limb and smiled. "Good idea."

He went into the ravine, walking as far as he could and then stopping to push or pull away whatever blocked their travel. It wasn't easy. Though it was shady and much cooler between the humongous, gritty walls, it was also a tight squeeze with little maneuvering room to rearrange materials so that they could be passed, stacked out of the way, or stepped over.

Ansel went second, clearing more space wherever she could so that Dixie's larger form could follow more easily. The anxiety of feeling hemmed in from all sides was almost overpowering. The further they walked, the more the light from behind dissipated, casting them in a shadowy, confining tunnel. Ahead, there was equally minimal light. Even looking straight up toward the open sky, which was nothing but a tiny blue strip between brown rock, didn't help. They were like rats in a maze.

"How long is this?" Dixie said.

"About a quarter mile. We're halfway through."

The ravine twisted to the right, and they rounded a curve which widened to five feet. This would have been refreshing for Ansel except she saw what the others did at the same time. Her stomach twisted. Parker stopped suddenly. When he turned to stare at her, his expression was one of exasperation. Already his long-sleeved shirt was dirt-stained and wet with sweat from all his exertions of clearing a path. The coolness without the sun couldn't compensate for the lack of breeze inside the channel. The air was incredibly close and smelly from their rising body odors under stress.

"Shit," Dixie exclaimed, staring at the fifteen-foot-tall oblong boulder completely blocking the ravine. Even if Parker somehow hoisted them up, there was still no way he could reach the top on his own afterward. Getting down on the other side would be difficult as well. Nobody could jump it without risking a broken bone or suffering some internal injury.

Parker leaned against the wall. "I can't move that."

Ansel looked at her watch. It had taken them an hour to traverse this far. She was hungry and very thirsty. A bad sign. She'd eaten no breakfast. The last time she'd even had liquids was the night before when she'd had two Cokes with the Black Angus take-out. Her own clothes were ringing with sweat, and the urge to strip off some clothing was like a kicking mule inside her head, but she knew that keeping her body covered with loose clothing was better for cooling her body than no clothing at all.

She licked her dry lips before speaking. "Going back is not an option. We need to get out of here and find water. We'll push it over. All three of us."

Dixie dropped her duffel. "That's going to be a tight fit, us in the same few feet of space. I guess we could go high, low, lower and all get our hands against it."

"We don't know what's on the other side," Parker pointed out. "It may not go over even if we have enough leverage to push it."

Ansel set down the briefcase and his duffel. "Let's find out."

He nodded and tossed his walking stick behind Dixie. "All right. I'll go high. You go in the middle, Dixie. Ansel, you're low."

They bunched up together against the backside of the rock and took positions at different levels. Parker asked them if they were ready and then counted to three. They pushed with everything they had for almost thirty grueling seconds, sweaty hands slipping against the stone surface and feet sliding or digging into the dirt on the ravine floor. The rock wobbled fiercely, then settled back in place with a crunching finality.

"Stop," Parker yelled. Ansel sat on her rump and Dixie fell back against the cliff wall, panting heavily. "Nice try, but it isn't going to work. Any other ideas?" He sat down on the ground beside Ansel and leaned back against the wall, face flushed with heat.

"I don't suppose you packed any rope," Ansel said with a grim smile. It felt good to rest, and she wished she could just lie down and sleep for a while.

Parker laughed. "No, I saved the space for my six-pack of spring water."

Dixie smiled for the first time. "Anybody bring a ladder? We could just shoot right up and over that old rock."

"Or some dynamite so we could just blow it out of the way," Ansel said. She saw Parker's strange look. "What?"

"That's not a bad idea," he said.

"Dynamite?" Dixie wondered aloud.

"No. Making a ladder. We've got plenty of old timber around here."

Ansel's face turned serious. "And rolls of gauze and tape in the medical kit for lashing the cross pieces. Or we could use bark strips from shrubs and fallen limbs if it came down to it."

Parker stood up, suddenly energized. "I'll collect the larger logs. Dixie can get the small crossbars. You get the lashing materials, Ansel."

The next hour was spent slowly accumulating the raw materials for the ladder. Parker had to walk back through the ravine a ways, but he came back with two near ten-foot lengths of sturdy pine logs about three inches in diameter. Dixie collected a few thick limbs of fallen spruce and broke them into fifteen-inch pieces. The white medical tape worked well as a first lashing material to connect cross limbs to the log sides. It was strong and very hard to tear. The corner ties were further strengthened with gauze strips.

Ansel was the most proficient at doing the final strengthening of the lashings by using peeled strips of scrub bark and timber hitches she'd learned to use on the Arrowhead for joining broken fence boards to posts when staples weren't available. Another hour and they were ready to lift the impromptu ladder up against the boulder.

Parker easily positioned the ladder and grabbed his duffel bag. "I'll go first. If it holds me, it will hold you two."

Ansel and Dixie held the leg struts steady for him, and he climbed quickly up the rungs, careful not to let his weight settle too long on any one cross limb. The ladder was a few feet short of the boulder top, but they could easily reach it by stepping on the top rung. Parker pulled himself up and stood on the boulder, arms outstretched to steady himself on the cliff walls.

"There's nothing on the other side except some scrub brush. Lift the ladder up to me. I'll position it on the other side and get down, then tip it back over the top to you. Use it to come up one at a time, and I'll help get you down again."

Ansel and Dixie lifted the ladder up so Parker could grab the highest rung and pull it up enough to let it see-saw over the flattened boulder top. A few seconds later, he turned around to face them and stepped down onto the ladder. He disappeared from view as he descended. After calling that he was down safely, he pushed the ladder top up and over the boulder again, sliding down so that Ansel could grab it and reposition it again.

Dixie went up next carrying her duffel. She repeated Parker's ascent onto the boulder. Ansel lifted the ladder up to her, and Dixie pulled on it enough to swing it past her and down to Parker. When she had descended, the ladder was pushed over again one last time.

Ansel grabbed the descending ladder end and carefully steadied it against the boulder for her own ascent. She realized that in order to get the ladder up behind her, she'd have to tie something on the top rung so that she could pull it up to her the last few feet and over the boulder top. There was just enough gauze left. She stooped to grab the cotton roll on the ground when the loud snapping sound of trampled foliage echoed behind her.

Ansel froze, disbelieving but knowing that her ears weren't wrong. The noise of footsteps on rock and breaking brush was undeniable. Somebody was coming down the ravine straight at her. Panic spurred her into action. She yanked the last long strip of gauze off the cardstock spindle, grabbed the briefcase, and went up the ladder as quickly as she could in her long skirt. When she was high enough to reach the top rung, she fumbled with the gauze, one hand through the briefcase handle loops, and hastily tied a double knot. Behind her she heard a man cough.

"Ansel, where are you?" called Parker.

Damn. Ansel turned to look behind her. Several yards away, a pale, red-haired man quickly rounded the ravine curve and stared at her in amazement. He carried a shotgun in his right hand. It was Rusty, and she could see by his expression that he now knew exactly who she was. Surprise and equal disbelief that he'd met her once before and hadn't recognized her as Chase Phoenix's daughter twisted his face into a wide-mouthed scowl. She bolted up the ladder, gauze in one hand, case in the other, and practically jumped up onto the boulder.

Without preamble, she tossed the briefcase down to Parker, who was gazing up at her quizzically. Then she yanked on the gauze and the ladder rose. Out the corner of her eye, she saw that Cyrus was running toward her, intent on grabbing the ladder. She couldn't let him get it. The boulder was the only thing standing between him and their lives.

Ansel latched onto the top rung and jerked the ladder roughly off the ground. Cyrus bellowed his anger as he half ran and half stumbled across the rocky earth in an effort to foil her. The ladder came up smoothly, almost beyond his reach, but he jumped for it and managed to catch the left leg with his free hand.

"Give me that." He yanked the ladder with a maniacal brute force.

Somehow she managed to hold onto it without being pulled off the boulder. She grabbed the next rung down and then the next, and used her own strength to pull and pivot the middle of the ladder onto the boulder. Gravity won out and the ladder tipped toward Parker and Dixie on the other side, slamming Rusty's arm with the resulting change in angle. He yelped and let go. Ansel let the ladder fall down freely, hoping Parker would catch it and get it instantly ready for her to descend.

"Get down here," Parker ordered, realizing that she was in serious trouble.

Ansel started down. Below her, Rusty had recovered and was sighting his shotgun at her chest. "I should have killed you the first time, bitch," he sputtered. Then he pulled the trigger.

Ansel's feet skipped a rung as she hopped downward and ducked at the same time. She barely slipped behind the boulder before the shotgun blast deafened her. A wash of hot air jetted over her head and hundreds of shotgun pellets hit the bluff wall to her left. Parker pulled her off the ladder and to the ground as rock shards rained down on them, and the smell of gunpowder fouled the ravine. Flynn's curses of frustration filled the air next as he stormed around on the other side, pounding on the rock with the shotgun butt and tearing up bushes in a tantrum.

Parker helped Ansel to her feet. "What the hell is going on?"

Ansel took a moment to catch her breath. "It's Cyrus Flynn. He came up behind me."

"Flynn? The copter must have come back and dropped him off to flush us out. Now we know that they're poachers. We've got to hurry. The pilot will be waiting for us on the other end if Flynn gets back to him and tells him we got away." Parker turned to reach for his duffel bag, but it was gone. Ansel followed his strident gaze.

Dixie stood several yards away. Parker's unzipped bag lay at her feet. Pointing Outerbridge's Magnum at both of them with one hand and clutching the agent's briefcase with the other, Dixie displayed her usual toothesome smile.

"Either of you lovebirds move and you'll be feeding the buzzards."

Chapter 32

"There is a hole at the end of a thief's path."
Lakota

"I heard that Captain McKenzie gave you a FLEAT enema when you got back from Billings this afternoon," Odie said. He steered the dusty sedan toward Cyrus' house.

Reid grimaced at the parodied acronym used by officers which described a "Federal Law Enforcement Ass Thrashing." Agent Broderick had complained to McKenzie about their public match-off, and his boss had gleefully run a goal with it up his end zone, so to speak.

McKenzie's Imperial Commandments were predictable. Thou shalt never pull a stunt like that again with a BLM official. Thou shalt never bring personal grievances into homicide investigations. Thou shalt be condemned to a suspension hell without pay if thou disobeys any of the above.

The fact that he'd found Cullen Flynn's vehicle, connected Cyrus to the sheriff's disappearance, exposed Jessie Frost as a poacher, and learned the truth about Operation Dragon and the mafia connection hadn't figured into McKenzie's gratitude factor.

"I'm steeping in my own regrets," Reid said. "Can't you tell?"

"Well, at least you'll enjoy the next few hours."

Reid cast a pleased glance at Odie as they rode up the dirt driveway. A deputy sheriff's car followed behind. He'd waited for this moment for the last two hours. The search warrant in his left hand, authorized by Judge Elizabet Ottey, empowered him to take some constructive action. The paper allowed him to locate Cyrus' car and to search it, as well as to search the residence for any evidence which might give them information about Cullen's whereabouts.

It hadn't hurt that Frost, who was cooling his heels in a Billings hospital after surgery to remove the bullet in his shoulder, had a criminal record as well. Though the stockyard foreman wasn't talking, his association with operations director Carigliano, who in turn was linked to mafia contacts, made the possible threat to Cullen Flynn's life even more pressing. Judge Ottey was Cullen's friend, and after reading Reid's request for a search affidavit, she signed the warrant in less than a minute.

The drive was empty. The windows were firmly shut. "Nobody home," Odie surmised.

"No surprise. Guess who rents this house to Cyrus."

"Frost?"

"Close. Carigliano. We need to find a gun or drugs. Let's toss it good."

Reid and Odie went up the disintegrating steps. The deputies trailed behind wearing bulletproof vests and carrying their guns ready. After knocking on the door and announcing their intentions to enter with a search warrant, Reid turned and nodded at the uniforms.

A stocky young officer, still smaller than Odie and ironically named Samson, stepped up and gave the doorknob plate a couple of good kicks. The ugly green door whipped open and slammed against the interior. A putrid odor composed of rotten food, a backed-up toilet, and other unidentifiable smells flew at them like a hot, invisible wall.

Samson gagged and stepped away. "Man, that's ripe."

Before anyone responded, a rat the size of a small cat ran out the front door and between their feet, raced across the porch, and dove off the planking into the grass.

"Damn, did you see that?" Heller, the older deputy, asked, his face twisted in disgust.

"*Rattus Norvegicus.* One of Flynn's roommates," Odie replied with utter seriousness.

Reid was more interested in the smell coming from inside. He walked into the living room, placed the warrant inside his suit jacket, and carefully put on his latex gloves. The joint looked worse than it had the first time. Flies buzzed around the coffee table filled with a mound of unwashed dishes, half-finished cans of beer, and plastic soda bottles. Unwashed clothes littered the floor as if Cyrus had simply disrobed and let the stinking apparel stay where it fell—none of them soiled in a way indicating he was a shackler on a kill floor. Rat turds littered the deteriorating carpet.

Reid walked to the sofa and switched on the pole lamp. It didn't come on, but a black object beside the base caught his eye. He reached down and picked it up. A series of numbers and letters was carefully written in yellow paint on one side.

"He's been gone for a while. Look at the souvenir he left behind."

Odie walked over and surveyed the three-inch black curving stone. "What is that?"

"I think it's a dinosaur claw. Guess we've just got evidence to link Cyrus to the poaching ring. Bag it and tag it." He passed it into Odie's gloved hand, then turned toward the uniforms. "Find out where that smell is coming from. Don't touch anything."

"Looks like the electricity is off," Odie said. He stared at the blank face of a plugged-in digital clock sitting on board and cinder block shelving. He placed the claw inside a manila envelope brought along for that purpose. "Probably didn't pay the electric bill, and the place is locked up tight. Could account for the smell."

Reid moved toward the cushions, pulled them up and found enough food crumbs to feed an army of rats, cigarette butts, unpaid bills, a sock, a pair of scissors, and an empty bottle of iodine tincture. He picked up the bottle.

Next he rifled through the coffee table, where cold medicines had been splayed around before. Among the liquid nighttime medicines, chest ointments, and nasal sprays, he found four empty pillboxes of Contac decongestant. Lower in the pile of trash, he discovered several boxes of wooden matches. From a gun magazine he flipped through, a pack of unopened coffee filters fell to the floor.

"Damn," he cursed. "I should have caught this before. Cyrus is getting tweaked. He's been mixing up personal batches of sidewalk meth with iodine and cold medicine."

Odie nodded when he saw the empty packages. "That's based on old Nazi formula to make small batches of speed. Some pseudoephedrine and other stuff cooked up with toxic chemicals like lye, muriatic acid, acetone, and red phosphorus, and you're set to stay awake for several days. The Germans developed that during WWII to keep the Reich going when their troops couldn't get the manufactured stuff provided by supply lines. Cyrus is lucky he hasn't burned himself with caustic chemicals or died from the fumes."

Reid shook his head. "Too bad he didn't just blow up the whole damn house with him in it. Keep an eye out for some crystal."

They continued their search of the living room and the kitchen. Aside from a wealth of filth, there wasn't much more incriminating evidence. Reid was going through Cyrus' bedroom, a dingy hole with nothing but a bed and a bureau, when Odie came to the doorway,

"Reid, you'd better come and see this."

"What is it?"

"The second bedroom."

"Something good?"

Odie's eyebrows lifted. "Maybe. Maybe not."

"Hokay." Reid accompanied Odie through the living room and down a dark hallway leading past the kitchen and toward the rear of the house. The uniforms were standing before a closed white door. "What's the problem, guys?"

"Got a locked steel door, Lieutenant," replied Deputy Sampson.

Deputy Heller nodded. "We think the smell's coming from in here."

Reid concurred. The stench of a wet foulness was stronger there than anywhere else in the house. The outside of the door had a regular doorknob as well as an exterior deadbolt lock. He knocked on the portal. It was indeed a multi-layer steel door not unlike those used in the construction of FEMA safe rooms. It also felt cool to the touch.

"Looks like a tornado shelter," Reid said.

Odie scowled. "Inside this dump? Rooms like that with temperature controls aren't cheap. Run about ten to twenty grand depending on the size."

"This is the east corner," Reid considered. He looked at Samson. "Go outside. I want to know what's on the exterior. Heller, you go to my car and grab the yellow Geiger counter from the trunk and your battering ram. Odie, give him the keys."

"Yes, sir," Samson replied. Heller nodded. After Odie passed over the key ring, they hurried down the hall, leather belt holsters squeaking.

"You think there's hot bones in there?" Odie queried.

Reid shrugged. He'd filled in everyone at the department that had to know about Outerbridge's task force and the details. "I figured it was better to be safe than sorry. Ansel was right about that."

Odie looked at the manila envelope resting against his groin. "Shit," he said, his eyes widening. He unceremoniously tossed the package down the hall as if it was poison. "You could have reminded me before I carried that around."

Reid started to laugh. He couldn't help himself. Seeing a strapping giant like Odie reduced to near panic was not an ordinary sight. "I didn't even think about it. Relax. I touched it, too. Besides, we had our gloves on. We'll check it."

"It's not funny. Radiation shoots through you like an invisible slug. Future generations of Fiskars could be hanging in the balance. Ivy and I are trying to have a baby, you know."

"Yeah, I know. How's that endeavor going, by the way?"

"None of your business."

The deputies returned and Odie's head jerked toward them. "Hey, check that envelope on the floor with the counter."

Deputy Heller stopped short, set down the heavy metal ram, and looked at the boxy, twelve-inch-long meter with dubious interest. At last he found the power switch and flicked it, pointing the front end toward the floor. The meter clicked occasionally but didn't go wild.

"Looks okay," Heller said. "What's the deal?"

Odie sighed. "Never mind, just bring the package here."

Samson had joined Reid. "The outside is wood siding like the front, but there's a wide steel door that locks from the inside. You could drive a small forklift through there if you had to."

Heller walked forward and scanned the steel door from top to bottom. The meter clicked more than it had in the hall, but it wasn't consistent. "What's in there?"

"Could be some dinosaur fossils containing high levels of uranium," Odie confided.

"Want us to open it?" Heller asked.

Reid looked at Odie. "Just for a second? If it's too hot, we'll close the door right away. According to Ansel, any time of exposure under a minute isn't lethal."

"I guess, but I'm standing back," Odie replied.

"Let's go for it," Samson intoned.

Reid nodded. "Give me the counter. I'll handle the door. You guys bust it and get back."

Reid and Odie moved down the hall to give the deputies room to work. The uniforms took handle positions on either side of the solid, four-foot-long metal device with a flat plate on the front. The first strike bounced off the door like it had never been dealt, but the officers pounded away at the center of the portal with fierce determination. The hallway resounded with a deafening reverberation of metal against metal. The white paint chipped off. More slowly the area around the lock buckled inward. Sweat poured down the deputies' faces and Reid called them to a halt.

"Let's take a breather and get some fresh air."

They took a five-minute break and then were back at it. The deputies removed their heavy black vests beforehand. They pounded away at the door for another ten minutes, then gave up, near exhaustion. The door was severely warped, and the doorknob gone, but it refused to open.

Odie, despite his earlier apprehension, yanked off his suit jacket and picked up the ram in his pumped, herculean arms, then single-handedly hammered the door with incredible power. Five blows later, the deadbolt bent inward and the steel barrier yielded. It rammed against the inside wall as if a tornado had flung it.

The interior was pitch black and warm. The smell of old rock, fresh plaster of Paris, and rotting meat wafted into their faces. Heller pulled a small flashlight from his belt, flicked it on, and handed it to Reid. "You know what that smells like," he said, rolling his eyes.

Odie moved quickly away so Reid could take a reading at the door frame. The meter needle spiked across the dial and clicked loudly at fifty rem. It was high, but not deadly. He flashed the light around.

All of the men peered into the gray-walled room which contained stacks and stacks of small and large plastered casings of all sizes and reached halfway up the eight-foot-high walls. The casings were marked with magic marker. Reid noticed a large, white form on the floor to his right. It was marked *Allosaurus skull. Vernal, Utah*. Above it on the quarter-inch-thick steel wall was a thermostat. It was set at thirty-two degrees Fahrenheit, but without electricity, the steel room had heated up substantially.

The only out-of-place item in the room was the incongruous, zippered black plastic suit bag lying on the floor in the middle of the room. From it came the overwhelming stench of death.

A man-sized lump filled it. Reid took a step inside.

"No," said Odie with concern.

The meter spiked another ten rem. Still bearable. Not Cullen, he prayed. "I've got to know," Reid replied as he moved quickly into the room and bent down.

The meter clicked louder at seventy rem. He pulled back the zipper and the smell of decay roiled at him. Cullen's defrosted face, looking serene despite its countenance of beginning decay, lay before him. Reid held his breath and moved the zipper downward, saw the blue shirt drenched with blood, then the monstrous, gaping chest wound with burnt edges. He thought of Cyrus' remark about gut-shooting deer.

Bile rose in his throat. He stood toward the back of the room and the Geiger counter spiked wildly, shocking him back to reality. The rem hit over a hundred, then fell down twenty points as he skittered toward the door.

Alarmed, Odie shouted, "Get out of there."

In seconds Reid was out of the room, pulling the door closed with fingers along the door edge. It would no longer fit in the frame, but it did stay closed.

"It's Cullen. Shotgun blast to the chest." He looked at the deputies. "I want an amended APB out for Cyrus Flynn. He's considered armed and dangerous. This time it's felony murder. I want Code 10-61 on everything. Limited radio communication with no details. Notify the office by phone to send an ME and forensics team out here pronto. If the feds find out the fossils are here, they'll bust in and take over. I want first crack at this."

"Yes, sir," Heller answered. "We're on it." They left the house, battering ram in tow.

Odie shook his head. "Poor Sheriff Flynn. How long you think he's been here?"

"I saw the wound. When we found the shotgun shell wad, it was already too late."

"If Cyrus was messing with these bones all the time, he could be a walking dead man. He was sick when we were here, but I

figured it might be drugs or a virus bug. You think he knows
about the radiation?"

Reid sighed. "We'll find out. Let's finish the walk-through.
We still have the basement."

Reid and Odie went down into the dimly lighted lower level
and simply perused the area. The whole basement smelled like
roasted nuts, and they knew they were onto something. Since the
house was now a crime scene, they were careful about disturbing
things. However, they easily spotted the open boxes containing the ingredients and glassware supplies used to manufacture
methamphetamine. Plus a box of syringes. All of this accounted
for the basement's smell.

Reid walked over to the water heater, where a small Pyrex
bowl sat on top. Circular white crystals stuck to the inside.
"Looks like two or three grams once it's scraped out."

Odie grinned from giant ear to giant ear. "Enough for twelve
doses. He's cooked himself another long stint in the slammer
with this alone."

A moment later, Samson came down the rickety basement
steps, a cell phone in hand. "Lieutenant, Sheriff Combs wants
to talk to you."

Reid grabbed the device. "Yes, Sheriff?"

"Reid, I just heard. Hell of thing about Cullen. That son-
of-bitch nephew will get a sodium thiopental cocktail if I have
anything to do with it. Did you find the gun?"

"No, sir. Haven't found any guns or ammo. We just got a
small quantity of sidewalk meth and the supplies for making it.
Another couple of nails in the coffin."

"Keep up the good work, Lieutenant. I have some other
news. Just got a call from the FBI in Glasgow. Seems Agent
Outerbridge's helicopter is overdue."

A chill coursed along Reid's spine. He looked at his wristwatch. It was almost five o'clock. All this time, he'd assumed that
Ansel was at the hospital tending to her father. He hadn't wanted
her to go with Parker, but he knew her reasoning was based on
getting to McCone the fastest way possible. Still he could have

made other arrangements for a sheriff's chopper to take her to McCone County if he'd had to, and if she'd given him an hour to set it up. He would have found a way to legitimize the action to Combs and McKenzie.

Reid kept his voice calm and impersonal. "What do they think happened?"

"Seems the feds got a call from the U.S. Air Force Rescue Coordination Center on the East Coast. They're the U.S. authority that receives notification when a satellite control center gets a serial number for an aircraft distress beacon transmitted to them from a satellite flyby. The satellite center got a fleeting signal from a beacon, but it died before they could get a location. A second confirmation flyby later didn't pick up any signal.

"Since the Air Force contacts a local rescue unit to go out and search, they try to avoid false alarms, most of them from beacon malfunctions. It's normal for them to call people who may know pertinent flight info first. The federales can't reach the task force by aircraft radio or cell so they want to speak with you about Outerbridge's departure. Call them. Ask for Agent Ralph Edison. Here's his number."

Reid scrambled for his notebook and pen as Combs read off the digits. "I'll call them."

"Find out more details, and let me know what they say when I arrive," Sheriff Combs announced with enthusiasm. "Looks like the feebees got hung up somewhere, and that's perfect timing for us." He disconnected a second later.

Odie noticed Reid's shocked expression. "What was that all about?"

Reid took a deep breath and swallowed before answering. Odie, if anybody in the department, knew how seriously he looked after Ansel since saving her life the year before. He handed the phone back to Deputy Heller, who discreetly left the basement.

"The FBI copter flying Ansel to the McCone County hospital may have gone down."

"Man, that's bad news. Where is it?"

"They don't know. I've got to talk to the FBI." Reid pulled out his phone. "I'm also leaving after this call. When Combs arrives, cover for me."

Odie scowled like an ogre. "Christ, how am I supposed to do that?"

Reid attempted a wan smile. "Tell him I'm chasing a lead on Cyrus."

"What lead?"

Reid took Odie's manila envelope. "This dinosaur claw. I've got to check something first, but I think I know where it came from."

Chapter 33

*"Misfortunes do not flourish on one path,
they grow everywhere."*
Pawnee

Ansel watched helplessly as Parker took his gun from the holster and set it on the ground in front of Dixie. His stare was one of chilly appraisal. None of this made any sense to her. She'd never related to Dixie, but had never suspected the woman was dangerous.

Cyrus had been listening too, and he called out, "Hey, let me over. Don't leave me here, lady. I was sent to help you."

"Now what, Dixie?" Parker demanded. "You join your buddies who tried to shoot you down in a chopper? They're either very stupid or very pissed at you."

Dixie lost her smile and leveled the Magnum at his head. "I've got Outerbridge's briefcase. They won't do anything to me." She stepped forward and grabbed up Parker's gun. "Honey, you'd better get Parker to shut up."

Ansel swallowed. The only weapon she had in her possession was the scissors in the medical kit inside her purse, but they had been badly dulled by her bark-stripping activities. Dixie had control over everything now: guns, cell phones, maps, GPS unit, emergency beacon, clothes, and Outerbridge's locked briefcase. God knew what was in there.

Ansel held up her hand in a calming motion. "Just go on your way, Dixie, and leave us. It would look better if we died in the Badlands anyway. You'd be clear of a murder charge and could tell the FBI any story you wanted."

Parker grinned. "So what's your real story? If you're not with the poachers, you must be with the mafia."

"Lady," screamed Cyrus. "Get me out of here. I'm not feeling good. I'm sick."

"Stupid doper," Dixie complained under her breath. "You can rot there for all I care," she screamed back. Then she focused on Parker again. "Neither. I'm leaving, and if you try to follow me, I'll kill you. It's that simple.

"You won't get away, Lady," Cyrus yelled, his voice sounding near panic. "I'll find you." There was the sound of a shotgun being cocked, then a gun blast as Cyrus angrily fired at the boulder. He seemed to go crazy and fired two more shots at the unmovable stone barrier.

Ansel covered her ears as the ammunition slammed into the other side of the rock. Parker suddenly rushed Dixie, who had momentarily squeezed her eyes shut and dropped the gun's barrel toward the ground. She recovered in an instant and the Magnum spit fire.

Another blast filled the tiny ravine before a bullet thumped into Parker's left thigh. He grunted and went down like a pole-axed bull, rolled on the ground, and clutched his leg. Blood darkened his jeans with a frightful scarlet plume.

"I warned you," Dixie sputtered.

Ansel didn't even think, simply rushed to Parker while Dixie stood surveying her handiwork. The wound was bad. Parker sat up, trying to stanch the blood flow with his hands. He didn't seem to be in too much pain, but his eyes were wide black spheres. She took off her windbreaker and twisted it tightly into a nylon tourniquet before tying it above Parker's wound.

"It's going to be all right," she said, not believing it. "This will help stop the bleeding."

Parker looked into her eyes and smiled. "Don't worry. It doesn't hurt that much."

He's going into shock, Ansel thought. Her icy gaze fell upon Dixie, who was gathering all the bags together. "At least leave us some clothes. The temperatures drop at night. I've got to keep him warm."

"I'll be all right," Parker insisted, even as blood continued to stain his pants leg and he began to shake a bit. Pain was slowly creeping into his consciousness.

Dixie gathered one duffel and the briefcase in one hand, the gun still poised in the other. She kicked the other tote toward Ansel. "You follow me and you're dead." Seconds later she backed down the ravine and disappeared around a brush-strewn bend.

Ansel could care less as she dug through the duffel and found another of Parker's long-sleeved shirts. She helped him put it on. "I'm got to dress the wound. Lean against the wall and rest."

Parker did as she instructed and said nothing as she pulled the medical kit from her purse and opened it. With great difficulty, she used the dull scissors to cut away a large hole in his jeans. Even that little bit of activity caused blood to gurgle from his thigh despite the tourniquet. She used one of Dixie's tees to clean away most of the blood around the wound, then used antiseptic wipes to clean it as carefully as possible. More blood surged out and Parker winced.

"Sorry I got us into this mess, Ansel," he whispered with great effort. "Bandage me up and get out of here. Just keep away from Dixie."

Ansel smeared the whole tube of double antibiotic ointment over the leaking wound. "I'm not leaving you." Three large, non-adhesive, sterile dressing pads went on next.

"Get help. We need water or we're history." Parker gritted his teeth against some unseen agony.

She unwound a spool of elastic bandage. "Don't argue with me. I've got to get this around your leg and keep some pressure on it. Ready?"

"Hard-headed Indian," he cursed but lifted the leg by pushing down on his boot heel just enough for her to start wrapping the bandage tightly under and over his thigh. Despite his grunts, Ansel didn't stop. Blood colored the bandages crimson, soaking through to the elastic wrap. Ansel loosened the tourniquet but left it on.

"Swallow these," she instructed, pulling two Tylenol tablets out of a foil pack.

Parker took them and gagged as they went down. He gazed at her sheepishly, eyes droopy. "No spit."

"How do you feel?"

"Like I'm in the Badlands with a cap in my leg. Get out of here, Ansel, please."

Ansel said nothing, but packed up what was left of the sparse medical supplies. She looked through the duffel bag again. A pair of Dixie's jeans caught her eye, and one of Parker's belts. "I'm going to change into these instead of this damn skirt. No gawking."

"Killjoy."

She took off her knee-length boots, unbuttoned her skirt front, and pulled the dust-stained black fabric off. She neatly folded it and placed it back inside the bag. The hot air swirling around her underwear and sweat-drenched legs felt wonderful. Parker watched for only a moment, then closed his eyes. He was losing consciousness, and she worried that the bullet had clipped an artery.

Dixie's jeans were too long and too wide, but she adjusted the cuffs and scrunched up the belt line with his belt, which flopped in front of her like a calf's tongue. The boots went back on. This getup was much better for the climbing and bushwhacking.

"Sounds quiet on the other side," Ansel said. Her head bobbed toward the boulder.

"So what. You're headed the other way." Parker's eyes were still closed.

"Wrong. I'm going back to the box canyon."

His eyes sprung open. "Are you nuts?"

"What I need is the other way." Ansel left the medical kit on the ground next to Parker, but situated her purse strap diagonally across her chest. She took one of the yellow ponchos from the duffel before positioning the ladder more firmly on the boulder. As she got on it, she hoped fervently that Rusty had left the ravine.

Parker started to get up when he saw her, then groaned and sat back down, clutching his leg in agony. "God dammit," he fumed. "Get off that ladder, Ansel."

She couldn't look at him so she went quickly up the rungs. At the top, she peered over the boulder very carefully, mindful of Rusty's shotgun. "He's gone. I'll be back in an hour." She got on the boulder, gauze strip to the top rung in hand, and pulled the ladder up.

Parker watched, eyes hard brown stones of anger. "What the hell are you after?"

"Medicine for your leg." Ansel let the ladder down on the other side and descended before he could say anything.

"Ansel, be careful," Parker yelled a moment later.

The boulder had been badly pockmarked by lead shot, some of which littered the ground. The tree limbs they hadn't used for the ladder were thrown all over, and the indigenous vegetation torn into pieces. Rusty's rage had been directed at everything in his path. She found Parker's walking stick and picked it up. It was a weapon of sorts.

Ansel stepped over the wreckage, used the stick, and moved along the ravine, her senses attuned for any unusual sound or movement that meant Rusty was near. She made good time, and the previously cleared path gave her a long line of sight. Nobody could ambush her.

Suddenly a stabbing pain shot through her abdomen, and she almost buckled on the trail. Heat cramps. The excessive heat without water was messing with her body salts. She should be resting in the shade, not walking. Gasping deeply, she waited a minute until the knot in her lower body eased before continuing again. Sweat coursed down her chest and back from the passing pain and yet more valuable body salts and liquids seeped out of her body. The light-headedness she now felt was not a good sign.

Ansel poured all of her concentration into watching the open prairie, and the closer she got to the exit point, the more she was sure that Rusty had returned to the black copter. By the time she finally neared the exit between the bluffs, her thirst was all-encompassing. She willed herself to keep her eyes only on the swatch of brown prairie now visible between the craggy ravine walls, and her feet shambling forward without passing out.

"Please help me find water," she said aloud before she realized it. As she reached the slotted entranceway, she noticed a shotgun lying on the ground amid a pile of brush and halted immediately. Rusty's gun.

Ansel approached it on her toes, Indian style, and carefully picked it up. A quick check of the weapon's chamber proved that it was fully loaded with two cartridges. She tossed her walking stick aside. Where was Rusty and why had he left the shotgun?

Her answer came when she moved through the brushy, dead fall of the entranceway. To her left, where the canyon wall made its turn along the bluff's inner rim, she saw Rusty's body. He was face down in the prairie grass, his long, scraggly red hair splayed across the ground. He was either unconscious or dead. There was no sign of the black copter.

Ansel cocked the trigger and walked toward him. Her mind was set that if he was alive and tried to hurt her, she'd shoot him on the spot. However, six feet away, she could see his chest expanding and collapsing. Her eyes immediately riveted to the round camo-cloth canteen lying beside him. Water. Her finger in the trigger guard was sweaty with apprehension and adrenalin. Damn, she didn't need this. She had to get back to Parker, but she wanted that canteen more than anything else at the moment.

"It's Ansel Phoenix. Turn over, Rusty." The barrel of the gun was aimed at his head. There was no response. "Don't play possum with me, you bastard. Look at me."

Still nothing. Ansel kicked him hard in the ribs with her right boot and his body shifted. He didn't make a sound. He had to be out cold to ignore that blow to his side. Her finger eased on the trigger but never left it as she moved closer, edged her boot under his ribs, and used all her leg strength to lift and kick him over onto his back.

Cyrus' face was deathly pale and blotchy. Garish brown freckles stood out against his bleached-out skin tones. His powder blue ranch shirt, the same one he'd worn in Billings, had ridden up his chest, and she saw the nickel-sized, hemorrhagic spots beneath the skin of his stomach. She remembered the smell of vomit on his breath when he grabbed her at the hotel, and he'd told Dixie that he was sick. Maybe he'd been delirious and dropped his gun and canteen, she reasoned.

A moment later, Ansel's blood turned to ice as it dawned on her that Rusty had the classic symptoms of radiation sickness.

The intellectual revelation both stunned and horrified her. Even more chilling was the fact that she didn't know how she felt about Rusty's condition on a personal level. What was she feeling right now, knowing that the man who had roamed through her psyche for years was dying an unimaginably horrible death? Did she feel vindicated or cheated? Was she happy or unhappy? Glad or ashamed? Those questions were too complicated for her now.

Ansel snatched up the canteen and paced backward where she could set down the shotgun and open the container in relative safety. It was half full, and an almost primal frenzy possessed her as she unscrewed the cap. She didn't spill a drop as she tilted the canteen against her cracked lips and took three healthy swallows.

The cool, sweet purity of the liquid shocked her senses but left her wanting more, even as she gulped a few mouthfuls. It was exquisite on her tongue, and she tore the canteen from her lips in order to prevent guzzling it all down. If she did, she'd really get sick, and Parker needed the water more. Ansel capped the spout and placed the canister over her shoulder as she had the purse. Then she picked up the shotgun and left Rusty. He could wait.

She walked directly to the dead fall where the eight-inch-wide puffballs grew. The fungi circle was still intact. Some were solid white, others brown with tiny holes beginning to open on the top. There were four of these.

She used one finger to gently poke through the first puffball, and a smoky whiff of thousands of spores flew upward. Perfect. After opening her saddle purse flap, she yanked the collapsible puffball from its stem, folded it up as best she could, and carefully pushed it into her bag. The three other puffballs followed. As she worked, she noticed that the air around her had become cooler and the sun wasn't as bright. A brisk wind jetted against her back, causing her long hair to flap angrily in her face.

Ansel turned to stare into the prairie. Above the north rim of the canyon, a strange creamy-white haze filled half the sky. Not clouds or the predicted edge of a squall line supposed to hit that afternoon. This was something more solid, like a wall of churning smoke stretching from west to east across the horizon with just the top part evident above the canyon walls. The slowly setting sun wasn't even visible through the haze. The creamy mass shifted within itself, eddied, and turned smutty brown. The cloud traveled quickly and spanned thousands of feet high.

Ansel stood as a sandy gust of air scoured her face and every hair on her body rose in atavistic alarm. Black blizzard, her mind screamed.

A dust storm.

Chapter 34

"The pathway to glory is rough
and many gloomy hours obscure it."
Chief Black Hawk

The dilemma of what to do with Rusty pounded in Ansel's skull. Leave him to the dust storm or drag him with her, if she could, back to the shelter of the ravine? He might tell her where Cullen was.

However, the child inside her wailed for revenge. Let him rot as Dixie had decided, the nearly drowned little girl deep inside her brain screamed. But there was a grown woman inside there, too. She heard her mother's voice as if her words of Blackfoot wisdom were being carried on the escalating prairie winds. Ansel wished she was wearing her Iniskim and listened.

"Obey the teachings of *iit-tsi-pa-tah-pii-op*, the Source of Life and the source of the teachings of the Grandfather and Grandmother Spirit. Love one another and help one another in all matters."

Decision made, Ansel got the shotgun and ran toward Rusty, bent down, and shook him roughly. "Wake up. You've got to move. Now."

To her surprise, Rusty's eyes opened, and he groaned angrily. "You. Leave me alone. I'm sick."

"You'll be dead if you don't. There's a dust storm coming, and you've got radiation poisoning. Some of those fossils you handled were full of uranium. You need a doctor." She rose and stepped back, gun pointed at him. "Stand up or I'll leave you."

Rusty's eyes had widened into fearful emerald orbs. He looked at the far horizon and then down at the horrible blotches on his body. "You're lying. I've got the flu."

Ansel shook her head. "I don't have time to convince you. If you can walk, get up. Try to hurt me, and you'll never reach a hospital, Rusty. I promise you that. You lead."

He winced profusely as he managed to stand with a wobbly effort. "You stole my gun and my water," he said, eyes dazed.

Ansel cocked the trigger. "Shut up and walk."

Rusty shuffled slowly to the ravine entrance and Ansel glanced behind her. The immense sand cloud was closer and larger, but hadn't yet rolled over the top of the box canyon. At this rate, they'd never get back to Parker before the storm hit and dumped tons of blinding, stinging sand on them. She couldn't warn Parker or make an impromptu shelter if she didn't get back in time. They all might succumb if that were the case.

"Hurry it up," she ordered as they entered the ravine.

Rusty continued to be slow, not because he was stalling, but because he was truly weak and unsteady on his feet. As Ansel followed, the vision of this pathetic excuse for a man whittled away at her icy, unsympathetic resolve to keep him alive only for Reid to deal with later. She was actually beginning to feel sorry for him with every dragging step, feverish back glance, and grunt of pain.

Ansel couldn't imagine what was happening inside his irradiated body. What she knew about radiation sickness was minimal. It could cause damage to the intestines and lungs, as well as mess with white blood cells. In severe cases, it caused cancer. How long Cyrus had been exposed, how acutely, and how long ago would determine his rate of death. Combine the radiation with his drug-wracked body and the terminal possibilities were endless.

Suddenly Rusty collapsed to his hands and knees between the craggy bluff walls and began vomiting up bile and blood. Ansel stood back watching, her heart bucking in her chest. She was afraid to get too close. If he tried to jump her in the close confines, her ability to manipulate the gun effectively would be impaired. Still, the urge to rush to his aid was there, but she couldn't give in to it.

When he was done gagging, Rusty lay on the ground panting. "I can't move," he said in a hoarse whisper. "Help me." He looked back at her, sallow death-face imploring. "I don't want to die in this ass crack. Those fuckers did this to me," he wailed.

Even now, he'd take no responsibility for his own actions, Ansel thought. She released the shotgun trigger and leaned the weapon against the wall, then pulled the pre-packaged yellow poncho out of the purse from behind the folded puff balls.

"Rusty, you can't go on, but I have to. I'm going to leave you this poncho and hood. It will help keep the dust out of your face so your tongue and jaws won't get parched by hot air. Otherwise let the sand cover you. It will keep you cooler. I'll be back as soon as I can."

"Man, don't leave me here alone. I never meant to hurt you. I was just joking at the pond. Don't do this to me."

Strangely enough, the mention of the stock pond didn't upset her. She walked toward him and tossed the poncho pack. "It's not personal, Rusty. I just can't drag you all the way. I'm not feeling good either and I've got to hurry. You'll be all right between these bluff walls. Do you want some water before I leave?"

Rusty shook his head. "I can't keep it down. You take it."

"You're sure?"

"Yeah," he whimpered, head on the ground. "Just get out."

Ansel stared down at him. "Before I go, I want to know what happened to Cullen."

Cyrus looked up at her, bright, greasy red hair flopping away from his once boyishly handsome features. He looked a hundred years old. "I killed him," he said. "At my house."

A lump fell into Ansel's nauseated stomach like a boulder. Her father had been right. "Where's his body?"

"Put him in the steel room at my house with the bones I've been watching for months."

"You killed your uncle because he found the bones?"

"Nah, he saw the dinosaur claw," Rusty babbled feverishly. "With the numbers."

Confusion danced through Ansel's heat-exhausted brain. "What dinosaur claw?"

"One I lifted from Yancy."

"Hillard Yancy?"

Rusty managed to nod, then collapsed again, his breath wheezing in and out like a dying animal.

Ansel picked up the shotgun. Cullen hadn't deserved a death like that, and the urge to shoot Rusty was a rampaging bull inside her aching head. She could do it, and no one would know the difference if she claimed it was self defense. Would it be a mercy killing or murder? She fingered the steel trigger with cold calculation. She knew she could do it.

Instead she stepped over the man and said, "Rusty, whatever happens, I forgive you for trying to kill me twice."

Then she forced her prickling limbs to jog through the ravine toward Parker, praying that he wasn't already dead.

◇◇◇

Parker was unconscious when Ansel finally got up the ladder and back over the boulder to reach him. By that time, the wind had started whipping through the ravine behind her as a moaning gust that sent loose dirt, leaves, and branches flying. The sky seen through the crack overhead was gray-brown. The dust storm wouldn't be far behind.

Parker lay on his back, legs spread. She bent over him, yanking the canteen off her shoulder at the same time. "Parker, I've got water." When he didn't stir, she surveyed his bandages. They were awash in blood, which pooled between his legs on the dusty ground. She pressed the canteen to his cracked lips. "Drink," she ordered roughly as the water tumbled across his face, none of it getting into his mouth. He was out cold.

"Damn."

At least his head was cool. No fever. Abandoning the effort to hydrate him, Ansel took some of the water herself. It was better to drink when she needed to. Rationing water was a fallacy. More water inside you from the beginning gave you the resilience to stay alive longer. When she felt somewhat quenched, she tightened the tourniquet again and went about the job of stripping off the bloody bandages. The wound looked puffy and ragged. A four-inch hole peppered with pellet shots around the edges.

She methodically pulled out the four puffballs from her purse, opened them and scooped out handfuls of smoky, microscopic yellow-brown spores, then dumped them into the open wound. Hopefully they would clot the blood that Parker hadn't already lost. Last she tossed the soaked gauze away and simply rewound the elastic bandage back around the spore-laden wound and loosened the tourniquet.

It took her fifteen full minutes to drag Parker's dead weight against the boulder. She then placed the ladder at a cross angle above him and against the ravine walls so that she could tie clothes from the duffel to the forward side railing. The impromptu roof with side panels might help reduce abrading dust after the storm hit full force. She carried the second poncho with her inside the grossly inadequate shelter. They'd need it to cover their faces.

Ansel settled with her back against the boulder and with Parker squeezed right next to her between the cliff walls. Her last effort to prepare herself to ride out the dust storm was to break apart the smaller white puffball she'd brought back and to eat some of the inner layer of soft white meat. The mushroom's outer flesh was dry and bland, but her stomach welcomed it and the few sips of water she used to wash the food down.

She finished the meal just as the sky above her turned a menacing earthen tone and a blustering wind howled through the ravine carrying a blast of dust so fine that it coated everything it passed upon first touch. Ansel closed her purse and readied the poncho to be held over their heads. Dust began to fall from everywhere: above, behind them, and in front of them.

Sand, rocks, and grit funneled into the ravine as a howling monster that could not only be heard but seen and felt. Ansel pulled the poncho over their faces and held onto it with all her strength, legs pulled against her into a tight ball. Parker didn't stir and she envied his oblivion. For her, each minute would be a torture of blinding dust, coughing fits, tear-stained eyes, gasping breaths, scoured skin, and straining muscles until the storm passed. Who knew how long that would be.

As the clothes canopy contracted, shuddered, and snapped, Ansel thought of Reid. By now he probably knew she hadn't arrived at the hospital and that the FBI chopper was missing, but he couldn't help her. Unless the copter emergency beacon had been received before the aircraft burned, the cavalry wasn't coming.

Soon the sun set and darkness swallowed the ravine like a dinosaur's maw. The dust was everything and it inhabited all available space as a swirling, choking miasma. Within two hours, it covered the landscape in a two-inch layer of grainy, talcum-fine particles that didn't miss a seam, crack, or crease.

Despite the poncho, with every breath Ansel sucked in grit that scraped the inside of her mouth and tongue before burning down her esophagus into her lungs. Parker slept fitfully, coughing and sputtering but never reaching consciousness. The corners of her mouth and eyes, her nostrils, and her lips were caked with dust as well, and the feeling of suffocation was a constant companion as she huddled behind the hot, stiff protection of the plastic poncho. Parker's bandages were coated with dust, and she could only pray that the puffball pollen had protected the injury from infection.

Just holding the poncho over Parker's face was fatiguing her arms and shoulders, which screamed with muscle pain. She didn't know how much longer she could stand this. She was tired and physically exhausted. But there was nowhere to go. Wandering into the blinding maelstrom would be fatal.

The winds had reached incredible speed through the ravine and the sound of flying debris hitting the bluff walls and the boulder was an endless succession of smacks, slaps, and booming rock crashes. She imagined that everything from the bluff tops was breaking loose and falling into the channel above them. A ray of hope sliced through Ansel's gloomy thoughts. If Dixie had been caught in the open by this storm, her chances of survival were slim. Maybe she was still close by, huddled within the ravine walls, riding out the storm. That meant that the briefcase was nearby and there was still a chance that Ansel could get it back from the paleontologist.

At last, Ansel's lids closed, and the poncho slipped off her head. Sleep stole over her in seconds. She dreamed of Reid. He was telling her something, but she couldn't understand him. His words were garbled and broken as if his voice were nothing but a static-ridden radio frequency.

"I'm coming," the dream Reid finally said quite clearly.

Ansel smiled in her sleep. "I know," she mumbled. "I'm waiting."

Chapter 35

"Seek the ways of the eagle, not the wren."
Omaha

"I'm here to see Agent Broderick," Reid Dorbandt said to the pretty blonde ranger standing behind the wooden counter at the Red Water station. Her name tag read P. EASTOVER, and Reid realized that she was the BLM station ranger who told Ansel about the fossil thefts in Glendive and Sidney. "Is he here?"

A shadow rolled across Eastover's face. "Yes, he is. He expects you?"

"I doubt it." Reid pulled the left side of his jacket aside and fully displayed his holster and sheriff's badge which hung from his shirt pocket. "Tell him Lieutenant Dorbandt wants to talk."

"Just a minute." Eastover left the counter and walked through a closed door.

Reid occupied his time surveying the room, which was nothing more than a tiny alcove with plaster walls, wood flooring, and square-beam trusses. The obligatory conservation and BLM guidelines for government land regulations filled the walls, tables, and rotating display stands throughout the tiny space. The whole place looked daunting and complicated. Uncle Sam in a box with too many instructions for the care and feeding, he thought as Eastover strode into the room looking annoyed.

"He can't see you. Would you like to make an appointment?"

Reid smiled and walked around the counter. "Yeah, I'll do it." He marched past the barrier's corner.

"Sir, you shouldn't go through there," Eastover said, without budging from her spot, "but I guess I can't stop you. Personally, I'd leave while I could." She smiled weakly, signaling that her duty as far as she intended to perform it was finished.

Reid opened the door and grinned. "Thanks for the warning."

He went down a hall leading to a quad of offices, one of which was occupied. Broderick shuffled papers from behind a desk. Reid hustled into the room, pleasure sparking at seeing the agent's surprised expression.

"Get out, Reid."

Reid closed the door behind him. "We're going to talk."

Broderick threw a sheaf of forms down on his gray metal desk. His eyes were bullets. "No, *we're* not, but you're going to get sacked for this stunt, Dorbandt." He reached for the black phone on his desk.

"You'd better hear me out, Broderick, because I'm going to make you a hero whether you deserve it or not."

The agent's scowl deepened, but his hand hovered above the device. "Oh, really? How's that?"

Reid pulled the claw from his coat pocket and set it, numbers side up, on the pile of forms. "With this. I'll also tell you everything you want to know about the FBI op."

Broderick moved his hand back and picked up the crescent-shaped rock. "Talk fast."

"I intend to." Reid sat down in a gray fabric chair in front of the desk. "A lot has happened in the last forty-eight hours so I'll start from the beginning."

It took him ten minutes to tell Broderick the abridged version of Ansel's cooperation in assisting Agent Outerbridge with the Operation Dragon sting, the Billings hotel shooting, the raid on Cyrus Flynn's house where Cullen's body was discovered along with irradiated fossils and, finally, the missing status of the FBI plane.

"So what has all this got to do with me?" Broderick demanded.

Reid took the fossil out of his hand. "This claw belongs to Hillard Yancy from Earthly Pleasures in Sidney. I know because it's listed in his sale catalog. I assume you've talked to him regarding his store break-in during your own investigation into the attempted museum theft?"

Broderick leaned back in his chair. "Of course."

"Then you know it wasn't one of the items Yancy lists as stolen."

"True. Get to the point."

"I found this at Cyrus Flynn's house. I think Yancy either gave it to him or Cyrus lifted it when he was at the store discussing their poaching plans together. It's no secret that Cyrus suffers from chronic light-fingers disease. Maybe this fossil is what got Cullen killed."

The agent shrugged. "That's pretty thin, Dorbandt. Yancy's an odd duck, but that doesn't make him a poacher."

"How about the fact that Yancy retired two years ago as a paleogeologist consultant for the Wonsits Valley Oil and Gas Field near Vernal, Utah? I did some digging of my own. His job was to test for naturally reoccurring radioactive materials in the oil and gas wells in the Morrison Formation so company excavators, preparators, and researchers wouldn't accidentally incur any health risks by handling hot rock. You think it's just a coincidence that a pile of uranium-laden Vernal fossils got swiped and ended up in Cyrus' house? I don't."

"How do you know the fossil cache inside Cyrus' house came from Vernal?"

"I saw the labels on the plaster jackets myself. They were stashed in a steel room built right into the house but disguised as a bedroom. A Geiger counter told me how hot they were. Shit, I'm surprised they didn't glow in the dark. Yancy knew exactly where the Vernal fossils were so they could be heisted, and Cyrus babysat them. Right now Flynn is probably dying from radiation exposure and doesn't even know it. Who knows how many other people have been made sick. Yancy's upscale gallery is nothing but a front for the sale of stolen bones to the mafia. I'd stake my reputation on it."

Broderick rubbed his beard thoughtfully. "You are staking your reputation. And mine, if I swallow this tainted bait whole. What do you want from me?"

Reid put the claw in his pocket. "I need you to take me into the Badlands. According to the flight plan Outerbridge's pilot filed in Billings, the ERT was going to fly over the Hell Creek area. That's approximately where the satellite control center got a brief emergency beacon blip before it disappeared. Get me a helicopter, and I'll let you take all the glory for finding and saving the FBI team, plus cracking open the poaching ring through Yancy."

Reid held his breath and tried to look pleased with the idea of handing the jerk his own case-breaking lead. He needed that chopper. Ansel was in trouble. He felt it in his gut. If the copter had crashed, Ansel could be lying injured somewhere without hope of medical care. He pushed away the unsettling and fleeting thought that Ansel could also be in the wilds with Parker Standback and enjoying every minute of it.

"Why don't you get a police copter?" Broderick fished.

"I don't have the time to push this through regular channels. We need to move on this."

The agent stared at Dorbandt. "Is Ansel Phoenix on that chopper?"

"I don't have any idea."

Broderick rolled forward in his chair, and it creaked mightily. "Bullshit. She is, all right. I can tell. You've got a real lightning bug up your butt over her, don't you? Well, I'm not as enamored of Miss Phoenix as you are, Dorbandt. I'm here to do my job. Something you've obviously lost your perspective about. You're pathetic."

Reid allowed the insults to roll over his back like water. "Yancy's got a Class 1 commercial pilot's license. That means he's chopper qualified. He may have forced Outerbridge's aircraft down. I sent a Sidney cop over to check out Yancy's shop. It's locked up tight. He's gone. Check the facts if you don't believe me."

"You're certifiable." Broderick rose from his chair and pointed to a map of Montana pegged to the stark white wall behind the desk. "Haven't you heard the news? There's a seventy-mile-an-hour dust storm blowing over the Badlands as we speak."

Dorbandt maintained his calm even though his mouth almost dropped open. "I've been busy."

"It came down from Canada on the leading edge of a thunderstorm. Right now there's a cloud wall sweeping over Hell Creek carrying seven million tons of dust with it. Nobody's flying until it clears up. That could be a few hours or a few days."

"The NOAA must have some idea when it will blow over. That's when we go in and find the helicopter."

"If it crashed," Broderick snorted. "Aircraft beacons go bad all the time, either from old batteries or electrical shorts. Hell, half the government planes never get overhauled and inspected when they should be, and equipment just disintegrates from overuse or neglect. It was a false alarm at best. Besides, it's a CAP job to search for crash survivors, not the BLM's."

"You're making a mistake. Something has happened to that plane. The FBI doesn't even know where it is. The Civil Air Patrol won't fly unless the Air Force Center tells them to. And they won't do that unless the satellite center says a beacon signal was primed. We've already lost five hours. People could be dying, Broderick. What are you going to do?"

"Me? I'm leaving. Tomorrow I fly back to the state office." Broderick grinned and grabbed his spotless Smoky hat from a rack beside the map. He carefully adjusted it on his bull-headed skull. "Your department has a face for the museum poacher, and it's only a matter of time before he's identified. I'll just let you mop up that mess while I take care of the Big Toe Museum footprints."

Angry heat flushed Reid's cheeks. "That's what this refusal to help is about, huh? The fact that Sheriff Combs got a photo of the museum poacher out on the wires before you could nab him?"

"No, before you got the facial reconstruction done. You've spearheaded the whole poaching investigation with the help of your Indian scout, Phoenix. She's been spying and reporting back to you like a loyal pet. Both of you can crash and burn as far as I'm concerned."

"But you're going to screw the museum, aren't you?" Reid growled. "Taking their fossils away will be your last vindictive act, won't it?"

Broderick walked past him. "Just adhering to BLM policies. And, Dorbandt, the next time I see you near this property, I'll arrest you for trespassing." He exited the office in seconds.

Reid didn't move. He couldn't. He was tired and partly paralyzed by the implications of Broderick's departure. Going to Sheriff Combs and requesting a plane or helicopter from the department was his last and only hope of finding the FBI aircraft. And he knew that the chances of convincing Bucky to support such a speculative, dangerous, and expensive course of action would have no more effect than pouring water on a drowned rat. Still, he would try.

"You okay?"

Reid turned in his seat. Ranger Eastover stared at him inquiringly. "I'm on my way out." He got up.

"You're a friend of Ansel Phoenix?" When he stared at her blankly, Eastover added, "I listened through the door. Couldn't help myself. He's such a prick."

"Yes, Ranger Eastover. He is a prick, but Ansel's my good friend. I think she's in trouble."

Eastover pulled a business card from her pants pocket and stared at it carefully. "She gave me this when I went with Broderick to interview her. I liked her. Sure would hate to see anything happen to her." She fixed Reid with a cunning gaze.

Reid nodded. "Me, too. Any suggestions?"

"My brother, Adam, is a duster. Keeps his plane at the Swoln agricultural airstrip. He'd fly you to Hell Creek in a blizzard if I asked him to." Eastover's face erupted into a broad grin. "Bet that would really piss Broderick off, don't you? Especially after he'd passed up the opportunity."

"And especially if you solved the poaching case and saved the FBI team," Reid added, eyes twinkling. "Can you stomach being a disobedient hero, Ranger Eastover?"

"Call me Pam. We're going to have one hell of a trip ahead of us if we're dodging a dust storm. Might as well be on familiar terms."

"Right, Pam. I'm Reid. You won't regret this. I promise."

"Have you got a copy of the FBI route filed with the FAA? Gotta make a call and fill in Adam before we head to Swoln."

"Sure. In my car. I'll go get it." Reid started through the door, feeling a great weight lift from his chest.

Pam stepped aside to let him pass. "Oh, speaking of stomachs, bring your Dramamine. If we don't stall from dust clogging the engine intakes, we'll still have winds trying to knock us into the ground."

Reid worried more about what would happen once they *were* on the ground rather than in the air. His return look was pensive as he spoke to the ranger.

"And you bring all the firepower you can. We won't have any backup."

Chapter 36

"The rain falls on the just and unjust."
Hopi

Ansel awoke violently and struck her head on the boulder pressed against her back. The poncho was gone, swept away by the wind. Through the swirling dust and darkness, she could see no sign of it. Overhead, lightning zigzagged across the sky-crack and illuminated the ravine for a several seconds.

As she rubbed her head through gritty hair, she saw that the airborne dust had thinned considerably along with the gale-force winds. Excitement and relief coursed through her. The dust storm was abating, and the thunderstorm Parker had told her about was right behind it.

Ansel turned and prodded the man, whose head and body were covered with dust. He hadn't stirred in hours, but his chest was moving. Lightning and thunder clashed again.

"Parker, wake up," she yelled.

He groaned and turned his head, causing dust to avalanche off his hat and down his face. Ansel wiped away the excess powder as best she could. Her motions prompted him to open his eyes at last. He coughed, spitting out dust through chapped lips and gagging up grit-filled phlegm.

"Ansel," he croaked. "What happened?"

"A dust storm. It's almost over. How do you feel?"

"Like sandpaper."

Ansel smiled. "If you're joking, you'll live." She picked up the dust-buried canteen. "Drink some water."

Parker weakly brushed powder off his chest. "Water? From where?"

"I found it and a shotgun. Probably Cyrus lost them," she lied. Parker knew nothing about Rusty, and she didn't have time to explain things. He looked at her dubiously but didn't argue.

With her assistance, Parker didn't waste a drop of water this time. She let him drink several gulps before taking it back. "Drink what you want but in small quantities." Next she pulled some edible puffball from her purse. "Eat this."

He scrutinized the canteen, the clothes-covered ladder crossways over his head, and then the white, spongy lump in his hands. "What is it?"

"Mushroom. It won't hurt you."

He shook his head. "You're amazing."

"I've got to look at the wound." Ansel lifted his leg a bit and began unwrapping the dirt-laden bandages.

"It doesn't hurt as much. I guess I passed out on you. Sorry."

Ansel shrugged. "I'm not surprised. It looks better though. I found plant medicine that helped the blood to clot, but you shouldn't move too far. I don't know how good this temporary fix is." She rewound the bandages.

Parker bit into the puffball and chewed hungrily. "Miracle medicine, too? The FBI should recruit you on a permanent basis."

"No, thanks. It's going to rain. I've got to get moving."

Parker's attention riveted to her. "You're leaving again?"

"We need help. Beyond this bluff there's two ranch roads." Ansel got her legs under her and crawled on her hands and knees from under the shelter. She stood stiffly and swatted great mounds of dust off her clothes, hat, and exposed skin and hair.

Parker stared hard. "How do you know that? I didn't see anything on the BLM maps."

"Ranch roads aren't on those maps. Besides, I saw them from the air before we crashed. They'll lead to people."

Raindrops fell into the wash through the sky-strip and pattered lightly on the dust-choked ground, dimpling the gully with mini-craters. Ansel looked up between the bluff walls as lightning flickered. Soon, the need for water would be solved by a capricious Mother Nature.

"I've got to go." She took nothing with her this time; the urgency to find help was her only interest.

"Take a poncho."

Since he didn't know that she'd left one poncho with Rusty, she couldn't mention the fact that the only one left had blown away. "I have one in my purse. Don't worry," Ansel replied, feeling comfortable with the white lie. "I'm leaving the shotgun."

Parker eyes grew hard. "Damn, I feel so useless. Listen to me, Ansel. Promise you won't mess with Dixie or the poachers. There's no way to beat them without weapons."

"I'll be careful." She pecked him on the cheek before he could say anything else, then turned away.

Never looking back, she headed down the wash, moving several quick paces whenever lightning revealed the twists and outcrops of the brush and rock-strewn path before her. As she walked, it seemed that the more the dust dissipated, the more the rainstorm increased. The thunder came closer and closer, as if trailing her along the ravine top. Raindrops changed from gentle splatters into large, heavy drops falling in a cold, gushing curtain.

Soon Ansel was sloshing through ankle-deep dust turned into a gooey quagmire. From above her, storm-ravaged ponderosa limbs and pine needles began washing down on her along with sandy grit. Once clear rainwater turned brown as it coursed down the bluff walls into the crack where she moved like a wet specter spotlighted by intermittent flashes of fiery orange hue.

Luck provided her with a break, however. Twenty minutes after leaving Parker she found her yellow poncho. It was snagged on a small boulder. She put it on, heedless of its muddy interior, and proceeded. Soon after, the sound of gurgling water rivulets across stone filled Ansel's ears along with the chattering of her teeth. Hours of scorching heat had been replaced by the new torture of frigid water against her sand-blasted skin. Her face, neck, and hands stung with pain. She pushed forward, determined to reach the southern Badlands opening to freedom.

All the while a primal panic threatened to consume her. The wet, the darkness, and the cold attacked all her senses. It was like being in the stock pond all over again. But she could breathe, and when she thought of Cyrus dying or already dead near the box canyon so far behind her now, the horrible flashback trigger in her brain eased up substantially. For now her childhood demon had been pushed behind a scabrous, closed door, and that was a first considering the environmental conditions. Maybe her psyche was finally healing.

Ansel trudged onward, sometimes with light, other times blindly using her outstretched arms against both claustrophobic walls. Time dragged and distances stretched into surreal lengths that didn't seem physically possible. Once she glanced at her wristwatch as lightning flickered. It had stopped at 9:10. She didn't know how long ago that had been, and still there was no exit point in sight.

Ansel halted abruptly. A red glow pulsed from behind a thick mass of scrub brush plugging the wash. Her view of what lay behind the wind-battered foliage was partially blocked by a sudden right-hand passage turn. She moved closer to the bushes while the mysterious neon light clicked on and off. What the hell was it?

Then it dawned on her. The emergency strobe light that Parker had mentioned. It was in his duffel. Was Dixie just around the turn waiting to shoot her? Why had the woman wasted the strobe battery by activating the light between two walls of stone where no one could see it?

Ansel moved closer to the brush as quietly as she could through the slimy water at her feet. It was like slogging through a streambed. She listened, but could hear nothing but pummeling water and thunder. Still the strobe flashed at her between the limbs and leaves of the scrub bush, beckoning in a rainbow of kaleidoscopic colors as the crimson light reflected off every drenched thing around it.

Freezing and unable to stand still for long in the drenching curls of water cascading from above, Ansel parted the brush and peered around the ravine corner. The sight rooted her to the spot.

Dixie was sitting against one cliff wall while water rose over her splayed legs. Parker's open duffel and Outerbridge's briefcase lay near her. Her face beneath a thick patina of pasty wet dust was deathly white, eyes open and staring toward nothing, mouth agape. On her lap sat a huge coiled rattler. Its head swivelled toward Ansel and the horny, multi-ringed tail rose shaking like a pebble-filled gourd. The strobe, near Dixie's blue, grossly swollen left hand, streaked over everything. Ansel could guess what happened.

Dixie's last act had been to set the light beacon when she knew she was going to die from snake venom. Perhaps she'd hoped to be found before it was too late. When the water got high, the snake had climbed upon her body for refuge and to recline in the last reserves of her dying body heat. It was the kind of death she'd warned Parker about before giving him the walking stick.

Ansel backed through the bushes and began breaking small limbs away from a scrub trunk. The rattler's ire increased. It coiled tighter on Dixie's lap and whipped the rattle faster than the eye could see. She worked while keeping one eye on the angry serpent. Soon she had a long weapon which she snapped away from the scrub base with the heel of her boot.

Her mind was calm and focused. No snake was going to stand between her and Parker's duffel containing all the electronics, or Outerbridge's briefcase. Ansel carefully moved through the bushes, stick outstretched. The snake's body shifted left to right upon coils that looked black and oily in the rain. Yellow eyes glowed like amber. She paused very close to the snake, the trunk tip poised several feet from the snake's head. When lightning flashed, she made her move.

Between flickers, Ansel jabbed the branch forward and down behind the snake's head, smashing the reptile's neck against Dixie's fleshy thigh as hard as she could. Before the lightning ceased, she'd rushed forward and used her left hand to snatch the snake in a vise-like grip behind the rear of the skull. The snake went wild, uncoiling and twisting as the heavenly fires died and blackness crept back into the ravine. Only the faithful strobe gave Ansel her bearings in relation to the slippery snake's gyrating, muscular form.

She lifted the six-foot-long rattler and stood. Its jaws opened, and two-inch fangs scythed outward, dripping venom. Her grip was strangling tight, and her left hand never budged as the rattler whipped its thick corded body in twisting loops around her arm. Ansel tossed the stick aside and headed for Parker's duffel, snake in hand, and making sure the deadly head faced away from her.

She bent carefully and pulled out Parker's gun with her right hand. She made sure the safety was off and the pistol seated properly in her palm. Licking her lips, Ansel shook the snake's body from her arm and threw it as hard as she could at the wall to her right. It smacked the sandstone like a wet mop. She watched as it slid down into the ravine, leaving a bloody smear behind. Before the rattler could even twitch on the ground, Ansel fired a bullet into its massive head.

Cordite flared and Ansel winced as the gun report deafened her and rebounded off the ravine walls as a crackling echo. The rattler's head evaporated into a ruddy mist. Soon there was nothing but the pummeling rain and the hellish strobe again. She lowered the gun along with her head as a soul-deep weariness crept over her.

The impulse to weep rolled over Ansel as a mini-waterfall thundered onto her boots from the Stetson's artificial ledge. How nice to be able to let all the frustrations consume her and just sit down in the rain like Dixie. To give up. To rest forever. The thought of going on seemed too much to endure.

But she had the duffel and the briefcase. Whatever secrets were on that surveillance video, they were safe now and could potentially bust a fossil poaching ring. People had died for that evidence, including Dixie. And somewhere farther west her father waited to see her, even if only for one last time. She had to go on. Had to keep moving. At least she had a snake to eat.

When she lifted her head, she was surprised to see another person standing in the ravine with her. She squinted, not sure her eyes weren't playing tricks on her through the pouring rain. No, it wasn't her imagination.

Ansel took a step forward. "Reid?"

Her relief evaporated. No, not Reid. Somebody else. Someone pointing a nasty-looking semi-automatic weapon at her.

Chapter 37

*"When man moves away from
nature his heart becomes hard."*
Lakota

"Nice shooting. Now lose the gun," Hillard Yancy ordered.

Ansel didn't move a hair. "I get it. No more pretending. I have to admit, you're quite an actor. All that indignant rage about being labeled a fossil plunderer really had me fooled. Tell me, when did you find that pilfering precious bones was more enjoyable than preserving them?"

"You don't know what you're talking about. Put down your gun, Miss Phoenix."

Ansel had to comply. She laid Parker's gun on top of the nearby duffel so it wouldn't be submerged in the rising gully water, already an unsettling depth just below her knees. Torrents of liquid poured down from the bluff rims as the thunderstorm raged.

Yancy stepped out of the shadows into the crimson wash of the beacon, and she saw that he wore a cowboy hat and an oilskin duster. She watched anxiously as he used one hand to push her weapon into the duffel, zipped it, then grabbed it up. The steel briefcase got wrenched up in the same hand. His rain-splotched glasses gleamed gold as he looked at Dixie with mild interest.

"You and Dixie were working together?" Ansel asked through clacking teeth.

His gaze darted back to her. "Hardly. I'm a victim of this mess just like you."

"How's that?"

"I owe the mafia money. A gambling debt. I'm just cleaning fossils for them until I pay it off. I'm not destroying anything," he protested.

Ansel thought of the preparatory work she'd seen at his shop. Good work. Professional. "So what did Dixie do?"

"She was a lackey for some guy in Helena. Told Cyrus and the other diggers where to get the best fossils. I never met her, but I heard about her."

It made sense, Ansel considered. Dixie located the bones via her access to national, state, and BLM databases and fed the info to the poachers under instructions from Cody Masterson. She also remembered the maps of northern Montana she'd seen on Yancy's workshop desk and Dixie's folder on the Medicine Line. After he cleaned the fossils, they were shipped into Canada for sale overseas.

"So you had fossils stolen from your shop by Cyrus to make it look like you were innocent of any local poaching crimes."

The surprised look on Yancy's face was unexpected, but Ansel relished it. Then she took a look behind her as inconspicuously as possible. A quick dash down the gulch and toward Parker might save her life. The blast of water from above was worse, and the fear of being crushed by the weighty run-off terrified her more than Yancy's gun. She took a step away from the center of the ravine toward a more protected wall.

"Don't move," yelled Yancy. He hastily resighted the pistol on her with a desperate determination. His fingers gripped and re-gripped the gun nervously. "If I'm going to make this as pain-less as possible, I need a clean kill shot."

His hesitation gave Ansel hope. "That's murder. Crossing another line, Yancy, or just scuffing it away so you don't have to see the difference between right and wrong?"

Yancy shook his head violently. "You think I want to shoot you? I don't, but I have to."

"Even if you kill me, you'll never get a copter off the ground," she yelled above the wind.

"Then neither of us will leave here alive. I'm sorry, Miss Phoenix. I really am."

Suddenly a thunderclap exploded. A massive, blue-white bolt filled the air above the towering bluff, and the smack of electricity hitting trees above resounded like the static-leaden finger of God poking the Earth. Electric energy filled the air as a palpable force, raising their hair on end. Ansel covered her ears. Yancy fearfully threw himself back against the opposite wall.

From behind Ansel, a vibrating rumble suddenly became audible above the horrendous power of the storm. She turned. A roaring, dissonant wave of slapping noise cascaded from the northern side of the crevice. In an instant, the roiling smell of black water slammed into her face. It was the acrid, organic smell of black dirt, pulverized trees, and decaying animals.

A wash-out, Ansel acknowledged with horror. Just when she thought there wasn't anything left to shock and demoralize her, nature proved her wrong.

The watery rumble shook the ground as speeding, pressurized water rushed toward them through a snaking space too impossibly small to accommodate it. The horrible sound of the undercurrent undermining the rock walls, felling chunks of rock, and filling the ravine with swirling sediments and debris was tremendous.

Just as she processed this frightening information, a wave of water turned the ravine corner. It was only two feet high, but it was a herald of bigger things to come. God, what about Parker, Ansel thought, but there was nothing she could do for him.

Her gaze leaped toward Yancy, who huddled against the wall, his face stretched in terror as he watched the preliminary surge of water. His paralyzed form emboldened her, and Ansel rushed him, heedless of the pistol. Before he knew what was happening, she yanked the briefcase from his hand and ran from the onrushing devastation.

Yancy moaned as the briefcase disappeared, but was unable to swivel around and fire the gun. Behind her, the wave struck his knees as an angry elemental force determined to remove everything from its path.

Ansel heard him scream as she splashed through the slippery ravine, dodging shifting piles of rocks, brush, and fallen debris of all types. Other times, she slid out of control and hit the ravine walls hard, only to bounce off running. Behind her, the wash-out waters rumbled and gurgled. The foulness of foam and wet dirt blew against her back like a salivating monster. She was keeping ahead of the surge by only a matter of seconds, and she knew she couldn't outrun it forever.

There was no place to climb up and no place to hide. Her panting gasps filled the path ahead of her as her legs tired with every pounding step. High water surged above her knees. She was losing speed and the safety gap was inexorably closing.

Ansel looked behind her only a for a second and saw a six-foot churning mass of foam only ten feet back. Water sprayed her backside like a warning slap as motivating as a whip crack. And it did spur her on for a bit more despite her near exhaustion. But there was no end to the ravine.

Then the main wave struck her and she lost her balance, buckling her knees and throwing her face down on the already water-logged ground. She fell on her chest hard, and the dirty waters rolled over her. Suddenly she was pushed forward in an underwater somersault. Tree limbs, tumbling rocks, and dirt rolled with her, scraping and thumping every part of her body as she held her breath and tried to distinguish up from down. Only the briefcase, still clutched in her fist, saved her. It was waterproof and buoyant. Her arm was wrenched upward and she went with it, her head popping out of the rushing water like a cork.

Ansel gagged out water and sucked in air as she was swept along with the surge. The ravine walls rolled by at a dizzying, roller-coaster speed. She tried to grab them with her free hand and hold on, but couldn't. Flotsam tumbled around her head. Once the dead body of a coyote whizzed by her. The worst part was being struck by the ravine outcroppings which protruded everywhere from the bluff walls. They were land mines of pain as they struck her legs and body during the journey.

Ansel didn't have time for fear. It was all she could do to keep her head above the rising water, already well over ten feet high. She held onto the briefcase for dear life. Without it she would drown for sure, a victim of the whirling undertow. She finally managed to clutch the briefcase to her upper chest with arms up and over it like a flotation ring, but she couldn't go on this way forever. Her weary limbs simply couldn't do it.

Without warning, she was jettisoned forward with tremendous power and the briefcase was almost pulled from her grasp. The feeling of being catapulted out a sling was both nauseating and exhilarating. Then she lost her grip on the case and went under. Water sped into her mouth, and she thrashed toward the air with her last reserves of strength. She never reached the top, but in her spinning, churning watery world, her feet skidded across the bottom instead.

As Ansel bent her knees and pushed off the ground with all her might, the waters above her head receded of their own accord. Once again her head struck air, just before she was thrown on her stomach with a mighty slam. She grunted and lay where she fell, hands outstretched and legs splayed, but apparently on solid ground with the ravine waters pooling around her in low gushes. The blinding rain had lessened substantially.

Ansel lifted her head and looked around. To her right, was a vast flat prairie with nothing but the black, sentinel outline of Yancy's grounded helicopter to spoil the view. To her left, black clouds roiled across the sky, but stars peeked out from behind the two scraggy bluffs through which she'd escaped. Water geysered over a huge pile of water-logged debris also trapped by the ravine entrance. Above, low-level lightning flickered in a tumultuous sky trying to clear itself of dust and rain.

Otherwise, she was too done-in to move. In the calming, six-inch waters around her, the red emergency beacon floated past, fully upright with crimson strobe pulsing like a hooker's signal of welcome. A sound to the south caught her attention next. It was a low buzzing noise filled with the rhythmic frequencies of a mechanical whine. The sound grew louder as she listened. Then from the pithy, low-level clouds burst a white object. A bird? she wondered near the point of insensibility. But the bird came lower and grew into a roaring monster with red eyes. It wasn't until the monster flew over her a couple hundred feet above and waggled its wings that Ansel realized it was a small plane.

Then blackness smothered her.

Chapter 38

"Life is as the flash of the firefly in the night,
the breath of the buffalo in the winter time."
Blackfoot

Ansel lifted her head and almost groaned aloud. Her neck was stiff, whether from her body-bruising adventures or from sleeping in a hospital chair, she couldn't say. Opposite her and next to her father's bed, Pearl snored softly in another chrome and vinyl monstrosity that passed for furniture. They'd spent the night together on what could be the start of a death watch.

A full day had passed since Reid, Ranger Eastover, and her crop-dusting brother had rescued her. After passing out on the prairie and then being taken into Reid's ministrations on the ride out of the Badlands, she'd recuperated quickly with food, water, and a few hours of sleep.

By the time Reid had driven her to the McCone County Hospital, she'd heard that a CAP rescue team had found Parker alive despite the dangerous wash-out. He was flown to a hospital in Glasgow and healing nicely after the wound in his thigh had been treated. He was well on his way to recovery and his future looked much better than hers.

Tears filled Ansel's already red and gritty eyes. As she had endured the trek out of the box canyon, so had Chase battled for life in ICU, and he now lay unconscious. His struggle had exhausted his body's reserves, and his condition was critical. Doctor Wellman had told her that if her father survived the first seventy-two hours, his chances of recovery would be good.

Still Ansel hardly recognized her father, a helpless spirit encased in damaged flesh that neither moved nor communicated. Tubes and catheters, beeping machinery, and strange smells filled the tiny room. Curtains drawn across the glass panels did little to dispel the aura of an encroaching catastrophe being monitored with microscopic scrutiny. He absorbed oxygen. He consumed nutrients. He eliminated wastes. All the scientific and biological parameters that she'd learned were the hallmarks of organic life were here, but they meant nothing.

For the first time, all of her scientific expertise failed her. There was no medicine for rejuvenating a weakened soul slowly slipping away. No tool for stitching the mind to the body so it couldn't separate. No equation for controlling time and altering the past. Though she'd been an innocent and traumatized young girl when her mother passed away, this was horribly different. Being a worldly, self-sufficient adult didn't mean crap when confronted with the lifeless husk of her father.

"You're up," said Pearl. She roused from her slumber, stretched painfully, and cast an anxious glance toward Chase.

"He's the same," Ansel said. She leaned forward and cupped Chase's cold, calloused hand into her sweaty palms. "You're going to be all right, aren't you, Daddy? I'm so sorry I yelled at you. I was being mean and spiteful. Don't leave me," she said, tears welling in her eyes.

"Ansel, he knows all that, and there's nothing you could do to make him not love you."

"I just want him to realize that I'm here."

Pearl stood and brushed a long lock of Chase's silver hair from his blue hospital smock. "We're both here, you old cowpoke. The ranch is fine. Seth is on top of everything. And it's raining, Chase. A regular gully-washer. No need to fret." She glanced toward the door. "Ansel, Reid's here."

Ansel looked over her shoulder. Reid, fully suited, stood in the door holding a folder and a brown bag. The last time she'd seen him, he was wearing civilian clothes and carrying enough guns to fight a battle. She stood, massaging her neck. "I'll be right back."

Reid moved away from the door as she approached. By some mutual, unspoken cue, they both migrated past the nurse's station and out of the ICU unit into the main corridor.

"Reid, what's up?"

He passed her the bag. "First, here's some stuff retrieved from the ravine. Your hat, purse, jewelry, and a few possessions that survived the flood. How are you?"

"I'm fine." The bag wasn't very heavy. At least she had her jewelry back.

"And Chase?"

Ansel frowned. "Not good. They're pumping him full of pain killers, blood thinners, and oxygen. I need to get back."

"I know. I wanted to catch you up on things. We found the bodies of Dixie LaPierre, Hillard Yancy, and Cyrus Flynn. Of course, Dixie died from snake venom, but Hillard and Cyrus drowned in the ravine. We also recovered the burned bodies from the FBI chopper."

How ironic that Cyrus had drowned in the end, Ansel thought with a shiver. She rubbed her hands along her arms. "Did anyone find Outerbridge's briefcase?"

Reid nodded. "Yeah, it was stuck in the debris outside the ravine. Got the computer disk safe and sound. It's been sent to the FBI. Who knows what was on it that everyone was trying to destroy. They'll be tracking down poaching ring and mafia drones for years."

"I just want to get back to my life." Ansel gazed toward the ICU. "If it's not too late."

"There are still some details my department has to deal with." He opened the folder and pulled out a large photo. "You deserve to see this. The museum poacher."

Ansel took the photo, their hands touching briefly. Even as mentally weary as she was, the contact held an emotional impact. She quickly withdrew her hand and glanced at the computer-generated portrait. Artistically speaking, it was very lifelike and expressive. She noted the name and address digitally imprinted along the bottom edge.

"Nice job. This Doctor Birch is very good."

Reid's face looked half pleased and half flustered. "He's a twenty-three-year-old named Noble Dawes. Comes from the Crow Indian Reservation near Hardin."

Parker's tribe. Ansel reviewed the drawing carefully. "You've identified him already?"

"Yeah, the tribal police phoned me late last night. Ever see him before?"

"No. Any information on him?"

"Not much. He doesn't have a rap sheet. Still don't know if he fits into the FBI case."

"You sound like you don't think he's part of the poaching ring."

"I have my doubts."

"Why?"

Reid shrugged. "Gut feeling. Have you talked with Parker?"

Surprised at the question, Ansel passed him the photo. Was he going to start some jealous tirade again? And jealous over what? She crossed her arms. "Once. He called to tell me he'd survived the ravine flood by climbing up on a boulder blocking the wash that was higher than the storm surge. How he did it?—an adrenaline rush, or just pure guts. His gunshot wound is healing."

"I was wondering if he said anything about the FBI's next move to you."

"Reid, I'm not someone the FBI confides in, and you know it. Stop two-stepping around me in order to ferret out my love life. I'm not in the mood."

Reid roughly pushed the photo back into the folder. "Gee, that's funny. I thought I came all the way from Mission City to do my job by following up on what you might know."

"I know when I'm being belly-roped," she countered, then walked away.

"He's no good for you, Ansel," Reid said under his breath.

She pivoted around and glared at him. "What did you say?"

Reid faced her squarely. "I see his type all the time in law enforcement. He's a social drifter. Oh, he's flashy and personable, and he's got that macho, federal fly-boy job, but he'll never settle down. Never commit to anything."

"Just like you, Reid?" She used her ebony gaze to pierce through him. "He may not be the perfect man, but he's a man. He knows when he wants to kiss me and does it damn well."

"Are kisses all you've given him?"

Ansel bristled. "That's none of your business. Stick to your job, remember?"

Reid's expression darkened into a bitter scowl. "Screw it. I don't give a damn what you do with your life." He whirled away and stomped toward the elevator, never looking back.

As Ansel watched him, an instant wave of regret enveloped her. He'd been brazen to question her about Parker, but why had she said that to him? It had been cruel and deliberate, a childish retort meant to pummel his ego. Her temper was her major character flaw, but lately it had been totally out of control. She'd give anything for a strong drink right now.

She started after him, willing to eat crow with mustard if that's what it took to get back in his good graces. She hadn't taken three steps when the cell phone in her jeans pocket rang. Worried that a distant relative or friend was trying to reach her or Pearl for information about her father's condition, she halted and dug it out.

"Hello?"

"Miss Phoenix. It's Noah Zollie."

For a moment the caller's name meant nothing to her. Then her brain cells jump-started. The lawyer. "Yes?"

"I hope I'm not calling at a bad time," he said carefully.

Ansel lightened her tone as she stared helplessly down the hallway where Reid had disappeared. "No. I didn't expect to hear from you so soon. I suppose you're calling about Dad."

"Your father? Not at all. I called concerning some interesting information about the Big Toe museum contract. Has something happened to Chase?"

"Yes. He suffered a heart attack two days ago. I'm here at the McCone ICU."

"My goodness. I'm so sorry. Please give Pearl my deepest sympathies. How are you two holding up?"

"We're just waiting and watching. What about the museum contract?"

Noah clucked his tongue. "Oh, I don't want to bother you. Call me when you're ready to discuss it."

Ansel looked out a wide plate glass window overlooking the front parking lot. Through the streaky, water-splattered barrier, she saw Reid shooting between the cars two stories below as he dodged the rain. He held the folder over his head, and his navy jacket flapped like a cape. *You can run but you can't hide. I'll find you.*

"Please, tell me now, Noah. I don't know when I'll be able to call again."

"Well, the museum contract is standard as far as BLM lease trusts go, and the execution looks solid and perfectly legal. I'm afraid that there's no way for the town council to contest the land tenancy clauses incorporated into the lease as presented, and the BLM has laid down the conditions upon which the contract can be terminated by them with great clarity. They are within their federal rights to divest themselves of the lease if they so choose under the auspice that the town council is unable to maintain the necessary protection and security for national antiquities."

Reid's white sedan pulled out of the parking lot. Ansel ran her fingers through her hair and angrily spun away from the window. "So there's nothing we can do to stop the closing of the museum and the seizure of the fossil tracks?"

"I wouldn't say that," Noah replied. "I've found a flaw in another legal document attached to the property. That's why I'm calling."

Ansel's indignation cooled, and a small tingle of hope vibrated through her body. "What?"

"The Dover ranch covers approximately three thousand acres comprising parcels acquired at different dates and under different circumstances. The BLM land leased to the town council, which contains the museum and tracks, encompasses one hundred and sixty acres. I've found a defect associated with the original land patent for that parcel. It's a lucky fluke that we can capitalize on if the town council wishes to forestall a lease foreclosure for a bit. In any event, this issue should be addressed at some point as it affects some of the heirs."

That tingle of hope blossomed into a full-fledged optimism. "You mean Chester Dover's children?"

Noah grunted. "Well, his children would be affected indirectly, but not to their benefit. Mr. Dover bought the land in 1950 through a real estate contract. He held a warranty deed on the property only. That's a state-generated document and is merely a 'color of title' which is the semblance or appearance of title, but not an ownership title in fact or in law. I'm talking about a land patent issued by the government which is permanent after its issuance to the bearer and his heirs forever. Most people don't know this, but a land patent is the only perfect title to land available in the United States. Your father inherited the Arrowhead through his family's original land patent, you know."

"No, I didn't. So who got the original patent for the museum acreage?"

"The patent was issued under the General Allotment Act of 1887 as part of a federal decree giving permission to reservation Indians to select pieces of land forty to one hundred and sixty acres in size for themselves and their children. A Crow Indian named Robert Dawes received partial ownership of the land with the government, which held it in trust for twenty-five years. After that specified time, as required by Indian homesteaders under the Allotment Act, Dawes bought the land outright through a fee ownership contract in 1914. That's when he received his land patent for the property."

Ansel hitched in a breath. She'd just stumbled upon the reason why Noble Dawes had tried to steal the dinosaur tracks. It was motivated by an old land dispute involving a relative.

"Are you all right, Ansel?"

"Yes. Just surprised. How does this help us?"

"Since Dawes held the original land patent, he could keep the property for as long as he liked, pass it on to his heirs, or sell it. For whatever reason, he chose to sell the acreage to a man named Lincoln Abernathy, who in turn owned the parcel until it was sold again to Chester Dover in 1950. I found the BLM paperwork that shows Abernathy to be the holder of an amended land patent spun off of the Dawes sale, but that document just didn't look right to me so I investigated further. Somehow the Abernathy land patent got unilaterally amended in 1915 by the county surveyor solely on the surveyor's affidavit and without the required re-survey of the parcel. I suspect that there was a concerted attempt to make Abernathy appear as the original land patent owner and not Dawes."

Ansel agreed. "You mean that Abernathy didn't want Dawes or his Indian heirs to ever come back in the future and say that the property belonged to them."

"Exactly. And proof of the first Dawes land patent didn't seem to exist until I found it misfiled in the BLM archives. To tell the truth, I was lucky to find it at all."

"Do you think the BLM knows the truth about the property's history and is attempting to hide it?" Ansel asked, aghast.

"I can't accuse the whole agency of that, but the defective, amended land patent renders the Abernathy-Dover and BLM contracts null and void. Technically, the Dawes land patent still stands. The property legally belongs to Robert Dawes and his living heirs."

Ansel frowned. "And so if the BLM never owned the land, they can't lease it. That's going to be quite a shot in the gut for them. Unfortunately, it doesn't bode well for the Big Toe town council either. They can't lease something from someone who can't lease it to them."

"True, but it gives the council a bargaining edge. They may be able to recoup their investment in the museum remodel, plus past lease payments, business expenses, and museum revenues. They contracted with the BLM in good faith and may have been a victim of federal incompetency or outright fraud. It's not what you were looking for, but it's definitely going to save the dinosaur tracks."

Ansel sighed, then had a thought. "Could you find Dawes' living heirs?"

"Not me personally, but I have resources at my disposal that could. Why?"

"It's some helpful information I can hand the town council along with the bad news."

"All right. I'll see what I can do, if you mention my name and number to the town council. I would be very interested in representing them in any legal pursuits," Noah unabashedly announced. "This kind of governmental tomfoolery gets my dander up."

"Agreed. Great job. I'll get back to you in a few days."

"Please wish Chase a fast recovery for me. Goodbye, Ansel."

Ansel pushed the cell into her pocket just as Pearl flew out the ICU doorway, her eyes wide. "Ansel, come quickly," she rasped.

Fear galvanized Ansel's body, and she could barely speak. "Daddy?"

Pearl grinned. "Lordy, yes. He opened his eyes and he's asking for you."

Chapter 39

"Stolen food never satisfies hunger."
Omaha

Ansel guided Chunky through the small cottonwood stand, then halted him with a tug on the reins. The swollen Red Water River lay directly in front of her, and across the bend was the Big Toe Natural History Museum. Water sped along the riverbed. Today was the first morning in three days without showers, though the sky was leaden and full to bursting with low, tumbling clouds. More runoff and the river would overflow completely. It didn't matter. She had to cross it before the sun was up and someone saw her.

Nothing had changed on the BLM land except that the terrain was soggy, and green shoots of prairie grass peeked out amid the brittle, brown vegetation. Otherwise, the museum was still closed, and the fence still chained and locked. Ranger Eastover had told her during the airplane rescue that Broderick would be gone by now, but she didn't want to get the woman in trouble by getting caught on restricted property a second time.

Because she risked arrest, Ansel had opted to approach the land on horseback via a more circumspect route. This isolated, adjacent property was U.S. Forestry land and publicly accessible if you knew how to find it. Her truck hauling an Arrowhead horse trailer was secreted behind the cottonwoods and invisible to anyone across the river.

Ansel kicked her heels against the buckskin's ribs, and he paced forward obediently. There was no incline leading into the river, just a sudden line of agitated water flowing speedily along. It was probably about ten feet deep in the middle of the hundred-foot-wide crossing. Not optimum conditions, but quite doable with a fast-swimming horse, Ansel reckoned. Chunky got one hoof into the river and stopped.

"Hup, Chunky," she urged, tapping her heels against his barrel body.

He didn't budge, just stood with ears pricked and nostrils flaring as he sniffed in muddy water scents. Ansel knew he wasn't scared. He'd be swinging his head from side to side or backing up if that were the case. Chunky was an experienced water crosser. He was being ornery.

Ansel turned Chunky away from the river. She walked him all the way back to the cottonwood line, then cantered him down to the riverbank again at another angle and place so he could view the waterway from a second perspective before going in.

This worked. Chunky went straight into the cold water without hesitation and plunged forward when the bank dropped off into deep waters. Foamy waves slapped against his broad chest as his legs kicked against the current trying to tug them downstream.

Water coursed up to Ansel's hips and a tiny bell of alarm went off in her head. The old primal fears wanted to run rampant, and she herded them back by concentrating on getting the horse across safely. A week ago she could never have accomplished this feat, and a sense of pride welled in her chest. She was in command of her phobia for the first time in her life.

They reached the other bank and Chunky got his footing, confidently pulling his weight onto the rocky incline. Streams of water poured off Ansel and the saddle as they hit land, splattering loudly on the flooded sandstone ledge. Ansel halted Chunky and peered down. The dinosaur tracks were near them but under three inches of swirling, opaque water. She couldn't see them at all.

A couple of heel taps and Chunky cantered over the incline onto the slightly mushy grassland. In seconds Ansel had reached her destination—the Allosaurus sculpture. She positioned Chunky sideways to the dinosaur's chest and leaned over the saddle to inspect its bumpy, dark brown-black skin. With the buckskin's fifteen hands of height added to her upper body length, she was staring eye-level at the model's lower chest, its clawed forearms just above her.

The puncture she'd noticed before on the pebbly skin wasn't easy to see because the area had been badly charred. Only sunlight glinting off silver that she'd previously seen from exactly the right angle had given it away. It would have been easy for the forensics team to miss it.

Ansel pulled a pen-knife from her jeans pocket and used the swivel blade to dig at the ashy crust of melted rubber. When she pried deeper into the fiberglass undercore, her blade struck something solid. She continued to enlarge the hole and exposed silver metal. It was wedged in hard, and it took her a while to realize that the metallic blob was of much larger diameter inside the fiberglass than out. Eventually, she released the large-headed object, and it fell into her hand.

It was a bullet. One of those wicked jacketed types with expanding heads that could penetrate almost anything and lodge deep inside flesh without leaving an exit wound. The head had mushroomed outward from the lower cylinder portion, leaving a jagged-edged pedestal of metal. She guessed it to be a forty-caliber, barrel-loader type of ammunition suitable for revolvers, and it created more questions than answers.

Who had fired the bullet and why? What did it have to do with Noble Dawes' attempt to steal the fossil tracks and the potential theft of his ancestors' land? Everyone believed that the Indian's death was caused by the rupturing propane tank. Were they wrong?

Ansel pushed the bullet into her pocket, reined Chunky over to the riverbank, then stopped on the fossil ledge. Water gurgled around Chunky's hooves. She still couldn't see the tracks, but in her mind's eye she could see the terrible two-foot-long sawcut.

She'd attributed the other disfigurements and pock marks along the ledge to flying shrapnel. There had been only that one narrow and whitish, skidding chip that looked peculiar. In retrospect, she imagined it was just the sort of mark that a high-velocity bullet skidding across stone might make.

Ansel looked behind her. It wasn't far from the ledge to the sculpture. She looked across the river toward the cottonwoods. It was entirely possible that somebody hiding in those trees had fired a shot toward the ledge which ricocheted and hit the Allosaurus. Despite so much rain, she needed to search the cottonwoods for sign of earlier disturbances or human activity.

Ansel nudged Chunky, and they entered the river again. In less than two minutes, they had crossed the waterway and were on solid land. This time the cold waters chilled her to the bone, and her weighty, water-laden clothing didn't help. She ought to change into some spare clothes stashed in the truck and warm up, but first she'd check the tree line for clues.

As she walked Chunky through the first compact growth of cottonwoods, she heard the unmistakable click of a cocking gun to her left side. In an instant, she yanked Chunky to a halt and peered anxiously in that direction.

Agent Broderick, out of uniform, was standing beside them with a revolver gripped in his right hand and a Cheshire Cat grin plastered across his face. Several thoughts spun through Ansel's head. First, every time she turned around, somebody was pointing a gun at her. Second, her Colt pistol was in the truck, though she doubted a gunfight with Broderick would be advisable, especially since he had a short rifle scope attached to the firearm barrel. Bolting wasn't an option at the moment.

"Get off the horse," Broderick ordered without preamble.

"You have no authority here," Ansel challenged. "This is public forestry land."

His grin morphed into a lethal scowl. "Don't start your Indian princess bullshit with me."

Ansel tightened her grip on the reins and Chunky's ears flattened against his head. Broderick's rough tone wasn't sitting well with the gelding. "What's your problem? You're not even supposed to be here."

Broderick leveled the gun at her chest. "I saw you across the river. You've been trespassing on BLM land."

It was her turn to smile. "You mean Indian land. In case you didn't know it, I've found out that parcel has legitimately belonged to a Crow Indian family since eighteen eighty-seven. Somebody messed up with the land sales since then. The Bureau doesn't have any rights to that parcel. You're going to find out all about it tomorrow. I've made sure of that."

Broderick actually stepped back from her in utter shock, but the revolver was still poised in her direction. "Shit," he hissed. "I can't believe you did this to me. Everything I've planned for months was about to gel, and you've blown it. All your God damned snooping. I should have gotten rid of you when I had the chance," he raged, his face turning redder by the second.

Ansel watched his accelerating anger with amazement. She didn't know what he was talking about. Unless…

"You know about the land? My God, you were the one that tried to hide the original Dawes land patent records in the state BLM files. But why?"

"Because it was my ticket to bigger things. I found out about the property months ago. I even went to Noble Dawes and told him about it," Broderick seethed. "I tried to help both of us. Him to get what was rightfully his and me to share in his good fortune. I would have been a media hit and gotten a good promotion to boot."

"This was all about a better job?" Ansel asked with disgust.

"A great job. We're talking about a BLM promotion to state director. I deserve it, but do you think Noble appreciated my information? No, all that has-been rodeo clown wanted was revenge. Some sort of Indian justice. He focused on the dinosaur tracks and saw dollar signs. I just helped him along with that idea to keep him quiet."

Ansel racked her brains for a means of escape as she talked. "So you gave him the concrete saw and the goggles and sent him off to vandalize the museum property. All the while you were planning to shoot him from these cottonwoods across the river."

"I didn't have to shoot him. I just had to hit the ledge and make a spark. The propane tank was rigged to leak. Made it look like some horrible accident blowing a thieving jerk to bits, which is essentially what he was."

"Did you use that revolver?"

Broderick's left hand grabbed Chunky's reins near the bridle, and the horse shook its head unhappily as he moved next to Ansel's side. The bore hole of the agent's gun came closer, too. It was only inches from her thigh.

"Do you know what a platinum-tip hollow point does to bone this close up, Miss Phoenix? Not to mention that it will go through your body and into your horse's belly. I saw you at the dinosaur. Give me the bullet you found or I'll give you the one in this barrel."

"I have to reach into my jeans to get it."

Broderick sneered. "Go ahead, but do it slow."

She pried open her right pocket and pulled out the slug. Reluctantly, she passed it to his open hand. Her leg muscles tensed.

"Good girl." He stepped away, gun pointed toward her chest again. "Now dismount on my side of the horse."

Ansel adjusted her seat as if to swing her opposite leg loose of the stirrup and dismount beside Broderick, then instantly changed tactics, freeing her left foot from the stirrup instead. Her sideways kick was well aimed. Her boot heel hit Broderick square in the groin. He dropped the gun, grabbed his genitals with his right hand, bullet and all, then bellowed in rage and pain. His left-handed grip on Chunky's reins, however, remained firm.

One hard kick on the horse's side from Ansel sent Chunky bolting forward, but Broderick didn't release his hold. He was yanked along with the gelding in a half-run, half-drag skid across the cottonwood copse as he fought to maintain his balance.

Ansel urged Chunky to pick up speed through the timber and lashed at Broderick's face with the reins in an effort to make him let go. Broderick was tenacious—grunting, cursing, and trying to pull her out of the saddle. For several yards, progress was slow as they both ducked low-hanging limbs and got whipped or slashed by leafy limbs.

Ahead, Ansel saw a humongous pile of dead fall blocking Chunky's path. They couldn't possibly jump it, and there was no way to go around given their blind plunge through the tree stand with a two-hundred-pound man leeched onto Chunky's side. The decision of what to do became moot as Chunky saw the debris and bucked to an immediate stop, front legs locked rigid and hooves shoveling up dirt in a death-defying slide.

The world spun as Ansel flew over Chunky's head in a free-flight roll. She landed hard on the dead fall with a sharp cracking sound that she thought might be her spine. When the dust settled, she realized that she was lying flat on her back and was relatively unhurt except for more bruises. The soft, rotten debris had actually saved her from serious harm.

Ansel lifted her head and stared past her boots. Broderick had regained his composure and looked furious as he approached her, hands fisted into grapefruit-sized knots of bone. He was going to kill her with his bare hands.

"Freeze," screamed a male voice from behind Broderick. "Or I'll shoot."

Ansel's eyes scoured the trees. She couldn't see anyone, but there was no way she could miss the withering look Broderick gave her before grabbing Chunky's reins. He was going to make a run for it. As he attempted to manhandle the gelding into a position where he could quickly mount, Chunky threw back his ears and rolled his eyes. A keening neigh echoed through the cottonwoods before Chunky whipped his head around and bit Broderick on the shoulder. This time the crunch of bone was very real. Broderick screamed and dropped to the ground as a torrent of blood gushed from his wound.

Suddenly, a handful of men wearing camo SWAT gear swarmed through the trees. One of the men bearing an assault rifle reached Broderick first and, after assessing that the target was down and unarmed, relinquished his weapon to bend down and attend the fallen man.

"Are you all right, Ma'am?" asked another husky officer as he helped Ansel up from the dead fall.

"I'm fine. Are you from the Sheriff's Department?" She hoped momentarily that Reid would be there soon.

"No. I'm Agent Farmer. DOI. We came in to find you."

"The Department of Interior?"

"That's right," replied another voice behind her. "I sent them."

Ansel spun around. Parker, wearing his usual attire, smiled back at her. He sported a shiny aluminum crutch under his left armpit. She almost ran over to hug him, then decided it wouldn't be appropriate under the circumstances. Instead, she gave him a warm smile.

He peered at her. "Are you all right?"

"Yes. I'm fine."

Parker eyeballed Broderick. "How is he?"

Broderick glared back and allowed Agent Farmer to stanch the blood with bandages from a portable med kit. He was standing again. Another agent had tied Chunky to a nearby tree.

Agent Farmer turned his helmeted head. "He'll live. Gonna need some antibiotics and stitches."

"Did you retrieve the bullet and his gun?"

"Yes, sir."

"Then let's get the trash outta here," Parker ordered.

Ansel and he watched as two agents handcuffed Broderick and escorted him away through the trees from which they'd miraculously appeared.

When the BLM agent was gone, Ansel said, "I can't believe it. What are you doing here?"

"Closing a case, thanks to you." He leaned over and moved a strand of hair away from her face. "I've missed you."

She stared deeply into his obsidian eyes. "Don't change the subject. What case?"

"Noble Dawes. I've been working to catch Broderick in the act for quite a while, actually. This isn't the first BLM monkey business we believe he's been involved in."

Her eyes narrowed into slits. "You knew all along who Dawes was and that he tried to take the fossil tracks?"

Parker nodded. "Yes, and before you go crazy on me, there's something you should know. I'm not with the FBI."

"No?"

"Uh uh. I'm a criminal investigator with the Bureau of Indian Affairs. It's my job to prevent suspected violations of law, programs, or property abuse on Indian reservations or Indian land that is within the Bureau of Indian Affairs' jurisdiction. Since Dawes lived on the reservation and his grandfather got his land allotment through the DOI, I became involved in this case. I was assisting Outerbridge because there was jurisdictional overlap between his poaching case and mine. He asked me to work with you for the Allosaurus skull buy. He also needed a local pilot."

"How did you know that I was here with Broderick?"

"I put a tracking bug on your truck the day I flew the FBI to your trailer. Same with Broderick's. I arrived in Mission City this morning and was concerned when I got a report that you two were headed toward the same destination. I knew Broderick was in real trouble then."

A wry grin grew across Ansel's face as she walked over to Chunky and untied his reins. "Is that so? FBI or not, you're a fed through and through, Parker Standback, but I forgive you for lying to me."

He pointed a thumb Indian fashion. "Hey, I never said I was FBI. You assumed."

She swept her arm eastward toward the river. "And you assume this is over. I'm attending both the Flynn funerals, and I'm not looking forward to them. Not to mention that the fossil tracks may be safe, but the museum might shut down just the same. There's no guarantee that the new owner will want to keep it."

She led Chunky toward the trailer beyond the dead fall.

Parker pursed his lips and crutch-stepped to keep up. "I forgot about that. What are you going to do?"

Ansel's laugh was mirthless. "I'm going to throw my own saddle, just like somebody advised me."

Chapter 40

*"Even when we lay down, we lay
down on our own path of life."*
Pawnee

"I'm lucky to be alive," Chase said as he sipped from his sun tea and leaned back in the patio chair. "And it sure feels good to be home. Sleeping in that hospital bed for two weeks was like bunking on clean straw. And I've been severely gut-shrunk by their food."

Everyone around the glass-topped table laughed, four heads nodding and laughter filling the rear veranda of the ranch house. Ansel, sitting between Pearl and Permelia, who had been invited over as their special luncheon guest, picked at her dessert and wished Reid were there.

She'd left phone messages at the Sheriff's Department for a week and never heard back from him. She'd even called his partner, Odie Friskar, who told her very politely that Reid was extremely busy, and that he'd certainly forward her message.

Otherwise, she was moderately happy at the moment. The funerals for Cullen and Cyrus Flynn were behind her. Luckily, her father had missed both of them. They had been excruciating and emotionally draining. He needed to do nothing more than rest and take a barrage of medicines including blood thinners and beta-blockers so he wouldn't overtax his heart.

And she'd completed her last drawing of the Giganatosaurus for the Argentine book. All twelve drawings had been signed, sealed, and delivered to the publisher. A nice chunk of money would be coming in for those.

Parker had returned to Hardin, a small town close to the Crow Agency, after Broderick's arrest, but he had promised to call as soon as things settled down. The question was, where did she stand with him when she was fretting over Reid? Was it Reid's friendship she was chasing, or something else?

"I think we've all had enough excitement for a while," Pearl intoned as a balmy breeze passed through the patio garden and dried cottonwood leaves skittered across the flagstones. She clasped Chase's hand in hers and gave a pointed look at Ansel. "For the rest of this year, none of the family is going anywhere without my permission. You two are always breaking range and getting into trouble. I can't keep track of you."

"Get 'em some neck bells," Permelia replied, waxy orange lipstick forming a gigantic neon circle around brilliant white dentures as she laughed. "That'll slow their stride. Though come to think of it, maybe it won't. I once had a horse of nervous disposition named Salado who'd get into the barn, eat the alfalfa hay, and then get colic. Almost killed him twice, but he kept doing it. I finally put a bell on him so we'd know when he was sneaking up on the open barn door. That bell drove him loco. He started running one day to get away from it and nearly broke down from exhaustion. Had to take the dang bell off, but I hung it on the barn door, and he never went near it again."

Pemelia hooted and then looked at Ansel. "Speaking of horses, your buckskin's a salty bronc, ain't he? Although biting a federal man is all right in my accounts book. Hope you're feeding him sweet feed and clover for his services."

Chase nodded. "Chunky may have his quirks, but he helped save Ansel's life."

"Chunky's always been an excellent judge of character," Ansel added. "He knows a murderer when he sees one."

"And I know a lady of substance when I see one." Chase lifted his tea glass once again. "I propose a toast to Permelia Chance, who has always been not only the Queen of the Mission City Maverick Parade, but should be more aptly known as the Queen of Lacrosse County. She has always had the foresight to know the true values of family, brotherhood, friendship, and lending a hand to others." Chase looked directly at Permelia. "Thank you for your offer to help save the Big Toe Museum from extinction."

"Here, here," Ansel seconded as they all clinked their raised glasses together, then sipped their drinks.

Pearl leaned across the table. "Yes, Permelia, tell us the details about the offer. Ansel's kept everything very hush hush."

Permelia's face was flushed with delight at all the attention, and she fussed with the collar of her apricot western shirt. "Shoot, I didn't do anything special. I just offered to swap my four hundred acres of quarry land for the new owners' hundred and sixty museum acres. I've never used that land anyway after Elam died."

"I know all about the land patent fraud from the newspaper, but who's the new owner?" Chase queried.

Ansel jumped in. "According to Parker Standback from the Bureau of Indian Affairs, Noble Dawes has a sister on the Crow Reservation. She's the next legitimate heir to the museum property. She's already hired Noah Zollie to handle her case against the BLM. Everybody seems to think that the government doesn't have a leg to stand on. Of course, it could take months to resolve the matter in court, but until then, the BLM has agreed to a provisional reopening of the museum during certain hours. It's not perfect, but it's something."

"It's wonderful," Pearl cooed. "At least Director Bieselmore won't be out of job, and the town council will make some money. Do you think this woman will consider the land swap after the litigation is finished?"

Permelia drained her glass of Coke before answering. "Zollie and I are talking turkey right now. Looks like this Ellen Dawes has no interest in owning a museum or managing one. As for the tracks, she thinks they should be left alone, and she's quite interested in my land. It's a workable quarry. She can dig for all the bones she wants, or sell the property for a nice profit. I'm offering her a parcel worth twice the land value of the museum parcel. She'll go for it."

Ansel grinned. "Plus Permelia wants to do a Starker exchange."

Permelia cackled. "That's right. It was Ansel's idea."

"That's brilliant," Chase said, peering at Sarcee.

"Well, somebody better educate me," Pearl interjected, "because I'm lost."

"It's an Internal Revenue real estate deal commonly called a 1031 exchange," Chase explained. "It allows you to buy or sell unimproved investment land or commercial property and defer the tax gains. A qualified intermediary holds your monies from the sale of one property in escrow until you buy another to replace it. For example, I could sell this ranch and buy another through a qualified intermediary because they're both commercial ventures, and I wouldn't pay taxes on my end-sale profit because I never touched the sale monies myself."

"That is perfect," Pearl said as she rose from the table to collect dessert dishes.

Permelia pulled out a Tiparillo from her shirt pocket and lit it with an old silver lighter. "All I have to do while the trial goes on is to get a business license, build a small office building on my property, have a few people pay me to harvest a few bones from it, and keep income tax records this year. That'll qualify it as an active commercial property so the Starker exchange will be legit."

Ansel beamed. "And guess who will be your first paying customer? Me."

The octogenarian chortled as blue smoke twirled around her head. "Wouldn't have it any other way. And if the federales get randy, I'll remind them that I'm one-quarter Cherokee. That's makes me a native according to the Cherokee Nation. Between a Crow woman and me, we can stir up some bad medicine."

"Well, I have a surprise for you, Permelia," Ansel said, standing. "I'll be right back." She went into the house and came back with her portfolio case. Once seated again, she pulled out a large watercolor sketch. "Here's my preliminary drawing for your book cover. Tell me what you think."

Permelia took the painting, her eyes widening with delight. Ansel saw her silent approval and relief surged through her. She hadn't been sure if she were on the right track for what Pemelia wanted. Where the Giganatosaurus head had been in the other pen and ink drawing, she'd placed a T-rex with gaping jaws, rapier teeth, and huge reptilian eyes. Instead of a fleeing Gasparinisaurus, she'd placed a cowboy with flaring leather-fringed chaps riding a horse, his body turned in the saddle to stare back at the onrushing carnosaur.

"It's Jim Dandy," Permelia exclaimed as she turned the sketch around for Chase and Pearl to see. "Tell me that doesn't make your eyes pop out."

Chase blinked, then smiled graciously. "It's an eye-catcher all right," he said, casting a sideways glance at Ansel.

"Very nice," Pearl replied. "I can't wait to read the book, Permelia."

Ansel leaned closer to Permelia. "Of course, this is the preliminary drawing. It will really stand out when it's completed in gouache. The three-dimensional perspective and coloring of that medium will be very realistic."

Permelia passed the sketch back. "I'm as tickled as a girl in a feather bed, Ansel. How much do I owe you for all this?"

"Not a thing." She replaced the sketch into her portfolio. "You're doing enough for everyone else." The sound of a doorbell echoed out onto the veranda and Ansel stood. "I'll get that. I've got to take this inside anyway."

She left the others talking rapidly about Permelia's plans for the writing of *Montana Chaps* and moved through the French doors into the cooler confines of the living room. She laid the case on the sofa in front of the stonework fireplace and hurried to the front foyer. When she swung open the heavy spruce portal, she expected to see a ranch hand or stockman associate of her father's.

"Reid." He stood on the wood decking staring back at her from beneath ebony shades. Her heart flew to her throat.

"Hi, Ansel. I took a chance you'd be here."

"I'm glad you did. Come on in."

He stepped inside. "I won't be long."

Disappointment stole over Ansel as she closed the door. "You're sure? We were just finishing lunch out on the veranda. Permelia Chance is here. She's going to try and acquire the museum land. You can meet her. Have some dessert and a drink with us."

"I'd love to, really," he said as he pulled off his glasses and fixed her with his sky-blue eyes, "but I've got a lot to do today. I'm taking a vacation starting tomorrow. I just wanted to let you know."

He was talking fast and Ansel sensed his nervousness, though his body language was self-assured. "You deserve it. Are you staying in town?"

"No. I'm going to Billings for two weeks. My family is there. I haven't visited them in a couple years. Sorry I didn't get back with you. It's been crazy at the department."

Ansel suspected he was going back to Billings for more than just his relatives. She'd never pinned him down about Outerbridge's comment concerning his knowing Cody Masterson's ex-wife. She didn't need to. She'd put two and two together by herself.

"If you see Dr. Birch, tell her that I'd like to meet her someday. We have a lot in common when it comes to artistic bents."

Reid's face went stoic. "Sure."

Ansel searched his eyes and saw that her arrow had hit the mark. He was going to see Chloe. All this polite conversation wasn't accomplishing anything. She decided to get down to the real issues between them.

"I'm sorry for what I said at the hospital, Reid. It was rude and insensitive. There was no excuse for it. I really thought you'd never speak to me again."

His new smile was genuine, and it made him boyishly hand-some. "Nonsense. I've got a shoe-leather hide. I blow up and I get over it. I should know better than to tell Ansel Phoenix what to do."

"You're just as bad," Ansel laughed. "We make quite a pair."

"Yeah, we do," he chuckled while he played with the shades in his hands.

The impact of their words hit them both at the same time. A pair. A couple. It was so glaringly obvious that neither of them was laughing anymore. The silence was deafening.

"I'd better get going." Reid reached for the doorknob.

"Okay. Have a safe trip."

It was such a pathetic comeback that Ansel wanted to curse out loud. Could she be any more stupid? *Say something else.*

She moved with him through the open door and onto the porch. Reid put on his sunglasses and stopped for a second. That was when she placed her hand on his forearm. "Call me when you get back?"

Reid smiled again and surprised her by leaning over and kissing her lightly on the cheek. "Sure." He bounded down the steps.

Ansel stood disbelieving against the hand-carved railing. She watched as his sedan flew down the paver-stone drive and onto the gravel ranch road leading to the Arrowhead's east exit. Corpulent Angus looked up from grazing as the vehicle sped between pastures. Soon the car became only a white spot beneath a beautiful aquamarine sky.

"Nice looking beau," said Permelia behind her. "If I were fifty years younger, I'd be all hot and bothered right about now."

Permelia had donned her color-coordinated orange cowboy hat and was toting a huge brown leather purse and a foil-covered plate. Ansel suspected it was piled high with tasty leftovers Pearl was sending home for her and Belle Starr.

"He's not my beau."

"Could've fooled me. I saw that smooch, and he was strut-ting like a peacock."

"Permelia, a peacock struts for every peahen in the roost."
She encircled Permelia's arm and assisted her wispy frame down
the deck stairs.

"Maybe, but seems to me your tail feathers were fluttering,
too."

"You obviously don't know Detective Reid Dorbandt."

"You're plum right," Permelia Reading Chance cackled as she
got in her neon pink Town Car, "but I sure know you."

As Permelia drove away, Ansel's cell phone rang. She tugged it
free of her pocket with one hand. The caller I.D. read *P. Standback*. She fiddled with her Iniskim and looked toward the road.
The phone trilled, insistent. She hesitated. Just a couple more
rings, Ansel decided, as she stared toward Billings.

Then she'd answer...

To receive a free catalog of Poisoned Pen Press titles, please contact us in one of the following ways:

Phone: 1-800-421-3976
Facsimile: 1-480-949-1707
Email: info@poisonedpenpress.com
Website: www.poisonedpenpress.com

Poisoned Pen Press
6962 E. First Ave. Ste 103
Scottsdale, AZ 85251